HEAVEN

BY ALEXANDRA ADORNETTO

Halo

~

Hades

~

Heaven

HEAVEN

Alexandra Adornetto

www.atombooks.net

To BELIEVERS

ATOM

First published in the US in 2012 by Feiwel and Friends, an imprint of Macmillan
First published in Great Britain in 2012 by Atom
This paperback edition published in 2013 by Atom

3 5 7 9 10 8 6 4

A CIP catalogue record for this book is available from the British Library.

ISBN 978-1-907410-80-2

Printed and bound in Great Britain by
Clays Ltd, St Ives plc

Papers used by Atom are from well-managed forests and other responsible sources.

I don't want to go to heaven. None of my friends are there.

—Oscar Wilde

If heaven ain't a lot like Dixie, I don't wanna go
If heaven ain't a lot like Dixie, I'd just as soon stay home

—Hank Williams Jr.

Contents

1

Till Death

EVERYTHING began to rattle.

I clutched the edge of the table and watched my engagement ring tumble onto the checkered floor of Sweethearts Café. The tremor lasted only a matter of seconds but the jukebox cut out and the alarmed waitresses teetered as they tried to balance their loaded trays.

Outside I saw the sky darken like bruised flesh and the treetops tremble as if shaken by an invisible hand. The blissful faraway expression on Xavier's face vanished, replaced by the hard, fighting look I'd seen far too much on him lately. I gripped his hand more tightly, closed my eyes, and waited for the blinding light that would surely come to return me to my prison in the sky.

But a moment later the earth was still again and normal activity resumed around us. Everyone had been bracing for something worse and breathed a collective sigh of relief when it didn't come. Now they were laughing, commenting on the unpredictability of Mother Nature while the waitresses hurried to clean up spilled drinks. Nobody was dwelling on what had happened—it would probably be newsworthy for a day or so and then forgotten. But Xavier and I weren't so easily fooled. Trouble was stirring in the Kingdom; we could feel it.

I considered telling Xavier that maybe this wasn't such a good idea after all, that we should return his grandmother's ring and drive back to Bryce Hamilton for the remainder of the graduation ceremony. If we hurried we'd probably arrive in time for him to deliver his valedictory speech. But the more I watched him, the more I faltered in my resolve.

My dutiful side recognized the wisdom of heeding the warning, meekly playing by the rules and not tampering with the will of Heaven. But I could feel a rebelliousness stirring inside me that told me it was too late to turn back. I let the timid girl I'd once been shrink into the shadows like a wallflower at a dance and allowed the new Beth to take over. I didn't know her too well, but somehow I felt like she'd been there all along, waiting in the wings, an understudy ready for her moment to shine.

It was this Beth who stood and snatched up her bag.

"Let's go."

Xavier tossed some bills down on the table and followed me into the street. He turned his face upward, squinting into the sun, which had quietly reappeared, before letting out a long sigh.

"Think that was directed at us?"

"I don't know," I replied. "We might be reading too much into it."

"Maybe," Xavier said. "But nothing like that's ever happened before and I've lived here all my life."

I looked up and down Main Street. People seemed to be

going about their business as usual. I noticed the sheriff was out, reassuring some nervous tourists. His level voice carried over to us.

"There's no cause for alarm, ma'am. Tremors might be rare in these parts but they're nothing to worry about."

The tourists seemed placated by his words but I knew the trembling earth couldn't be a mere coincidence. It was clearly a warning from above, not designed to do any real damage, just get our attention. And it had succeeded.

"Beth?" Xavier faltered. "What do we do now?"

I glanced at the Chevy parked across the street—it would only take us five minutes to get down to the water's edge where Father Mel was waiting for us in the chapel. I remembered visiting him along with Gabriel and Ivy when we first arrived in Venus Cove, and although it had never been openly discussed, he had known what we were. The look on his face had told us everything. I found myself thinking that if a man as pious as Father Mel had agreed to marry us, he must believe in our union. It was comforting to know we had at least one ally in our camp.

I wrestled internally for a moment before catching sight of an elderly couple sitting on a wooden bench in the square. The man held his wife's hand cupped in his own and smiled to himself as the breeze ruffled his white hair, while the sunshine warmed the back of his neck. I wondered how long they'd been together, how much of life's journey they'd shared. It was a glittering afternoon and the birches on the sidewalk twinkled in the sun. I watched a jogger go by, plugged into his iPod, and a little boy making faces at pedestrians through a car window. I may not have been born into this world, but I knew I had earned the right to be here. I was not about to relinquish that right so easily.

I took Xavier's face in my hands. "If I recall . . . you just asked me to marry you."

He regarded me uncertainly for a moment until understanding dawned. Then his face broke into a smile. He grabbed my hand with renewed fervor and we dashed across to the waiting Chevy. In the backseat lay the academic caps and gowns we had abandoned earlier but neither of us noticed them now. We didn't speak as Xavier stepped on the gas and the car sped off toward the shoreline. Any doubts we might have had evaporated. Come what may we were sticking with our plan.

SAINT Mark's was a bluestone chapel, built by European colonists just after the Civil War. A wrought-iron fence surrounded it and a cobbled path lined with bluebells led to its arched oak doors. It was the first Catholic church in the county, and a memorial wall lined the side garden, commemorating fallen confederate soldiers. Saint Mark's meant a lot to Xavier and his family. He'd taken bible study there since he was a boy and performed in every Christmas pageant until he was old enough to be embarrassed by it. Father Mel knew each of the Woods children personally. In just a few weeks he was going to marry the eldest daughter, Claire. As her brother, Xavier would stand up as one of the groomsmen.

As soon as we stepped through the arched doorway, the bustle of the outside world was completely obliterated. Our footsteps echoed on the red-veined marble of the chapel floor, and stone pillars towered to the domed ceiling above us. A statue of a crucified Christ dominated the nave, His crowned head bent, but His eyes turned Heavenward. Mosaic portraits of martyred saints stared down at us from the ceiling. A muted gold light filled the chapel, gliding off the golden tabernacle that held the consecrated hosts. On the walls, paintings of the fourteen Stations of the Cross hung in heavy carved frames. The pews were polished redwood and the smell of incense permeated the air. The stained glass window above the altar depicted a golden-haired Gabriel, stern-faced and red-robed as he delivered his message to a bewildered kneeling Mary. It was strange seeing an artist's interpretation of my archangel brother. The real Gabriel was so beautiful and formidable that his likeness could never truly be captured. Still, the colors rippled, bringing the figures to life before our eyes.

Xavier and I stopped at the entrance to dip our fingers in the font of holy water, crossing ourselves in tandem. A soft rustling of fabric preceded Father Mel's appearance. When he emerged, he was wearing full vestments that brushed the floor with a swishing sound when he walked down the carpeted steps to greet us. He was a balding man with twinkling eyes and didn't look surprised to see us. He embraced Xavier warmly and then folded my hand in his as if we were old acquaintances.

"I've been expecting you," he said encouragingly.

Father Mel ushered us to the front of the church where we both knelt before the altar. He searched our faces, looking for confirmation of our sincerity.

"Marriage is a serious commitment," he said. "You're both very young. Have you thought carefully about what you are about to undertake?"

"Yes, Father, we have," Xavier replied in a tone that would have convinced even the most ardent skeptic. "Will you help us?"

"Hmmm," came the gravelly reply. "What do your families have to say about all this? Surely they'd want to be present at such a momentous occasion?" Father Mel's gaze grew stern when he met my eyes.

"This is our decision," Xavier said. "I wish they could be here . . . but they just wouldn't understand." Father Mel nodded as he considered the full meaning of Xavier's words.

"This isn't some teenage crush," I cut in, worried that he might need more persuading. "You have no idea what we've been through to get here. Please, we can't go another day without belonging to each other in the eyes of the Lord."

I could see Father Mel was finding it hard to ignore our urgency, but the little voice in his head advocated caution. I needed to try harder if I was going to convince him.

"It's God's will," I said suddenly, and watched his eyes widen. "He brought us together for a reason. You of all people should know He has a plan for everyone and this is ours. It's not for us to question Him, we just want to embrace what He has created between us."

That seemed to seal the deal. He couldn't reject what seemed to be a blatant directive from above. Father Mel fluttered his hands in a gesture of consent.

"Very well then. It won't do to keep you waiting any

longer." He beckoned to someone who had until now been hidden in the gloom. "I've taken the liberty of asking Mrs. Alvarez to act as witness."

We turned our heads to see a woman who'd been silently praying at the end of a pew. When she stood up and approached the altar, I recognized her as the presbytery's housekeeper. Mrs. Alvarez smoothed out imaginary creases in her print blouse. She couldn't help looking excited about playing a minor role in what must have appeared to her as some wild and romantic escapade. When she spoke, she even sounded a little breathless.

"You are the son of Bernadette, yes?" she asked with a heavy Hispanic accent. Xavier nodded and dropped his gaze, anticipating a reprimand. But Mrs. Alvarez only gave his arm a complicit squeeze. "You don't worry; everyone will be happy for you soon enough."

"Shall we begin?" Father Mel asked.

"Please . . . *un momento*." Mrs. Alvarez shook her head and surveyed me unhappily before excusing herself. We waited in confusion for a moment until she returned and presented me with a posy of daisies hastily picked from the chapel's garden.

"Thank you." I smiled at her gratefully. In our hurry to get there, Xavier and I hadn't given much thought to details. Both of us were still in our crisp school uniforms.

"You are very welcome." Her eyes crinkled in delight.

The sunlight pouring through the stained-glass window washed Xavier in golden tones. It wouldn't have mattered if he'd been wearing his old gym shorts. His very presence was dazzling. Out of the corner of my eye I caught a glimpse of my own tumble of chestnut hair, streaked with copper and bronze. My reflection seemed to be glowing. A small part of me wanted to see this as a sign that perhaps our union might find favor in the eyes of Heaven. After all, the earth had stopped shaking and the ceiling was showing no sign of caving in. Maybe, just maybe, ours was a love that even Heaven had to accept.

When I looked at Xavier, I realized something in me had changed. I wasn't overcome with my usual flood of emotion—a love so intense that I sometimes felt my body couldn't contain it without exploding. Instead, I felt entirely at peace, like my universe was coming together exactly as it should. Although I knew Xavier's face like the back of my hand, every time I looked at him, it was like seeing him for the first time. There was so much depth and complexity in the graceful lines of his face: his full lips curving into a half smile, his swooping cheekbones and almond eyes that were as turquoise as the shallows of the ocean. Fingers of sunlight danced across his honey gold hair, making it glow like burnished brass. His school uniform, its dark blue blazer with the Bryce crest emblazoned on the pocket, seemed fitting for the solemnity of the occasion. Xavier reached up to give his tie a final adjustment. I couldn't tell if he was nervous or not.

"Gotta look my best today," he said, giving me a playful wink.

Father Mel spread his hands and held them ceremoniously aloft.

"You have come together in this church so that the Lord

may consecrate and seal your love through holy matrimony. May you both assume the duties of marriage with mutual respect and lasting fidelity. And so, in the presence of the Church, I ask you to state your intentions. Will you love and honor each other as husband and wife for the rest of your lives?"

Xavier and I both glanced up as if suddenly aware of the sanctity of this moment. We didn't hesitate, though, and answered in unison as if our individual selves had already intertwined.

"We will."

"Join your right hands and declare your consent before God and His Church. Xavier, repeat after me."

Xavier enunciated every word carefully, as if each one carried so much weight it could not be rushed. His voice was like music. I felt so giddy I had to tighten my grip on his hands for fear of floating away. His eyes did not leave mine as he spoke.

"I, Xavier Woods, take you, Bethany Church, for my lawful wife, to have and to hold, from this day forward, for better, for worse, for richer, for poorer, in sickness and in health, until death do us part."

Then it was my turn. I must have been nervous because I heard my voice quaver as I uttered the same vows while Father Mel looked gravely on. Mrs. Alvarez withdrew a lacy handkerchief that she kept tucked in one sleeve and dabbed at her eyes. As I spoke, even I couldn't keep the tears from falling. But I'd never understood until that moment what it meant to cry tears of happiness. I felt the pad of Xavier's thumb stroke my hand and for a second I lost myself in the depth of his eyes. Father Mel's voice brought me back to the present.

"It's time for the rings, which you give to one another as a symbol of your love and fidelity."

Xavier took my hand and slipped his grandmother's ring onto my finger. It fit snugly, as if it was attaching itself to me for good. Wishing we'd had more time to plan, I covertly slipped off my class ring and tried to slide it on Xavier's ring finger. Of course it was too small and I could only make it fit onto his pinkie. Xavier and I froze, thinking we'd ruined everything. But we both relaxed again when Mrs. Alvarez covered her mouth and started to giggle.

"May your union find favor in the eyes of the Lord," Father Mel concluded. "May it bring peace and harmony to your lives. I now pronounce you husband and wife."

And that was it. The ceremony was over and we were married.

All my life I'd felt like the outsider, looking in on a world I could never be part of. In the Kingdom I'd existed, but never really lived. Meeting Xavier had changed all that. He had let me in, loved me, and looked after me. He'd never cared that I was different, and he had brought my whole world to life just with his presence. I knew we still had struggles ahead of us, but my soul was now inextricably tied to his and nothing, neither Heaven nor Hell, could tear us apart.

We forgot to wait for the formal directive from Father Mel and melted instantly into a kiss. There was something completely different about the nature of the embrace we shared. This time, it felt sacred. My wings began to hum beneath my shirt and every inch of my skin began to tingle, spreading a warm glow across my body. Then, the light from my skin fused with the sunshine filtering through the stained-glass window. It exploded in a flash, locking Xavier and me inside a shimmering prism of light. Father Mel and Mrs. Alvarez gasped in surprise but a second later, the prism shattered as the sun dipped behind a cloud.

Mrs. Alvarez was so overcome with excitement that she broke into a stream of congratulations in Spanish and kissed us both as vigorously as if we were her long-lost relatives. She only stopped when Father Mel steered us discreetly away to the altar to sign the license.

I'd just laid down my pen when the chapel doors flew open with a crash so resounding it made everyone jump.

The loose-limbed figure of an adolescent boy with an effeminate face and a cowlick stood in the entrance. He wore a hooded black robe and three sets of black wings fanned out behind him. He bowed formally, never taking his eyes off Father Mel, and approached the altar with a gait so rehearsed he might have been on a catwalk. A gleaming scythe swung at his side. I knew at once what he was: a Grim Reaper, trained by the Angel of Death himself. Hysterical screams broke from Mrs. Alvarez as she scrambled for refuge behind the altar. Frantic prayers uttered in Spanish could be heard from her hiding place. Traditionally, reapers are only visible to those they seek, but in this case etiquette had been abandoned. Every movement seemed deliberate, designed to issue a clear message to us. This death was on our heads.

Instinctively, I pushed Xavier to the ground. At the same

time my wings snapped open, shielding him; a reaper could never claim a soul while its guardian was watching over it. But I soon discovered it wasn't Xavier the young reaper had in his sights.

His intense gaze was fixed on Father Mel, and his slender finger was pointing straight at him. The priest blinked in confusion before cowering backward until he was pressed up against the altar, his horn-rimmed glasses askew on his face.

"I meant only to help. I meant only to help," he repeated.

"Your intention is irrelevant," replied the reaper coldly.

Father Mel paused for a moment, then righted himself. "I was called by the Lord and I answered."

"Do you know what she is?" the reaper asked. "She is not human."

Father Mel did not seem surprised. He had known all along I was different, although he had never questioned me or treated me like an outsider.

"God works in mysterious ways," he replied boldly.

The reaper inclined his head. "Indeed."

I watched transfixed as he held one hand aloft and Father Mel instantly doubled over in pain, clutching his heart. He gasped for breath as he fell to the floor.

"Leave him alone!" Xavier screamed, trying to extricate himself from my grasp. I had him pinned, using strength I didn't know I had. The reaper seemed to look at us for the first time and turned his languid sleepy eyes to Xavier. The smile on his rosebud lips was almost insolent.

"My business is not with you," he answered. Then he closed the distance between himself and the priest lying prostrate on the marble floor. Xavier struggled, but my angelic power held him fast.

"Beth, let me go," he pleaded. "Father Mel needs help!"

"We can't help him now."

"What's wrong with you?" he implored, looking at me with a strange expression, like he didn't recognize me.

"You can't fight a reaper," I whispered. "He's acting under instruction. If you get in his way, he'll take you too. Don't make me your widow within minutes of becoming your wife."

That seemed to get through to him. Xavier stopped struggling and fell silent, though his eyes were full of anguish as he stared helplessly at his childhood priest and mentor. Father Mel's body twitched briefly and then was still. The reaper glided away only to reposition himself at the head of the body. I knew what he was waiting for. A smoky shadow emerged from Father Mel's open mouth and hovered in the air—a filmy replica of the lifeless form on the floor.

"Follow me," instructed the reaper tonelessly. He sounded almost bored. Father Mel's soul looked lost for a moment, searching for direction, and then complied. Together reaper and mortal soul ascended toward the domed ceiling of the church.

"Where are you taking him?" I demanded, dreading the thought of Father Mel being cast into the pit for trying to help us.

"His motives were pure, so his place in Heaven remains intact," the reaper replied without looking back or pausing in his flight. "But his days on this earth are over."

{ 2 }

Run, Baby, Run

ONLY when the reaper had disappeared did I feel comfortable enough to release Xavier. He rushed and fell to his knees beside Father Mel's inert body. The priest's eyes were still open, now dull and glassy.

A breathless Mrs. Alvarez emerged from behind the altar, shaking and looking at us with an expression of dread. She paused in the aisle, her quivering hands clutching at the jewel-encrusted crucifix around her neck.

"*Santo cielo!* God have mercy on us all," she whimpered before stumbling blindly out of the chapel.

"Wait!" I called after her. "Mrs. Alvarez, please!" But she didn't look back. She was too fixated on getting as far away as possible from what she'd just witnessed.

Once she was gone, Xavier looked at me, his face ragged with pain.

"Beth, what have we done?" he whispered. "We killed someone."

"No, we didn't." I knelt down beside him and took his hands in mine. "Listen to me, Xavier, this isn't our fault."

"They took him as revenge," Xavier murmured, averting

his face so I wouldn't see how upset he was. "For agreeing to this marriage. If he hadn't tried to help us, he'd still be alive."

"We didn't know that." I turned his chin, trying to make him look at me. "We're not the killers here."

I passed my hand over Father Mel's eyelids, closing them forever. I could feel anger swelling in my chest at the injustice of it all, but I knew that wouldn't help any of us. So instead, I sent up a silent prayer that Father Mel's soul would find rest. Xavier was still staring, bereft at the body on the floor.

"It's only his earthly life they've cut short," I told him. "He's at peace now—you know that, don't you?"

Xavier nodded and tried to blink back the tears that were gathering on his long lashes. The sound of a car screaming to a halt outside drew our attention. It was immediately followed by the sound of doors slamming and feet pounding on the gravel path.

When Ivy and Gabriel stormed into Saint Mark's, it took them a fraction of a second to appraise the scene and work out what had transpired. They flew down the aisle in a blur, and only came into focus when they were standing directly in front of us. Gabriel's beautiful features were pained and he passed a hand through his sand-colored hair in frustration. Ivy's loose golden mane was mussed and she wore an expression as black as thunder.

"What in God's name have you done?" she said in a tone I'd never heard her use before. Her voice had dropped several octaves and seemed to come from deep in her chest. Gabriel only clenched and unclenched his jaw without speaking.

"We're too late," he said finally. His eyes traveled over our wedding rings and the body on the floor. He didn't even flinch, evidently not surprised to see the first casualty of our ill-fated love.

"This is a travesty." Ivy shook her head in dismay. "This rebellion shall not go unchallenged." Her usually cool gray eyes had turned a strange amber hue and I thought I saw tiny flames in her irises.

"Not now." Gabriel motioned toward the exit. "We must leave this place."

They grabbed us both by the shoulders and half dragged us along with them down the aisle. We were too dazed to resist. The black Jeep was waiting outside the church. Ivy threw open the doors using more strength than was needed. For a moment it made the whole car lurch to the right. "Get in," she commanded. "Now."

"No," I objected, pulling feebly away from them. "I'm sick of everybody telling us what to do!"

"Bethany, I wish you'd come to me first," Gabriel said, his voice heavy with disappointment. "I could have helped you make the right decision."

"This is the right decision, Gabe," I said resolutely.

"You have betrayed the laws of Heaven and caused the untimely death of a man of the cloth," my sister said through clenched teeth. "Have you no regrets?"

"We didn't know that would happen!"

"Of course not," Ivy said, and suddenly I understood what it meant to have someone shoot daggers at you with their eyes. "Do you expect us to keep defending you no matter what you do?"

"No. I just wish you could see things from our perspective!"

"We only wanted to be together," Xavier said. "That's all."

His explanation only seemed to fuel my sister's discontent. "Get in the car!" she yelled. Her abruptness took us all by surprise. Then she turned her back on us and leaned against the passenger door, her shoulders tense with rage.

"We'll come with you," I said steadily, trying to restore a modicum of calm to the escalating situation. "Just tell us where we're going."

"You both have to leave Venus Cove. Right now. There's no time to lose," Gabriel said. "We'll explain on the way."

I realized suddenly that the veins in Gabriel's neck were throbbing. Ivy was wringing her hands and darting little nervous glances down the street. Was I missing something? I understood why they were worked up about our impulsive decision to marry, but I could see there was more to it than that. If I didn't know them better, I'd say they were scared.

"Gabe, what's going on?" I touched his shoulder with growing alarm.

The look on his face was one I hadn't seen before. It was a look of defeat. "It's not safe for you here anymore."

"What?" Xavier instinctively put an arm around my shoulders. "Why not?"

"I know we've made trouble," I said. "And I'll never forgive myself for what happened to Father Mel, but I don't understand! This shouldn't involve anyone but us. We just wanted to be married. Why is that so wrong?"

"In the eyes of Heaven it is," Ivy said, her rainstorm eyes meeting mine calmly for the first time.

"That's not fair," I protested, and at the same time felt tears threatening to spill. I climbed into the backseat, devastated that our happiness had been shattered so soon.

From the front seat, Gabriel spun around. He fixed Xavier with a hard look. "Listen to me carefully."

Xavier's face paled and he swallowed hard.

"You don't just have to leave," Gabriel said. "You have to *run*."

My brother drove out of town toward the hills at breakneck speed. Ivy bit down hard on her lower lip and clutched the dashboard. Despite their promise to explain, neither of them was saying a word. Xavier and I held on to each other and tried not to assume the worst. This wasn't exactly the honeymoon I'd had in mind. I just hoped Xavier wasn't having doubts.

I craned my neck and watched my beloved town shrinking through the rear window. The last thing I saw was the spires of the bell tower at Bryce Hamilton rising above the undulating hills before my brother made a sharp left onto a scrubby dirt road and Venus Cove disappeared from view. The only place I'd ever called home was gone! I wasn't sure how long it would be before I'd see it again or if I ever would. The thought made my head spin.

It hit me suddenly why Gabe was in such a hurry to leave the road behind. He wanted us completely concealed from view. Even then he didn't slow down. The ride was bumpy; pebbles flew under the tires and low branches kept thrashing at the sides of the Jeep. Even the trees seemed to be plotting against us. I watched the clouds turn elastic, twisting and forming into strange images. A mass of dense clouds stretched until it looked like a hand was reaching through it, the index finger extended and pointing straight down at us. A second later the finger retracted to become a swirling mass of cloud again. Imagined or not, I knew it was a symbol of judgment. That's what my marriage to Xavier would indubitably be seen as: an act of rebellion, treason against the Kingdom, punishable by laws I wasn't old enough to understand. Besides, my human traits were so dominant now, all of Heaven's laws would have seemed foreign. Meeting Xavier had shifted my loyalties; I no longer felt any ties to my native home.

I knew we were moving into higher ground because the air coming in through my window felt lighter. I tried counting the number of horses grazing in the paddocks to keep my mind off what lay ahead. I hoped my siblings would direct their anger at me and not Xavier. I knew I should apologize and concede we'd made a mistake. But I wasn't sorry for what we'd done. Not yet, anyway.

The day that had felt so perfect just hours before now lay in ruins. We were in the car so long I lost track of time. I wondered how many hours we'd been driving. Had we crossed state lines? I had a feeling we'd left Georgia behind. The terrain had definitely changed. The trees were thicker and taller. The air was as crisp as new-season apples. We were heading north; I could see the hazy blue contours of mountains in the distance, but I didn't dare ask which they were. Xavier stared out the window without speaking. I knew he was still thinking of Father Mel, replaying the scene over and over in his head and trying to work out if there was something he could have done differently. I wished I could comfort him, but nothing I said would make a difference now or ease the pain and guilt crashing down on him.

Finally, we pulled up outside a log cabin so in tune with its surroundings I didn't even notice it until we were right outside its green painted door.

"Where are we?" I asked, inhaling the pine-scented air.

"In the Smoky Mountains." My brother's voice was a low rumble. "North Carolina."

I only had time to take in the name of the cabin, Willow Lodge, and the two rustic rocking chairs on the front porch before Gabriel hastily fished some keys from his pocket and ushered us inside. The floor was scrubbed pine and there was an open fireplace with a quarry stone hearth and mantle.

I knew I ought to be grateful to Gabriel for coming to our rescue, but by now I was tired and found myself becoming more and more irked by his attitude. This was so like the Gabriel of old, looking at us like criminals, scolding us like children. I might be one of its indentured servants but what right did Heaven have to dictate Xavier's life? Xavier was human and in his world our actions were legitimate, even laudable. And his was the only world I cared about now. Maybe Xavier and I had been rash and impulsive, but that didn't warrant the damning looks we were getting. What gave my siblings the right to judge us? We shouldn't have to feel ashamed.

Inside the cabin, it was Gabriel's turn to lose his composure. He took me unexpectedly by the shoulders and shook me roughly.

"When are you going to grow up?" he demanded. "When are you going to realize that you're living a stolen life that doesn't belong to you? You are not human, Bethany! Why can't you get that through your head?"

"Take it easy, Gabriel." Xavier stepped forward defensively. "She's not your responsibility anymore."

"Oh, really? And whose responsibility is she? *Yours?* How do you plan to protect her?"

"I'm no one's responsibility," I declared. The last thing I needed was a face-off between my brother and my husband of a few hours. "I made a decision and I'm willing to deal with the consequences. Xavier and I love each other and we're not going to let anyone stop us from being together."

It made me feel strong saying it out loud, but I heard Gabriel let out a stifled groan.

"You're delusional."

"I can't live like you," I answered. "I can't bury my emotions and pretend they don't exist."

"You do not experience emotion, Bethany—you wallow in it, you are controlled by it, and everything you have done is based entirely on self-interest."

"Just because you don't understand love doesn't make it wrong!"

"This isn't about love anymore. It's about obedience and responsibility. Two concepts you appear not to understand."

"Will everyone please just settle down?" said Ivy. They seemed to be taking turns at venting their frustration. Now that Gabe was riled, Ivy seemed calmer, as if to counter his mood. "Arguing won't get us anywhere. What's done is done. We have to find a way to help Beth and Xavier now."

Her unruffled demeanor made us stop and take stock. Gabriel gave her a questioning frown and I saw a look pass between them, an unspoken secret. Then the moment passed. When Gabriel spoke again, it was in a much more measured tone.

"Ivy and I have to go, but we'll be back soon. In the meantime, stay out of sight and, Beth, stay away from the windows. Your presence will easily be picked up by . . ." he trailed off.

"Who's looking for me?" I demanded.

"Later." The prickly way he said it told me how bad things were. But when his eyes met mine, I saw how real his concern was. I felt a sudden onslaught of guilt. I couldn't blame Gabriel for being irritated. He was forever cleaning up my messes, consulting higher authorities and apologizing for someone else's mistakes. Our decision to run off and get married had created a drama that nobody needed right now, just when things were getting back on an even keel.

"One last thing," Gabriel added, his hand already on the door handle. "If it's not beyond the realm of self-control, I suggest you refrain from . . . physical contact."

He made it sound as if the request were the most natural thing in the world! As if he were asking us to remember to turn the lights out.

"What?" I asked, scowling. "Can we at least know why?"

Gabriel frowned, hesitant to share his rationale.

"They may look on you more kindly if the marriage is not consummated," Ivy answered for him.

"It may make no difference," Gabriel said. "But instinct tells me it would be wise for Bethany and Xavier to send out a message of . . ." He paused, searching for the right word. Again Ivy finished his thought.

"Repentance?" she offered, and Gabriel inclined his head, indicating she'd guessed right.

"That would be a lie!" I said without even thinking. "We're not sorry." The thought of Father Mel brought me up short. "But we never meant for anyone to get hurt."

"Be smart," Gabriel admonished. "This is a small sacrifice." He clearly didn't want to enter into a debate about it.

"I don't think you're in a position to pass comment on that, do you?" Xavier flashed him a defiant look.

"We're trying to help you," Ivy said wearily. "Before we can, we need to find out what's going on." That comment unnerved me more than anything that had happened so far.

"You mean you don't know?" I was amazed. Gabriel and Ivy were always attuned to the will of Heaven.

"There's no precedence for this," explained my sister. "It's only happened once before and that was a long time ago." Xavier and I both looked blank. If we were meant to divine her meaning, she'd have to speak more plainly. Gabriel unexpectedly came to our aid.

"Ivy is referring to the Nephilim," he said bluntly.

"Oh, come on!" I burst out. "This is totally different."

"Who the heck are the Nephilim?" Xavier interjected.

"They were progeny created a long time ago when 'sons of God' descended from Heaven and were captivated by the beauty of the 'daughters of men,'" I explained. "They mated with them, creating a half-human, half-angel race."

"Seriously?" Xavier raised his eyebrows. "They must've skipped that section in Bible class."

"It's not a generally accepted doctrine," Gabriel said drily.

"And what does all this have to do with us?"

"Nothing," I said emphatically. "This is *not* the same thing. Those angels who lay with mortals were fallen from grace. They rebelled against God. Heaven couldn't possibly consider this as serious a transgression . . . could they?"

"I don't know," said Ivy softly. "You have tied yourself to the mortal world, just as they did."

I had to admit Ivy was right. It was to the mortal world that I now felt the deepest loyalty. Gabriel saw me finger the precious contours of the ring on my left hand. I stole a glance at it, the soft sheen of the diamonds reflected in the waning light. Already it felt like a part of me, as if I were destined to wear it always. I certainly wasn't going to part with it, not without a fight.

"You should probably put that in a drawer," came the blunt suggestion.

"Excuse me?"

"It might be wiser not to flaunt it." Gabriel remained stone-faced.

"I'm not taking off my ring," I told him steadily. "I don't care if it makes the whole Kingdom angry."

Gabriel began to argue but Ivy swept past and murmured something in his ear too soft for us to hear. We caught only the tail end.

"Leave it, Gabe," she said. "Taking off the ring won't change a thing."

In spite of my bravado, I felt myself begin to tremble. Xavier, who had one hand protectively around my waist, felt it too.

"Are you okay?" he asked with concern. He couldn't know this, but I'd just remembered that the angels responsible for creating the Nephilim had met with a very bleak fate. Had I just put a death sentence on my own head . . . on both our heads? My brother and sister guessed precisely the turn my thoughts had taken.

"Don't jump to conclusions," said Gabriel more gently this time. "Nothing is certain yet."

"You need to just wait and be patient," Ivy said. "We'll find out what we can and tell you everything just as soon as we get back."

She reached for the car keys on the hall table but Gabriel closed his hand over hers.

"Leave them the car." He must have read Xavier's mind because he looked knowingly at him. "Don't worry; we'll know if you run into any trouble. If you do, get out fast. We'll find you."

"Got it," said Xavier, more ready to accept their directives than I was. He strode across the room, pulling the curtains tightly shut.

"We'll be back as soon as we can," said Gabriel. "Remember—stay away from the windows and bolt the door behind us."

"Hey, wait," Xavier called out as a new thought suddenly occurred to him. "What am I supposed to do about my parents? They must be getting pretty worried by now."

Gabriel stared at the ground for a moment and I knew he was thinking of the Woods family with regret. Would they ever see their eldest son again?

"I've already taken care of it," he said.

"Whoa, how?" Xavier took a step forward, suddenly riled. Up until now his family had been kept out of our dilemmas and I knew he wanted it to stay that way. "They're my family. What did you do?"

"As far as they know you were last seen at Bryce Hamilton before graduation," Gabriel said stiffly. "You disappeared and there is no further record of your whereabouts. In twenty-four hours the sherriff's department will file a missing person's report. In two weeks they will assume you don't want to be found."

Xavier stopped short. "You better be joking. . . . You want me to let my parents believe I've just skipped town?"

"It's for the best."

"No way."

"Call them if you like," Ivy cut in, more dismissively than was characteristic of her. "But you will be putting them all at risk. It is not safe for anyone to know your whereabouts."

"Are they in danger?" Xavier's eyes widened with rising alarm.

"Not as long as they're in the dark," my sister said. "If they find out anything, then they become useful. Do you understand? Right now, they have no information worth extracting."

The way Ivy and Gabriel were talking, we might have been watching a scene from an espionage movie. None of it made sense. But however confused he was feeling, Xavier swallowed hard and said nothing. He had no choice but to accept their edict. There was no way he would put his family at risk . . . even if it broke his heart to let them worry and grieve for their imagined loss.

"You'll see them again," Gabe told him. "When all this is over." Then he and Ivy stepped lightly through the door and disappeared.

"I hope so," Xavier murmured after them. I knew how much Xavier loved me; I just wished it hadn't come with such a high price tag. His voice sounded so forlorn that I wished I could do something to make his pain go away. I tried to move toward him, but Xavier turned away from me and fixed his attention on the clock on the mantel.

I knew he was lost in his own private grief.

I was curious to see where Ivy and Gabriel were going and whether they planned to fly there in plain sight. I crouched at the door and peered through the keyhole. I watched my siblings disappear hand in hand into the thatch of trees that surrounded the cabin. From between the twisted trunks, I caught a shimmer in the air and suddenly, two glowing beams like spools of yarn shot into the sky and vanished into the dense cloud. Gabriel and Ivy were visible only as periodic pinpricks of light, such as might be emitted by fireflies. A moment later, they disappeared completely from view. I turned and pressed myself against the door, wishing I could disappear. Without my siblings to protect us, I felt exposed, like the cabin itself was a flashing neon sign, advertising our presence.

3

Men in Black

I suddenly felt light-headed and flopped down into an armchair by the fireplace. All my nerves felt frayed and a few times I wondered if I might be on the verge of throwing up. My teeth chattered, and I couldn't stop myself from shivering uncontrollably. The sound must have snapped Xavier out of his thoughts because he turned and looked at me as if he'd just remembered my presence. Instantly, he was kneeling at my side.

"Hey, are you okay?"

"I'm fine."

"You don't look fine." Xavier surveyed me carefully.

"Everything will be okay," I said, and repeated it soundlessly to myself like a mantra.

"You know what Ivy and Gabriel are like," said Xavier, trying hard to appear optimistic. "They always predict the worst-case scenario."

I jerked upright when I heard a soft rustling of leaves outside. Even the ticking of the old mantel clock sounded exaggeratedly ominous.

"Beth." Xavier felt my forehead with the back of his hand.

"You need to calm down—you're going to make yourself sick."

"I can't help it," I said. "Everything's turning so hideously wrong. We should be on our honeymoon right now. Instead, we're locked up here in the middle of nowhere with someone—or something—hunting us down."

"I know. Come here." Xavier sat on the edge of the chair and pulled me close, resting my head against his chest. "Baby . . . aren't you forgetting something? You've been to Hell and back. You survived. You've seen your friends die and almost died yourself too many times. Nothing should scare you now. Don't you know how strong you are . . . how strong *we* are?"

I swallowed hard and pressed my face into the crisp fabric of his school shirt, letting his heartbeat as well as his familiar woody scent comfort me. It was working; I could feel my resolve coming back. My emotions were reeling like a yo-yo, up one minute, down the next.

"I love you so much, Xavier," I whispered. "And I don't care if the whole universe is against us."

We sat together in the cabin and watched the light begin to fade through the crack under the door. On the outside, we might have looked still and tranquil, but inside we were readying ourselves to face another battle, another struggle to preserve what was ours.

This seemed to be the story of our lives. Would fate ever look on us favorably, even for just one day?

THOSE first days we spent in Willow Lodge were some of the most nerve-wracking of my life. As the hours trickled past and every new day drew to a close, we remained imprisoned in the tiny cabin. Ordinarily, this would have been the sort of place I dreamed of visiting with Xavier: We would make hot cocoa, snuggle up in front of a log fire, and feel like the rest of the world didn't exist. But now we longed to return to civilization and escape our surreal lockdown. Too many questions remained unanswered for us to derive any pleasure from our picture-perfect surroundings.

Willow Lodge was nestled behind a blanket of trees, with low eaves and a cozy porch. Chintz curtains with ruffled edges hung in the front windows. The sitting room was filled with plump plaid sofas and firewood stacked neatly in a wicker basket. There was a pine kitchen with copper pots hanging from long hooks attached to a beam above the counter. The bathroom had a cast-iron tub and daisy-embossed wallpaper. Several steps led to a mezzanine level, which contained a vast canopied bed with a quilted bedspread, and a window overlooking the misty treetops.

But all that was lost on us. Under different circumstances, it might have been the ultimate romantic retreat. But right now, it was more like a jail.

Xavier and I sat cuddled together in one of the vast linen armchairs. I could guess what he was thinking: It was his lack of judgment that had landed us in this mess. He met my gaze and gave me a tight grimace of apology. But he needn't have worried. I didn't regret a single thing.

"Stop it," I told him sternly. "Stop blaming yourself."

"It was my idea," he replied abjectly.

"It was *our* idea," I corrected. "And no amount of

guilt-tripping from anyone will make me regret becoming your wife. If we have to fight, we will."

"Wow, you're turning into a little solider, aren't you?" Xavier said.

"You're the one who used to say *go hard or go home.*"

"I was talking about football," Xavier said. "But I guess the same applies here."

"We can think of it like a game," I replied. "Winning the right to be together . . . that's our goal, and we're just playing against an especially difficult team." Xavier was forced to smile at my analogy.

"Reckon we can beat 'em?" he murmured, tucking a stray lock of hair behind my ears. His touch warmed me and made me forget my fear.

I closed my eyes, distracted by the feel of his fingertips against my skin. "Of course," I murmured. "They don't stand a chance."

Our bodies pressed closer together and Xavier's thumb traced the outline of my mouth. I felt my lips part involuntarily. The mood was about to change. The air was seconds away from turning electric. We both sensed it and moved quickly apart. Xavier rocked back on his heels, putting a safer distance between us. *Nothing quells desire like fear,* I thought to myself. *Especially when the fear is that your beloved will come to harm.*

"This sucks," I said. "Gabriel shouldn't ask this of us now."

"It's nothing we can't handle," Xavier replied.

"You have so much self-control I think you should be the angel."

"No, thanks." He smiled. "I don't like heights."

"Really? You've never told me that."

"I was trying to impress you. I had to hold some things back."

"And now you don't have to impress me anymore? It's a bit early for complacency. We've only been married a few days."

"For better or worse, remember?"

"I wasn't expecting the worse to come quite so soon." Xavier stroked my head to placate me, but it triggered other feelings.

"I want to kiss you," I said suddenly. "I want to kiss my husband."

"I think you need a distraction." Xavier sighed.

"I completely agree. . . ."

"Not *that* kind of distraction."

Xavier stood up and began to rummage through the cupboards on either side of the fireplace. They were full of dated copies of *National Geographic* and *Reader's Digest* as well as an old wooden train set. I pressed my face into the sofa and groaned. Xavier persevered, determined to find something that would take our minds off the tension hanging in the air.

"There's gotta be something useful in here," he mumbled before withdrawing a couple of battered-looking board games and holding them up triumphantly. "Trivial Pursuit or Monopoly?" he said brightly.

"Trivial Pursuit," I said glumly.

"Oh, not fair," Xavier objected. "You're like a walking encyclopedia."

"Your sisters say you always cheat in Monopoly."

"Mortgaging properties when your cash flow's running low is not cheating. My sisters just hate to lose."

Outside, a spray of rain began, accompanied by the occasional rumble of distant thunder. I couldn't see the rain but I could hear it pattering on the steps outside. I shifted position on the sofa, playing with the fringed pillows.

"We don't even know who's looking for us," I whispered.

"Doesn't matter," Xavier said stoutly. "They won't find us. And if they do we'll run."

"I know," I replied. "I just wish I knew exactly what was going on. No one ever tells us anything. And I can't bear the thought of anyone trying to separate us again. . . ."

"Let's not think about it now," Xavier jumped in before the mood turned too gloomy.

"You're right. Let's just play."

Xavier nodded and began to set up the Monopoly board in silence. For a while the game managed to absorb us, but I could tell we were just going through the motions. Both our heads jerked up in unison at the slightest rustling of leaves outside or the snap of a twig. At one point, Xavier turned his phone on to find twelve missed calls and several frantic texts from his parents and sisters. Claire's message read: "Xav, I don't know where you are but you really need to call us as soon as you get this." Nicola's text message on the other hand reflected her feistier personality perfectly: "WTF? Where are you? Mom's flipping out. Call her." Xavier threw his phone at the couch in frustration and it slipped down between the cushions. I knew how hard it must be for him to ignore his family when a few simple words could ease their suffering.

I didn't know what to tell him, so I didn't say a word. Instead I rolled the dice and silently moved my token to Trafalgar Square.

It was only once we heard the Jeep pull up outside that we realized how cold and hungry we were. Luckily, Ivy and Gabriel had brought supplies with them.

"It's freezing in here. Why didn't you get the fire going?" Ivy asked.

I shrugged. I could hardly tell her all our energies had gone into keeping ourselves distracted so we wouldn't consummate our marriage, thereby incurring further heavenly wrath.

Gabriel waved his hand over the hearth and a roaring fire sprang up. I drew closer to it and rubbed my arms, which were covered in goose bumps. They'd brought Chinese takeout and we ate it straight out of the cartons on our laps, and washed it down with cider. If it weren't for the somber faces and heavy silence, someone looking in might have concluded we were a group of friends on a weekend getaway. We all knew there was a conversation hanging in the air, waiting to happen, but no one wanted to broach it.

I could have guessed Ivy would be the first to break the silence.

"The Seventh Order has assumed control," she announced, spreading her hands flat on her thighs, as if she needed to physically brace herself. "They're always sticking their noses in where they're not wanted!"

I vaguely knew what she was referring to. The Seventh Order was a faction of angels created to act as custodians over the nations of the world, but I was still struggling to grasp what they had to do with us.

"I can't believe this is happening." My comment was directed at no one in particular.

Gabriel turned his head to look at me. "What did you expect? A honeymoon suite at the Four Seasons?"

"No, but it's hard to imagine that they're coming here. Because of us."

"They're not *coming*," Ivy said gravely. "They're already *here*."

"What do they want?" Xavier cut straight to the more pressing issue. "Whoever they are, I won't let them anywhere near Beth."

"Still a hothead," muttered Gabriel, staring into the fire.

Ivy continued without him. "The two of you have to lie low and stay hidden. Word is they've already started hunting."

"Hunting?" Xavier echoed. "We're still talking about angels, right?"

"They are soldiers first and foremost," Ivy said. "With one objective . . . find the renegade."

It took me a second to realize the renegade was me.

I racked my brain to remember what I knew about the Sevens. That was the nickname we Guardians had coined for them, and it'd stuck. Formally they were known as the Principalities—or sometimes the Princes—because of their status. After a number of years as Guardians, angels were permitted to apply to train as Sevens, but it wasn't for everyone. It was like Heaven's version of military service—a strict existence of rigorous training with little to no interaction with human souls—so its appeal was limited.

Talking about them triggered a sharp memory from a long time ago. I hadn't thought about Zach since I'd come down to earth but back in the Kingdom he was once my friend. Zach had been a gifted Guardian. We jokingly called him the Pied Piper because he couldn't move without being followed by a troop of children's souls. For reasons he didn't really share with us, Zach soon became disillusioned with his role and set his sights higher. Perhaps it was the lure of prestige that spurred him to join the Sevens. He never told me. And I never saw him again after that. I couldn't help but think what a loss to our ranks his departure had been. Zach had made the transition from an earthly existence to a heavenly one seem as effortless as a game and children trusted him entirely. Not many Guardians could boast that. And yet it hadn't been enough to satisfy him. I could still picture his pale skin sprinkled with a dusting of freckles and his clear eyes like he was right in front of me. Zach seemed such an unlikely soldier I couldn't imagine what he must look like now.

Gabriel's voice snapped me back to reality.

"Our only chance is to confuse them," he was saying. "Keep moving, change locations."

"That's your solution?" I asked in disbelief.

"For the short term," my brother replied icily. "Have you got a better idea?"

I knew Xavier well enough to know he wasn't going to be satisfied with this. He needed to have all the facts, and my siblings seemed to be holding something back.

"I'm not really following," he persisted, struggling to keep the frustration out of his voice. "Look, I know we didn't get permission from upstairs for what we did, but they did give us the green light to be together once. All we did was take the next step."

"Except that step wasn't yours to take," Ivy said. I barely recognized her. She sounded like a Seraphim talking now, and not my sister. "Your relationship was tolerated. You should not have taken the step you took without authorization."

"Beth's committed a serious transgression," Gabriel added in case further clarification was needed. "Marriage is an indissoluble covenant between man and woman. You two have pushed your luck in the past but this time . . . you were way out of line. You cannot overturn the order of creation without repercussions. So get ready for a reaction. And I don't think it'll be pretty."

4

The Cover of Trees

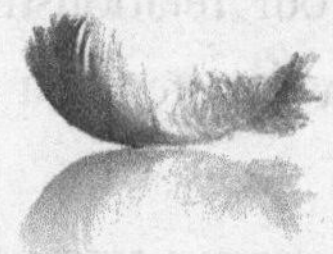

DESPITE his harsh words, Gabriel's eyes were sorrowful. I had the feeling that deep down he blamed himself for my actions. I remembered the quizzical look he'd given me just days ago on the lawns of Bryce Hamilton as Xavier and I were moving away from the students assembled in their caps and gowns. But then one of his eager young choristers distracted him with a question and his focus had shifted back to being the music teacher, and away from us. When he looked for us again, we would have been gone. Gabriel liked to see himself as infallible. His failure to pick up on what was happening under his nose would rankle.

Xavier gave my brother an exasperated look. "I'm so over this crap," he said finally.

"You're not the only one," Gabriel replied coolly. "But Bethany, as you insist on forgetting, is not from this world."

"Oh, I haven't forgotten." There was something about his tone that bothered me. Was he regretting his decision already?

"If you'd had the sense to come to us first, we might have found another way," my brother reflected.

"We're not children," Xavier said emphatically. "We can make our own decisions."

"Well, you're not very good at it," Gabriel replied. "Why don't you think more carefully next time?"

"Why don't you butt out of our lives?"

"I would gladly, if your decisions didn't have repercussions for everyone around you."

"For goodness sake," Ivy said. "We're all on the same side here—we need to stop pointing fingers and focus on the best way to handle this."

"You're right. I'm sorry," Xavier said. After a moment he directed his attention to Gabriel. "I suppose the real question is, could you take out one of these Sevens if you needed to?"

One thing I remembered hearing about the Sevens was that they considered themselves an elite group; they would network and swap information until they'd tracked down their prey. We couldn't elude them forever; eventually they'd catch up to us. I hoped Gabriel was working on a long-term plan.

"One-on-one, my powers would outstrip theirs," Gabriel answered. "But there is every chance I would be outnumbered. There are dozens of them and they're trained fighters."

"Super."

"What exactly will happen if they find us?" I asked.

"That's a good question," Ivy replied. Her face told us she didn't have the answer.

"You can't expect us to just sit around and wait for them to show up!" I said.

"You won't be able to stay here long. We're just buying time until we decide what to do," Gabriel said. "In the meantime there's nothing you can do except stay alert." I could see the possibilities ticking over in Xavier's mind.

"Can you at least tell us what these Sevens look like?" he said. "Could we pick one out of a crowd?"

"A long time ago they used to appear wearing robes and golden girdles," Ivy explained.

"They sound like losers," Xavier muttered.

My sister sighed impatiently. "They've adapted to fit the times. These days they tend to appear as men in black."

"So there's nothing we can do to prepare?" Xavier pressed.

"There are signs that usually precede their arrival," Ivy said grimly. "Look out for a blood moon or the sighting of a white phantom horse. If you see one, a Seven won't be far behind."

"A blood moon or a white horse?" Xavier asked dubiously. "Really?"

"You doubt the veracity of all this?" Gabriel sounded affronted.

"I don't mean any disrespect, Gabriel, but you don't honestly think I'm gonna let some dude in a girdle riding a white horse take Beth, do you?"

A sound of exasperation escaped from Gabriel's lips. He was on the verge of saying more until Ivy's raised hand silenced us all. She looked earnestly at Xavier.

"Your valor is admirable," she said. "But promise us one thing. If you do see one, don't try and fight it; just get Beth as far away as you can."

"Okay," Xavier said, his eyes deadly serious. "I promise."

A few minutes later, Gabriel and Ivy took off again. They said they were going to investigate and seek out information that might help us. But really we had no idea where they were going or what their plans involved. We were like children, following orders and being kept in the dark. I knew it was for our own protection but it still stung.

Xavier and I went upstairs that night with heavy hearts. We sat together on the green velvet sofa facing the window and looked out over the quivering treetops of the silver forest. An unsettling wind had started up, making things rattle in the roof and causing the boughs leaning over the paling fence to creak.

"I guess we won't be getting much sleep tonight," I said.

"I doubt it," Xavier replied, kissing the top of my head. I propped myself up, watching the dark outline of the trees through the window. In the cool blue moonlight Xavier's face was pale, almost unearthly, and the color of his eyes was vivid when he flicked them across to look at me. "I know you didn't need this," he said. "Not after everything that happened last Halloween."

"What can you do?" I replied. "Bad stuff is never well timed."

"I wish there was someplace I could take you," he said, turning his gaze upward in frustration. "Where I know you'd be safe."

"You shouldn't worry about me," I said. "I've seen a lot now. I'm not so fragile anymore."

"I know." He adjusted the throw on the sofa so that it covered my bare shoulders. "We've never talked about it, you know," he continued in a tentative voice. I knew he didn't want to push me. "The time you spent in . . ." Xavier petered out. But I wasn't afraid to say it.

"Hell?" I prompted. "There's not much to tell. It was everything they say it is."

"Some people say you don't remember a traumatic experience," Xavier said. "Your subconscious blocks it out. I kind of hoped that might be true for you."

I shook my head sadly. "I remember," I told him. "I remember everything."

"Do you want to talk about it?"

"I wouldn't know where to start." I shifted position, fitting myself around him like a puzzle piece. The warmth he radiated made me feel confident enough to continue. "The worst part is that I left my friends behind . . . Hanna and Tuck. Wouldn't think you'd make friends in Hell, would you? But they were like my family down there. Hanna was the kindest girl I've ever met, and Tuck was the one who showed me how to project so I could come and visit you."

"I wish I could thank him," Xavier said.

"I hate to think what they've done to him." I winced involuntarily. "When they're angry, they're capable of anything."

Xavier swallowed audibly. "Did they . . . did they do anything to you?"

"They tried burning me at the stake."

"What!" Xavier's whole body went rigid and he jerked upright. His face changed suddenly and I knew my words must have dredged up painful memories for him. Only a few years ago, his girlfriend Emily had died in a fire at the hands of demons.

"It's okay." I tugged him gently back down toward me. "The flames didn't touch me. I think someone was protecting me, someone from above."

"Whoa." He exhaled loudly. "That's not easy to get your head around."

"I know. But that wasn't the worst part."

"You mean there's something worse than burning at the stake?"

"I saw the Pit."

"The Pit?" Xavier echoed. His eyes widened. "You mean like the medieval pit of fire where . . ."

"Souls are tortured," I finished for him.

"Beth, I'm so sorry . . ."

"Don't be," I cut him off. "It's not your fault and it's not some problem you can solve for me. It's just something that happened and I have to deal with it."

Xavier looked at me, a strange expression in his bottomless blue eyes. "You're a lot stronger than people give you credit for."

I gave him a wan smile. "If my time underground taught me anything, it's that nothing is permanent. Everything and everyone you know can change at any moment. That's how I see things now—except for you. You're the one constant in my life."

"You know that won't ever change, right? I'll always be

here." Xavier pressed his forehead against mine. "You can bet on that. Besides, fending off these Sevens should be a piece of cake after what you've been through."

I thought about that for a second and decided he was right. What could be worse than being dragged into Hell and trapped in an underworld where those you loved couldn't find you? There might be legions of Sevens on the lookout for us, but Xavier and I were still together. And we had Gabriel and Ivy exhausting every possibility to help find us a solution.

"We should try and get some sleep," Xavier suggested. We moved over to the bed, kicked off our shoes, and curled up on top of it. After what Gabriel had said, neither of us felt comfortable enough to get under the covers. I closed my eyes but there was too much commotion in my head. I couldn't turn it off. It felt oppressive in our loft bedroom and I would have liked to open the window just enough to let in the night air but I knew I couldn't risk it. Would the Sevens pick up on our scent? Could they smell the fear and uncertainty hanging over us? I didn't know, but I wasn't about to take any chances. When dawn finally broke I couldn't remember whether we'd slept or not, but it was a relief not to have to fight consciousness anymore. Besides, the dark only added to my growing sense of claustrophobia. Who knew what might be out there . . . waiting for us.

The next couple of days and nights passed in the same manner. We lost track of time. Being on alert made us anxious and agitated, but a deathly lethargy also settled over us. At night we slept fitfully, but what we needed—real, restful sleep—continued to elude us. It was hardly surprising given that we usually spent all day cooped up inside with little to do but wait for updates from Ivy and Gabriel. They usually appeared without warning around mid-afternoon, bringing fresh supplies but little in the way of news. I was growing impatient and Gabriel's pronouncement that *no news is good news* did little to reassure me. Xavier, who had engaged in some form of physical exercise every day for most of his life, was also going stir-crazy.

Being in lockdown brought back painful memories for me. On the odd occasions when I did fall asleep, I would wake in tears shortly after descending into a nightmare. I dreamed the cabin was underground and we were running out of air. When I tried to open a window, a river of earth tumbled in, threatening to bury us alive. At the same time, I knew it wouldn't matter if we escaped, because what awaited us aboveground was no better. My strangled sobbing always woke me first. Xavier would wake in turn and comfort me, stroking my hair until I went back to sleep.

On our third night together my dream changed; legions of faceless Sevens were galloping through the skies holding flaming swords. Their horses' eyes rolled back in their heads as their hooves pounded the air. Their hooded riders pointed them toward our cabin where they lined up like rows of dominoes. There were so many that I lost count. They charged forward at the same time my eyes flew open. I clutched at Xavier's sleeve, rousing him immediately. His arm, already resting around my shoulders, tightened immediately. The weight of it made me feel protected and I nestled into him.

Thinking about the new nightmares that awaited me made it hard to settle and I kept wriggling restlessly and shifting my position on the bed to get comfortable.

"I know it's hard but please try to relax," Xavier coaxed. "We're going to be okay, Beth." Even in the moonlight streaming through the loft window I could make out his sky blue eyes. The unflinching way he looked at me reminded me that I was prepared to follow him to the ends of the earth.

"What if something happens while we're sleeping?"

"No one is going to find this place in the dark."

"Maybe not humans . . . but angel soldiers?"

"We have to trust that Gabriel's got this covered. If we're careful, we'll be fine."

I wanted badly to believe him, but what if Gabriel was out of his depth this time? And being careful alone was certainly no guarantee that we'd be fine. The truth was, we didn't know what was going to happen from one day to the next. On the spot I made a decision to be focused on the future rather than stressing over things I couldn't change. I tried to picture our life together when all this was behind us. I forced myself to imagine what kind of conversation we might be having right now under normal circumstances and decided to give it a try.

"Xavier?" I snuggled closer to him, pressing my cheek against his smooth, warm shoulder. "Are you going to sleep?"

"Trying to."

"Love you," I said.

"I love you too." Things always felt better after hearing those words.

"Xavier?"

"Yeah?" he answered in a sleepy drawl.

"How many babies do you want to have?" With any other teenage boy, that kind of question would have set off major alarm bells. But as usual, Xavier was unfazed.

"Probably no more than a dozen."

"Be serious."

"Okay. *Seriously*, is now really a good time to discuss this?"

"I'm just curious," I said. "Besides, it might take my mind off things."

"Fine. I think three's a good number."

"Me too. I love when we're on the same wavelength."

"That's good."

"Do you think there's much chance of it happening?"

"Of what happening?"

"Us having kids."

"Sure. Definitely. One day."

"Can we call our first born Waylon if it's a boy?"

"No."

"Why?"

"Because he'll get the crap kicked out of him, that's why."

"Okay, what names do you like?"

"Normal names, like Josh or Sam."

"Fine, but I get to name the girls."

"Only from an agreed list."

"I think I want my daughters to have strong names . . . strong but pretty, y'know?"

"Sounds great. Can we go to sleep now?" Xavier turned and

curved his body into mine. I could hear his breathing become deeper but I was still wide awake. I knew I should let him sleep, but I wasn't ready to part with his company just yet.

"If I give you some examples of girls' names, can you tell me if they make it onto the list?"

"If you insist." Xavier blinked hard and propped himself onto his elbow to face me, trying to take my game seriously.

"Caroline?"

"In."

"Billie?"

"No way, she'll be gender confused."

"Isadora?"

"Is she from Middle Earth?"

"Fine. How about Dakota?"

"Place names are out."

"That's not fair." I pouted. "Most of my favorites are places."

"Then I get to throw in some places of my own."

"Like?" I asked curiously.

"How about Ohio?" Xavier said. "Or better yet, Milwaukee."

I had to giggle. "Okay, we can ditch the place names."

"Thank you." When Xavier stifled a yawn and flipped over onto his back, I feigned indignation.

"Did you just yawn? Are your unborn children boring you?"

"No, but they are making me sleepy."

"All right." I laughed. "I'll stop now. Good night."

"Night, Mrs. Woods."

That reminded me. I was Mrs. Woods now. Xavier's wife. I felt an overpowering urge to reach out and wrap myself around him, to absorb his warmth and find comfort in his touch. But I held back, knowing it was too risky. I didn't want to make things harder than they already were. Instead I turned over and cradled my pillow. We'd made so many sacrifices already. How much longer could we go on living like brother and sister?

Before I closed my eyes, I couldn't help looking at the midnight sky through the window. A few flashes of lightning illuminated the clouds. I wondered whether a storm was far off. Then I saw a beam of light that didn't look like lightning. I thought about waking Xavier, but he was finally sleeping so soundly and I knew it wouldn't be fair.

The beam lingered and moved lazily across the trees, scoping the forest . . . looking for something.

5

Walking on Water

IN the morning I woke to a chorus of birdsong and the scent of pine. In my half-conscious state I felt around for Xavier in the bed and was startled when I couldn't find him. The sound of a kettle whistling reassured me that he was already downstairs making breakfast.

Xavier had turned on an old Bakelite radio and tuned it to a classic rock station.

"Good morning," I said, unable to repress a smile as I watched him whisk eggs to the beat of "Blue Suede Shoes" on the radio. He was wearing boxer shorts and a white T-shirt and his hair was still rumpled from sleep. Living under the same roof with Xavier over the last few days meant I got to see a side of him I'd only ever caught glimpses of before. For as long as I'd known him and before he'd got dragged into our supernatural mess, Xavier's life had been crammed with more activities than he had time for. I realized now how much of a homebody he was at heart.

"I hope you're hungry."

Even in my oversized flannel pajamas I was still shivering. I grabbed a throw from the nearest sofa, wrapped it around my shoulders, and sat huddled in a kitchen chair. Xavier poured me a mug of tea and I wrapped my fingers around the china to warm them.

"How can you not feel cold?"

"It's time you knew the truth. I'm a werewolf," he joked, hunching his shoulders and narrowing his eyes.

"A very domestic werewolf," I teased. "Why didn't you wake me?"

"Thought you could use the sleep. It's been a rough couple of days. How are you feeling?"

"Fine."

Xavier studied me thoughtfully. "You'll feel better once you have something to eat."

"I'm not really hungry," I said, hoping I didn't sound too unappreciative.

"You're passing on the famous Woods' fry-up?" he said. I couldn't bring myself to deflate his enthusiasm. Besides, it had been awhile since I'd seen this old carefree Xavier and I didn't want him to disappear just yet.

"I wouldn't dare." I grinned. "Can I help with anything?"

Looking around I saw bacon already sizzling in a pan and the table had been set with country-style plates and silverware.

"No, ma'am. Just sit back and enjoy the service."

"I didn't know you liked cooking."

"'Course I do," he said. "And cooking for your wife is half the fun."

He cracked an egg and it sizzled as it slid into the pan.

"A good husband wouldn't make fried eggs when his wife

likes them scrambled," I said playfully, drumming my fingers on the counter.

Xavier glanced up and fixed me with an amused expression. "A good wife would appreciate her husband's speciality and not complain."

I smiled and rocked back in my chair, wishing I could throw the windows open and invite the fresh air in. It was getting seriously stuffy in here.

"You called me Mrs. Woods last night," I said suddenly, recalling the conversation we'd had.

"Yeah?" Xavier looked up. "So?"

"I'm still getting used to it," I said. "It's strange to think that's me now."

"You don't have to take my name if you don't want to," Xavier said. "It's completely your decision."

"Are you kidding?" I said. "Of course I want to. It's not as if I've even been Bethany Church for that long. Besides, I've changed so much I don't even know who she is anymore."

"Well, I do," Xavier said. "She's the girl I married. Even if you lose sight of her, I never will."

The fire hadn't managed to chase away the chill in the air, so I moved into the living room to warm up. I didn't think I could face another day idle on the couch.

"Can we drive into town today?" I called out to Xavier, trying to sound blasé. "I really want to get out of the house."

Xavier came into the living room, frowning. "Beth, you can't be serious! It's too dangerous for us to be seen anywhere in public. You know that."

"We don't even have to get out of the car. I'll wear a blanket over my head if you like."

"No way. It's too risky. Besides, Gabriel will blow a fuse when he finds out."

"Might do him good," I grumbled, and Xavier's face lightened.

"True as that may be I don't think we should push our luck right now. Don't worry; we'll find something to do right here."

"Like what?"

"Why don't you have a look around while I finish getting breakfast ready?"

I suddenly realized how petulant I must sound. "Okay."

"That's my girl."

It occurred to me that Xavier was much better at staying upbeat than I was. I couldn't help complaining about being trapped. I shouldn't even be mourning the loss of "normal" life when it wasn't supposed to be mine to begin with, but I found the isolation disconcerting. Ever since I'd come to earth, there had always been people around. Milling around in the town square, walking their dogs, eating snow cones on the pier, waving across the street as they mowed their lawns. Now their absence made me uncomfortable. I desperately wanted to hear the hum of human voices in the background or watch people from a distance, even if we couldn't speak to them. But Gabriel's instructions had been clear: Stay out of sight.

I hated that after all Xavier and I had been through we still couldn't be a normal couple, which was all we wanted.

But I tried to remind myself that however difficult things were, at least Xavier and I were together. When Gabriel and Ivy had found us in the chapel, I was almost certain we'd be separated. I wouldn't exactly have been in a position to argue with them and I was relieved it hadn't come to that. They must have known neither of us would cope well with being apart.

I decided to take Xavier's advice and find something that would help fill the hours and at least give the illusion of normality. I checked the stack of magazines on the mantel of the stone fireplace but they were mostly dated and on the subject of interior decorating. Then my eyes happened to fall on the old travel chest in the living room that doubled as a coffee table. Up until now we hadn't thought to open it, but when I lifted the lid I found some DVDs hiding under a stack of old yellowing newspapers. The movies were mainly Disney cartoons, so I figured the family who owned the cabin must have young children. I tried to imagine them sitting in this very room, drinking hot chocolate and watching their favorite films.

"Hey, Xavier, I found something," I called out. He poked his head around the corner before coming over to examine my find.

"Not bad."

"I know, right? How can we be bored when we can watch a movie about . . ." I turned one of the DVDs over expectantly. "*Fish?*"

"Don't knock *Finding Nemo,*" Xavier teased, taking the DVD from my grasp. "It's a modern classic."

"Is it seriously about fish?"

"Yeah, but really cool fish."

"What about this?" I held up a battered copy of *Beauty and the Beast*. "It sounds romantic." Xavier wrinkled his nose.

"Disney . . . I don't think so."

"Why not?"

"Because if anyone found out, I'd never live it down."

"I won't tell if you don't," I pleaded, and Xavier shook his head in defeat.

"The things I do for you," he said with an exaggerated sigh.

After breakfast we finally got the DVD player to work after we found a missing cable. I kept interrupting the movie by asking a lot of questions that Xavier managed to answer with endless patience.

"How old do you think Belle is supposed to be?"

"I don't know, probably our age."

"I think the beast is sweet, don't you?"

"Do I have to answer that?"

"Why does the crockery talk?"

"Because they're really the prince's servants that the beggar woman put a spell on." Xavier frowned suddenly and looked mortified. "I can't believe I know that."

Despite being captivated by the magic of the story and having the lyrics of "Be Our Guest" set on permanent replay in my brain, I was restless again as soon as the movie was over.

I got up and began flitting around the room like a caged

bird. Just like Belle, I wanted to be out in the world living my life. Even Ivy and Gabriel had failed to make their routine appearance so we couldn't even get an update on how the *negotiations* were going. I knew they were working as hard as they could to obtain some sort of reprieve for me. I was grateful for everything they were doing but I just wished I knew what was going to happen, one way or another. At least if I knew what my fate would be I could begin to prepare for it.

"I wish my life was more like a Disney movie," I said heavily.

"Don't worry; it is. Didn't you notice all the crap those two had to go through before they could be together?"

"That's true." I smiled. "And there's always a happy ending, right?"

Xavier fixed me with his brilliant gaze. "Beth, when this is over, we're going to have so many adventures. I promise."

"I hope so," I replied, trying to sound more positive than I felt.

A shaft of sunlight peeked through the curtains like a gold bar falling across the kitchen table. It seemed to be taunting me, trying to lure me out of the house.

"Xavier, look—it's sunny out," I began tentatively.

"Uh-huh." Xavier was noncommittal but I knew he hated seeing me unhappy.

"I really need to get out of here."

"Beth, we've been through this."

"I only want to go for a walk. It's such a simple thing."

"Except that our lives aren't simple. At least, not right now."

"This is ridiculous. Can't we go outside just for a few minutes?"

"I don't think that's a good idea," Xavier said. But I could see his resolve wavering. He longed to make a decision and exercise some control over our lives as much as I did.

"Who's going to see us around here?" I persisted.

"Nobody I guess, but that's not the point. Gabriel and Ivy were very clear."

"We'll go as far as the yard and come straight back," I said. The idea of freedom, no matter how fleeting, had cheered me up so much that Xavier could hardly say no.

"Fine." He sighed heavily. "But if we're going outside you need to cover up to make sure you're not recognized."

"By who?" I asked sarcastically. "The paparazzi?"

"Beth . . ." Xavier said warningly.

"Okay, okay! What did you have in mind?"

Xavier didn't answer but strode out of the room and I heard him searching through the upstairs closet. When he returned, he was carrying an oversized military jacket and a hunting cap.

"Put these on." I gave him a skeptical look. "And don't argue."

I knew Xavier was just playing it safe, but so far nothing out of the ordinary had happened. Of course there'd been the mysterious lights in the sky, but I'd conveniently neglected to mention that. Xavier was tense enough already and besides, there was every chance it was nothing to worry about. We'd seen no white horses and no surprise visitors had knocked on our door. In fact, the last few days had been so uneventful it was hard to believe we were in any real danger. I even started wondering whether my siblings had somehow got it wrong. Maybe their contacts weren't as attuned to Heaven's will as they thought they were.

But I should have known that in our lives any period of calm usually preceded a storm.

WE made our way around to the tangled yard at the back of the cabin, where we found herbs growing out of a barrel tub and a tire swing hanging from the sturdy limb of a live oak. There was a rickety moss-covered footbridge leading to a lake that cut across the back of the property. I inhaled deeply, feeling my body shiver with sudden energy. We squatted by the clover-covered banks at the lake's edge and ran our hands through the rippling water. It was icy cold and so clear we could see straight through to the polished pebbles on the bottom. There was the hum of bees in the air and a gentle breeze wafted around us. The sun warmed our faces, and after being locked inside for so long the light was so bright it almost hurt our eyes.

We walked unhurriedly. At that moment it was hard to believe we were being hunted; the idea that I was an angel with a price on her head seemed almost absurd. For a moment we were just a couple in love. We looked around as if we were seeing the world for the first time. Xavier picked up some stones to test how far he could ski them across the lake. I tried to emulate him when he made a stone dance across the water but mine just seemed to hit the surface with a dull splash. There wasn't a doubt in my mind that I would trade my immortality in a blink to have the chance to grow old with Xavier. I hoped Ivy and Gabriel understood that. Of course, I didn't expect the Sevens to understand. I could never explain it to them. In my mind's eye I envisioned them as a pack of wolves hungry for the prize. Whichever one succeeded in finding me and delivering me to whatever retribution awaited would no doubt be hailed as a hero in the Kingdom.

Although all angels were created to be without ego, the Sevens were an aberration to this rule. Some said they were driven by their need for recognition. Thinking back on how much Zach had changed just before his promotion just confirmed this theory. I knew how the hierarchies that existed on earth were mirrored in Heaven and what lengths some—human or angel—would go to in pursuit of power. I had fought demons before and won. But demons were fundamentally simplistic beings. Their motives were transparent—manipulate humans and lead them astray. An ambitious rank of angels driven by a thirst for justice might be a lot harder to deal with.

We couldn't have been walking around for more than ten minutes when I caught Xavier sneaking a glance at his watch. I noticed the sun rose and set early in this part of the world. I too was suddenly conscious of the waning light.

"C'mon, Beth. We better head back."

"Already?"

"Yes. We've been out too long."

"Okay. I'm coming."

Although I knew Xavier was waiting just ahead, I allowed myself a few more seconds to enjoy my surroundings before returning to the imprisonment that awaited us in the cabin. The thick woods surrounding us had such a magical quality and I longed to explore them. The sun breaking through the wispy clouds sent shards of light dancing over the water. I took one final look around. Who knew when we'd be able to spend time surrounded by the beauty of nature again? If Gabriel got wind of our escapade he might decide we could never be left unsupervised again.

I turned my back on the idyllic scene and made my way to where Xavier was standing. He reached out his hand to help me climb up a steep part of the embankment. He pulled me toward him and adjusted the cap that was falling over my eyes.

"Do you think it might be safe to lose the hat now?" I asked playfully.

Xavier didn't reply. At first I thought he objected to my tone but then I saw the color drain from his face and his jaw clench as something on the other side of the embankment fixed his attention. When he spoke, his mouth barely moved.

"Don't turn around," he said.

"What? Why?" I gripped his hand more tightly as panic set in.

"There's someone on the other side of the lake."

"A local?" I whispered hopefully.

"I don't think so."

I dropped to my knees, making a show of retrieving something I'd lost. When I straightened I turned my head a fraction and stole a look across the lake. I shook my head, thinking I must be hallucinating. At some distance from us, tethered between two sturdy trees, was a white horse. Its coat and mane were a silver unearthly color and it pawed at the ground with gilded hooves.

"A white horse." The words seemed to tumble out of my mouth, now slack with shock.

"Where?" Xavier sounded incredulous as he peered into the surrounding woods.

Xavier hadn't seen the horse because he'd been so focused on its rider. The immaculately groomed figure was dressed as if he might be going to a funeral. Despite his empty eye sockets, I felt he was looking right at me. I'd never seen one before but I knew the creature staring back at me was a Seven. There was no doubt about it.

This was the moment I'd convinced myself would never come. I was finally face-to-face with a member of the Seventh Order, beings who up until now I'd only known through reputation.

He stood by the water at its broadest point, just as it flowed around the bend. Ivy's words rang through my head and I knew I should be running from him, but I couldn't move. I was frozen. I noticed the Seven had very white hands and they were folded calmly as he watched us. Then without warning, he began to approach us. A moment ago he was standing on the other side of the water. Now, he was moving steadily closer, the weight of his feet gently rippling the surface of the lake.

"Beth, am I dreaming or is he . . ." Xavier broke off and took a few cautious steps backward, pulling me along with him.

"You're not dreaming," I whispered. "He's walking on water."

6

We Need to Talk

THE Seven was headed straight for us. It was like watching something happen in a dream: One minute he was across the lake and the next he was standing only meters away from us. In the distance his white horse whinnied and reared its head, but its rider paid it no attention.

I remembered what Gabriel had told us; Sevens were hunters, trained to stalk their prey. But this one seemed unconcerned by the fact that we'd seen him. Instead he continued calmly forward. It was as if he understood there was no need for him to hurry, because we had no chance of outmaneuvering him. If I hadn't been desperately trying to calculate a way out, I might have been annoyed by his conceit. The Seven only paused once and cocked his head slightly, as if to confirm my identity. There was something mechanical about the movement, like a device was being activated. It made me imagine his brain was wired to pick up everything from the shape of my skull to the smell of my skin. There was nothing human about him. But there was nothing angelic about him either.

Like others of his kind, this Seven was faceless. His lips and nose blended so seamlessly, it was almost impossible to distinguish them. He had no eyes, just empty sockets covered over by a white milky membrane of skin. The perfect contours of his face reminded me of the mannequins I'd seen in department store windows.

Suddenly my thoughts began to blur, sinking like melted butter into bread. I tried but couldn't shake myself free. The Seven seemed to have me trapped in an invisible vice-like grip. Luckily, he couldn't exert the same power over Xavier, who quickly realized what was happening. He didn't bother trying to snap me out of the trance. He just picked me up, threw me over his shoulder, and made a break for it. After a few moments, I felt the Seven's hold over me loosen. I slid off Xavier's back and, bolstered by adrenaline, we pelted down the path together, running without turning back to check our pursuer.

My siblings and I had long been able to communicate telepathically, and we were always attuned to each other's needs. I silently called out for my brother's help. "Gabriel! They're here. They've found us!" There was no response.

As soon as we made it to the gravel path outside the cabin, Xavier stopped to rummage in his pocket for his cell. He fumbled through his list of contacts, his fingers clumsy from stress. He was just about to hit the CALL button when we both came to a sudden halt. I was already halfway up the porch steps when I backed up suddenly, collided with Xavier who was standing right behind me, and knocked the cell phone right out of his grasp. Before either of us could attempt to retrieve it, the front door opened. The Seven was already there, waiting for us.

I looked around frantically for somewhere to hide but I knew there was no point.

"Leave us alone!" I shouted instead, backing away from the immaculately groomed figure. In response, he took a single step forward, as if to remind me that he could not be commanded. A loose board creaked under his feet and I remembered the sound being impossibly loud in the sleepy afternoon.

Where were Gabriel and Ivy? Hadn't they heard my plea for help? Or had they been intercepted? A shiver ran through me when I realized how much could change in the next few seconds. Staying calm was our only chance. I just hoped Xavier didn't do anything rash in a bid to protect me. The Seven would take his life in a heartbeat. The moist white membranes that covered his eyes made it impossible to tell exactly who or what he was looking at. I wasn't expecting it when he extended an elegant hand toward me.

"We need to talk," the Seven said. His voice was toneless, a dull vibration in the air. "Would you care to step inside?" He stepped aside, allowing room for me to enter. Up close the planes of his face were so smooth they might have been made of plaster. The way he smelled struck me as odd; it was the scent of cheap cologne mingled with a hint of gasoline that burned my nostrils.

"Think again, buddy," Xavier snapped. "Beth's not going anywhere with you."

"Xavier, please," I whispered. "Let me handle this."

The Seven seemed not to notice that Xavier had even spoken. Although I'd never encountered one before, I sensed how dangerous it would be to show overt resistance.

"It won't take long," the Seven continued in a parody of politeness. We both knew that if I followed him inside I'd never come out again. I took a hesitant step forward, my feet like lumps of concrete beneath me.

"Beth, wait!" Xavier caught hold of my arm and stared at me, his bottomless blue eyes full of horror. "You're not seriously gonna go with this . . . *freak,* are you?" If the Seven was at all offended it didn't register on his face, which remained as perfect as a digital picture.

"Do not make this more difficult than it needs to be," he warned. He kept his face turned in my direction. I had to think quickly. I had to do something to stall him, catch him off guard. I kept asking myself, *What would Gabriel say?* I knew he wouldn't have to think about it. Maybe that was the key.

"You're turning on your own kind," I said suddenly. "You know that, right?" I wondered how shrewd the Seven was. Would he see through my ploy? If I could delay my interview with him even for a few minutes, maybe Gabriel and Ivy would make it back in time.

"I'm sorry, Miss Church, I'm not the one here who's turned." He spoke with such cold authority that it shook my confidence, but I wasn't about to let him see that.

"Actually, it's Mrs. Woods now," I said brazenly.

The corners of his perfect mouth seemed to twitch into

a tiny smile, the first display of emotion so far. Was he mocking me?

"I advise you, *Mrs. Woods,* to comply with my request and there will be no need for bloodshed," he replied, casting a fleeting glance in Xavier's direction. I knew that beneath the courteous and businesslike exterior was a soldier with no other objective than to fulfill his mission . . . whatever the cost. Again I had the feeling that my thoughts were clouding over.

"Of course," I said mechanically. "I understand."

Xavier grabbed my hand. "I'm not letting you go."

"It's okay," I lied. "It's just to talk." Xavier didn't look convinced but before he could react further I wrenched my hand away and moved toward the Seven. I knew Xavier couldn't protect me. It was my job to protect him now. If I had no choice but to ascend with the Seven, then I was going to make absolutely sure Xavier stayed behind unharmed. But Xavier wasn't about to take any chances with my life either. He ran forward and pulled me behind him so that he was the one face-to-face with the Seven.

"If you want to talk to anyone, you can talk to me." The Seven was forced to address him.

"Boy, what makes you think you can counter the will of Heaven?"

"Just arrogant, I guess."

"Step aside. I have no business with you."

"Beth's business is my business."

The Seven gave a sigh of impatience, or was it boredom? "Don't say I didn't warn you."

"Don't hurt him, I'll do whatever you say!" I cried out, but it was too late.

The Seven raised his palm upward and a string of light poured from it. The thin beam, which I knew was tough as steel, wrapped itself around Xavier's throat. I watched his eyes widen and his hands grasp at his neck, but the struggle was in vain—he was choking. This was not a fight he could win. Xavier fell to his knees and I could see his body begin to slacken as he had lost consciousness fast.

"No one can divert the will of Heaven," the Seven said.

As I watched the scene before me, I felt the fog in my head begin to clear, replaced by something much more powerful: rage. The anger was coursing through me, pushing back everything in its path. I felt it swelling like water in a dam after torrential rain. In a moment it would burst its banks.

"I told you not to hurt him." I didn't raise my voice but I could hear the venom in it. Something inside of me had changed.

Rage often distorts one's perception of reality, but at that moment, I had never seen things with so much clarity. It released me from any hold the Seven had over me. I could almost feel the cogs in my mind turning and for a split second I felt like I was seeing the world through X-ray goggles. I could see the molecular composition of the cabin, pinpoint exactly where its weak spots were, and sense the places where the damp was creeping through the walls. I knew things nobody could possibly know, down to where the last raindrop from a summer storm had touched the ground. I was still looking at the Seven but now I could see through him. In that moment everything about me that was human seemed to dissolve and I felt at one with the universe—I was air, rock, wood, earth. I knew then what I needed to do, what I was capable of doing.

Quick as a flash, I stooped to pick up a loose brick from the few I knew were scattered at the bottom of the steps. I threw it like a Frisbee, so fast it collided with the Seven's neck before he even saw it coming. His finely tuned reflexes should have allowed him to catch it midair and throw it back with enough force to knock me out cold. If he were capable of expressing sentiment, the Seven would have looked surprised. But he wasn't prepared for retaliation and my attack had caught him off guard.

His head seemed to snap backward and he took a couple of teetering steps into the house. With a sudden burst of force I thrust my hand out and pulled the front door shut behind him. My fingertips started to tingle and before I knew it, the roof was beginning to smoke. What happened next was almost out of my control. The fire blossomed before my eyes, twining around the porch posts and shattering the windowpanes. In a matter of seconds, Willow Lodge was engulfed in flames. As the walls began to collapse, I saw the Seven, standing in his flaming suit. The fire wouldn't kill him. . . . It probably wouldn't even leave a mark. But it had temporarily slowed him down. I didn't know for how long and I didn't plan to stick around to find out.

I had one thought and one thought only: get Xavier to safety. If the Seven caught up to us now, he would probably kill him out of spite. I rushed to Xavier's side; he was passed out but still breathing. I couldn't rouse him, and carrying him on foot was out of the question. Through the window I could see the Seven already moving toward the door like a blazing torch.

My wings flew open with a resounding crack. The sound reverberated through the forest and the birds scattered from the treetops. I grabbed Xavier from behind, wrapped my arms around his chest, and lifted us both off the ground. My wings were so powerful, he felt weightless in my arms. I headed for the road, flying low to avoid detection; the treetops brushed the soles of Xavier's feet.

My thoughts weren't all that coherent but I planned to land somewhere and flag down a car. Instead my heart lifted when I saw the familiar black Jeep speeding down the dirt track that led to the mountains. My brother and sister saw me at exactly the same time. The car shuddered to a halt and Gabriel was at my side in an instant, taking Xavier in his arms and laying him gently in the backseat.

"Where have you been?" I said, tears trickling down my ash-smudged face.

"We came as soon as we could," said Ivy, sounding breathless. I pointed at Xavier.

"Can you help him?"

Ivy placed a cool hand on Xavier's forehead and a moment later he began to regain consciousness. He groaned and instinctively put a hand to his head.

"You're okay," I told him. "We're okay."

As the memory of the last half hour came back to him, Xavier tensed and quickly sat up.

"Where did he go?" he asked. "Where are we?"

"Ivy and Gabriel are with us," I said. "We got away."

"How?" Xavier asked. "The Seven was going to take you . . ."

"I think . . ." I hesitated. "I think I sort of set him on fire."

"*No way.*" Xavier looked stunned for a moment and then couldn't hold back his laughter. "That's awesome. He really had it coming."

Ivy had a slightly different reaction. "Have you lost your mind?" Her silver eyes were almost metallic with shock. "Using powers like that on a Seven. It's treason against the Kingdom!"

"I didn't mean to," I protested. "He was trying to kill Xavier!"

"Well, now that you set him on fire, I'm sure we're well on the path to reconciliation," Gabriel said drily.

The wind rustled in the treetops and I was suddenly conscious that the Seven might still be out there.

"Do you think he'll try to follow us?"

"No, he's lost the scent by now. He'll need to start over. But we should leave anyway." Gabriel turned the key in the ignition and reversed across the overgrown track.

I couldn't help feeling a little bit smug. I'd succeeded in thwarting the plans of Heaven's most formidable agents. Gabriel seemed to read my mind.

"Don't get too confident; you managed to fend off *one*. There are legions of Sevens. We can't fight them all."

"How *are* we going to deal with them?"

"We've convened with the Arch and the Seraphs," Gabriel said. "That's why we were late getting back to the cabin."

"And? What's the verdict?"

I knew the news was bad when Gabriel remained silent.

"The Sevens are out for blood. They are not willing to compromise," Ivy said. "They want your marriage dissolved."

"I thought angels were supposed to be fair and just," Xavier said. "Since when do they go around trying to kill people? Since when does Heaven condone that?"

"What makes you think Heaven condones it?" Gabriel asked sharply.

Xavier was unapologetic. "They're not exactly doing much to stop them."

"What you must remember about the Sevens is they were created to be Heaven's watchdogs, designed to keep order. They have no understanding of human behavior, so it's easy for their power to get out of hand."

"You're defending them?" Xavier was taken aback. I could hardly blame him. Everything he'd ever been taught about Heaven and its inhabitants was being turned on its head.

"I'm not defending them," Gabriel replied. "I'm trying to explain how they work. In their minds they're only doing their job."

"Well, somebody needs to fire them."

"The Covenant is working on ways to limit their power."

"And in the meantime they're out of control?" I asked skeptically.

"Essentially," Ivy replied. "Their perception of justice is perverted. Once they have a mission, nothing else exists."

"You'd think they have better things to do," Xavier muttered. "Worry about world peace or something."

"Exactly," I seconded. "Why is our marriage so high on their agenda?"

"I don't know," Ivy said simply. But I got the distinct feeling she was holding out on us. She pressed her long, white fingers together and fixed her rain gray gaze on the seat in front of her.

Gabriel concentrated on the road ahead, his face rigid with some internal struggle that was waging. I pushed myself up between the two front seats and studied him.

Finally he took his eyes off the road and met my gaze. When I saw the expression in them, I guessed immediately what he wasn't telling me. "They've asked you to turn us in, haven't they?"

Gabriel frowned and closed his eyes for a moment. I would have told him to watch the road only I knew he could drive with flawless precision even if he was blindfolded.

"Yes," he admitted. He pressed his lips in a severe line. "That's exactly what they've asked."

"How dare they!" I was outraged on his behalf.

"They claim that any faithful servant of the Kingdom wouldn't need to think about it."

"So they're questioning your allegiance now?"

"They have told us surrendering you is our only option."

"I can't believe they've put you in this position," I fumed.

"Wait." Xavier held up his hands, his voice uncertain. "Gabriel, what did you tell them?"

My brother went silent.

"Gabe?" Xavier repeated, his voice now tinged with doubt. When he spoke again, Gabriel's voice was heavy with sorrow.

"I said I would."

There was a beat of dead silence.

"You what?" I asked softly.

"They're waiting for us right now. They believe I am bringing you to them."

It only took a moment for panic to set in.

"No!" I cried. "How could you?"

I realized then that the doors of the car had automatically locked. There was no way out, unless we tried to break a window.

"Bethany, please." My brother's voice was calm. "You are not a prisoner with me." He turned his head and I saw his flawless face was pained to think I had doubted him. A wave of guilt washed over me.

"You mean you're not . . ." I faltered.

"I am not turning you in to the Covenant. I have not betrayed you."

"Wait." I clamped a hand over my mouth. "That would mean you lied to them?" The idea was incomprehensible. It went against everything I thought I knew about my brother. I couldn't believe he had willingly put himself in such a compromising position.

"I had no choice."

I was overwhelmed by the sacrifice he'd made. "They could throw you out for this. I can't let you do it."

"It is done." He spoke the words gravely, as if someone had just died—maybe a part of him had. All I could think was that I'd never seen so much emptiness in his eyes before.

For as long as I could remember, Gabriel had been one of

the most dedicated and faithful archangels in the Kingdom. His allegiance went back thousands of years. Time had tried and tested his resolve, but he had remained true. He and Michael represented the two pillars upon which the Arch was founded. Was he really willing to turn his back on everything just to protect me?

How would I ever repay him?

"So you intend to renounce them?" I whispered, aghast. I couldn't imagine what fate awaited my brother were he to be stripped of his angelic identity. I didn't want to think about it.

"No," Gabriel replied. "But they will renounce me once I fail in my duty to serve."

7

College Kids

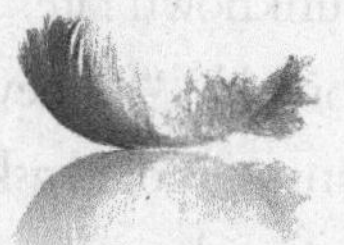

"I can't believe this is happening," I said. "I can't believe God could be so angry with us that He would unleash the Principalities." I couldn't make the idea gel in my head.

"Bethany," Ivy said, her oval face full of sadness. "This is not God's doing. Surely you know that?"

"How?" I asked in confusion. "Everything that happens only happens because it is His will."

"On earth that is true," my sister said. "But the angelic hierarchies settle their own disputes; they have not sought His counsel."

"The Sevens especially," Gabriel cut in, "are a rebel faction; the Covenant struggles to keep them under control."

"Are you saying God has no idea what's going on?" Xavier asked.

"I cannot speak for Him," Gabriel said. "But you must not blame Him for your troubles. It is the Sevens who seek retribution."

Gabriel leaned forward over the wheel and rubbed his temples, scraping back the blond locks that fell in front of his sculpted face. Ivy looked equally glum. I knew she was worried about their future. This was not the outcome either of them had hoped for.

"You don't have to do this, Gabe," I said earnestly. "I know how much this is costing you both."

"You are my family, Bethany," replied Gabriel. "I won't just hand you over to some unknown fate."

"Thank you," I said humbly. "I'll never forget this. You are by far the best brother anyone could ask for, human or angel."

Gabriel seemed unsure of how to respond to such praise, but I saw the corners of his mouth lift in a smile.

"So what now?" Xavier asked, steering the conversation in a more practical direction.

"We keep running, I suppose," said Gabriel.

That just didn't sound like my brother. Since when had Gabriel ever *supposed* anything? He was the one I consulted for answers when I had none. Life might be a constant puzzle for mortals, but Gabriel knew the reason behind everything. Among angels his wisdom was unquestionable. His uncertainty now cemented my deepest fears. The Sevens were going to try and tear Xavier and I apart, and everything so far indicated that they would eventually succeed. There was only so far you could run, only so many places you could hide. If I were taken away, I knew I wouldn't get Xavier back until his soul eventually ascended to Heaven. That was if I could find him . . . Heaven was vast. And by that time I might be nothing more to him than a faded memory. I knew I ought to feel devastated, but instead I was tired. Tired of fighting, tired of arguing, tired of always second-guessing.

"So, if you're not taking us to the Covenant . . . where

exactly are we going?" said Xavier, trying to dispel the grim silence that had descended over us.

"You need to go into hiding again," Ivy said.

"Oh, no," I groaned.

"But this time it'll be someplace harder for them to track you."

Xavier was skeptical. "Does a place like that even exist?"

"I'm not sure yet," Ivy replied.

"I don't care where we go so long as Beth doesn't have to be locked up. She didn't handle it well."

Xavier's comment seemed to trigger something in Ivy. A sudden spark appeared in her eyes as a new idea took shape.

"Maybe we need to do the opposite," she murmured cryptically.

"The opposite?" I echoed. "What are you thinking, Ivy?"

"The Sevens expect us to hide you in some remote location. Those are the areas they search out first. Maybe it's better to get lost in a crowd."

"That could work," said Gabriel, catching Ivy's drift before either Xavier or I did. "The Sevens have finely tuned sensors that pick up electrical currents emitted by angelic beings. The more humans around, the more diluted those currents become."

"So where're you taking us—China?" Xavier asked.

"Actually somewhere a little closer to home."

"I don't get it." I frowned.

"Think about it," replied Gabriel. "If circumstances were normal right now, where would you two be going?"

"Home?" I asked.

"Think harder," Gabriel urged. "Where is Molly planning to go this fall?"

"How would we know?" Xavier said, irritated with the code cracking.

I touched his hand suddenly. "Wait. Molly's going to Bama . . . to college."

"You're joking, right?" Xavier sat upright, as if the prospect had ignited something in him. "You want us to go to college?"

"The Sevens will never see it coming," Ivy replied. "You'll be right under their noses and they won't even know it."

"Are you sure about this?" Xavier's brow creased.

"You won't use your real names," Gabriel said. "That way you can't be tracked through records."

"This could be like starting a whole new life," I said. I could feel the excitement building. "We can be anyone we want to be."

"I thought college was going to be on hold for us for a while," said Xavier. He sounded like someone had just handed him back a part of his life.

"Well, don't get too excited. Who knows how long you'll be able to stay."

"I guess we'll take it one day at a time," Xavier agreed.

"Does it matter where we go?" I asked Ivy. She read my thoughts.

"Why not go where you planned to go before everything got so screwed up?"

Going to college was still a fantasy in my head, like a picture-perfect world inside a snow globe that I could never reach. In my mind it embodied everything there was to love about the human world. I had never thought I'd be lucky enough to experience it firsthand.

"Well then," I said. "I guess we're Oxford bound."

I deliberately wound down the window and took a deep breath as the wind unravelled my hair. Mentally, I was bracing myself for the next challenge in our unpredictable lives.

We had a brief stopover in Venus Cove overnight to get organized, which proved harder than I thought. I got to see Phantom again and realized how much I'd missed him. Xavier had to deal with the frustration of being within reach of his family yet barred from contacting them. He kept pacing around the living room and balling his hands into fists.

"I'm sorry it's happened this way," I said, trying to be of some comfort.

"They're my parents," he said. "I can't just cut them out, pretend the last eighteen years of my life never happened. And my sisters, I want to be there for them. I want to see Jasmine and Maddy grow up."

"You will," I said forcefully. "You'll be back someday, I know it."

"And I'll just be the brother and son that ran out on them."

"They'll love you no matter what. And maybe one day you'll be able to tell them the truth."

Xavier laughed humorlessly. "Somehow I doubt that."

"I know how hard this must be for you," I said, taking his

hand, but Xavier pulled away from me. That was not something that happened very often and it took me by surprise. When I couldn't offer him comfort, it meant something was really wrong.

"How would you know?" he asked. "You've never had parents."

I was quiet for a moment as I thought about what he said. Xavier pressed his head into his hands. "Beth, I'm sorry, I didn't mean that."

"It's okay," I said, sitting down on the edge of the coffee table. I could see that the anger in his voice and in his eyes wasn't directed at me. He was staring out the window at the invisible enemy that could be anywhere. "You're right," I told him. "I've never had parents like yours and I don't know what it's like to be part of a human family. But I do have a father and right now He's seriously angry with me. Everything I do just disappoints Him more when all I really want is to make Him happy. I don't know if my Father is ever going to forgive me, in fact He may cast me out of my home . . . but yours will never do that, I know that much. Your father will always love you." I smiled to myself. "In fact, my Father will always love you too. You're His child as well."

Xavier looked up. "And you're not?"

"I have a slightly different relationship with Him," I said lightly. "Your kind was created to love, my kind was created to serve. He has always loved humans above all else. He sacrificed his only son, remember? So you see? He will protect you."

Xavier wrapped an arm around my shoulders. "Then I guess it's up to me to protect *you*."

IN the end Xavier settled for writing his parents a letter. He didn't read it to me and I didn't ask what it contained. I wasn't even sure whether Ivy and Gabriel would decide it could be delivered, but I thought it was probably just as important for him to write it.

Ivy took charge quickly, organizing and packing what she thought was necessary for college life. Of course we had to focus on the essentials. There wasn't time to pick out comforters and wall hangings like the other freshman girls, and I figured I could get anything else I needed once I got there.

I knew our college experience was going to be vastly different from everyone else's. There would be no emotional parents, no prolonged good-byes, and no time to stress over rec letters and signing up for classes. Even so, I was nervous. Xavier had been prepping for college his whole life. His father and grandfather had both pledged Sigma Chi and college football was a family tradition. I, on the other hand, had no prior experience and no family history to guide me. I had only just found my place in the world of high school and the idea of adjusting to a new and even more mysterious world worried me a little. I knew I'd have Xavier to guide me through it, but I needed to do some homework of my own if I wanted to be self-reliant.

"What exactly is a sorority?" I asked finally as Xavier loaded our bags into the trunk of the car.

"It's like a sisterhood," he said. "They have houses on campus and you do most activities with them. Fraternities are the male equivalent."

"Do you just pick one?"

"Not exactly. They have to choose you and you have to choose them."

"What happens if a girl picks a sorority that doesn't want her?"

"Then she doesn't get into that one," Xavier explained. "You're supposed to choose carefully."

"How do you work out what each one's like?"

"During rush week," Xavier said. "Over seven days all freshmen get to visit the sorority and frat houses. You sort of get interviewed. Then you get a card that tells you which ones have invited you back. You have to rank your preferences and get a bid."

"Aren't there hundreds of students?" I asked. "How can they possibly know who they want?"

"They'll check up on all the girls before they let them in," Xavier said.

"How am I supposed to learn if you won't take my questions seriously?"

"I'm not kidding. That's what they do."

"Isn't that going a bit far to recruit members?"

"That's just how it works. It's a long-standing tradition. For example, say there was a girl coming from Alabama to Ole Miss. The Tri Delts at Ole Miss would contact the Tri Delts at Alabama who would know someone who went to high school with her. Of course, they wouldn't find much if they tried to check up on you."

"Thank goodness. It sounds mean."

"They do a lot of good stuff too—support charities and

work in the community. Anyway, you don't have to worry about it; I doubt we'll get involved."

I knew next to nothing about Greek life. In high school I only knew the sorority my best friend Molly wanted because she talked about it all through senior year. Hallie had even told her she needed to cut it out because she risked putting all the other sororities off. At the time I didn't really listen because it sounded like they were speaking a foreign language. But it was funny how a conversation you thought was lost came filtering back when you needed it.

"Who's doing your rec letter for Chi O?" Hallie had asked Molly.

"Ryan's mom. She was a Chi O at Duke."

"Are they your first preference?"

"It's my only preference," Molly had declared. "They're the only sorority worth being in."

"That's a big call," Hallie had snorted. "There are plenty of others."

"Not for me."

"You do know Chi O has the highest GPA requirement, right?"

"Are you calling me a grade risk?"

"No, I'm just saying you might want to be careful spreading that around. If you get dropped from Chi O, no other sorority will touch you."

"Don't be stupid. I won't get dropped."

I remembered tuning out. Now I wished I'd asked a few more questions. Despite his initial excitement, Xavier was withdrawn on the drive to college. Because he hadn't been able to go home, he'd been forced to leave his beloved Chevy behind. I knew he wasn't happy about it even though there'd be a new car waiting for him when we arrived as compensation. He just wanted his old life back. I wanted to take Phantom with me and cried when I had to leave him even though Ivy reassured me that Dolly Henderson would take responsibility for him while we were away. I hoped she'd find time to walk him in between visiting the tanning beds and catching up on neighborhood gossip.

I would miss not having Molly with me at college. She would have made the transition a whole lot easier. A new thought occurred to me.

"Hey, Gabe, won't there be kids from Bryce Hamilton going to Ole Miss this fall? They're bound to recognize us."

"They're mostly headed to Alabama and Vanderbilt," said my brother. "There were one or two from Venus Cove but they've been taken care of."

"Oh my God, you didn't—" I gasped and Gabriel glared at me.

"Don't be so ridiculous. We made sure they were offered scholarships they couldn't refuse at other SEC schools."

"Oh," I said, impressed. "You're good."

THE road trip to Mississippi was peaceful except for the debate that ensued about the choice of music. Gabriel had a habit of playing hymns no matter what the occasion, while Xavier's Chevy was set permanently on classic rock. I voted for country, while Ivy said she preferred silence. Gabriel's idea of a compromise was setting the station on Southern country gospel. Although I didn't say so aloud, I quite enjoyed it.

I was struck by how green the landscape lining the highway was. It flowed around us like a mantle. Cattle grazed in paddocks, squirrels scampered up the trees, and cotton fields quivered in the wind. Every so often we'd catch a glimpse of deer darting through the woods.

When we took the turn for Oxford, my mood lifted and I could feel excitement starting to simmer. I'd never seen the town, but I'd heard enough about it. I knew it was the birthplace of William Faulkner and home of the Ole Miss Rebels. I opened my window and sweet Southern air washed in. It smelled fragrant and dewy and I already knew I was going to like my new home.

The town square was as pretty as a postcard. I felt like I'd stepped back in time. Everything was perfectly preserved, not dusty and rundown but polished and well kept like it had just been built. I wasn't prepared for how manicured and quaint all the stores were. Oxford reminded me a little of Venus Cove.

The eateries and the streets were full of eager freshmen and their proud parents. When we pulled into the University itself, I peered out the window at Fraternity Row, admiring the stately pillared homes and the gold letters of the Greek alphabet that marked each one like a badge of honor. Boys in polo shirts were gathered on the front porches, talking and laughing among themselves. It was an oasis for the preppy, elite children of the South. It was its own secluded little world and nothing within it felt real. I fell in love with it almost immediately. The humid air was syrupy sweet and relaxed me. I liked the way it slowed things down, made it impossible to do anything in a hurry. My skin moistened the moment I stepped out of the car but the air was so clean it didn't matter.

Just before Gabe and Ivy dropped us off to find a parking space they handed us each a manila folder.

"These are your new identities," she said. "Everything you need is in here—birth certificates, student ID, high-school transcripts."

I flipped through the enrollment papers Ivy had handed me. "Good-bye, Bethany Church and Xavier Woods," I said. "Hello, Ford and Laurie McGraw."

"Hold up," Xavier said. "We share a last name? Seriously?"

"You're brother and sister while you're here," said Gabriel. He made an apologetic face. "We thought that made sense seeing as you're going to be spending so much time together."

"Great," Xavier said, rifling though the papers.

"It's not ideal," Ivy acknowledged. "But it's the best we could do."

"Okay," Xavier said, leaning over to show me our transcripts. "We're from Jackson, Mississippi. You're an honors student fresh out of high school and I'm a junior transfer from Bama in Sigma Chi." He stopped and looked at Gabriel. "You remembered?"

Sigma Chi was the fraternity Xavier's father and grandfather had been in before him. I was surprised at my brother's thoughtfulness. Gabriel only inclined his head as if to say *You're welcome.*

"A junior, huh?" I asked. "What does that make you, like, twenty?"

"Twenty-one." Xavier smirked. "As you can see, I'm older and therefore wiser so you better be respectful."

"Everything's been taken care of," Ivy said. "All you need to do is pick up your keys and books."

"Thank you," I said. "You don't know how much this means to us." I was fully aware that Ivy could have turned her back on us, but she had chosen to take our side. It wasn't something I took lightly. "You're taking a big risk helping us out," I said. "This ought to buy us some time to figure things out. But whether it lasts months or only a day, I want you to know I won't forget it."

She nodded. "If you need us you know what to do."

"So I'm your brother?" Xavier said as we lugged our duffel bags in the direction of the dorms. "That just feels weird. What were they thinking?"

"I think they were just taking precautions."

"They could have gone for cousins."

"How would that be any different? Don't worry, it's just for show, we can still be us when we're alone."

"How much alone time do you think we'll get at college?" Xavier sounded dubious.

"We'll get used to it," I told him breezily.

"You think you'll get used to me being a single frat boy?" Xavier smirked. "Because that could get messy."

"You're a frat boy on the run," I reminded him. "I'd try to keep a low profile."

As soon as we hit the dorms I realized that I stood out.

Not because of any angelic radiance but simply because I was dressed totally wrong. In my floral sundress with its ruffled hem I was distinctly out of place amid the Nike shorts and oversize T-shirts the other girls were wearing. Everyone we passed gave me a second glance. If the objective was to blend in with the crowd, this was not a great start. When we found my dorm, I held the elevator door for a woman carrying a cardboard box piled with pillows and picture frames.

"Oh, I can wait," she said emphatically. "You're so nice and pretty, I don't wanna mess you up."

Xavier smothered a smile as the doors slid shut behind us. In his navy polo shirt and cream shorts, he fit in perfectly. He shook his head.

"Nobody told me there was a dress code, did they?" I grumbled.

"You are *so* not prepared for college," he said.

"It can't be any harder than high school," I replied stubbornly. Xavier hit the button for the ninth floor, where my room was located.

"Okay then, define this term: *freshmen fifteen*."

"Well," I said indignantly, "I suppose freshmen fifteen might refer to a group of fifteen students with a particular interest or . . ."

"Nope." Xavier laughed. "Not even close."

"What then?"

"It refers to the fifteen pounds freshmen put on from a college diet of fried chicken and beer."

I grimaced. "I take it that means food is going to be a problem?"

"Food's always a problem in college but don't worry; we'll find you something healthy."

I realized we hadn't talked about the Sevens and our situation since we'd arrived at Ole Miss. It was a relief to put all of that aside for a moment. Xavier was cracking jokes again, preoccupied with normal things like finding the campus gym.

I couldn't quell the hope that coming here would mark a new episode in our lives. Of course I knew that in reality nothing had changed. We were still on the run, although being surrounded by students somehow gave the illusion that we'd got our lives back on track. Apart from the whole brother and sister thing, everything felt surprisingly normal. I was absorbing every detail—after being hidden away in the cabin, the world of Ole Miss was coming to life before my eyes, like a black-and-white sketch suddenly filling with color.

8

The Roomie

THE dorm wasn't as bad as I predicted it would be. I didn't know how I'd fare with communal showers but I knew I'd muddle through somehow. The freshmen girls couldn't help but sneak admiring glances at Xavier as he slung my heavy bag over his shoulder and sauntered casually through the corridors. I was glad he was there to help me. Xavier's purposeful stride and confident air contrasted with the nervous looks and anxious questions being fired around us. I was grateful that we'd been given the chance to attend college together. I was noticing a lot of lost girls looking overwhelmed and glancing up hopefully every time someone walked past.

"Hey there." Xavier addressed them all by half-raising his hand. They smiled shyly, averting their eyes and fiddling with their hair.

I'd managed to land a corner room at the end of the passage. Xavier told me they were always a fraction larger and I wondered whether Ivy had had anything to do with it. But once I let myself in I realized that even her angelic influence wouldn't help me here. I looked around in dismay. From the linoleum floor to the dusty venetian blinds, it was basic, to say the least. The beds had been stripped and were nothing but two stained pale blue mattresses on rickety wooden frames. The painted brick walls were bare and the spaghetti-string pattern on the ceiling couldn't help but put one in mind of a prison. My brother and sister arrived and silently surveyed the room. Ivy moved to sit down in one of the plastic chairs by the built-in desk, but thought better of it and opted to stand.

"You know you could fix this just by snapping your fingers," I told Gabriel, imagining how easily he could transform the dorm from dungeon to hotel room.

"I could." My brother smiled smugly. "But that would defeat the purpose."

"The purpose being?"

"Giving you an authentic college experience."

I grimaced and went to tentatively inspect a miscellaneous stain on the mattress.

"I'm going to need some disinfectant wipes."

Xavier burst out laughing and kissed the top of my head.

"Wait a minute," he said, and set to work, rearranging the beds so they were pushed against either wall, creating the illusion of more space.

"What do you think? Any better?"

"It all looks the same to me." I shrugged. "There's not much you can do with a place like this."

"You'd be surprised," Xavier told me. "Some girls go all-out. They loft the beds, carpet the floors; some even hire interior decorators."

"They do not! That's crazy."

"That's college."

"Oh, boy," I said. "Maybe I'm not ready for this."

"Welcome to the world of freshmen," Gabriel said. "Good luck."

"Wait, you're leaving already?" I was surprised.

"We can't hang around," Ivy said. "Our presence is too easy to detect."

"And mine isn't?"

"You are shrouded by the world of humans."

"Really?"

"Of course," said Gabriel. "You act like a human, you think like a human, you even feel like a human. That level of interaction helps you blend in with them."

"But . . ." I wasn't ready for them to leave. "We need you."

"Don't worry, we won't be far away."

Ivy turned to leave, but Gabriel lingered, biting his lower lip as if he wanted to say something more but was searching for the right way to phrase it.

"Are you okay?" I asked. He ignored me and glanced at my sister. A look of collusion passed between them and without speaking it aloud, Ivy knew what was on his mind. He seemed intensely uncomfortable with whatever it was, but he finally exhaled and just spat it out.

"Remember my advice from a few days ago?"

Was he being deliberately cryptic? "No," I said. "You give a lot of advice."

"About the wisdom of abstinence," Gabriel said with a heavy sigh.

"Oh, that. What about it?"

"Feel free to ignore it." Gabriel shrugged off the mystified looks Xavier was giving him.

"Umm . . ." I wasn't entirely comfortable discussing my sex life with my brother. "Why the change of heart?"

"I hardly see the value in denial now. It's too late to placate Heaven. It's time we played on our terms."

"What about the whole 'don't add fuel to the fire' strategy?" Xavier reminded him.

"I'm done with strategies. If they can't play nice then neither shall we."

Xavier and I watched open-mouthed as Gabriel turned and strode away down the corridor, disappearing out of sight a moment later. With my siblings gone, the mood between us became suddenly awkward. Xavier sat stiffly on the end of the bed with his hands on his knees while I made a beeline for the closet and focused intently on hanging up my clothes to avoid the conversation now hanging in the air. I wondered what was going on in Xavier's head. It felt like a hunger strike had just been lifted but we were both afraid to take the first bite. It wasn't that temptation had seized us right there in the dorm room, it had simply been a taboo subject for so long that neither of us really knew how to discuss it openly. I was relieved it was Xavier who decided to broach the subject.

"Is it just me or was that really weird?"

"It's not just you," I said, coming to sit cross-legged beside him on the bed.

"What's come over Gabriel?"

"I'm not sure." I frowned. "But I reckon he must be pretty pissed off at someone."

"Do you think he was serious?" Xavier paused. "You know . . . about us?"

"He was serious," I said. "Gabriel doesn't know how to joke around."

"Right." Xavier was thoughtful. "So he's saying it would be okay?"

"Not necessarily," I said. "I think he's saying we're already in so much trouble it's not going to make much difference."

"So do you think we should?"

"Do you?"

Xavier let out a deep sigh and stared at the ceiling. "We've been so controlled for so long I'm not sure I know how to be anything else," he said.

"I guess that's true." I must have sounded a little disheartened.

"But we could try," he offered more encouragingly, "and see what happens. If you want to, that is."

"I want to," I told him. "I think we've waited long enough."

Xavier looked dejectedly around the dorm room with its fluorescent lights and peeling custard-colored walls. I had to agree it was far from a romantic setting.

"Not here." I laughed. "I still want it to be perfect." Xavier looked visibly relieved.

"So do I."

"HEY, y'all! I'm Mary Ellen, it's so great to meet you!"

Xavier and I both looked up as a girl appeared in the

doorway. She was taller than me with straight fair hair and wide brown eyes. She was tanned and athletic looking and dressed in the same Nike shorts and oversize T-shirt I'd been seeing all day. "Are you my roommate?" the girl continued. She was quiet for a moment and then broke out in a huge smile. "I've been dying to meet you! I tried Facebooking you, but I couldn't find anything! Where are y'all from? What's your name? What's your major?"

Before I could begin to formulate an appropriate response, faces began to pop up behind her in the doorway like jack-in-the-boxes. Unlike us with our meager belongings, this girl had arrived loaded with possessions as well as what seemed to be a team of assistants to help her settle in.

"I'm Mary Ellen," she repeated. "Did I already say that? And this is my mom and dad, my brother, Jordan, and my twin cousins, Jay and Jessica."

I was so taken aback by her familiarity as well as the information overload, that I was at a loss for words. Xavier took the lead to dispel the sudden silence.

"Hey," he said. "Nice to meet y'all. I'm Ford and this is my sister, Laurie. I'm helping her get settled in."

I was glad he'd spoken first; I'd already forgotten our aliases and would have introduced us by our actual names, blowing our cover within the first hour.

"Oh, well, don't you worry," said Mary Ellen's mom. "We'll have this place looking like home in no time."

As it turned out, they had plenty of ideas for adding homely touches to the stark dorm room. They'd bought a fluffy pink carpet and a minifridge that doubled as a whiteboard, polka dot curtains for the window, and matching wastepaper baskets. Mary Ellen had also made framed collages of about a hundred friends, which took up most of the wall when she hung them up.

"I hope I've left you enough space," she said apologetically.

"I really don't need much," I replied. "Feel free to put up anything you like."

"See, baby," her mother said. "Told you we'd find a sweet girl for you to room with."

Mary Ellen was obviously relieved. She must have been expecting a roommate from hell who would refuse to coordinate decor and play heavy metal music long into the night.

"I'm from Germantown," she said eagerly. "How bout y'all?"

"Jackson," Xavier said, with an adorable shrug and a half-smile. "Like half the population of Ole Miss. I was a junior at Bama, but I decided to transfer."

I was surprised at how easily he slipped into the role and how naturally he could flesh out his assumed identity. But then I remembered that Bama and Ole Miss had been part of his life before I showed up and turned things upside down.

I could almost see Mary Ellen's eyes mist over when he spoke to her.

"I'm glad you did," she said in a high-pitched, fluty voice. I rolled my eyes behind her back. It was starting already. The female attention that Xavier received was going to get on my nerves fast, especially since I couldn't take his hand or do anything that would make our relationship blatantly clear.

"Yeah, sis." Xavier slung an arm casually around my shoulder. "Aren't you glad to have me?"

Mary Ellen giggled and I narrowed my eyes at him.

"Not really," I said, shrugging him off. "How am I supposed to meet boys with you around?"

"Oh, you won't be meeting any boys," Xavier said. "No one's going near my little sister."

"I hear you, man," Jordan chimed in as he helped his father unload a batch of Mary Ellen's clothes. He was cute in an Alabama visor and dark blue polo shirt. He had the same wide hazel eyes as his sister. "Frat boys only want one thing."

Jordan peered closely at one of Mary Ellen's dresses on the hanger he was holding. It was a strapless minidress in a stretchy denim fabric with a zipper that ran from top to bottom—one strategic maneuver and the whole thing would come undone and crumple to the ground.

"What is this?" he demanded, holding it up. It really was more of a top than a dress and I saw Xavier smother a smile behind his hand. "You're not going out in this."

"You sound like Granddaddy," Mary Ellen whined as her brother tucked the offensive garment under his arm. "What am I going to wear to frat row?"

"I'm confiscating this." He tossed her an oversize sweatshirt and some baggy sweatpants. "You can wear these to frat row instead."

Mary Ellen flounced across the room, sulkily set up a mirror on her desk, and began fluffing her hair vigorously. She grabbed a bottle from one of her bags and a moment later a thick cloud of hair spray enveloped her. I looked questioningly at Xavier.

"Big hair." He shrugged. "I think it's a Mississippi thing."

"So." Mary Ellen's mother leaned against the bed frame and fixed Xavier with an inquisitive gaze. "If you were a junior at Bama you must know Drew and Logan Spencer; they're from Madison."

"Hmmm." Xavier pretended to think. "Doesn't ring any bells."

"Oh, no?" Mary Ellen's mother looked confused. "Everybody knows them! I'm actually their godmother and their aunt is married to my sister's best friend. And Logan is dating a girl called Emma, whose mother is from my hometown!"

"I'll ask some friends." Xavier gave her his most charming smile. "I'm sure I've seen them around." His lips brushed past my ear as he bent down to pull my suitcase onto the bed. "Everybody knows everybody here."

"Another Mississippi thing?" I asked.

"You're a quick study." Xavier winked. "The whole of the SEC is like an extended family."

I knew the interconnected lives of these people wasn't limited to Mississippi, it was a Southern thing. I thought of Dolly Henderson, who lived next door to us in Venus Cove. No matter who you were or where you'd come from, she would manage to find some distant connection. She knew everybody in town and all their business. I liked the way the town was linked together. Secrets might not stay secret for long, but when it came down to it, you could count on these people. I wanted very much to be part of a community like that and being Laurie McGraw from Jackson gave me a chance to try . . . even if I was living a life meant for someone else. I knew eventually our past would catch up with us and we'd be forced to flee again, probably without so much as a good-bye or a thank-you to the people who had briefly touched our lives.

"This weekend is going to be wild." Mary Ellen's voice interrupted my train of thought. "There's a rave at the Lyric and the Levee and almost every frat house is having a throw down."

Her brother glared at her. "I think it'd be a whole lot smarter if you had a nice early night."

"Whatever, Jordan." She rolled her eyes and turned to me. "I reckon we start at Sigma Nu then follow the crowd."

"Okay." I tried to match her level of enthusiasm. "Sounds awesome."

"But we've got to be so careful!"

"We do? Why?" I automatically tensed up.

"Everything we do will get back to the sororities. So don't hook up with anyone who's not a freshman. Just because a guy says he's single doesn't mean it's true and if he's dating a sorority girl, you'll be screwed. Oh, and I heard that Pike had some drink spikings at North Carolina so we better watch out."

"Right." I nodded dutifully. "I'll keep that in mind."

Xavier and Jordan both scowled at the prospect of their little "sisters" in the hands of drunken frat boys. Mary Ellen playfully twirled her hair around one finger and focused on Xavier.

"So, Ford, will you be there tonight?"

"I sure will," he said.

"Ugh." I tried to sound convincingly irritated but inside I

was deeply relieved. There was no way Xavier could leave me alone with these girls—they were almost speaking another language and I needed him to translate. All the girls at Ole Miss had been prepping for college for years. Xavier and I might have shortlisted the school back during our days at Bryce Hamilton but I still knew next to nothing about college expectations.

The other girls were preoccupied with Greek life and good grades, but I didn't care about those things. Even though I'd only been here a few hours, I was already realizing how different I was in every respect. It wasn't that I couldn't fit in; my situation simply wouldn't allow it. How was I supposed to be intimidated by sorority girls after the things I'd witnessed? How was I supposed to care about being judged by my peers when Heaven and Hell had judged me?

"Are you excited?" Mary Ellen gave a little squeal. "The rest of our lives start right now."

My first thought was that my life had already begun; I didn't need to embark on some journey of self-discovery. But then again, I rationalized, maybe college would help me—after all, I wasn't sure I even knew who I was anymore.

When I went to collect extra hangers from a box in the hall, I saw a poster on a door that read WE LOVE OUR REBELS. I stopped for a moment and thought about it. Maybe I would fit in here because that was who I'd become now. A runaway. A rebel. But not without a cause.

{ 9 }

Starry, Starry Night

NIGHTFALL came fast, and eventually Xavier had to leave me to meet his own roommates. As a junior he got to live in an off-campus apartment, although I knew he wouldn't be too far away.

After the isolation of the cabin, it was strange to hear the halls alive with the chatter of teenagers. I went to investigate the bathrooms to discover they weren't as bad as I'd envisioned, though they were a far cry from the gold taps and marble vanities I was accustomed to at Byron, my home in Venus Cove. But I was capable of shutting out my surroundings and turning my focus inward; Hades had taught me that much.

While I filled the basin with warm water to wash my face, I stared at my reflection in the mirror that ran across the length of the wall. I supposed I could pass for a college girl, if I teased my hair and slapped on a little fake tan. The only thing that didn't fit was the look in my eyes—that look that said *I know something you don't*. It was a faraway expression, as if my mind were elsewhere. Some might misconstrue it as boredom and others might simply conclude I was a dreamer.

Despite my intense earthly connections, the reality was that I was still bound to a supernatural life and my soul—my very essence—was not human. It was impossible to hide it.

When I got back to my room, I discovered that Mary Ellen had wasted no time in inviting our neighbors over to get acquainted. The girls, Missy and Erin, were both from the same town outside Fort Worth, Texas. They were equally enthusiastic to begin college life and keen to make a good impression. Missy was a perky Rebelette who smiled a lot and Erin declared she was only there to find a husband. Mary Ellen decided on the spot that we were all going to be best friends and immediately took to walking into their room without knocking.

As it turned out, I did not possess any attire halfway appropriate for a frat party and was forced to borrow some items from Mary Ellen. If the girls dressed down in the daytime, they certainly made up for it at night with sky-high heels and hemlines well above midthigh. Mary Ellen lent me a midnight blue silk shift and strappy satin heels. The loose cut of the dress made me look tall and lean and my hair fell in chestnut twists down my back.

"Y'all look so pretty," said Erin. "Let's make this a first night to remember."

The girls took forever preening in front of the mirror and it was after ten P.M. before we could actually make a move. I was already tired and ready for bed, though I'd never admit as much. I pretended to fiddle with my hair and reapply my lip gloss and join in with their chorus of physical discontentment.

"My thighs look so fat in this dress."

"Uh, at least you're not so pale you practically glow in the dark."

"Whatever, have y'all seen my ID picture? I have to keep that for the whole year!"

"I can't get my hair to coiff," I chimed in, and the girls nodded sympathetically before Mary Ellen attacked me with a bottle of hair spray.

When we finally set off for Fraternity Row, I discovered the frat houses themselves were quite beautiful. We stopped at a stately whitewashed Southern home with gold lettering that read ΣΝ planted firmly on the eave of the house. Rocking chairs were positioned on the front porch, occupied by boys eating pizza and swigging from bottles of beer. Inside was the dining room with a long oak table and a wide staircase leading to the bedrooms and common area. There were college kids everywhere, lounging on the couches, chatting in the hallway, sprawled on the beds and out on the back porch. There was a keg underneath the pool table and red plastic cups scattered on the floor, which was already sticky with beer.

The freshmen girls were easy to pick out. They looked terrified, standing in awkward circles, afraid to drink or even speak for fear of annoying the dreaded sorority girls. They talked among themselves, straightening their posture slightly and adjusting their hair whenever the boys passed by. It was hard not to be entertained by them. Problems that seemed inconsequential to me were life changing to them. I even found myself wishing I could trade places with them—if only life were that simple.

"Hey ladies, how y'all doing?" The boys on the porch addressed us with disarming smiles and the girls giggled nervously and shuffled a little closer.

When Xavier arrived, he was a whole different person. I was so used to seeing him in his usual defensive mode with all the problems of the universe to keep him occupied. But in the space of a few hours, he had already changed and I could see he was in his element. He arrived with a group of boys, all dressed smartly in polo shirts and smelling of expensive cologne. It was easy to see that these boys were unafraid, they knew who they were, where they were going, and there was no doubt that they belonged. People stopped talking to watch them pass. They called out to their friends as if they'd been here for years rather than a few hours.

"Oh Lord." Mary Ellen clutched my arm. "They're juniors. You have to get your brother to introduce us."

"Which one is your brother?" Missy and Erin craned their necks eagerly.

"The one in white . . . with the dark blonde hair." Mary Ellen waggled her eyebrows mischievously.

"Dang, that's your brother?" Missy drew a sharp intake of breath. "Wow."

"I know," Mary Ellen hissed back. "And he's a Sigma Chi."

Xavier waved and sauntered over to us.

"Hey, sis." He elbowed me gently in the ribs and smiled at the others. "How y'all settling in? These are my roommates, Clay and Spencer."

"I don't see the family resemblance," Spencer said, inspecting me.

"We think she was adopted," Xavier joked, and the girls doubled over as though he'd just cracked the joke of the century.

A boy carrying a cooler passed us and stopped to talk to the boys.

"Y'all want anything?" he asked.

"No thanks, I don't drink," I told him.

Missy and Erin accepted some beers but insisted on pouring them into cups to trick the sorority girls into thinking they were drinking soda.

It took awhile but eventually Xavier and I found an opportunity where we could slip out of the frat party unnoticed. He pulled a set of keys from his pocket and approached a big black, jacked-up truck.

"Um . . . are you hijacking a car?" I asked.

"Yep," he said. "College has made a criminal out of me already."

"Xavier!"

"Relax, Beth." He laughed. "It's mine. Ivy and Gabriel left it for me."

"They did?"

"Yeah, they felt bad I had to leave the Chevy behind. And if we need to leave in a hurry we can't exactly rely on Rebel Ride."

"On what?"

"Never mind, let's just get out of here."

Xavier pulled out of campus and drove along the highway lined with lush forestland. When he was sure we were clear, he pulled into a dirt road and parked the truck, cutting the lights immediately, and making sure the car was hidden by the shadows of the trees. Ever chivalrous, he jumped out and came to open the passenger door for me.

"Where are we going?" I asked.

"I don't know," Xavier said. "Someplace no one will find us."

It was warm and dark amid the trees and the moss-covered forest floor muted our footsteps. Every so often I would catch a glimpse of headlights through the trunks and smile at the fact that no one could possibly know we were there. I was glad to escape the noise and humidity of the party.

"So how do you like being Ford McGraw?" I asked.

"It's all right." Xavier moved behind me and I felt his hands come up to rub my shoulders. Any tension I'd felt melted away instantly. "But I think there's a lot more perks to being Xavier Woods."

"Like what?"

He bent his head and I felt his lips brush against my neck. "Like this . . ."

"That's not very brotherly behavior," I told him while at the same time reaching back to twine my fingers in his hair. I could feel my breathing getting heavier as our bodies pressed closer and Xavier's hands slid down to my waist.

"Are you sure we should be doing this? I hope we're not crossing the line."

"I don't care anymore," Xavier murmured in my ear, sending shivers down my spine. "I want to show my wife how much I love her." He stopped for a moment and turned me around, taking my face in his hands. His turquoise eyes were full of something so intense I thought I couldn't bear it.

"What did you call me?" I whispered, needing to hear it again.

"My wife," he repeated softly.

Xavier gently slipped one of the shoestring straps off my shoulder. His touch, usually so familiar, startled me. I felt as if he were touching me for the very first time and it made me realize how careful we'd been up until now. We had gone out of our way to avoid intimate contact. Now, with our bodies wrapped together, I realized how easy it would have been to give in. I didn't know how we'd lasted so long and showed so much restraint. How had we ignored the spark that ignited at every accidental touch? How had I pretended the fire in my belly didn't exist? It was strange to feel the air charged with electricity and know this time we didn't have to ignore it. I took Xavier's hand and placed it on my pounding chest so he could feel my heartbeat in his palm. He closed his eyes and I thought I saw an almost pained expression cross his face.

Around us the majestic oaks rose to the sky and the delicate perfumed air seemed to embrace us. The breeze felt good against my feverish skin. I felt so overwhelmed I thought I might faint in his arms.

"It's okay," he whispered. "The sky isn't going to open and rain down fire on us."

Our chests were pressed together now, so I could feel our hearts thudding into one another. Xavier buried his face in my neck and I felt him inhale deeply. My body seemed to sink down and he caught me in his arms, lowering me onto the moss-covered ground. It was soft beneath my skin and I imagined silk sheets couldn't have felt smoother. Xavier lowered himself gently on top of me and our bodies fit together like pieces of a puzzle. I knew I would never feel like a separate entity again. For the first time in my existence, both angelic and human, I felt truly whole.

"Crap!" Xavier abruptly pulled away from me and sat up.

"What's wrong?" I was seized by a wave of self-consciousness. Had I done something wrong? I wracked my brain, trying to remember every move I'd made so far, but I'd been too lost in the moment to remember.

"We don't have protection. I didn't think we'd need it."

"Forget it." I tugged him back toward me, searching for his mouth, unwilling to let anything break the mood. Moments ago it had been so perfect, but I could feel it about to shatter. Xavier firmly resisted my advances.

"Beth, we can't just forget it; we have to be responsible."

I sighed heavily and sat up. I'd been under such an intense spell that nothing else had crossed my mind. I hated how quickly our perfect night could be shattered.

"Does it honestly matter?" I asked.

"Of course it does! Do you really want to get pregnant now? Don't you think we have some issues to sort out first?"

"Xavier, I probably can't even get pregnant!"

"You have a human body, Beth," he said. "It's a very real possibility."

"Fine," I conceded. "You're right." I paused as a more troubling thought entered my head. "As long as there isn't another reason . . ."

"What do you mean? What other reason could there be?"

"Well, we've avoided this for so long . . . do you still . . . do you even still see me that way?"

Xavier groaned. "Are you crazy? Of course I see you that way. I've had to actively try not to see you that way."

I lifted my chin and looked him square in the eye. "I want you to show me."

"Beth, come on . . ." Xavier began but I pressed a finger against his lips.

"No," I said. "No excuses. I'm your wife now, remember? And I'm asking you to show me how much you love me."

Xavier gazed at me for a moment and then in one swift movement he lifted me up and pulled me on top of him. This time, his kiss was deep and fathomless. Even though I technically didn't have one it felt like our souls were fusing and a tingling feeling spread over my skin where he touched me. I felt his muscles tense and his breathing grow heavier. The kiss seemed to last forever. Time stood still as we pressed into each other. Finally, our mouths separated and he moved his mouth along the curve of my neck, imprinting smaller kisses there.

"Still having doubts?" he whispered. I shook my head as my mouth searched for his again. His lips were warm and full and perfect. His kiss was smooth and enticing. As usual, it left me wanting more. Time and space seemed to blur as we lost ourselves in each other's embrace. I felt the intensity of our passion swell in the air around us, threatening to obliterate the world and all its problems.

"I don't want you to stop," I murmured into his neck.

"I don't either." Xavier leaned back and looked at me, his turquoise eyes bright and beautiful. This time it seemed plain stupid to resist the pull of something so powerful.

"But . . . what about . . ." I didn't want to finish the sentence for fear Xavier would revert back to his old cautious self. I was so intoxicated I could barely keep my thoughts coherent. Xavier gazed at me for a moment, and then said, "I'll be careful."

Our first night as husband and wife felt like exploring a magical underwater world where nothing existed save the two of us. I was only aware of the feel of his warm skin beneath my fingers and the press of his lips as they explored my body. The forest felt like our own private kingdom where no one else could enter. Everything came to life before my eyes that night; the moss-covered boughs of the trees and the ferns on the forest floor were all glittering silver as the moonlight washed over them. The air seemed alive, dancing around us, bringing with it the sweet smells of the earth.

Afterward, when I opened my eyes, I saw a dazzling array of stars unspooling across the night sky like fireworks. Thinking back to that night, I remember glorious, fragmented images rather than a whole sequence of events. I remember my arm lying outstretched and looking pale as stone against the mossy ground. I remember Xavier's fingers trailing their way across my shoulder and feeling my veins pulsing with supernatural energy. I remembered his shirt crumpled on the ground and my hands pressed against his smooth chest. I remembered feeling like I was filling up like a balloon until I felt like I was about to burst. Most of all I remembered not being able to determine where Xavier's skin ended and mine began.

When a dam breaks, what can you do to stem the torrent of water? Perhaps the water can be redirected but it can never go back to being contained. That was how I felt then—unencumbered by heavenly dictates and tied to Xavier by bonds not even death could break.

10

From Dixie, With Love

WHEN I woke, Xavier and I were a tangle of limbs on the forest floor, but I couldn't have felt more comfortable. I lifted my arms above my head and stretched, relishing the giddy feeling in my head. We'd slept a dreamless, exhausted sleep by the base of an ancient oak while the gibbous moon kept watch over us, peeking between the treetops.

I sighed dreamily as I watched the sky flush with rose. Pre-sunrise the hills were black silhouettes and everything was silent, interrupted only by birdsong. The human inhabitants of Oxford were still in bed and minus the hum of traffic the scene had a primordial quality. I propped myself up on my elbows and studied Xavier. He looked different somehow. His face was even more striking in sleep when he wasn't frowning or on alert. Contentment wasn't something I was used to seeing on him. I wished the moment would last forever.

"I don't like being watched when I'm sleeping," Xavier murmured, adjusting his position. His eyes were still closed but the corners of his lips were already curling into a smile.

"Bad luck," I said, snuggling back down beside him. "I like

watching you. Besides, we should leave soon, before people start waking up."

"Why?" Xavier's eyes flashed mischievously. "Nobody knows we're here."

We fell back onto the ground, all sensible thoughts abandoned. There was less urgency in Xavier's kiss this time but I still felt like I was diving from a great height. The same feelings from last night washed over me as I descended back into the coral sea of vivid colors and warm sensations, a place where only the two of us existed in a fantastical dimension.

WHEN the sun rose properly, it flooded the forest with a light so bright it hurt my eyes. Although we were both reluctant, we needed to get back to campus before people started to notice we were gone. While I was sure Spencer and Clay wouldn't pry, I knew Mary Ellen was going to be full of questions.

In the early hours of the morning, the campus was deserted. Only the empty red cups littering Fraternity Row served as a reminder of the revels of the night before. I knew that once the students woke up and got some food in them the celebrations would start all over again until class began on Monday morning. When I found my dorm, the woman at the front desk gave me a strange look. I caught sight of my reflection and saw I still had tiny twigs caught in my hair. I flushed and hurried past her, opting to take the stairs rather than wait for the elevator. I slipped into my room as quietly as I could . . . but not quietly enough.

"Laurie, where have you been?" The tone was a combination of curiosity and accusation. Mary Ellen sat bolt upright in her bed almost the second the door clicked shut behind me. "I looked everywhere for you!"

"I'm sorry," I told her. "Did you get home okay with Missy and Erin?"

"Yeah." She shrugged. "Where were you?"

"I ran into some old friends from high school and we hung out."

"Really?" Mary Ellen asked nosily. "Who were they?"

"Just some sorority girls," I replied lightly, and could have immediately kicked myself.

Mary Ellen's eyes widened with admiration. "You're friends with sorority girls? But they're not supposed to talk to freshmen. Which sorority?" she asked eagerly.

I'd gone and dug myself a hole but luckily, it was one I could climb out of. I let my mind travel back to when I arrived—the letters on the houses flashed through my mind with an unexpected clarity. I blurted the first one that came to mind. Delta Gamma.

"They're DG's." I was surprised at how easily I could lie. "I would have called you to come with us but I didn't have your number."

"Oh." She looked disappointed. "Maybe next time. Did Ford go with y'all?"

"Who?" I asked.

"Um . . . your brother?" Mary Ellen said, frowning at me, like she thought I might have knocked my head.

Saying our new names aloud was like putting on a new outfit for the first time. It was too crisp and not quite comfortable because it hadn't softened with wear. I'd thought that being a new person might offer a whole new perspective on life. Instead I just felt confused—I was one person on the outside, another within. I was also worried that I'd slip up and say or do something that would set the whole delicate balancing act tumbling to the ground.

"Right," I said, forcing a laugh. "Mental blank. I don't know where Ford was, probably off with some girl. He's like that."

Mary Ellen gazed into space and I could almost read her thoughts: *I could be some girl.*

"Do you think you could hook me up?" she asked with doleful eyes.

I was a little taken aback by the suddenness of the request. I'd expected her to build up to this, ask me in a few weeks when we knew each other better, but she'd dived right in.

"With Ford?" I asked.

"Yeah," she said. "He seems to know all the right people and he's really good-looking . . . but you probably hear that a lot."

"Look." I sat down on the edge of my bed and pretended to think. "I'd hate for you to get hurt. I don't think Ford's looking for a serious relationship."

"Hmmm." Mary Ellen frowned and sank back onto her pillows. I could tell she wasn't about to give up so easily. "Maybe we could come up with a plan?" she said.

"I don't know," I hedged.

"What if you told him you think we'd be good together? He'd listen to you."

"I'm probably the last person he'd listen to."

"Right." Mary Ellen looked pensively into space. "I'll think of something."

"What about Spencer or Clay?" I asked, trying to distract her with another proposition. "They both seem cute."

"Maybe," Mary Ellen mused, reaching down to grab her laptop. "I'm going to Facebook stalk him."

I had to actively try to hold back the possessiveness that rose within me. I wanted to tell her it was never going to happen, but of course I couldn't. I was starting to dislike Mary Ellen already; she was too pushy and demanding. I mentally chastised myself for being so negative; one of the basic edicts of Christianity was tolerance. I guessed my defensive side kicked in when it came to other girls chasing after Xavier.

I climbed into bed and pulled the covers over my head, trying to ignore the sound of Mary Ellen clacking away on her laptop. I tried recalling Bible verses in my head, but stopped short. Did I even have any right to seek guidance from the Word anymore? I didn't know and I felt guilty trying. My mind went suddenly into panic: Was it possible that the law of God didn't apply to me anymore? If I couldn't live by that, what would I live by? There was no one else I wanted to serve. I didn't want to reject His sovereignty; I only wanted to keep Xavier. But maybe I couldn't have both. I realized my breathing had quickened and I recited the words of a hymn Gabriel used to play under my breath to calm myself.

"Heart of my own heart, whatever befall, still be my vision, O ruler of all."

THE next few days passed in a blur. I soon came to realize that college didn't leave a spare moment to think about troubles. Floor meetings, shopping for game-day dresses, raiding Walmart for dorm supplies, and learning our way around campus took up every minute. Classes began on Monday and I took notes, but absorbed nothing. I couldn't help scanning the faces as they filed into the lecture halls, watching and waiting for signs of the Sevens.

Mary Ellen was very quickly getting on my last nerve. Her interest in "Ford" soon developed into an infatuation and then a full-blown obsession. She warned the other girls off by calling "dibs" on him. She would peer over my shoulder whenever I got a text and creep up behind me when I was sending e-mails. When Xavier came to visit after our first night together, she made it nearly impossible for us to talk. When he poked his head through the door, she nearly pushed me out of the way in her eagerness to get to him. Xavier was all politeness despite the fact that her behavior must have annoyed him.

"Ford!" She clutched at his arm. "How did you get past the front desk? They're being so paranoid about boys being here right now."

Xavier gave an easy shrug. "I gave them my ID. It's all good." He turned to me, his eyes twinkling with a smile. "Hey, Laurie. What's up?"

"Hey." I felt almost bashful as flashes from the previous

night flooded my mind. I averted my eyes and smothered a grin with the back of my hand. "Not much," I replied lightly. "Y'know, just hanging out."

"Yeah?" Xavier said. "Did you have fun last night?"

Luckily, Mary Ellen was too starry-eyed to pick up on the intimate note in his voice.

"It . . . wasn't what I expected," I said slowly. "It was so much better."

"You were only there like five minutes," Mary Ellen's amplified voice cut in, determined not to be excluded from the conversation. Xavier sighed; I could tell he was feeling uncomfortable. "As for you . . ." She pointed an accusing finger at him. "I hardly saw you at all!"

"Yeah," he replied. "I was kind of preoccupied."

"Preoccupied with what?" she asked without taking a breath.

"This girl from my hometown. We had some catching up to do."

That was not the answer Mary Ellen wanted to hear. She was silent for a minute before letting out a forced laugh.

"Is she an ex-girlfriend? Awkward!"

"No," Xavier replied. "I actually know her pretty well."

"So was it good catching up?" I asked sheepishly.

Xavier held my gaze. "That's an understatement."

"Are you going to see her again?" Mary Ellen asked, trying hard to sound casual.

Xavier flicked his turquoise eyes over to her. "Probably not," he said. "I'm not looking for anything serious."

I couldn't help smiling at the shared joke that was only apparent to us.

"You're too busy living wild and free, right?" I said.

"Exactly, sis." Xavier winked at me. "You know me too well."

As Mary Ellen became more agitated, I saw red blotches spread across her neck and chest. Thankfully, the conversation was cut short when our neighbors, Erin and Missy, knocked on the door.

They were sweet girls and seemed to like Mary Ellen, but I caught them on a few occasions rolling their eyes behind her back. When they weren't comparing notes on boys, I noticed the girls spent their time discussing prospective sororities. I tried to feign interest but usually got bored within the first few minutes and had to tune out. I was too busy absorbing the thriving atmosphere of the campus and adjusting to the new culture. I was constantly taken aback at how carefree everybody seemed. It was a sad indictment of how troubled my life with Xavier had been.

"I am so excited for football season," Mary Ellen told me as we were walking to the grove one afternoon. "I mean, we won't win, but who cares."

"Why not?" I asked, a little surprised at her defeatist attitude.

"Ole Miss never wins." She laughed. "Everybody knows that."

"But I'm sure we stand a chance!" I said, feeling strangely upset by the thought of my adopted team losing.

"Not really." She shrugged again. "Bama and Auburn are where you go if you want to win football games."

"Humph," I said. "Maybe our luck will turn around this year."

"Haven't you heard?" Mary Ellen grinned at me. "We might not win the game but we never lose the party."

Mary Ellen and I stopped in the Grove where we found Xavier sitting with Clay, Spencer and a group of boys from the baseball team. They were having an in-depth discussion about Rebel sports. Spencer looked up and waved when he saw us. I slid in next to him while Mary Ellen made a beeline for Xavier. I hadn't noticed before, but Spencer was good-looking, with a swatch of blond hair and hooded blue eyes.

"So, how was your first weekend?" he asked.

"I survived," I told him. "It was pretty crazy."

"Yeah, frat row was just about exploding with freshmen."

As he talked, two squirrels began chasing each other around the trunk of a tree and caught my attention. Their movements were so quick they seemed almost computerized. One was clearly in pursuit of the other and I couldn't help smiling.

"He just won't give up, will he?" I said.

Spencer glanced up to see what I was looking at and grinned. "Maybe she's been giving him mixed signals," he replied. "He's all confused."

"Nope." I shook my head. "I think it's pretty clear she's not interested."

The first squirrel finally halted his pursuit and the other stopped as if in confusion. She then darted past again, daring him to pick up the chase.

"See, now she's just playing games," Spencer said. "Manipulative bitch."

I burst out laughing. I liked Spencer already; he was so relaxed and normal. Sitting there in the Grove I almost felt as though there was no such thing as heavenly soldiers called Sevens, and everything we'd been through so far was just part of a hideous nightmare.

Then my cell phone rang. I had only just switched it back on, ignoring the barrage of messages and missed calls from people wanting to know where I was. But this was a number I didn't recognize.

Xavier tensed up immediately, although no one noticed but me. The phone lay on the picnic table vibrating and spinning in circles until Mary Ellen finally looked across at me.

"Aren't you gonna get that?"

"Hello?" I said tentatively, feeling my heart thumping in my chest.

"Beth!" The squealing voice on the other line sounded relieved and all-too familiar. "I didn't think you'd pick up. I've been calling for days!"

"Molly?" I asked, and watched Xavier breathe a barely perceptible sigh of relief. "Is that you? Where are you calling from?"

"Of course it's me, I got a new phone," she replied. "But more important, where have you been? You just took off and left town, we were all so worried. Things have been so weird. First you disappeared and then Father Mel died suddenly. They're saying it was a heart attack? It was awful. We all thought Mrs. Woods was going to have a breakdown."

"I know, we heard," I said. "And it is awful. I wish I could be there but things are just too complicated right now."

"Why? Are you okay?"

"I'm fine," I assured her. "It's hard to explain."

"Well, you better try! Where are you?"

"Just hold up," I said. "I know you're mad but I promise to come visit you soon and tell you everything. How's Bama?"

"I wouldn't know." Molly snorted. "I left."

"What? You dropped out?"

Xavier widened his eyes at me as if to say *seriously*?

"Yeah, something kind of happened. . . ." Molly's voice petered out. "I had to transfer."

Why did I immediately assume it had something to do with us? It was probably because bad fortune was haunting us these days.

"Why? What happened? Where did you go?"

"To Ole Miss," Molly replied. "I'm gonna be a Rebel."

"Oh, boy . . ." I glanced across at Xavier.

"What?" Molly demanded. "Hello?"

"Where are you right now?" I quizzed.

"In the Crosby parking lot. I actually just got here."

"Okay, stay there," I told her. "We're going to come meet you in five minutes."

"Wait, are you . . ." Molly began but I hung up on her.

"What happened?" Xavier mouthed at me, and I smiled nervously in response.

"Molly's here," I said. "I've got to go find her."

"Who's Molly?" Mary Ellen barked, concluding it was another long-lost girlfriend making a reappearance in Xavier's life. I didn't bother to respond. I was too anxious. I needed to find Molly straightaway and explain the situation before she called someone and accidentally gave us away.

"I'm coming with you."

Xavier stood up and Mary Ellen tried to tug him back into his seat.

"Why do you need to go?" she whined.

He extricated himself from her grasp like one might shrug off a demanding child and followed me toward the dorm. I was almost jogging in my hurry to reach Molly. Why had she left Alabama? Had the Sevens shown up and tried to interrogate her? I sent a silent message out to Gabriel and Ivy, letting them know to be on hand in case we needed their help.

ALL four of us arrived at the same time and found Molly standing alone by her car. Gabriel and Ivy closed in protectively around her. She was unchanged with her baby blue eyes and pert little nose, holding nothing but her pink cell phone and a matching purse.

"Molly!" I threw my arms around her and hugged her tight. "I'm so glad you're okay. Whatever happened, I'm so sorry and you don't have to be afraid. We'll take care of it."

"Yes," Gabriel said, his voice deepening with concern. "We'll make sure you are protected."

"Just tell us what happened and who came looking for you," Ivy said.

"What did they do to you?" Gabriel asked. "What did they say?"

Molly put her hands on her hips and inspected us closely. "What are y'all talking about?"

I realized then that she didn't appear scared or shaken at all. "You mean the Sevens didn't find you?"

"The who?" Molly stared at me. "Apart from being seriously mad at you, everything's fine."

"Molly." Gabriel fixed his penetrating silver gaze on her. "If everything's fine then what on earth are you doing here?"

"I had to leave," she said simply, and Gabriel's eyebrows knitted with concern.

"May we know the reason? Did you run into difficulty?"

"No," Molly said. "I ran into love."

For a moment Gabriel's face clouded over as he recalled Molly's infatuation of last year and the tension that followed as a result. But it wasn't Gabriel Molly was thinking about. I could tell by the way she was looking at him that she had struggled to master her obsession and forced herself to think of him as a friend. She was looking at him now in an open, generous way that suggested she had smothered her previous expectations.

"You changed schools for a *guy*?" Xavier blurted out. He missed my signal to show a little more sensitivity. "Are you *insane*?"

Molly was too elated to take offense. She gave Xavier a condescending sigh.

"Not just a guy, *the guy*."

"Who is he?" I prompted.

"He's name is Wade Harper and he's a junior. He's going

to be a doctor and the course here at Ole Miss is more specialized or something."

"He asked you to come with him?" Xavier asked. I could see he was worried about Molly having made such a momentous decision without serious thought.

"Don't worry; he wants me here. He was totally buzzed when I told him. I can't wait for you to meet him. He's the best."

"We're very happy for you, Molly," said Ivy. Gabriel didn't say anything but a tiny frown had appeared between his brows.

"Thanks," she said, beaming.

"May I offer one word of advice?" my sister said.

"Of course."

"Take your time with this boy." I could hear genuine affection in my sister's voice. She didn't want to see Molly getting hurt again.

"Oh, I plan to," Molly replied. "I'm the one slowing him down, can you believe that? He's already talking about having kids and everything! He's super respectable, goes to church and all that."

"He sounds great." I smiled.

"He's very serious. He dropped his fraternity because it was taking time away from study and he doesn't party *at all* but I'm working on that. Hey, I'm meeting him right now in the Union. Why don't y'all come?"

"We can't stay," Gabriel said.

"That's okay. Beth, you'll come, won't you? We haven't hung out in forever!"

She remembered Xavier's presence and cast him a fleeting glance. "You can come too if you like." She slipped her arm through mine, claiming my attention.

"Uh . . . Molly, I have a few things to tell you before we go."

"Yeah," she agreed. "Like where the heck you disappeared to on graduation and why you haven't answered any of my calls."

"It's complicated," I said. "We kind of got married."

"Shut *up*!" Molly let out a scream of excitement and I frantically shushed her. "You did *not*."

"Yeah, we did," said Xavier. "But here's the best bit: You can't tell anyone here because they think we're brother and sister."

Molly blinked in confusion. "Huh?"

I patted her on the arm. "It's a long story. I'll explain on the way."

"Wait!" Molly shook her head in dismay and stopped dead in her tracks. "You got married and didn't invite me?"

Xavier looked over his shoulder and shared a look with my brother and sister. "Good to have you back, Molly," he said.

I turned back to see Gabriel still standing by Molly's car. His hands were deep in his pockets and even from my distance I could see his frown had deepened. I'd never seen quite that expression on my brother's face before and wasn't sure I was reading it right. Perhaps I was imagining things but Gabriel looked a little lost.

11

Hello, Stranger

IN the Union, Xavier detached from us to go and talk to a table of friends. I didn't know who they were or when he'd even had a chance to meet them but Xavier had always operated with such a cool, confident air that people seemed to gravitate toward him and seek out his company. Molly and I lingered at the salad bar.

"So . . . just married and having to play brother and sister. That must be fun," she teased.

"It sucks," I confessed, ignoring her levity.

"I guess you can't even hold hands."

"That's not the worst part. It's the other girls. I see the way they look at him."

"That's nothing new—Xavier's always had girls falling over him."

"Molly, there are a lot more girls here."

"Yeah," she agreed. "And Ole Miss students were voted the most attractive in the country."

"Thanks," I said. "That's very helpful."

"C'mon, don't stress about it," Molly reassured me. "Xavier's never even looked at another girl. Why would that change now?"

"Well, some of them are really pretty and *normal,*" I said. "Xavier must wonder sometimes how much easier it'd be if he'd just picked one of them instead."

"He doesn't think that. You're just being paranoid."

"I wish they'd be a bit more subtle about it, y'know? They just drool over him, it makes me so mad!" I clenched my fists involuntarily.

"Well, you can't blame him for that. As soon as he starts showing any interest in one of them then you have my permission to get mad."

"I know," I agreed. "What makes you so wise all of a sudden?"

Molly's face became suddenly distant. "I know what it's like to want someone who doesn't want you back. I see how Xavier looks at those girls—he doesn't see them."

"How can you tell?"

"Because someone once looked at me in exactly the same way."

I didn't have to ask who she was referring to. It still pained me to think of the unhappiness she'd endured in regard to my brother. I had tried to warn her at the time but my warnings had fallen on deaf ears. Months had passed but I sensed the wound was still raw.

"And how do you feel now?" I asked, hesitant to say his name. "About Gabriel?"

"It was hard to move on," Molly admitted, examining the

salad dressings with unnecessary focus. "But I'm with Wade now."

"What changed?"

"I just woke up one morning and realized how desperate and pathetic I'd become," Molly said. "I don't want to be that girl. Life's too short to waste loving someone who doesn't love you back. And then Wade came along and I knew he was going to be good for me."

"Wow, you sound so mature these days," I teased. "Who *are* you?"

"Are you saying I was immature before?"

"I wouldn't say immature exactly—more like psycho."

Molly feigned shock. "Well, I'm boring and stable now."

"That's good but please be careful, Molly," I said. "Don't rush into anything you might regret. If this guy is as good as you say he is, you should be able to take your time."

"Oh, you don't have to worry," Molly said breezily. "Wade's not like that—he doesn't even believe in sex before marriage. Nothing physical is really important to him—he says all that can wait."

"Really?" I was genuinely surprised. This boy didn't sound like the type Molly usually went for. In fact he sounded like . . . well, like Gabriel. I hoped she hadn't gone out and found a human substitute for him. "Is that what you believe too?" I asked.

"I think I've made a lot of mistakes," Molly said. "Wade's been teaching me how I've been on the wrong path this whole time. He really understands."

"Understands what?" I asked.

"Everything." Molly sighed. "I told him everything about my past and he just gets it. There are no secrets between us."

"You didn't tell him about me, right?" I hated to ask, but I had to be sure Molly hadn't fallen so hard for this boy that she'd thoughtlessly blurted out our family secret.

"No, are you joking? I don't want him to think I'm crazy."

"That's a relief." I broke off as I watched two girls move to where Xavier was standing with the pretext of getting fries. One deliberately brushed past him on the way to the counter.

"Uh-oh," Molly said. "The competition is closing in."

Even though Molly was joking, I was uncomfortable with the whole situation—it just didn't sit right. And if I was completely honest, I was starting to feel insecure. These girls were gorgeous, with blond highlights and long, tanned legs. I could pick the type a mile away. They were the sorts of girls that were well connected, drove a Lexus, and went skiing in the winter. They had a profile at Ole Miss and I watched them fall easily into conversation with Xavier and the boys. Even from my distance, my sensitive ears could pick up threads of the discussion—they were talking about the first game of the season. Some of the references went right over my head, but Xavier seemed engaged. They spoke the same language. I knew right away I could never befriend them. They reminded me too much of my own shortcomings. When Molly saw my face, she marched over to Xavier and prodded him on the shoulder. I saw the girls raise their eyebrows and exchange looks.

"Come on," Molly said bossily, leading him away. "Let's go."

She didn't give an explanation and Xavier didn't ask for one. He merely shrugged and followed her.

When Wade turned up, he was not what I'd expected. He had carefully tousled hair, clear eyes, and an impish grin. He wore a blue checked shirt and worn leather boots. He looked outdoorsy and next to him, Molly seemed like a pampered princess. I smiled at the thought of her pretending to enjoy camping just to please him.

"This is Ford and his sister, Laurie," Molly announced, enunciating slowly to make sure she got our names right. "They're like, my best friends ever."

"Hi, how you doin'?" Wade shook hands with both of us. "Nice to meet you."

"Likewise," Xavier said.

"Hey, baby," Wade began, "weren't you going to introduce me to your other friends that go here? Beth and . . . Xavier, wasn't it?"

Molly gave me a worried look and I knew that she must have mentioned us to Wade before she knew about the terms of our new arrangement.

"Those guys changed their minds at the last minute," she said quickly. "They wanted to go to school in . . . Wyoming. I hardly talk to them anymore."

"Why Wyoming?" Wade asked with a confused look.

"I dunno." She shrugged. "Fresh air and all that. Who cares anyway?"

"Didn't you say she was your best friend?" Wade persisted.

"We're in college now," Molly told him lightly. "Everything's changed."

Wade didn't look convinced but Xavier cut in smoothly and changed the subject.

"So we hear you've been taking good care of our girl," he said, slinging an arm around Molly's shoulders.

"Doing my best," Wade replied, his face serious even though Xavier had been joking. "I've been taking her to my church and this weekend we're going to see some healers in Tennessee."

"Healers?" Xavier asked, glancing at Molly. "Are you sick?"

Molly opened her mouth but Wade answered for her.

"Not physically," he said. "But spiritually we have some work to do. It's okay though." He gave Molly a comforting smile. "I'll be there every step of the way."

Molly gazed up at him like he was her savior and tucked herself under his arm.

"What kind of work?" Xavier asked doubtfully.

"We're all broken, brother," Wade said knowingly. "Only the Lord can heal us. I think Molly understands that now."

"I've learned so much from Wade," Molly told us with a broad smile. "Everything is going to be okay from now on."

THE days passed and I fell into a familiar routine. Nothing out of the ordinary happened. No faceless horseman stampeded the Grove, no ash and smoke pervaded the air over the football stadium, and no apparitions appeared in the Johnson commons. My biggest concern was Molly's relationship with Wade. I knew she believed he was going to save her and she seemed more than willing to follow his directives. Molly might not be perfect, but I didn't think she was going to find

God by following Wade's step-by-step instructions. He made her sound like a project—a damaged damsel in distress he needed to rescue. I remembered something Gabriel had once told me.

"There are some people who seek Christ only to serve their own means," he'd said. "But Christ will not be used. You have to come to Him with complete humility, a complete willingness to accept Him into your heart and give Him reign over every aspect of your life. If you try to use Christ as a solution to your problems, it will not work. You have to serve Him in order for Him to serve you. Standing up in church for an hour on Sunday doesn't make you a Christian."

That was my fear—that Molly was turning to Wade and seeking refuge in religion when she didn't really believe it in her heart of hearts. It was bound to backfire if she wasn't careful. She didn't bring up Gabriel anymore. I wondered if she had locked those memories away someplace where they couldn't torment her.

When Molly first met Mary Ellen, a mutual if tacit hostility sprang up between them. There wasn't enough room for the both of them in my life and Molly had prior claim to the position of best friend and confidante. Besides, for the most part Mary Ellen only talked about boys, or more specifically, Ford. She wanted to know if he'd said anything about her, what kind of music he listened to, and what his favorite color was. She only stopped short of asking for a lock of his hair to keep under her pillow. She'd somehow tracked down his cell number and sent him a text to ask if he wanted to hang out in the Grove after class. When she received no reply, she bombarded me with questions.

"Why won't Ford text me back?" She waved her cell under my nose. "Here, read this message. It doesn't sound too desperate, does it?"

"It sounds fine," I said, swatting her away and hoping to cut the conversation short.

"Then why hasn't he responded?"

"I don't know." I scowled. "Maybe he's busy."

"Doing what? He'd always have his phone with him."

I'd never met a girl quite like Mary Ellen who simply refused to pick up on hints. It was clear that Ford wasn't showing signs of interest and I clearly didn't want to discuss the matter, but still she persisted.

"Do you think maybe he's scared to get emotionally involved?"

"Yes, probably," I said in the most dismissive tone I could muster.

"You have to help me, Laurie," she said. "You have to talk to him for me."

"Look," I said, trying hard not to let my mounting irritation show. "I try to stay out of Ford's love life. No guy is going to listen to his sister anyway."

I tried to spend as little time in the dorm as possible. It was confining and claustrophobic and we often woke up to find the bathroom sinks splattered with vomit. After living at Byron for most of my earthly life, this was a rude awakening to the real world of teenagers and their habits. I avoided

Mary Ellen as much as I could. But whenever she found me, it was impossible to shake her and no matter what topic I brought up, the conversation inevitably found it's way back to my brother, Ford.

MARY Ellen wasn't the only girl causing me grief. I soon had a bigger problem to deal with.

Three weeks into the semester, Xavier met Peyton Wynn. Peyton Wynn was perfect in every way and she was in Xavier's biology lab. She came from the right family; she was a Delta Gamma, a devoted Christian, an honors student, and occasionally supplemented her earnings by working as a model for Abercrombie and Fitch. Her résumé was impossibly impressive and she was the rumored candidate for the title of Miss Ole Miss, nominated for her charity work and involvement in campus life. Ordinarily she was the sort of girl I might have become friends with . . . if she hadn't asked Xavier to formal.

She approached us one Friday afternoon as we sat together in the Grove.

"Hey, Ford."

As soon as we heard the voice, Xavier's foot, which had been playing with mine under the table, instantly jerked away. We both turned to see her standing with her backpack slung easily over one shoulder. Every strand of her long fair hair was in place and she looked fresh as a daisy despite the heavy humidity in the air. It wasn't fair—not sweating was supposed to be my thing.

"Hey," Xavier greeted her warmly. "How you doing?" I could see he genuinely liked her and wasn't simply tolerating her presence like he did with Mary Ellen.

"Good, thanks." Peyton smiled a perfect smile. "Finally done with class for the day."

"Ready for the weekend, I'll bet," Xavier said. "This is my sister, Laurie, by the way. Laurie, meet Peyton, she's in my biology class."

"Hi!" Peyton shook my hand. "Are you going out for rush?"

"I'm still thinking about it," I replied.

"You'll meet some of your best friends in a sorority," she told me. "Speaking of which, Ford, I was wondering if you want to go to the formal with me?"

She asked so confidently, without a hint of nervousness or hesitation. Xavier looked taken aback.

"I didn't know any formals were coming up so soon," he said uneasily.

"Yeah, we're having one before we get all the pledges in," she said. "It's two weeks away."

"Oh," Xavier said, casting a glance in my direction. "Cool." I could tell he was tongue-tied and that didn't happen to him very often. He was being asked on a date right in front of his wife.

"So, are you in?" Peyton asked.

"Sure," Xavier said with a slightly pained expression.

"Great, what's your number? I'll text you the details."

I glared at Peyton as Xavier gave out his cell number—only I could detect the note of reluctance in his voice. Peyton probably mistook the whole thing as nervousness. I was sure she was accustomed to intimidating boys all around campus with her baby blue eyes and beauty-queen smile.

"Thanks," she said, slipping her phone in her back pocket. "I'll see you in class. Nice meeting you, Lauren."

"It's Laurie," I corrected humorlessly.

When Peyton was gone, I folded my arms and glared at Xavier. He groaned and put his head down on the table.

"What just happened?" I demanded.

"*That* was awkward," he said.

"Are you seriously going to go out with her?"

"What was I supposed to say?" Xavier said helplessly as I stood and circled our bench restlessly.

"How about *no thanks?*" I suggested.

"Beth, it's not that easy," Xavier said. "It's pretty rude to turn down an invitation for no reason."

"It's pretty rude to ask out a guy who's married," I said, digging the toe of my shoe into the dirt in frustration.

"That's hardly fair. She doesn't know—"

"Whatever. I don't like her."

"Come on," Xavier said. "She's a nice girl, this really isn't her fault."

"Couldn't you have just made up an excuse?" I said. "Told her you were busy, going out of town, something!"

"I went blank." Xavier held up his hands in defeat. "I'm sorry."

"Ugh," I said, sitting stiffly down beside him. "This is not okay."

"You know I would never do anything," Xavier said. "You should trust me enough to believe that."

"I trust you," I said. "But it's still giving out the wrong message."

"I know," Xavier said. "I just don't know how I'm going to get out of it."

To make matters worse, by the end of the day everybody knew that Ford and Peyton were going to the fall formal together. Mary Ellen sent me a devastating text message: "*F and Peyton going to formal?!?! How did that happen? I heard she can be a real bitch sometimes. Maybe he couldn't say no???*"

I ignored her. Even if I wasn't a member of the Peyton Wynn fan club, I didn't like the way Mary Ellen felt the need to tear her down to soothe her own ego. The boys on the other hand, were nothing but complimentary.

"Nice going." Spencer slapped Xavier on the back when he got back to his apartment. "She's a great girl."

I didn't like the way people were acting as if they were already a couple.

"This is good for you too, Laurie," Clay said. It took me a moment to realize he was addressing me.

"How so?" I asked drily.

"Peyton can get you a bid to DG," he said. "And she's a great role model."

"That's true," Clay's girlfriend, whose name I couldn't remember, chimed in. "Peyton Wynn is like, everything you want to be as a woman. She'll totally take you under her wing."

"Great," I said, trying not to look like I'd just sucked on a lemon. "Can't wait."

12

Twisted Sister

I slept fitfully from then on. I dreamed of Peyton and Xavier's wedding, full of rapturous guests and bouquets of flowers just as it should be instead of substitute rings and a dead priest like ours had featured. Xavier's entire family was there and Peyton's father gave her away at the altar. Mary Ellen was there too, tugging on my sleeve incessantly and crying when Xavier failed to acknowledge her presence. Then the scene shifted and I watched as Wade proposed to Molly. I saw her accept without hesitation and he carried her across the dance floor. She seemed to be dancing while standing on his feet so he was propping her up like a ragdoll. None of the moves she made were her own and her head lolled eerily to one side like she was a puppet full of stuffing. When her vacant eyes met mine, they were looking right through me.

Throughout the dream, I felt a peculiar itching at the back of my neck like I was developing a rash, an allergic reaction to something or someone in the room. I kept spinning in circles, searching for the eyes that were hiding in the shadows but I only caught a glimpse of a figure for a split second before it vanished. It was only moments before I woke up that I saw him. He was a Seven, but different from the others. He wore an iron mask to cover his face and fingerless leather gloves. The mask had a slit for a mouth and two eye-holes through which I saw nothing but blackness. I thought I could hear his rasping breaths even from where I stood. I had the strangest feeling that I knew him from somewhere. The dream left me rattled and glancing over my shoulder for the rest of the day.

WHILE Xavier was in class, Ivy and Gabriel turned up to give me an update. Luckily, Mary Ellen had gone to the library and was absent from the dorm. It wasn't safe for her to meet Gabriel; I didn't know how she'd react and we didn't have time to waste fending off her attempts at flirty banter.

"I dreamed about them," I told Gabriel as he leaned against the bed frame wearing a serious expression. The ring on his index finger clinked as he drummed his hand against the bed frame. The daylight spilling through the window seemed to mingle with the gray of Gabriel's eyes, turning them a dazzling reflective silver. They were so deep and clear sometimes I thought I was seeing right through to his soul. Only I knew he didn't have one. Souls belonged exclusively to mortals; angels only had an essence.

"They're trying to read your location through your dreams," he said.

"So as soon as I dream of Ole Miss, they'll know where I am?" I asked in alarm.

"Dreams are rarely specific," Ivy said, patting my back. "If you dream of a college dorm, you could be in any dorm in any college across the country."

"I suppose," I said uncomfortably. "But as soon as I dream of the Lyceum or Colonel Reb, the game's up. I'll have given everything away."

"Relax," Ivy said. "Your subconscious is preoccupied with other things."

"I hope you're right," I said gruffly. "So what's the latest? Have you heard anything more?"

"As far as we know, the Sevens are still searching."

"Well, that's good," I said, reaching out involuntarily to close the dusty venetian blinds. "And you're sure they won't come after you?" I hated the idea that my brother and sister might come to harm on my account.

"They're too smart for that," Ivy said. "They know we'll put up a good fight."

"But you could handle them, right?" I asked skeptically. I didn't doubt the strength of my siblings; Ivy's slender forearms could be as strong as steel and carry more force than a speeding truck, but I didn't like the idea of them going up against an army. Nothing could change the fact that they would be outnumbered.

"I don't know," my sister said gravely. "If they attacked en masse, we might be in trouble. But they won't risk it, they'd lose too many."

"So we just stay put?" I asked, relieved we wouldn't have to pack our meager belongings and flee again so soon.

"For now," Gabriel said. "We have been trying to reach the Covenant to inform them of what the Principalities are doing. They may be able to stop them. Or at least restrict their powers."

"What about Our Father? Where is He?" I asked breathlessly.

"Occupied," replied Ivy, casting a nervous glance at Gabriel. "He has His hands full at the moment."

"What are you talking about?" I was confused.

Gabriel sighed and squeezed his eyes shut for a moment. "I suppose you were going to find out eventually," he said. "Hell has retaliated, the demons are running riot."

"What?" I whispered, feeling my heart turn to lead.

"Their influence has spread, and their numbers have tripled in the last few weeks," said Gabriel. "The world is in serious trouble."

My sister nodded dourly in confirmation. "The death of an Original has caused quite an uprising. Lucifer is sending his agents out like the plague."

I felt my stomach sink to my shoes. Was this my fault? Were people now dying because of me, because I'd been stupid enough to make Lucifer angry? My hands crept up to cover my mouth but Gabriel seemed to read my thoughts.

"You are not responsible for the actions of the underworld, Bethany," he said. "They need no excuse to cause pain and suffering."

I rolled onto my bed and lay facedown on my pillow, wishing I could just hide and wait for all this to be over. I didn't move until I felt Gabriel gently touch my back.

"Remember, it was not your hand that killed Jake," he said. "It was mine."

Those words did little to console me. It didn't matter who had struck the final blow, people were still suffering because of us. The demons were sadistic and vicious enough when they had no lust for revenge. I couldn't imagine the agony they'd now be inflicting on innocent people just to spite us. And if Our Father had no time for other concerns, then things must be bad.

"This is a disaster," I whispered.

"Yes," my brother said truthfully. "But we must not lose hope. Heaven may be busy right now, but He will answer our prayers."

"What about the demons?" I asked. "Are they looking for us too?"

"We can't be sure," said Gabriel. "Right now there is no discernable pattern to their attacks, they seem to be in free fall. However . . ." He hesitated, unwilling to go on.

"I'm sure they haven't forgotten about us," I finished his thought.

"I doubt it," said my brother grimly. "But let's focus on one battle at a time."

When Ivy and Gabriel left, I wanted to find Xavier immediately, but first I had to escape Mary Ellen, who had returned to the dorm, as bubbly and over the top as always.

"Where are you going?" she asked, bounding off the bed and practically attaching to my side.

"To meet a friend," I said warily.

"Oh, great!" She grabbed her purse. "Just let me fix my make-up."

I tried not to let my exasperation show on my face. She

was so tactless sometimes. My tone clearly indicated I didn't want her company, as did the fact that I hadn't invited her.

"Actually," I said awkwardly, "I'm going to meet Molly and she's having some boy trouble. I don't think she wants to see anyone else."

"But I'm good at giving relationship advice," Mary Ellen said. I wondered if she was being deliberately obtuse.

"Yeah, Molly's not all that comfortable around new people," I said.

"But . . ."

"Sorry! See you later." I cut her off and darted out of the room before she could protest further. I knew I was probably being callous and hurting her feelings, but I was so eager to see Xavier that I couldn't stop to worry about it. I decided to make it up to her later.

I jogged lightly to the baseball field, where I knew Xavier had gone to practice with the boys in his fraternity. The place was abandoned when I got there, but Xavier was waiting for me inside. I hated having to meet with him in secret. We only got to be ourselves for a few stolen minutes each day. The rest of the time we were living this double life as Ford and Laurie McGraw. Sometimes I wished we really could trade places with these fictional characters and live like normal for a while. I wondered what it would be like to worry about things like grades and not being beaten too badly by a rival football team instead of the wrath of Heaven or Lucifer on the warpath.

I ducked quickly into the locker rooms hoping I wouldn't be seen. Xavier was sitting on a bench wearing a white

T-shirt. He scraped his fingers through his honey-colored hair that was damp from the shower. He looked up and smiled when I arrived—the same winning smile that always took my breath away.

"Hey, Beth," he murmured softly. I went over and sat in his lap, nuzzling my head into his neck and breathing in his clean scent. His skin was so soft beneath my fingers.

"You smell good," I told him, my arms wrapping around his torso, which felt solid and secure. "Kinda fruity."

"Thanks." Xavier rolled his eyes. "That makes me feel so manly."

I laughed, before growing thoughtful. "This place really feels like home, doesn't it? I wish we were here under different circumstances."

"I know," he said. "But things were never gonna be normal for us. I guess it makes us appreciate what we have."

"We have to stick together," I said earnestly. "Even if things get worse before they get better."

"Of course," Xavier said. "I'm in this for good. Even if the world falls apart at our feet, I'll never leave you, Beth."

"Good," I said. "Because I just talked to Ivy and Gabriel . . . and you're not gonna like what they said."

Xavier ran his finger gently across my cheek and let it trail down to my lips. Usually, a comment like that would have put him on alert. He'd want to know details, know exactly what was said and what we needed to do next. But I sensed tiredness in him now, a reluctance to fight anymore.

"Is it a problem that Ford and Laurie have to worry about?"

I frowned. "No."

"Then it can wait," he said. "I never see you smile anymore. I miss that."

I nodded and tipped my head up to look him in his brilliant turquoise eyes. His eyes used to sparkle, like he was laughing at a private joke he wouldn't share with anyone else. Now he just looked weary.

"I don't want to be Ford and Laurie right now," I said. "How about we try being ourselves? But let's go back to the way we were at the beginning, before any of this happened. Let's go back to that night on the beach in Venus Cove, the night of the bonfire."

Xavier and I both remembered that night with clarity. It was the night I had leapt from the cliff and let my wings break the fall. Although it had been the most frightening and daring revelation I could make, we had both been entirely at ease afterward. We had lain together in the sand for hours and by the end of it we had known we were meant to be together. Not even the anger of my brother and sister had detracted from the warm feeling that spread through me that night. Although Xavier was familiar to me, he was still spectacular, my own Prince Charming that had wandered right off the pages of a fairy tale and set my world ablaze. When I closed my eyes and felt the warmth of his hands on me, fireworks and shooting stars exploded behind my lids, leaving a trail of glittering cosmic dust in my mind.

I tipped my head up and nudged Xavier's chin with my nose. He leaned toward me and his lips tickled my ear, sending little shivers down my spine. I wanted to see the carefree eighteen-year-old boy again, not the man weighed down by the woes of the world.

My hands came up and wound around the base of his neck, feeling the heat of his body spread through me. As our lips met, I felt a familiar bolt of intoxicating energy burst inside me and the fireworks exploded across my field of vision. The feeling never dulled no matter how many times I kissed Xavier, it was always as if I were kissing him for the first time. His arms closed around my waist, pulling me closer. He took my face in his hands and we were lost in a world where only the two of us existed, outside space and time. We were too distracted to hear the footsteps on the concrete outside until it was too late.

A strangled gasp broke the magic. I jerked away to see Mary Ellen standing in the doorway, both hands clapped over her mouth in shock. I jumped up and backed away but she had already seen everything. She must have been suspicious and followed me.

"I can explain," I said as my back collided painfully with a locker. I felt the metal scrape across my shoulder blade, but I ignored it. It was a horrible cliché but I couldn't think of anything else to say. Besides which, it was a lie. I couldn't explain. I didn't think the excuse *He's really my husband and we're on the run* was going to help our cause much.

"I don't believe it," she spluttered, backing away from us as if we were contaminated. "This is disgusting!"

"Mary Ellen, please listen . . ." Xavier stood up and held out his hands in supplication, but she cut him off.

"You're sick! She's your sister. How could you do that?"

"She's not my sister," Xavier tried to make her understand. "She's my wife."

"You got married!" Mary Ellen clutched her chest, like she were having a heart attack in what I thought was an overly theatrical gesture. Suddenly she narrowed her eyes. "So that's why you never texted me back and why you wouldn't return any of my signals. I thought I was being too subtle!"

"Too subtle?" Xavier asked incredulously, starting to get angry now. "You were about as subtle as a raging bull!"

"Well, sorry I couldn't compete with your *sister*," Mary Ellen shrieked.

"Shut up for a second," I burst out, exasperated. "We haven't done anything wrong."

"You might think that," Mary Ellen said triumphantly. "But this community disagrees!"

"He and I are not related," I said emphatically. "We were lying to you before. Lying to everyone."

"Look." Mary Ellen held up her hands. "I understand how you might think this is okay, but that's because you're not right in the head. I have to tell someone about this . . . for your own sake. You'll thank me later."

"Mary Ellen, wait!" Xavier cried out, but she had already turned and fled the locker room.

Xavier pressed his face into his hands, but I was already halfway out the door, ready to give chase.

"We have to go after her," I said, going back to try and haul him to his feet.

"Why?" Xavier stared at me blankly. "She'll never listen to us."

"Xavier, think about it," I said. "This is Mary Ellen we're talking about . . . she's going to tell *everybody*."

"Let her." He shrugged. "She's got no proof. It's her word against ours."

"Doesn't matter." I grabbed his hand. "No one can ignore an accusation like that. Even if we deny it, it's going to attract so much unwanted attention. We've spent all our time here trying to go unnoticed. If we let Mary Ellen put us in the spotlight . . ."

"They'll find us," Xavier concluded in a tight voice.

"Exactly!" I squeezed his hand. "Come on."

It was hardly fair, I thought, as we pelted across the baseball fields. Ole Miss was more than just a hiding place for us. It represented everything we wanted but couldn't have: a future together on earth. I didn't want to leave and I wasn't prepared to let Mary Ellen drive us away. I picked up the pace, running so hard I could no longer feel my feet hitting the ground. I was moving with speed I didn't know I possessed. All I knew was that I couldn't let anyone put us in danger, especially not someone as ignorant about our history as Mary Ellen. To anyone watching, I would have appeared as a blur. I soon left Xavier behind and caught up with Mary Ellen in the Grove. I grabbed her shoulders from behind and she let out a strangled squawk.

"Get off of me!"

"No!" I spun her around and forced her to look at me. "Not until you hear me out."

But Mary Ellen was beyond listening. "Help!" she shrieked. "I need help!"

Something inside me snapped then. I was not going to let this happen. Xavier and I had been through enough and there was no chance I was going to let some frivolous freshman screw up the one place that was still safe for us. I pointed a finger at Mary Ellen's mouth and a second later a thick layer of skin began to creep across her lips, sealing them shut. Her eyes widened and she clawed at it with her fingers for a moment, before realizing it would be painful to break the skin and tear her lips apart. She trembled and looked up at me with fear in her eyes. It was not an expression I was used to seeing directed at me but I didn't have time to worry about that right now. For the moment I had succeeded in rendering her silent.

I could feel power coursing through me, setting my arms and legs on fire. I felt my whole body straighten and right itself, alive with the energy that was taking over. I reached out and placed a now-glowing hand on Mary Ellen's head. She sank to her knees at my feet. I could feel her thoughts and memories swirling under my touch. When I closed my eyes, I could see them, taste them, as if I were right there in the moment. I saw Mary Ellen at her sixth birthday party, dressed as a Disney princess and knew I'd gone too far back. It was hard to sift through the memories, seeing as there were so many of them. In fact, every moment in time is a memory and so I had to steer my way through waves of them until I found the exact one I wanted to erase. I knew that's what Gabriel did but he had it down to a fine art. I was new at this and my technique was not so refined. I managed to zone in on the week that included our encounter at the baseball field. That was going to have to do. I felt the memories being lifted from Mary Ellen's mind and sucked up into my fingertips. I made sure everything was gone, right down to the last few minutes in the Grove. Then I simultaneously released her and removed the seal from her lips, just as Xavier came running up behind us.

When my hold had loosened, Mary Ellen slumped to her hands and knees.

"Hey!" I said, bending down to scoop her up. "You all right?"

She stood there trembling and looking completely disoriented.

"How did I get here?" she asked. "I was in the dorm. I thought it was morning. . . ."

I realized the last memory she had was of waking up to go to class. Xavier flashed me a look of concern. I ignored him and felt Mary Ellen's forehead.

"I think you may be coming down with something. We better get you back to the dorm."

"What are you both doing here?" she asked, still dazed.

"We were taking a walk and we found you," I said. "You really shouldn't be wandering around by yourself at this time of night."

"But I wasn't . . ."

Xavier propped her up against his shoulder, which seemed to distract her from her previous train of thought.

"C'mon," he said. "Let's get you home. I'm sure you'll feel better in the morning."

"I don't feel well," Mary Ellen said suddenly, as if Xavier hadn't spoken. Gabriel had once told me that fiddling around with someone's memories could leave them with a throbbing headache or a feeling of nausea.

"I know," Xavier said. "Laurie's right—you probably are coming down with something. We'll get you to the health center first thing tomorrow."

"Okay. Thank you."

Mary Ellen took a few shaky steps in the direction of the dorm before dropping to her knees and vomiting at the base of an old oak. Xavier caught her on the way down and I pulled her hair out of the firing line. She gave a low whimper. It must be scary to find yourself wandering around alone in the dark and have no idea how you got there.

"It's okay," Xavier said, keeping one steadying hand on her back and the other wrapped around her middle to keep her from falling forward. He threw me a look that was almost accusatory.

"Was that really necessary?" he hissed into my ear as he helped Mary Ellen to her feet.

Ordinarily, I would have felt regret or guilt over what I'd done, but today I looked into Mary Ellen's alarmed face and frightened eyes and felt nothing. *Yes, it was necessary*, I thought to myself. *I had done what was necessary to protect us.* I was starting to think like my siblings, concerned less about the individual and more about the overall picture. If Mary Ellen had gone screaming to town with the ammunition we'd given her, we'd be in serious trouble right now. I met Xavier's gaze with a resolute look.

"She'll live" was all I said.

13

Here Comes the Bride

WHEN Mary Ellen woke up late the next morning, I was waiting for her with a cup of hot coffee and a bacon biscuit. I felt bad about traumatizing her the night before, even though I knew she wouldn't remember it. She awoke with a moan and buried her head under her pillow.

"What time is it?" she croaked.

"Around noon," I answered, setting my offerings down on her desk. "How do you feel?"

"Like I got hit by a bus," she replied theatrically, shielding her eyes from the light. "What happened?"

"You got sick," I said, trying to keep the information to a bare minimum to avoid questions I wouldn't be able to answer. I felt like I had performed surgery, only I'd messed it up.

"Was I drinking?" she asked, rubbing her temples.

I took in her sunken eyes, ringed with purple, her dry lips, and tangled hair. Alcohol seemed as good an explanation as any for her current condition. It was the only plausible thing that might have left her wandering around Ole Miss, incoherent and uncoordinated.

"Yeah," I said. "I think so." Lies came so easily these days.

I no longer stumbled over them or betrayed my true feelings with my body language. I was growing accustomed to weaving a tangled web of deceit wherever I went. But now was not the time to chastise myself. First I needed to cover our tracks.

"Wow, I must have really gone heavy," she said. "I don't remember a darn thing."

"You were pretty far gone when we found you," I told her, giving little away. "But all that matters is that you got home safe."

"Laurie . . ." Mary Ellen asked sheepishly. "Can I ask a favor?"

"Sure," I sighed, eager to make amends in some small way.

"Please don't mention this to anyone. If people find out, my reputation will be shot."

I was taken by surprise but readily agreed. I'd expected Mary Ellen to blab the story all over campus. With her penchant for overexaggerating, I had thought she would tell everyone who'd listen about her ordeal and how she barely made it back alive. But this would work out much better. In fact, Mary Ellen's fear of sorority girls was the first stroke of luck we'd had in a while.

Once I was convinced she was safe to be left to her own devices, I went to find Xavier at his apartment. Spencer opened the door. I could see past him to Clay sprawled on the couch, his chunky biology textbook propped up on his chest.

"Hey, mini-McGraw," said Spencer with a lopsided grin. "Welcome to the man cave."

"Thanks. I think." I smiled at him and stepped tentatively

inside. With four boys living there, Xavier's apartment was really more of a shrine to life in a fraternity than actual living quarters. Xavier was by habit pretty neat, but the living room was a mess of pizza boxes, cans, and game consoles. None of the furniture matched, it was all thrown together and clearly only there to serve a purpose, and that purpose was functional. Nothing there was intended to be decorative. The Mississippi state flag was hung up on one wall along with the Sigma Chi crest and a wooden cutout of Colonel Reb.

"This whole place smells like boys," I said, and Spencer laughed.

"Are you saying it smells bad?"

"Nope," I said. "Just . . . manly."

"We are very manly men." Clay nodded in agreement. "Your brother's in the shower, but don't lie . . . you're here to see us."

"You got me," I said. "I can't stay away."

"Ha, yeah, right." Spencer winked to let me know they were joking. "So did you hear, Ford refused to come out with us last night? We think he has a secret woman in his life."

"Oh, no," I said in mock seriousness. "That boy needs to get his priorities straight."

"I know." Spencer shook his head. "You better have words with him about it. Imagine putting a girl above your fraternity brothers."

"It's a disgrace," I agreed, and settled on the couch to wait for Xavier. A few moments later he emerged from the bathroom, his hair wet, and nothing but a towel wrapped around his waist. For a moment, his body took me by surprise and I had to keep from staring. I hadn't seen him shirtless in a while and was taken aback by his taut and chiseled form. I felt like I was being rocketed back to our early days, when we had first started dating and I had to make a concerted effort not to make my feelings blatantly obvious. Now I had to pry my eyes away from his muscular chest before anyone noticed.

"Hey," Xavier said. "Thought I heard your voice."

"Nice of you to get dressed," I said pointedly.

"Yeah, man, what kind of show you think we're running here?" Spencer said.

"Nothing you haven't seen before." Xavier shrugged but he grabbed an Ole Miss T-shirt from a pile of fresh laundry and disappeared into his room to get changed. When he came back, he offered me his hand and hauled me up from the sofa.

"C'mon, sis, I'll buy you lunch," he said. I knew he was looking for an excuse to get out of the apartment so we could spend some time alone.

"You never buy *us* lunch," Spencer grumbled. "How come?"

"Don't like you," Xavier called over his shoulder. Spencer hurled a cushion after him as we disappeared through the doorway.

IN Xavier's pickup truck, I settled back, finally able to be myself for a while. As he started the engine, the chords of Brad Paisley filtered through the stereo and my feet started tapping of their own accord.

"Do you see what Ole Miss has done to me?" Xavier said.

"I'm voluntarily tuned in to a country music station." He drummed his fingers against the wheel as he mouthed the words: *"Listenin' to old Alabama, drivin' through Tennessee . . ."*

"You're a country boy at heart," I told him. "Just accept it."

Xavier plucked at my baggy checked shirt. "There's only one redneck in this car," he said playfully.

"You know they think you have a secret girlfriend," I told him, catching hold of his hand and playing with his fingers. I missed being able to touch him whenever I liked and wanted to take full advantage of the moment.

"Who, them?" He used his free hand to jerk his thumb back toward the apartment. "Who cares? They'll have a tough time guessing who."

"Do you ever just want to tell everyone?" I sighed. "About us."

"Yep," Xavier said. "Especially since Spencer told the whole frat house about my smokin' little sister."

"He did not!" I couldn't help laughing. Spencer was such a character.

"Oh, he did. They all want to meet you now." Xavier shook his head. "Not gonna happen."

"Whatever," I told him. "I've got it worse. The girls are pretty much obsessed with you."

"That's ridiculous," Xavier scoffed. "They don't even know me."

"They know your star sign, all the sports you play, where you worked last summer, and who you went on senior camp with," I said.

"Huh?" Xavier looked at me blankly. "How?"

"Don't underestimate the art of Facebook stalking."

"That is messed up," Xavier laughed.

My cell phone vibrated and I looked down to see a text from Molly wanting to know what I was doing.

"Here we go," Xavier groaned. "Can you tell her you're studying?"

"She says she has news. . . ."

"Probably something about the Kardashians." Xavier rolled his eyes.

We decided to go get lunch and worry about Molly later. We found a quiet booth at the back of a diner and settled in. I ran my hands over the cracked burgundy vinyl and watched the colored egg-shaped lights overhead. It was dark and noisy inside the diner and I felt like we could truly hide away from the world. The walls were covered in dusty framed photographs and variations of the flag and the ceiling was studded with toothpicks, their tips twinkling with cellophane.

"This is great," I said. "I love being at college."

"Yep." Xavier stretched and kicked back in his seat. "Most carefree days of our lives."

"How long do you think it'll last?" I tried not to look downcast.

"Doesn't matter," Xavier said. "What matters is we're here together. If it lasts a year or just one more week, at least we got to experience it. And who knows, maybe we'll be back someday."

"What would you be if you hadn't met me?" I asked suddenly. "I mean, what would you be doing?"

Xavier didn't hesitate to answer. "I'd be Xavier Woods, pre-med, secret Bama fan, Sigma Chi legacy . . . total man whore."

"I'm being serious!" I scolded.

"What kind of a question is that?" Xavier said. "Everything would be different if I hadn't met you."

"Yes, but how?" I insisted.

"Well for starters, I would never have seen as much as I've seen, which means I wouldn't value what I have as much as I do. I'd probably still be searching for the right girl and I'd probably end up in some white-collar job, in a nice neighborhood, with a nice family."

"That doesn't sound so bad," I murmured.

"I said *nice,*" Xavier emphasized. "Not extraordinary. It would never be like what we have."

"I guess not," I said halfheartedly. I couldn't stop imagining the family he might have one day, if I wasn't around to cause upheaval in his life. It wasn't that I couldn't give him children; I just couldn't provide the stable environment in which to raise them. At least not yet and maybe not ever. That picture-perfect life was everything I wanted and Xavier was throwing it away without a thought. Was he underestimating its value? I couldn't let him do that.

Xavier reached across the table and took my hand.

"You want to know what the biggest difference is?" he asked softly, and I glanced up. I could almost feel the warmth from his blue eyes feeding into me. "I'd still be questioning my faith. I'd be struggling like everyone else, trying to make sense of the world. But because of you, I have conviction like

I never thought possible. I've seen the power of Heaven; I know what angels can do. Because of you, Hell isn't just a place I hear about in Bible study—it's a reality. Because of you, I know there's a God above and He's watching over me every step of the way. Because of you, I now believe there's a Heaven and one day we will get there . . . together."

"The white place," I whispered, and I felt his fingers squeeze mine. "You know, when I look at you, I feel this presence . . . like Our Father has special plans for you."

It was true, Xavier's energy seeped into everything around him, and it was impossible to be unhappy in his presence. Sometimes I felt like I could even taste him. He tasted like sunshine. Like love.

"I don't feel like we're two separate people anymore," Xavier said, smiling dreamily over the rim of his sweet tea. "It's like I live inside you and you live inside me. We're pretty much the same person."

"That's how Our Father intended man and woman to live and love," I replied. "Mimicking the relationship of the trinity, in unity with one another."

I noticed the girl at the next table staring at us and abruptly pulled my hand away. It was difficult to remember that we couldn't have these intensely personal moments in public anymore. Xavier coughed slightly and seemed to shake himself like he was waking from a dream.

"So anyway," he said in the most offhanded tone he could manage. "Should we see what Molly wanted?"

We both recognized it was a lot safer to hang out with Molly than to risk being on our own. The temptation to get lost in each other was just too strong. I sent a text telling her to meet us at the diner and she turned up fifteen minutes later, bouncy as ever in a white "Harvard of the South" T-shirt and bright pink shorts. She flopped into the booth and looked at us both, grinning from ear to ear.

"Guess what?"

"What?" Xavier looked like he was regretting this already.

"I have news."

"We heard."

"Big news," Molly emphasized. "Life-changing news."

"Come on." I laughed. "Just tell us already."

Molly suddenly whipped her left hand from her lap and placed it triumphantly on the tabletop. It was impossible to miss the sparkling engagement ring on her finger. My mouth dropped open and she beamed from ear to ear.

"Say hello to the future Mrs. Wade Harper the Third."

"Oh, good Lord . . ." Xavier didn't know what to say.

"I know, right!" Molly squealed and threw herself at me in a hug. "Isn't it amazing?"

"Well . . . yeah," I said, trying to sound enthusiastic. "But are you sure you're ready for this? You're only eighteen."

"So are you, and you married Xavier," Molly protested.

"Yes but I . . . that was . . . I guess you're right." I didn't know how to tell her that Xavier and I were different without sounding conceited. But it was true, we were in a very different situation, we had seen a lot together, our relationship had well and truly been tested. We hadn't made some spur-of-the-moment decision. I felt awful thinking it, but to me Molly's rash engagement seemed the equivalent of a drunken

Vegas wedding. Did either of them really know what they were getting into?

"Molly . . ." Xavier leaned forward and he adopted his older-brother voice. "Are you sure you've thought this through? Do you really know Wade that well?"

"You sound like my father," Molly retorted.

"Have you told him?" Xavier wanted to know.

"No, but I bet that's what he'd say. My parents are supposed to criticize, my *friends* are supposed to be happy for me." She glared at us both, clearly disenchanted by the mildness of our reaction.

"We are happy for you!" I said, flashing Xavier a look. "You just took us by surprise, that's all."

Molly's face softened. "Well, Wade took me by surprise." She twirled her hair around her finger like a schoolgirl. "It's going to be so romantic. You'll see. Wade and I are going to be just as happy as you are."

I didn't tell her that our happiness came at an expense. On the outside, we might appear like the ultimate couple in love, but we'd been to Hell and back, literally, fighting for the right to be together. Love wasn't so much a feeling anymore, but a lifelong commitment. That was love. That was marriage. And I wasn't sure Molly was quite there yet.

14

Showdown

"I'LL walk you to class," Xavier offered. I was wearing his oversize Sigma Chi T-shirt that came down to my knees. I had to keep hitching it up so you could see that I was in fact wearing shorts underneath.

"You don't have to."

"It's on my way," Xavier said. One of the few upsides of having to keep our relationship secret was that Xavier had taken to courting me again; walking me to class and picking me up from my dorm so we could sneak off to lunch together. Everybody accepted that we were close as siblings could be.

"Can we go to the square to eat?" I asked.

"Sure. Why don't you bring Molly?"

"Seriously? You really want me to?" Xavier never suggested we bring Molly anywhere.

"No," he said, sighing, "but it can't be just the two of us all the time. We have to be aware of that."

"We never get alone time anymore," I grumbled.

"We'll get some time soon. A lot of kids will be leaving this weekend."

"How come?"

"It's an away game." I gave him a blank look. "It means the Rebs are playing at another school."

"How come football determines everything around here?" I asked, and Xavier looked at me as if I'd just said something deeply offensive.

"Beth, football is like a religion here."

"Well, I don't get it."

"I'll take you to the next game and you'll understand."

"You know how I feel about crowds," I hedged.

"Don't worry," Xavier laughed. "It'll only be about sixty thousand."

My jaw dropped and he gave my shoulder a fraternal squeeze. "Oh, Laurie, you have much to learn."

We walked past the imposing façade of the Lyceum, the university's first building, with its towering white columns, which I knew from my reading had once served as a hospital during the civil war. The surrounding flowerbeds were awash with color, planted with daffodils and purple pansies. I marveled at the pristine state of the campus grounds and the efforts that must go into keeping it that way.

We made our way to the old lecture theater with its tiered wooden seats and polished gray linoleum floors. It was already teeming with students pulling laptops out of backpacks and chatting casually as they awaited the arrival of the English professor. I noticed Xavier didn't seem in a hurry to leave.

"So I'll come find you when I'm done?" I ventured.

"I might just stick around if that's okay. I want to see what your class is like."

"Don't you have study group?"

"I'm sure they'll manage without me."

"Is something wrong?" I asked suspiciously.

"Nope, I just don't feel like leaving you right now."

I didn't argue. I knew what he meant. After the last conversation with Gabe and Ivy, I also wanted us to stay close to one another. If anything were to happen, I wanted us to face it together.

We edged our way past students standing in clusters and veered toward the back row. It might have appeared antisocial but I wanted to dodge any questions about what we were doing there together. But I was fairly certain nobody knew me well enough to pay much attention.

I didn't know why, but I was on edge that day. Something had changed; a few times I caught a whiff of something foul carried in the air. I sat upright and tense in my chair, the back of my seat rubbing uncomfortably against my spine. Xavier, on the other hand, looked comfortable in the aisle seat, his legs outstretched and crossed at the ankles.

When Professor Walker finally arrived with his thatch of silver hair that stood upright on his head like a cockatoo's crest, he carried no notes, only a battered copy of the *Norton Anthology of Literature* under his arm. He peered at us in a world-weary way over round tortoiseshell glasses that had slipped midway down his nose. As soon as silence fell, he directed us to turn to the page containing Keats's "Ode on a Grecian Urn." Beside me I heard Xavier let out an audible groan. A couple of girls in front of us turned around, giggling and pulling faces in empathy.

"Poetry?" he whispered. "Why didn't you warn me?"

"It was your idea, remember?"

"Is it too late to make a run for it?"

"Yes. You have to stay now. Besides, you might even learn something."

"This better not really be about an urn," he said, scowling.

I jabbed his arm with my pencil to silence him. Xavier slunk lower in his seat and cupped his face in his hands as if he wanted to make himself invisible. His usually piercing blue eyes flashed me a look of betrayal. I gave him a contented smile in return. Boring as he might find what Professor Walker had to say, I was going to enjoy having him beside me for the next hour.

But as it turned out, class that day was not as uneventful as Xavier expected.

IF we harbored any doubts before, the fact that the Sevens chose a public venue to launch their attack on us confirmed how little they valued human life. When I looked back on it, I realized their actions went against everything they were created to do. They were supposed to maintain harmony on earth, not wreak havoc. But it seemed a handful of mortal lives lost was a small price to pay for the capture of an errant angel. After that day, I began to harbor serious doubts about the Creator's involvement in the events that unfolded. That day felt like the work of a celestial vigilante group, a rebel faction that had taken matters into their own hands.

The first tangible thing that alerted me to trouble was the rumble overhead that everyone assumed to be thunder. Only

I remembered how cloudless the sky outside had been just minutes before. This was followed by a barely audible hum that sounded vaguely familiar. It bothered me so much I strained to hear it above the resonance of the professor's voice. I so badly wanted to believe it was due to faulty air-conditioning, but then I saw something that made my blood run cold. When I looked up at the vaulted ceiling, I saw the solid plaster become as ductile as dough. The whole roof seemed to be quivering like jelly, as if the entire room had suddenly become malleable.

That was when the door of the lecture hall burst open and I saw it, a gilded white horse snorting and pawing at the ground. He appeared like a rough sketch, not properly filled out. I grabbed Xavier, slamming my hand down over his on the desk. I caught sight of a jeweled saddle as the horse reared its head, the white mane fanning down its back. Under ordinary circumstances it would have been beautiful, but it was nothing but a warning sign, preceding the arrival of its masters. The other students looked curiously at the door, oblivious to its presence. The horses appeared only to those who understood their significance.

"It's back," I whispered. "Xavier . . . it's them."

No sooner had I spoken those words than the masked figures appeared like phantoms in the lecture hall. Their hands and feet were concealed under swirling black robes. Whatever semblance of a face they possessed was hidden behind masks of white plaster, which seemed to adhere to their faces. They had slits for eyes through which there was nothing but empty sockets to be seen. There was not even a hole through which they might draw air; they had no need to breathe because they weren't of this world. The only skin exposed was their calloused hands; a hoary color, like decaying flesh, half covered by fingerless leather gloves. They were the Sevens from my nightmare, only in the dream there'd been just one. Now there were at least a dozen.

I felt Xavier go rigid beside me. The other students sat up straighter and pointed, some concerned, some intrigued, and some laughing at what they assumed to be an elaborate, high-tech hoax perhaps executed by some creative frat boys. Few could have understood how real the threat they were facing was.

In the next moment, Xavier was out of his seat and shoving me down onto the hard floor, trying to conceal me from view. I didn't resist and crouched under the folding seats with the metal bars pushing into my shoulder blades, my heart racing uncontrollably. They were so close, was it possible they hadn't seen me? Surely their storming of this particular class hadn't been mere coincidence. They must have known I was there. But if they hadn't seen me yet, maybe we still had a chance of getting out alive.

From my crouching position I only had a fragmented view of what was happening. I heard Xavier take charge, urging people to move.

"Get out!" he shouted. "It's not safe here. Run!"

Everybody reacted differently. Some refused to heed his warning, determined to see for themselves what the spectacle was all about. Professor Walker had stopped speaking and stood in open-mouthed wonder. The heavy anthology he'd been reading from slipped from the lectern and thumped to the floor. The Sevens were blocking the exits; they seemed vast and unmovable in their voluminous robes. The sound of the scratchy, labored breathing coming from beneath their masks filled the room. The black hoods that concealed their faces were ruffled by an invisible wind and flapped against their plaster cheeks.

Some hysterical girls turned to Xavier for help, desperate for an authority figure to give instruction when everybody else appeared to be rendered useless.

"What do we do?" they screamed, clutching one another. "What's going on?"

Xavier could see immediately there was no safe way out of the lecture theater. He put a hand on a girl's shoulder, the one who seemed least hysterical, and looked her dead in the eye.

"Get down and stay low," he instructed, and threw a glance at the other two who were a mess of tears and smeared mascara. "Look after them, they need you."

The girl nodded and swallowed hard. She guided the others who were still whimpering to the ground and I watched them crawl away on their hands and knees to the safety of some nearby desks. Other people were still stumbling around the aisles or hastily trying to bundle their belongings into backpacks.

The Sevens reacted swiftly on hearing Xavier's voice and they began to advance toward us. They couldn't see us; I knew that for a fact—they were like blind animals that relied on other finely tuned senses to hunt. Their heads creaked eerily from side to side as they surveyed the room. What were they using to detect us? Was it smell or voice recognition or could they pick up the vibration of our souls and know instinctively who we were? Either way, Xavier needed to get out of sight. I reached forward and caught hold of his ankle. He nearly yelled out but stopped himself just in time when he saw my face peeking out at him from ground level, and he managed to back away silently and slide under a desk beside me. We both lay as still as we could, holding our breath and hardly daring to move a muscle.

The Sevens reached inside their capacious black robes and withdrew long bars of metal that glinted in the light. It took me a second to realize they were swords, the jeweled hilts gripped in their gloved hands. Against the stark white walls of the lecture hall, I caught a flash of the shadow of wings, dark and tattered, almost skeletal. The feathers seemed to be falling away, leaving the wings bald, only the bone structure with wisps of residue still clinging to the frame.

At the appearance of the swords, it didn't take long for the human survival instinct to replace curiosity. Students began to panic, running in all directions and shielding their faces with books. The swords the Sevens carried seemed to ripple slightly and appeared to emit a powerful heat. Soon the room began to feel like a sauna.

The Sevens swept up and down the aisles. One of them passed by the desk under which I lay hidden, so close I could smell the odor of damp, rotting leaves that clung to the hem of his robes. He held the sword by the hilt at his chest, its tip pointing toward the ground. I could feel the heat radiating from the metal, as if it had been held under an open flame. From the tip I could just make out a thin beam, like a laser, that seemed to be searching for something. I didn't have time to jerk back and the beam traveled across my hand, which I hadn't tucked back under my body after reaching out to Xavier. I felt a blinding flash of pain as the skin sizzled, the heat burning deep into my flesh and leaving my hand smoking with the burn. I bit down hard on my lip to stop from crying out and felt my eyes begin to water. An angry blistering stripe now marred my hand from my wrist down to my knuckles. I tried not to look at the bubbles of skin and red, raw flesh. The Seven stopped for a moment and I thought I heard a wolf-like sniffing. Could he smell the injury, smell my fear, or both? Slowly, and with great difficultly, I turned my hand over and pressed it into the carpet, hoping it might block out whatever the Seven was detecting. I gritted my teeth and tried to ignore the little prickly fibers now digging into my exposed flesh. A moment later the Seven moved on and the beam from the sword continued . . . only now it was heading for Xavier's ankle. He braced himself, ready to face the pain, but nothing happened. The beam passed over him, harmless as a blowfly. I realized then that the swords were designed for me—to ferret out my hiding place. If one came in direct contact with my body, it would sear me until I had no choice but to scream and reveal myself.

The masked creatures continued to scope the faces in the crowd with their unseeing eyes. I could hear the breathing of the one beside me, rasping like he suffered from advanced emphysema. I was surprised at their ability to ignore the fearful cries and wild scampering of the human students around them and I wondered if they could even hear them at all from behind their plaster masks.

Amid the confusion, a figure began to walk toward the lectern. At first all I could see of him was a pair of heavy black boots, each step hitting the ground as heavily as if they were made of stone. I pressed my face against the floor, trying to get a good look at this mysterious newcomer. He was tall and built solid as a rock. His rich ebony skin had a slight sheen and long matted dreadlocks hung to his shoulders. His black eyes were hooded and expressionless. He had no cause to wear a mask—I could never have doubted his identity. This was Hamiel, the leader of the Sevens and a prophet of doom. Wherever he went, suffering was sure to follow. He looked around the lecture hall and a small smile began to play on his lips.

"Come out, come out wherever you are," he said in a deep, rumbling voice that had a curious singsong quality. "You can't hide forever."

Xavier's hand curled protectively over mine and I turned my head a fraction to look at him. His honey-colored hair fell over one side of his face. He couldn't speak but his brilliant, electric blue eyes held all the unspoken words. His hand tightened over mine and I knew he was saying, "*Don't you dare. Don't even think about giving yourself up.*"

I flicked my eyes desperately toward Hamiel's boots and back again. He wasn't going to be patient for long. If I didn't surrender myself, I had no doubt he would slaughter every person in the room until he found me. Hamiel's tar-black gaze fell on a girl cowering nearby. She screamed as his massive presence approached her and picked her up by the scruff of her neck like a dog. I didn't know the girl's name but I recognized the curtain of red hair and pale skin from my dorm. Susie, was it? Or Sally? I couldn't remember and it didn't matter. All that mattered was that Hamiel would kill her if I didn't step forward. He tossed her down on the ground and swung his sword in a gentle arc so the flat side of the gleaming blade thudded dully against her neck. He was playing with us. All he needed was to change the angle and put a little more force behind it and she'd be dead in an instant.

It was time for me to act. I pulled my hand away from Xavier and leaned across to awkwardly kiss his cheek. It wasn't the farewell I would have chosen, but I had no choice. I wasn't going to let some poor girl die in my place. I might be a disgrace to Heaven, but I was still an angel and it was my job to protect human life. I hadn't forgotten that.

I couldn't speak to Xavier and risk giving him away, so I gave him a look that I hoped conveyed a fraction of what I felt for him. It was hard to break away; I felt like I was trying to leave my own body behind. But the petrified look on the face of the redheaded girl spurred me into action. The heartbreak at leaving Xavier made my whole chest tighten. But there would be time to grieve later. Right now I had to be strong. I wriggled out from under the desk and folded my arms across my chest.

"Hey there," I said casually to Hamiel. "Looking for me?"

15

Class Dismissed

HAMIEL'S face broke into a grin, his teeth stark white against the rich sable tones of his skin. There was no amusement in his expression, only victory. He had won, smoked me out of my hiding place and right into his clutches. He signaled by clapping his hands and the Sevens stopped dead, turning in a formation to face him and await instructions. They were like trained dogs, acting blindly at their master's command. He needed only to say the word and they would end me.

I felt a slight movement at my shoulder and then Xavier appeared at my side. I could almost feel my heart breaking as he protectively took his place beside me. More than anything I'd wanted him to stay safe. But I should have known he'd never let me face the music alone. My condemnation was his condemnation. There was no separating us now. I wanted to cry, but I would not show weakness by breaking down in front of Hamiel. Instead, I reached out and took Xavier's hand, entwining our fingers and holding on tight. Taking his cue from me, Xavier refused to be intimidated. He leaned against a desk and drummed his free hand against the wood.

"You boys need to get out more," he said. "And really, what's with the masks? C'mon, this isn't *Scream*."

Despite whatever horrors might have been laying in store for us, I forced myself to give a defiant smirk. The whole situation was so unthinkable there was nothing left to do but show them they couldn't wear us down completely. Hamiel narrowed his eyes.

He was clearly not expecting this sort of reaction from us and although his face remained unmoved, I could see the flicker of rage in his black liquid eyes.

"Who do you think you are, boy?"

Xavier shrugged. "I'm with her."

Hamiel flicked his gaze back to me. "I've heard."

"So what are you gonna do about it?" I asked almost tauntingly.

Hamiel gave a nasty smile. "You're about to find out."

The room was plunged into darkness, resulting in more high-pitched screams of terror from the students who we had all but forgotten about. Xavier and I grabbed one another, ready to face our comeuppance, whatever it might be. We were prepared for pain, for emptiness, even for death so long as we could face it together. On the surface, we appeared unarmed, but we were each other's greatest weapons.

When the lights came on again, I sensed something wasn't right. Hamiel looked angry, almost confused. He hadn't been the cause of what had just happened. That was when I saw Gabriel, standing barefoot in the center aisle, his golden hair streaming behind him like a flag in the wind. Traditionally, he should have been wearing a robe of white to denote his position in the angelic hierarchy, but he had thrown away protocol and wore a pair of faded blue jeans instead. Light spilled from his skin so the students closest to him had to look away. His white T-shirt was glowing so bright it had transformed into what looked like white-hot armor.

Silence descended as everybody examined the newcomer. The students seemed to realize at once that help was at hand. One look at Gabriel told you whose side he was on. There was not a shred of darkness in him and the look on his face was fiercely protective. He was here to back the victims. The screaming settled into whimpers broken by the occasional tearful plea for help.

Hamiel twitched a finger and the vast ceiling rose overhead, giving a deep groan, and then was wrenched from its place, leaving a gaping hole. It hurtled toward Gabriel, who merely threw out an arm to intercept its fall, directing it to shatter against a wall out of harm's way. For several long minutes nothing happened as Gabriel and Hamiel stared at each other while plaster dust settled on the ground around them. The Sevens, who were still awaiting command, remained as motionless as statues.

For what seemed like an eternity, the two celestial warriors watched one another, each trying to calculate the other's next move. I knew how precarious the situation was. At the moment the balance of power was even, but if it tipped even a little in the wrong direction, things could end in disaster. Gabriel also knew that if the situation escalated, their combined power could cause the entire building to collapse on top of us. I knew he wasn't about to risk letting that happen.

I looked at the students, who no longer knew what to think and were just waiting for the ordeal to be over. Some of the boys were trying to comfort the sobbing girls, shielding them with their own bodies while others cowered uselessly in their seats, faces in their cupped hands. I could hardly blame them; it must have looked like the end of the world.

"You have no authority to invade this place," Gabriel said in a voice like steel. "Your presence here is unjustified."

"As is yours, brother," said Hamiel. "Tell me, how does Heaven feel about traitors these days?"

"Protecting the innocent doesn't make me a traitor," Gabriel snarled. "Tell me, under whose instruction are you acting?"

"We work to serve the Kingdom," said Hamiel proudly.

"Do not lie to me," Gabriel thundered. He swept a hand around the room in disgust. "He would never condone this."

Hamiel pointed a gloved finger at me. "That angel has broken the law. Her actions will not be exonerated."

"And neither will yours," Gabriel replied.

"You could have avoided this game of hide and seek." Hamiel gave a contemptuous laugh. "How long did you think you could keep us guessing?"

"This is about saving face for you, isn't it?" Gabriel said in disgust. "Pride is a dangerous thing, brother. We should all know that."

"It is about justice."

"Then why don't you step down?" Gabriel suggested. "Let Him deal with them as He sees fit. I assure you it will not be like this."

"No," Hamiel replied smugly. "He can't come to the phone right now. It's up to us to issue punishment."

The conversation was going in circles. Hamiel was deftly avoiding Gabriel's questions about Our Father. He knew the Sevens were acting out their own crazed idea of justice. I wondered at what point the ranks that were employed to maintain peace on earth had become a rebel force, to be feared rather than respected.

Gabriel let his wings unfurl slowly and I heard the students gasp.

"You will not be the one to judge them," he said.

"You have no authority here, Arch," Hamiel replied dismissively.

"You know I could destroy you," Gabriel snarled.

"Undoubtedly, but not without incurring loss of human life. I know how much that bothers you." In case he hadn't made his meaning clear, Hamiel glanced pointedly at the helpless teenagers on the floor.

"Then open the doors and let only those involved remain," Gabriel said. But his appeal to the Seven's sense of justice didn't seem to be working.

"Too late," Hamiel said. "They all must perish."

Some of the students began to cry harder and beg for mercy. Others squeezed their eyes shut, willing this to be part of some terrible nightmare.

"These people are innocent." The authority seemed to have leached from Gabriel's voice. Now he just sounded astonished by Hamiel's indifference to human life.

"Your attachment to these creatures of clay weakens you,"

Hamiel said darkly. "I suggest you stop thinking about them and worry about your own future. Besides, they are not innocent. They carry the guilt of Adam's sin."

"And why do you think Christ was sent?" Gabriel boomed. "He paid their debts, their sin was washed clean by His blood. Why do you manipulate the truth?"

"Are you really going to try and stop me?" Hamiel challenged.

"Indeed," my brother replied. "You will regret this."

As he spoke, a glowing ember appeared in the air beside him and began to shift to form a figure. I knew before I saw the tumble of golden hair and eyes the color of raindrops that it was Ivy. She belonged to the highest of angelic orders and could transform into a glowing orb and travel great distances in a matter of seconds. Hamiel took a step backward. Ivy raised a hand and from her dainty palm, bolts of lightning now blasted through the air, connecting with each Seven in turn and setting their black robes ablaze, the tongues of fire licking at their expressionless plaster faces. They beat a hasty retreat, taking flight and disappearing one by one into the hole that had appeared in the ceiling above us, until only Hamiel stood, deserted. He was their leader and not so easily intimidated.

"I will destroy you," he roared.

Ivy raised one delicate, golden eyebrow. "With what army?"

Hamiel bared his teeth and hunched forward like an animal about to strike. Then without warning, he reached inside his robe and withdrew a scepter. It all happened so fast I hardly had time to react. He knew he couldn't touch Ivy and Gabriel, but he could punish them in his own way. He pointed the scepter at a girl crouching in front of us and I watched her try to hide her face. A bolt of energy burst forth, literally rocking the room. The boy beside her threw his body protectively over hers. When the beam from the scepter pierced his side, I heard the same sickening sizzling sound that skewered meat makes on a barbecue. His arms fell lifeless to his side and I choked back a scream seeing his limbs become charred beyond recognition. When he fell back, unmoving on the carpet, I realized that the face, now blackened and covered with red welts still hissing with heat, was Spencer. All that had remained intact was the thatch of blond hair and his eyes. They were open and staring lifelessly at the ceiling. But I could see no fear in his face, only conviction.

Xavier stared at the body of his fraternity brother on the floor.

"No, damn you!" I heard him shout in a voice choked with emotion. Spencer had been his roommate, his ally, his friend. And now he too was dead because of us. Xavier took an unsteady step back and sagged against a desk. I didn't know how much more death he could handle. All the fight seemed to go out of me in that moment.

I could see that Gabriel was about to bring down the ceiling with fury. Ivy seemed to withdraw into herself for a moment and when she opened her eyes, she opened fire on Hamiel, hurling deadly lightning bolts in his direction. Hamiel somersaulted through the air, dodging the attacks nimbly despite his colossal size. Gabriel focused on protecting the other students and webs of blue light began to form over each cowering body, looking fragile, but in reality as strong as an impenetrable steel cage. But Hamiel didn't care about them anymore. Now he had his sights on us.

I wanted to summon the strength I knew must be dormant somewhere inside of me, but I was so numb from what I'd witnessed that I couldn't do anything. When Hamiel reached for me, I feebly threw up my hands to protect myself. He caught my wrists in his clublike hands and twisted them backward, snapping the bones like twigs. The sharp cracks were loud and Hamiel hurled me away. I flew through the air like a ragdoll, rolling across desks, my head thudding repeatedly against the wood. I landed on my broken wrists and gagged from the pain. Gabriel's arms were around me in an instant, lifting me up. My head was foggy but I was still able to remember what was important.

"Xavier," I whispered, struggling to get free and being reminded of my inability to help him by the throbbing pain in my hands. Xavier had been left unprotected.

"Beth!" He had all but forgotten Hamiel's presence, concerned only about my safety. He was on the other side of the lecture hall and couldn't reach me. When I was in danger, he shut down and had only one focus. But from my position, I could see everything that was happening. I watched Hamiel's looming form appear right behind Xavier, a hungry expression on his face. Victory had come sooner and more easily than expected. There were so many things I wanted to do: beg, plead, scream out at Xavier to run, to fight. But when I opened my mouth all that came out was a pitiful cry because everything that meant anything to me in this world was about to be taken away. Hamiel's black eyes met mine and he gave a small, satisfied smile before he casually reached out with his scepter and a bolt of lightning stabbed Xavier in the back.

Xavier stopped dead and his hand flew up to clamp over his heart. Confusion registered on his face for a moment as he slowly sank to his knees. His eyes were still looking right into mine and I saw them reflect shock, then pain, then a dull look of acceptance. A moment later his lids fluttered shut and he slumped to the ground.

I screamed so loud, my lungs hurt as Xavier crumpled before my eyes. It had happened almost too fast to register, but I'd heard his heart stop beating and seen the light go out of his eyes. Ivy turned to Hamiel, a look of unadulterated wrath on her face. But the leader of the Seventh Order crouched and then sped upward with the speed of a bullet and was swallowed up by the hole in the ceiling. The last thing we saw were his robes swirling around him and the flash of a triumphant look on his face. Pieces of plaster continued to dislodge, raining around us like pale shrapnel and enveloping us in clouds of white dust.

Gabriel was still holding me tight, but my wings burst open with such force they knocked him back and carried me over to where Xavier lay. I put my lame, broken hands on his chest and shook him, no longer aware of the pain. I felt Ivy and Gabriel at my side, talking rapidly to one another, but their words didn't register. I felt as if I were far, far away, and a loud ringing in my ears drowned out all thought. My brain refused to comprehend what had happened. Fog was engulfing me, swirling around in my head. All I could feel was a hideous gaping hole inside me. Gabriel put a hand at Xavier's neck, searching for a pulse. I saw him look at Ivy and almost indiscernibly shake his head. This couldn't be real, and yet deep down I knew it was.

Xavier lay on his back, his perfect face so beautiful and yet still as stone. The turquoise eyes I loved so much gazed unseeing at the ceiling. I touched his hand, which was still warm, and heard the familiar clink as our wedding bands knocked together. But when I shook him hard, he did not respond. When I repeated his name again and again there was no answer. When I laid my cheek against his and willed him to come back to me, I realized I could no longer reach him.

Hamiel had killed him deliberately and mercilessly before my very eyes. Xavier was gone.

16

The Sleeping and the Dead

IVY and Gabriel lifted Xavier and carried him into the empty office adjoining the lecture hall. They laid him gently on a worn leather sofa while Gabriel turned back to face the traumatized freshmen still inside. I could see from his face that he was steeling himself for the task ahead. Gabriel had the power to collectively erase their memories. I didn't know how he planned to explain the wreckage or Spencer's charred body. But that seemed immaterial to me now. I couldn't tear my eyes away from Xavier's inert form. He lay limp on the sofa, his slender hand trailing on the floor.

His heart had already stopped, but perhaps there was still time in the precious seconds before his soul left his body to do something . . . anything. I held my broken wrists out to Ivy. In one touch my twisted hands became straight, the bones knitting together and clicking back into place. I set to work on Xavier immediately. Buttons spun into the air as I tore open his shirt and spread my hands over his smooth chest, but I was trembling so much I couldn't focus. I tried sending out the healing currents that might restart Xavier's heart, but my own was racing so fast it kept blocking my concentration.

I looked frantically at Ivy kneeling beside me. Although she'd resumed her earthly form, shiny pearls of light still dripped from her flaxen hair, dissolving once they hit the carpet. What was she waiting for? Ivy was a healer. I knew she was the only one who could help him now. I shifted position to allow her room to work and squeezed myself onto the sofa with Xavier's head in my lap. As I stroked his hair away from his eyes, I saw that a deathly pallor was already settling over his beautiful features.

I looked imploringly at my sister. "Do something!" I begged.

She gave me a stricken look. "I don't know what I can do. He's already gone."

"What!" I almost screamed at her. "You've done this before, you've brought people back! I've seen you do it!"

"People who were close to death," my sister said, nodding frantically. "On the brink. But he's . . . past that point now."

"*No!*" I yelled, leaning down and pumping Xavier's heart vigorously with both hands. Hot tears poured down my face and dripped onto his unmoving chest. "We have to save him. I can't let him die."

"Bethany . . ." Ivy began, looking at us both like a mother might look at her injured children. The acceptance I read in her face horrified me.

"No . . ." I cut her off. "If he dies, I die."

My words seemed to snap her out of her reverie and return her to the present.

"Okay." She quickly looped her hair into a loose bun at the nape of her neck. I'd seen Ivy heal many times by now but I'd never seen it cost her so much effort. A fine film of perspiration appeared on her brow. She kept her eyes closed but I could see the strain growing on her face. She was silently mouthing an invocation in Latin of which I caught only the words *Spiritus Sanctum*. It grew in fervor every time she repeated it until she finally paused to draw breath.

"It's not working," she said, amazed at her own failure. She sounded so composed while I felt like my heart was being wrenched out of my body.

"Why?" I said weakly.

"Either my energy is spent or Xavier's resisting."

"Try harder!"

Could Xavier's soul be resisting? Perhaps he thought giving his life to spare mine was a good compromise. Perhaps he thought the wrath of the Sevens would now be satisfied. I imagined what he'd say: "*Doesn't seem like such a bad deal.*" Maybe even in death he was still trying to protect me. It did make sense that with one of us dead, the separation would be complete. The Seven's job would be done. Had Xavier known all along that Hamiel was going to kill him? Could he really have offered himself up like some kind of sacrificial lamb? No way was I going to stand for that. He had forfeited the right to act independently when Father Mel married us.

Suddenly I was aware of another presence in the room. I turned to see the same youthful reaper that had appeared at our wedding. He was lounging in the doorway, the same impertinent, slightly bored look on his effeminate face. He tossed his head and began tapping his foot impatiently as he waited for his cue to enter. The fanning of his black wings created a breeze in the office and emitted a strange smell like scented oils.

"Sorry, is my timing off?" he drawled. "Shall I come back later?"

I had no time for his sarcastic remarks. Xavier was slipping further away with every second that lapsed.

"Don't you come near him!" I warned as Ivy's whole body clenched with the effort of trying to revive him. I prayed that she would stay strong, that she wouldn't give up and relinquish him to Heaven. A golden light the color of corn surrounded the spot where her palms lay on Xavier's chest. It glowed then waned in rapid succession. I knew she needed time to restore her healing power; time Xavier didn't have. Suddenly I knew that what remained of her energy was not going to be enough to get Xavier through this crisis.

"That's no use," the reaper said as if it were obvious. "Can't you see? His soul has already detached."

"Give him back to us," I cried. "Get away from him!"

"Always making me the bad guy." The reaper sighed.

"Please don't take him," I begged. "Tell him I need him, tell him . . ."

"Why don't you tell him yourself?" the reaper said, and I saw his gaze flicker to the space at the end of the couch. I looked up and my mouth dropped open in shock.

He was nothing but a faded outline, but he was standing right in front of me. Everything about him was washed out and if you weren't concentrating, you could have missed his presence entirely. Xavier's spirit stood at the foot of the sofa, looking lost, like he was trying to find his way. I sucked in my breath so loud that Ivy jumped and the reaper rolled his eyes.

Ivy crossed over to the spirit, who was standing very still. "Xavier? Can you hear me? You need to come back to us. This is not your time."

Xavier's spirit looked at her uncomprehendingly and then turned to look at the reaper.

"Sure you don't want to come with me instead?" the reaper said smoothly. "Don't worry, you can trust me, I'm a professional." Ivy threw him a furious glance. "Hey," the reaper protested with a smirk, "this job gets old. Why not let me have a little fun with it?"

The spirit stood motionless, as if it barely understood what was going on. I knew Xavier was caught between the worlds of the living and the dead. It was a hard transition to make. That was what reapers and guardian angels were for, to lead people out of this world and into the one beyond. Only now we needed to get him back and that was no easy feat.

"Look at me," Ivy said, reaching for him. "You know who I am, you can trust me. I'll take you back to the life you knew."

When her fingers connected with his pale, ghostly ones, Xavier seemed startled and took a step back.

"That is one pathetic sales pitch," said the reaper. He turned to Xavier, tossing his head in an overly theatrical way and grinning. "I can make all the pain go away. All of those worries that were weighing you down, you can forget them. I'll take you someplace you'll never have to worry again. No more death, no more destruction, no more suffering. All you have to do is follow me."

He threw a triumphant glance at Ivy, clearly impressed with his own performance. Xavier's spirit tilted its head slightly as if the reaper's words appealed to him and the air shimmered as he moved away from us. Instinctively, I looked around for my brother. I was so used to Gabriel coming to our rescue, solving all our problems. But today he had problems of his own. What could I do? I couldn't grab hold of a ghost. Xavier's body now lay deserted and there was no way to slay the reaper. I couldn't kill Death himself.

Xavier's spirit gazed at me, confused. It looked around as if trying to determine which way to go. The reaper smiled coyly.

"Looking for the way out? Come with me. I can show you." His voice was full of promise.

"Don't listen to him!"

Xavier's spirit looked at each of us in turn, unsure who to trust. I knew how vulnerable he was in this moment, how easily he could be influenced. "You don't want to go with him," I insisted. "You'll never get back. We need you here."

"She's lying," said the reaper. "She only wants to keep you because she doesn't want to be alone. Come with me and nothing will ever trouble you again."

It had become a contest between the reaper and me with Xavier's spirit caught between us. But there was no way I would let the reaper steal him from me.

"Just take my hand," I urged. "I'll show you how easy it is."

But it wasn't working. He only looked more lost and confused than ever. At any moment, I could lose him and he'd slip away for good.

I felt Ivy's lips at my ear. "Only you can help him now. Do it!"

But how? I wanted to cry out. I had nothing on their strength or power. I was a weakling in comparison. But I didn't have time to dwell on that. I ran forward and planted myself firmly in front of the spirit, hands on my hips. It stopped as recognition slowly dawned on its face.

"You listen to me, Xavier Woods," I yelled, trying to grab hold of his shoulders. But my hands passed right through him and fell uselessly back at my sides. "Don't you even think about leaving me behind! What happened to *we're in this together*? We had a pact: *Wherever you go, I go.* If you die on me now, I have to find some way to follow you. Are you trying to kill me? If you don't come back to me right now, I'll never forgive you. Do you hear me? You can't leave me here alone!"

My outburst was so personal I could see Ivy felt like an intruder. Even the reaper cast his pale gaze at the ceiling as he waited for me to finish. The spirit gazed for a moment and then stretched out its hand to me.

"Come on," I whispered. "Come back."

When Xavier's fingers connected with mine, they were solid and I was able to grip them tightly. I knew it wouldn't last for long, but I couldn't rush him. Slowly, I coaxed him away from the reaper and back toward the couch, where his lifeless body lay. When Xavier stood looking down at his own death scene, Ivy took over. She moved her lily-white hands so that they now hovered over Xavier's temples. It created a nimbus of light around his head. The light began to creep down, spreading across his body like a fine mist. It continued to extend until it reached the spirit, coiling around it like tendrils of fog, drawing back in. Suddenly, Ivy fell to her knees and threw her arms up to the sky. There was a flash as the gentle mist morphed into a blazing sheet of lightning and then vanished, taking the spirit with it.

From the couch, Xavier let out a gasp like he'd been stuck underwater and had just broken the surface. His eyelids flew open and a moan escaped his lips. Sobbing, I threw myself at him, my arms clamping around his neck and refusing to let go. From the doorway, I saw the reaper pout.

"You win," he said with a slight bow. He turned and disappeared into the hall, muttering something about reaping not being anywhere near as much fun as it used to be.

Xavier still seemed disoriented, so Ivy had to pry me off him.

"It's okay, Beth," she said, handing me a wad of tissues. My face was a mess of tears and a running nose. I was crying so hard I felt my skin tighten and my eyes swell up. "He's going to be fine," Ivy repeated soothingly. Still, I watched the rise and fall of his chest fixedly, doubting my own eyes and refusing to take Ivy's word for it.

"Beth?" Xavier asked groggily, his eyes struggling to focus.

"I'm right here," I told him, overcome with a fresh wave of tears.

"Are you okay? You're not hurt?"

"I'm fine so long as you are," I said, lying down beside him. "How do you feel?"

"My body feels weird," Xavier said, and I automatically sprang back up.

"Relax," Ivy said. "It's completely normal. He just needs to rest."

Xavier mumbled something incoherent before closing his eyes and falling into an exhausted sleep. I wrapped my body around his, relishing his warmth and made a promise to myself. As long as I was living and no matter what it cost me, I would never let anybody hurt him again.

NOW that I knew he was okay, he could sleep for a month and I wouldn't mind. Gabriel strode back into the room with his wings retracted. He paused to shake the dust from his robes and plaster fragments from his hair and smiled when he saw Xavier.

"How's Lazarus doing?" he asked.

"He'll be fine," Ivy replied, sinking back on her heels, exhaustion showing on her face. "It wasn't easy."

"I'm sure it wasn't." Gabriel inspected my tear-stained cheeks and bloodshot eyes. I noticed that Gabriel too looked exhausted, his face drained.

"How did it go?" I asked.

"It is done," Gabriel replied. "The students are blaming Mother Nature and emergency services are on their way."

"What about Spencer?" I asked, my eyes stinging with fresh tears as I recalled the last look we'd exchanged before his death.

"He was never there." From the curt way my brother spoke, I knew it was wiser not to probe him for further details. I didn't know what he'd done with Spencer's body, but it must have been difficult for him. Altering states of mind and erasing memories was one of the things he found hardest. He only did it when there was no alternative. I knew he had to be feeling pretty uncomfortable right now. Ivy turned the subject to more practical matters.

"We'd better leave," she said. "Before anyone starts checking these rooms."

For now at least the crisis had been averted and all four of us had come out relatively unscathed. I didn't know whether the Sevens were enforcing God's law or not but I still sent up a silent prayer. *Thank you, Father, for delivering Xavier from the hands of death and returning him safely to us. Keep him from harm and I'll do whatever You ask of me.*

WE were sitting around a traditional room in a local inn on the outskirts of town where we'd taken refuge, putting a healthy distance between us and the campus where the Sevens had just launched their attack. We weren't worried yet about retaliation. We knew it would take them awhile to regroup.

"Move away from the beast." Xavier opened his eyes and we saw immediately that he was completely rattled.

"Welcome back," said Gabriel with a puzzled look. Xavier glanced up at him without a glimmer of recognition. His eyes wore the glazed look that comes with fever. I touched his forehead to find it burning hot under my fingers.

"The beast is rising out of the sea," Xavier said. He was writhing uncomfortably on the bed and kept looking toward the door even though it was bolted.

"What's going on?" I demanded.

"I'm not sure," said Gabriel. "He's quoting from Revelations."

"It's okay Xav," I said, thinking he must be suffering from some kind of post-traumatic stress. "There's no beast. You're safe here."

Xavier fell back onto the pillows, his chest beginning to shine with sweat. He gritted his teeth like he was in pain.

"Beth, no." He reached out and grabbed my hand in an iron grip. "You have to leave. Go, now! Promise me you will?"

"The Sevens are gone," I said calmly. "Gabriel and Ivy dealt with them. They won't be back for a while."

"Why don't you get it?" Xavier suddenly sat up arrow-straight, alarm in his eyes. "Nobody is safe. He's here."

"Ivy, what's he talking about?" I turned to face my sister. Nothing coming out of Xavier's mouth was making any sense. "What's wrong with him?"

"Calm down, Beth. Give him a minute. I think he's just disoriented. He was dead, remember?"

Xavier tried to stand up and all the color drained from his face. He swayed dangerously and had to grab the bedpost to steady himself.

"Take it easy," Gabriel said, a look of concern spreading across his features. "There's no rush."

Xavier looked at each of us in turn in complete confusion. Then suddenly, his expression shifted.

"Well, that was fun. Can we do it again real soon?" At first I wasn't sure where the biting voice was coming from. I'd heard Xavier use sarcasm before, but this didn't even sound like it was the same person speaking. I held a hand out to him, but shrank back immediately. Nothing had changed and yet everything had changed. The softness was gone from his face, as if someone had just remodeled the contours to take on a hard, brittle look. His cheeks were more cavernous and I'd never seen him narrow his eyes in such a mocking way. An uneasy look passed between Gabriel and Ivy.

"What? What's happening?" I looked from one to the other but whatever they were thinking they chose not to enlighten me.

"Are you feeling okay?" Gabriel asked gently. He seemed to have a sense of what was happening but wanted to make completely sure. Perhaps he wasn't ready to accept it.

"Never better!" Xavier smiled pleasantly. He slid off the bed and slunk around the sofa, never taking his eyes off my brother.

"Xavier?" I watched the smile fade from his face as he returned me a level gaze. I wanted to walk over and shake him to his senses. To let him know we could overcome this hurdle if only he would be himself again. But I had a feeling my words would be lost on him right now and any gesture of affection would not be welcomed.

"I could really use a run." Xavier was pacing now, flexing his arms and bouncing on the balls of his feet. He wasn't the hyperactive type. I didn't recognize him like this—behaving as restless as a caged tiger.

"Maybe you should lie down," I said, taking a tentative step forward.

"Beth, don't," warned my brother.

"No, I don't want to *lie down*," Xavier said. His voice was shrill as he parodied mine and was colder than a snowstorm. I took a step toward him and felt Gabriel's ringed fingers squeeze my shoulder. I looked up into his silver eyes.

"Xavier would never hurt me," I protested.

"No," Gabriel said. "*Xavier* wouldn't."

There was something about the inflection in his words I didn't like.

"He's just worn out is all," I said loudly, refusing to accept any other alternative. My emotional threshold had been reached when I'd seen Xavier die before my eyes. I didn't know how much more I could handle.

This had to be a reaction to extreme stress. After all, humans, unlike angels, didn't have limitless reserves of energy they could tap into. Xavier had coped with so much in the last few weeks it was a miracle he hadn't fallen apart sooner. But everyone had a breaking point and Xavier had just reached his. I remembered reading about this in psychology books. If you put someone under enough pressure, cracks were bound to show and they would start acting out in bizarre ways. But I hadn't expected Xavier's meltdown to result in anger that was directed at me. What was happening to him? The hostility in his voice now was worse than a scorpion's sting. It was hard to ignore the way he was looking at me, like I was his worst enemy.

"There must be something I can do," I whispered to delay the tears that were threatening to spill. I needed to stay strong right now for the both of us.

"As a matter of fact, there is." Xavier had never spoken to me so formally. How hard had he hit his head when he'd fallen to the ground? I looked at him expectantly, eager to accommodate whatever request he might have. I walked across to where he stood behind the sofa, cutting himself off from us. He cocked his head as he cupped my face in his hands, studying me as if he were seeing me for the first time.

"Tell me what I can do," I repeated.

Xavier bent his mouth to my ear and whispered in a low voice, "You can stay the hell away from me, you whiny little bitch."

And then I knew. The voice speaking to me through Xavier's body wasn't Xavier's but I recognized it instantly. I would have known it anywhere. It hadn't changed since I'd last heard it in a place I wanted desperately to forget.

Lucifer's voice was still that odd combination of gravel and velvet, syrup and whiskey.

17

Bad Tenant

I clutched my stomach as if someone had just stabbed me there. It seemed a childish reaction but hearing the venom in Xavier's voice felt like a violent physical attack.

I stepped away from him and walked numbly toward the window. Outside, the sun was still shining and cars passed by in a colorful blur, their drivers oblivious to what was happening just yards away from them. Jumbled thoughts collided in my head like a meteoric storm. How could this have happened? What were we going to do about it? Could Xavier be set free before something disastrous happened? But what could be more disastrous than what we'd already faced in the last twenty-four hours?

"How could this have happened?" I said it aloud this time and whipped around to face my siblings. "I don't understand."

"Possession can happen to anyone," Ivy said softly.

"No." I shook my head vigorously. "Things like this don't just happen to people like him. He's supposed to be protected by his faith. There shouldn't have been an opportunity for his body to be invaded like this!"

"Bethany, think about it," said Gabriel gently. "Xavier

died. . . . Those minutes on the brink between life and death were more than enough time to let darkness in."

"But . . ." I felt my chest constrict and my eyes sting because I knew my brother was right. "I just got him back."

"Don't give up hope," Ivy said. "This just means the fight isn't over yet."

I was barely listening to her. The thought that Lucifer had been watching us, waiting for the opportunity to strike was enough to make me shiver. We had been so focused on avoiding the ire of Heaven I'd forgotten we were being targeted by another, perhaps more dangerous predator. Heaven wanted us separated, but it seemed Hell wanted to exact its own revenge. The faceless Sevens were nothing compared to what I was about to deal with. A chilling memory fought its way into my conscious mind: the image of Sister Mary-Claire's face, the nun from the convent in Tennessee. Amid the blood and scratches, bitten lips and ground teeth, there had been a look in her eyes. A completely vacant look that suggested she wasn't present at all. The demon had completely overrun her mind, body, and spirit. That experience had been damaging enough when I'd only been present in astral form and the person involved was a perfect stranger. This time it was happening to Xavier. I wasn't sure I had the courage to deal with that.

I kept my face averted from Gabriel and Ivy, knowing how easily they'd be able to read me. I wasn't naïve enough to think I could hide anything from them—I just needed a moment to absorb what was happening and get my raging emotions under control.

"Come on," Ivy said. "We need to get moving. We can't stay here." She tried to sound businesslike but there was an edge to her voice that hadn't been there before.

"Where are we going?" Xavier asked cheerfully. His perkiness was almost child-like and it sounded wrong coming out of his mouth.

"We're taking you back to our house," Gabriel said, his gaze flickering over Xavier's condition. "You can stay there until you . . . feel more like yourself."

"Wait, you have a house?" I cut in. "Where?"

"Here," Ivy replied. "In Oxford."

"Since when?" I demanded.

"Since you got here. We've been closer than you thought, keeping an eye on things."

"Why didn't you tell me?"

"We thought it was safer if you didn't know. If we were in constant contact, it might have given us away. We just wanted to have a base close by in case you ran into trouble. And it's a good thing we did."

"I feel fine now," Xavier interrupted, not bothering to keep up with our conversation. To prove his point, he began flexing his limbs like an athlete warming up before a workout. There was something showy about it, nothing like how he normally behaved. It made my skin prickle with discomfort. Xavier turned his attention to me. "I'm so lucky to have a girlfriend who won't give up on me." There was something mocking in his tone and his smirk didn't help matters either.

"You're right, we should get him out of here," I said flatly. So much was wrong, I didn't have the strength to do anything but agree with my siblings. "Before he does something to attract attention."

"Gracious!" Xavier exclaimed loudly. "So much for sticking together. What a bad wife."

I nodded at Gabriel, who crossed the room in two strides and gripped Xavier's shoulders.

"Ivy . . ." he said. "I might need your help."

"Whoa, whoa, take it easy papa bear," Xavier said in a singsong voice, holding up his hands to show his cooperation. "I'm not a flight risk, this is too much fun to miss out on." He laughed and began singing under his breath: *"I'm sticking with you, like I'm made out of glue."*

Gabriel pushed him roughly in the direction of the door, where Ivy hovered uncertainly. Was he going to make a break for it? Somehow I didn't think so. The demons wanted to hurt us and the best way to do that was to stick around and make us watch. As Xavier tripped toward the door, he paused and looked at me, his blue eyes suddenly filled with disarming familiarity.

"You're coming, aren't you, Beth?" he asked. "You're not leaving me with them?"

When he looked at me like that, with such wide-eyed sincerity, it was hard to tell who was speaking anymore.

"I'm coming," I said, trying to keep my voice level, but my restless hands betrayed me. I silently followed my siblings out to the parking lot with Xavier right behind, humming an irritating tune. I felt like he was a ticking time bomb, ready to blow at any minute. I realized then how vital it was to get him out of sight. He couldn't stay at a hotel and we couldn't let him anywhere near campus. We really had no idea what he might do next.

Xavier's behavior continued to be unpredictable on the drive to the house where Gabriel and Ivy now lived. Despite his earlier determination to have me with him, he now acted as if I were his worst enemy. He sat as far away from me as possible in the backseat of the car, his chin cupped glumly in his hands, his body curved away to the point of looking contorted. He kept his gaze fixed on the buildings we passed, only looking away to throw vicious glances my way over his shoulder.

I decided to test Xavier's reaction by reaching out and placing my hand gingerly on his knee. His whole body went rigid and he made a low growling sound like an injured animal in the back of his throat. I almost thought he was going to bite me and I quickly withdrew my hand.

Soon Gabriel was turning into a long driveway and pulling up in front of a pale blue house with a pitched roof and wraparound porch. Fall chrysanthemums in pots stood outside the screen door. I looked around with some curiosity. Up until then I hadn't seen where my siblings had taken up residence. In fact, I'd hardly even thought about it. The house was old and like most Southern homes, felt like it belonged to the past, like it had a story of its own. I could almost picture the wife of the confederate soldier faring him good-bye as he went off to fight for the Old South. But it also had a strangely familiar air, like it was a friend welcoming us home. We walked through a short hallway to a country-style kitchen with white cabinets and stippled blue walls. Antique lights hung over the island bench and white shelves above the sink displayed a collection of colorful old china. I spotted Gabriel's guitar propped against a painted dresser. Just for a moment I allowed myself to pine for Byron and the happy times we'd all spent there. Then I turned my attention back to the troubling present.

I slid onto one of the rush-seated stools at the bench and waited for someone to say something to diffuse the mounting tension in the room. Gabriel was watching Xavier like a hawk.

"Cool pad," Xavier commented as he walked around, uncharacteristically picking up books, cups, and candles and turning them over in his hands. "What is there to drink around here? Where do you guys keep the good stuff?" He flopped down full length on the window seat in the breakfast nook, ignoring Ivy's look of disapproval.

"We don't keep liquor here," she said, going to the fridge and retrieving a bottle of soda. Without warning, she hurled the bottle like a discus, aiming it straight at Xavier's head. It whizzed through the air but just before it hit him, Xavier casually threw out a hand and caught it. He hadn't even bothered to adjust his reclining position. No mortal athlete, even one as skilled as him, had the reflexes to do what he'd just done.

"Nice throw." He twisted off the cap and downed half the contents without taking a breath. When he was done, he stood up, propping the bottle on the floor.

"Where's the bathroom?" he asked with a winning smile. "I really need to take a shower."

"Upstairs, first door on your left," said Ivy. She threw Gabriel an uneasy look.

But Xavier never made it out of the kitchen. A split second later, Gabriel's wings snapped open, sending objects on the countertop crashing to the floor. He flew at Xavier, grabbing him around the waist and wrestling him to floor. Gabriel had him pinned within a matter of seconds but Xavier wasn't so easily subdued. With what seemed like a show of supernatural strength, he used his legs to propel Gabriel across the kitchen. He slammed into the counter so hard a crack appeared in the marble. A moment later, they stood facing each other, arch-nemeses poised for a fight.

"Stop it! What are you doing?" I yelled at them both. I made a move forward, hoping to come between them and make them come to their senses. But Gabriel turned to me, the intensity in his face stopping me in my tracks.

"Stay out of the way. He will hurt you."

Unintentionally, I had distracted Gabriel long enough to give Xavier the advantage. He lunged forward and I heard a sharp crack as his fist collided squarely with Gabe's jaw. It caught him by surprise, stunning him for a moment, before he retaliated with a thudding blow to Xavier's ribs. Xavier doubled over, winded, but recovered in time to duck the next blow. Seeing that the front door had been left open, Xavier spied a chance at escape and darted down the hall toward the entrance. Gabriel ran after him, impeded by his wings colliding with the walls. He pulled them back and threw himself after Xavier, grabbing him by the ankles. They crashed through the screen door together, tumbled over the porch railing and landed in the carpet of dead leaves in the front yard.

Angel and mortal wrestled in the dust while Ivy and I stood helplessly watching. Across the street two ladies sat drinking sweet tea in white rockers on their porch. Their necks stretched out like cranes when they saw the commotion and they squinted over at us, not believing what they were witnessing. I doubted they saw many brawls in this neighborhood. In fact, I got the feeling it was the first time any sort of scuffle had happened in their respectable street. One stood transfixed with her hand over her heart while the other grimaced and then scuttled inside.

"Miss Bishop is calling the sheriff," Ivy announced, sounding like she had half a mind to call him herself.

"Should we go over and try to stop her?" I asked apprehensively.

"Not now; Gabriel needs us."

We watched as Gabriel picked Xavier up and threw him sprawling face-first into the gravel. I wanted to run to his aid but Ivy restrained me.

"Gabriel's hurting him!" I yelled in her face. "Make him stop!"

"He's trying to help him." Ivy grabbed my shoulders and shook me. "If Xavier leaves there's no telling what he might do . . . how many people he might hurt, including himself. You have to trust us, Bethany."

I looked into her ice-gray eyes and nodded, trying to keep my eyes averted from the scuffle. My loyalties had never felt more divided. There was very little I wouldn't do if my brother asked it of me. At the same time, I couldn't be expected to abandon my husband when he needed me most.

Xavier got up looking dazed, which gave my brother the opportunity he needed. He quickly maneuvered himself behind Xavier. I wondered what he was doing until I saw him slip both arms underneath Xavier's armpits and lock his hands behind his neck. In this position, Gabriel was able to render Xavier immobile long enough to herd him back into the house. I wondered whether the poor Bishop sisters across the road would ever recover from hearing the profanities Xavier was shouting.

"You're nothing but whores," he screamed as he passed us. "Whores with wings! I'll see you all in Hell."

"Er . . . he's a distant cousin," Ivy called to the gawking woman across the road, who looked on the verge of collapse. "He's having a bad day. So sorry."

Then she quickly shut the door behind us.

"OPEN the basement!" Gabriel yelled once we were back inside the house. Ivy did as he asked and Gabriel and Xavier stumbled their way down the narrow concrete steps that led into the bowels of the house. I peered into the dark nervously. I didn't like being belowground.

"Can't we talk up here?" I asked.

"With the racket he's causing?" Ivy shook her head. "We might as well broadcast it on the seven o'clock news."

I trudged down the steps behind my brother, keeping a safe distance from Xavier's thrashing legs. His attempts at a struggle had no effect on Gabriel, whose body it seemed had turned to stone.

I shivered. The basement was cold and had a dank smell. The whole place, with its stained floor and spiderwebs dangling from the rafters, was reminiscent of a tomb. There were no windows, only a small ventilation grate, too narrow to let in much more than a sliver of daylight. The basement walls and floor were reinforced concrete, typical of many in the area designed to withstand the force of a tornado. There were the usual items one might expect to find: storage boxes, a washer-dryer, and a freezer. But there was also an old iron bed with a moth-eaten striped mattress and springs protruding from the stuffing. Seeing the iron manacles hanging from its posts gave me a sick feeling right down to my bones.

It seemed Gabriel and Ivy had anticipated such an emergency because they knew exactly what to do. Gabriel struggled to hold Xavier down on the bed long enough for Ivy to bind his wrists and ankles. Xavier thrashed around and hissed like a wild animal. Finally they both stood back. Xavier must have exhausted himself because he was now lying spread-eagle on the bed, perfectly still, his eyes fixed on the ceiling.

"Ivy, can you go and deal with that?" I wondered what Gabriel was referring to until the sound of sirens reached us seconds later. Xavier laughed softly to himself, pleased to be causing trouble.

"You sure you're okay here?" Ivy asked, and my brother nodded.

"Just make it quick."

Ivy went silently but Xavier, alerted to the possibility of escape, began shouting so loudly that Gabriel had to clamp a hand over his mouth. We could hear car doors slamming and voices at the front door. I heard Ivy's voice, deferential and apologetic. I caught fragments of her explanation of her young cousin's relapse after a spell in rehab. She was a good liar, blaming the fact that he traveled in the wrong circles and promising to keep him under watch until he made a full recovery. The sheriff's voice in turn was all sympathy. He was evidently charmed by her and made clucking sounds with his tongue, called her a "brave young lady," and urged her to hang in there during tough times. He also reminded her to call him anytime she needed assistance. Ivy thanked him politely and shut the door firmly.

She came back stony-faced, carrying an armful of salt containers from the kitchen. She proceeded to spill the salt in a careful circle around the bed.

"What are you doing?" I quizzed.

"Salt and iron repel demons," she said matter-of-factly. "We need all the help we can get here."

I wanted to tell her this was no ordinary demon but I didn't think that would prove very helpful.

"Do you remember why?" she asked. My basic training as an angel flashed back to me.

"They're pure compounds, and demons, being the essence of impurity, can't handle being near them," I recited.

"Good." Ivy nodded curtly.

"It won't be enough, though, will it? It can't be that easy."

"Unfortunately, no. The demon has already gotten inside him. But this will stop it from escaping, until we work out how to destroy it."

"Can I stay with him?"

"Definitely not," Gabriel said bluntly.

"Why not!"

"Isn't it obvious? You're too emotionally involved. That makes you vulnerable. We can't risk you being tricked."

"I won't let that happen."

"Bethany . . ." said Gabriel in such a warning tone that I knew to let it go.

"Fine," I snapped. "But you can't stop me speaking to him."

Gabriel didn't try to prevent me from approaching the bed. Xavier's eyes were still riveted on the ceiling and there were gravel scratches on his face from when he'd fallen outside. Even with his battered body and wild eyes, he was still achingly familiar and it still made my heart stop just to be near him. I leaned carefully over him so I could whisper even a fraction of what I felt, but the words failed to come. The person lying on the bed was a stranger. What could I say to him that would make any difference to his plight? I was wracking my brain for the right words when Xavier suddenly turned his head and gave me a look so penetrating I couldn't tear my gaze away. I forgot all about Gabriel and Ivy standing there frowning at me. I looked deep into the crystalline blue of Xavier's eyes searching for a sign of recognition. Just for a second a strange thing happened. I thought I saw *him*. The expression in his eyes softened and I caught a brief glimpse of the boy I loved. I could see what it cost him though. It was like watching a drowning man claw his way to the surface, only to be pulled under again by a wave more powerful than his will to survive. Then he was gone and the flinty look was back. But it didn't matter. I knew Xavier was in there somewhere. It was the only incentive I needed. Even though every fiber of my being was telling me to run, I knew I would never leave him to face this alone.

18

Things That Go Bump

GABRIEL frowned, looking lost in thought. I sensed there was something about our current predicament he wasn't telling us.

"Let's go upstairs," he said suddenly. "We need to talk." I shook my head adamantly.

"I'm not leaving Xavier."

"He'll be fine."

"You think he's *fine*?" I asked incredulously.

"I didn't say he *was* fine; I said he'd *be* fine down here for a while. Now, are you coming or not?"

I decided to stand my ground.

"Not," I said stubbornly. "You and Ivy know what you're doing. You don't need me."

Gabriel's sigh was audible. I knew he was tired and I was trying his patience.

"And what exactly do you hope to achieve by staying down here?"

I shrugged. "I don't know yet," I said tartly. "I'll be up in a minute. I'd just like some time with Xavier alone if that's okay with you."

"It most certainly is not," Gabriel said irritably. "Have you gone insane?"

"Isn't it time you stopped telling me what to do?"

"He's just worried about you," Ivy said. "You can't help Xavier right now and it's probably safer if you weren't alone with him."

"He's in chains!" I exclaimed. "What's the worst he could do?"

"Bethany, this isn't a time to argue. Xavier needs us to work together. The longer we waste time, the longer that thing stays inside him. Now, are you going to help us or not?"

Unlike Gabriel, who had yet to learn the skill of tact despite centuries of interaction with humans, Ivy always knew just the right thing to say. As usual, she succeeded in making me feel petulant and shortsighted. I reluctantly followed them up the steps, looking back to check on Xavier's condition. He hadn't stirred and was still staring unblinking at the ceiling. I paused at the top of the stairs.

"What if something happens?"

"I promise, we'll hear him."

"All right," I said gruffly. "Let's make this quick."

But it wasn't quick. I should have known my siblings well enough to realize they weren't going to make any snap decisions. When dealing with something so delicate, it was like walking a tightrope. Human life was fragile and demons were destructive. One mistake could cost us everything. I stood in the kitchen, my frustration mounting as Ivy drifted around the kitchen putting together some kind of herbal infusion. She was calmly picking leaves off stalks and mixing them in hot water. Gabriel too was rummaging through cupboards, pulling out boxes of salt and lining them up on the countertop. They were both behaving like eccentric witch doctors rather than angels with the power to tear the demon out of Xavier if they chose.

"It'll kill him, you know," Gabriel said, reading my thoughts. "If we try to rip it out . . . it would be like ripping stitches from a wound. He won't survive the pain. We need to weaken it first."

"Okay," I said stiffly. I could hardly argue with that. I kept my ears trained on any sound coming from the basement but there was only Xavier's breathing, which sounded more rhythmic now. I only hoped it meant he'd exhausted himself into sleep. It killed me to think of him like that, chained underground, trapped inside his own body. I knew we couldn't rush things, but we didn't have all the time in the world either. As neither Gabriel nor Ivy had any understanding of human love, they didn't understand my urgency. They didn't understand that it was my husband down there, being torn apart from the inside out.

"I think we're going to need backup," said Gabriel pensively. He said this casually, as if he might have been discussing what we were going to have for dinner.

"I agree," said Ivy, only she looked less comfortable with the idea.

"Aren't you guys big shots? Can't you handle this?"

"Ordinarily, yes, but this is different."

"How?" I asked, and Gabriel glared at me impatiently.

"I think you know how."

"You mean because it's *him*?"

I didn't know why I was unable to call him by name. Perhaps his name and everything it called to mind was so distasteful I couldn't bring myself to say it aloud. Maybe there was also the fear that if I acknowledged him, it would bring back a flood of memories I'd been trying desperately to obliterate. Part of me was still hanging on to the childish notion that if evil doesn't have a name, you can convince yourself it exists only in your imagination. Whatever the reason, I knew I had to keep it together for Xavier's sake. It was an impossible situation, having the person I loved most and the thing I despised most within one body. Which emotion was I supposed to feel, love or hate?

It took Gabe awhile to answer me, as if he'd had to consider his words carefully.

"Because we cannot afford to fail."

"What does that mean?"

"It means if we fail, Xavier may not come out of this alive."

The thought short-circuited my train of thought and the world blacked out for a moment, but I managed to recover.

"Why would you fail? Expelling demons—that's your thing. It's what you do, right?"

"Yes." Gabriel hesitated. "But only through the power vested in us from above."

Suddenly the fog lifted. "Oh, I get it." I felt my fists clench. "Given recent events, you can no longer be certain of corporate backing."

"That's one way of looking at it."

"So Heaven isn't on our side. That puts us in a pretty vulnerable position."

"We don't know that for sure," Ivy said. "We can still find allies."

"Assuming we have any left," I muttered, and my sister raised an eyebrow.

"Don't think that way."

"We're outcasts." I tried to keep my voice from becoming shrill. "Nobody is coming to help us! Why would they?"

"Because we're all part of the same family."

"We're screwed," I mumbled.

"Have you no faith left at all?" my brother remarked in surprise.

"How can I, when God seems to have abandoned us?"

"That is when you need faith the most," Gabriel said. "Not when everything is going your way, not when you have much to be thankful for, but when there is darkness all around. He is always there, He is always watching, and one way or another, He will set you on the right path."

I hated my brother sometimes for being so wise. Everything he said made sense and I knew he was right, but we weren't out of the storm yet. I, of all people, should have had faith but I was so tired and learning fast that even angels are not infallible. But somewhere inside me, through all the layers of worry and hurt and anger, I did feel a comforting hand, like a whisper on my back, guiding me forward and letting me know I wasn't alone.

The basement door was still tormenting me and Ivy caught

the glances I kept darting in its direction. She finally took pity on me.

"Bethany isn't going to be much use to anyone until she checks on Xavier."

A slight inclination of Gabriel's head indicated that he understood. I thanked them and forced myself to walk slowly rather than bolt for the hallway.

"Five minutes," Gabriel called after me. "Make sure you leave the door open. And no matter what he says to you, do not untie him."

"Got it," I said.

"Wait!" Ivy said, and handed me a pottery mug that gave off a strange pungent aroma. "See if you can get him to drink this."

"What is it?"

"Mandrake tea."

"It doesn't smell too good. What's it for?"

"I'm hoping it'll knock him out for a while. That way we won't have to keep vigil all night. Things will be clearer by morning."

"Maybe," I said.

"By then we should know if help is available." Ivy tried to sound encouraging. "After you check on Xavier, you should get some sleep. You look beat."

"Good idea." I gave her a tight smile, knowing full well how little chance there was of that happening. "I'll be right up. I'll just make sure Xavier's okay and then I'll crash." I'd play along with Gabriel and Ivy right up until the point I could sneak back to sit by Xavier's side.

Walking into the basement for the second time, I found it hard not to fall apart seeing Xavier shirtless, bloodied, and shackled to a bed. Despite his taut and well-defined body, he'd never looked so vulnerable to me than he did at that moment. His face was exhausted, his lips chapped, and a five o'clock shadow was already visible on his chin. But it was his lost expression that was the hardest to take. I knew how maddening it must be for him to be aware of what was happening and not be able to do a thing about it. Xavier was never one to shirk from a challenge and would always choose to confront his enemies rather than run from them. But how could you fight an enemy that lived inside you?

I carried the steaming drink and placed it carefully to cool on the old record player beside the bed. I went to the rusty sink and moistened a towel Ivy had brought down and used it to carefully tend the scratches on Xavier's face.

At my touch, he opened his eyes. At first he looked relieved to see me, then the memory of the last few hours crashed through his consciousness and a look of horror clouded his features.

"Beth," he choked out. "I'm so sorry!"

"Xavier, what's wrong?" I touched a hand to his forehead, out of habit.

"Those terrible things I said! I didn't mean it . . . any of it!"

It was hard to believe it was actually him I was talking to. I didn't know how long we had before the darkness took over again. I could see the effort of fighting it was costly, he was breaking out in a sweat and gritting his teeth. It was remarkable that he had succeeded at all in the struggle—one could not simply push Lucifer out of the way. Xavier must be stronger than any of us realized. But I couldn't waste time marveling over that right now.

I put my finger over his lips to silence him. "It's okay. It wasn't you. Don't think about it. Here . . ." I held the mug of tea up to his lips, knowing that in a few minutes, maybe even seconds, the heinous creature inside him would resurface and he'd be lost again. "You need to drink this, it'll help."

Xavier lifted his head obediently and took a few sips before making a face.

"Sorry," I said. "Does it taste as bad as it smells?"

"Yep."

The muffled voices of my siblings deliberating in the kitchen reached us.

"What are they doing?" Xavier croaked. I knew he must be wondering why they weren't here, taking charge of the situation with their customary authority.

"They're just trying to figure things out." I squeezed his hand. "They'll fix this, I promise. You just have to get through the night."

Xavier squeezed his eyes shut and gave a groan of pain as something invisible twisted inside him, fighting to regain control.

"The night?" he repeated, and I caught the note of rising panic in his voice. "Why do we have to wait? Can't they do something now?"

"They're working on it, Xav," I whispered, searching for something more reassuring to say. "It won't be much longer."

I hoped my words might hold some comfort for him, but Xavier turned his face away.

"You should go. I don't want you to see me like this."

"I'm not going anywhere," I pressed, inching closer to him as if to prove my point. "This is what marriage is about. The good, the bad, and the ugly."

"I think this might be too ugly," Xavier said with a pained expression.

"I don't care, so quit arguing," I said resolutely.

"Beth . . ." His fingers clamped down hard around mine. "I don't know how long I've got before . . . before he comes back. I can't stop it, it's like someone flicks a switch in my brain and I lose control."

I leaned down so our noses were almost touching. "No one can control you, Xavier. You're too strong for that."

"What if I'm not?" he whispered.

"I know you are. Want me to tell you how I know?"

He looked at me with the first glimmer of hope I'd seen since we'd brought him back here.

"How?"

"Because this is *you* talking to me right now. Do you know how hard that is? How impossible? But you wrestled him down and that's a bigger feat than anyone could hope for. You're strong enough to fight this; you just have to believe you can. Will you do that for me?"

Xavier gave a distant smile. "I'll try, Beth."

"That's more like it."

"But I want you to do something for me." Xavier's eyes seemed brighter than usual. Was he on the verge of tears? "If things don't work out the way we hope . . ."

The rest of the sentence choked in his throat.

"What is it, Xavier?" I asked, although I already knew what he was about to say and the emotion that washed over me was almost too much to bear.

"Promise you won't get upset?"

"Mmhmm," I said, not trusting myself to speak.

"I know Gabriel and Ivy will do everything they can but if they can't help me . . ."

"They can, Xavier," I insisted. "Of course they can."

But he hardly heard me, he was so focused on getting out what he wanted to say.

"There's something deadly inside me, Beth. I'm gonna fight it hard but if I don't win, you have to promise to lock me up, to keep me somewhere where I can't hurt anyone."

"It won't come to that."

"But if it does . . . I'd rather die."

"Don't say that." My voice was breaking, but Xavier pressed on, determined to finish this.

"You have to let me die."

"I won't!" I cried.

"If it's between my life and someone else's, you have to let me go, Beth. I don't want any more deaths on my head. I can't live with that."

"I promise I won't let you hurt anyone," I said. "That's the best I can do. Please don't ask more of me."

"Okay," Xavier murmured. He looked like he was losing consciousness. "I'll see you again. Don't forget me."

"What?" I asked, but he was already asleep. Ivy's brew was one powerful concoction.

"I won't forget you," I whispered, pressing my lips against his temple. "I'd sooner forget myself."

I went upstairs to collect a duvet, which I wrapped around my shoulders and settled in a dusty wicker chair in the basement to keep watch. Ivy and Gabriel didn't try to stop me this time—the silent tears running down my cheeks must have been a signal for them to leave me alone. In the dark, I dozed intermittently, always jerking awake at the slightest sound or twitch of movement. It seemed every time I opened my eyes I was witnessing a physical transformation on the bed before me. Xavier's cheeks looked more hollowed and there was sullenness around his mouth that was unfamiliar. But I told myself it was the gloom in the basement playing tricks on my mind.

I only knew dawn was approaching by the strident crow of a rooster in someone's yard. It stirred Xavier from sleep and he opened his eyes to look at me. They were still bright and brilliant and blue, but they were not his own. When he spoke, it was in a throaty voice so unlike his own it made me jump.

"A magnificent vessel."

"What?" I wasn't sure I'd heard him right and I inched a little closer.

"This." He tilted his chin to look down at his body. "It's almost a shame to ruin him."

"You . . ." I began in a sudden fit of rage, but all the things

I wanted to say, to scream at him, seemed to lodge in the back of my throat and I couldn't get anything out. I knew Xavier was gone, there was a new tenant occupying his body now and boasting about his new lodgings.

"Cat got your tongue?" He smiled and rattled the chains that bound him like they were nothing but toys. His voice had a low Texan drawl. "It's good to see you again, little angel. You've done well for yourself. It feels good in here. In fact, I like it so much I might stay."

"You won't be staying," I said, sounding so calm I surprised even myself.

"Oh, really? What makes you so sure of that?"

"You can try but you won't win," I said dismissively. "Not against us."

"Depends how you define winning." The voice became lower and more spiteful. "I'm in here, aren't I?"

"Not for long." I shrugged, but my devil-may-care attitude wasn't rattling him. I supposed it didn't work so well against the actual devil.

"You'd be surprised how tenacious I can be."

"Gabriel is a pretty powerful arch," I said. "He'll deal with you soon. You may as well give up now because you don't stand a chance."

"*My brother will deal with you. We have to help poor Xavier because I love him sooooo much.*" The shrill voice and bitter laughter stung like a whip. "Oh, Bethany, my dear, your naivety is adorable. Now I think I do stand a chance; you know why? Because I ain't budging and as long as I'm here, lover boy is at my mercy. I'd advise against trying to evict me. I can do a lot of damage from the inside—literally speaking."

Xavier's head lolled from side to side as if he were trying to wake from a nightmare. His eyes were open but unfocused. Suddenly his body became racked by violent spasms like someone in the throes of a seizure. "See what I mean?"

"Xavier!" I screamed, my hands reaching out to his chest.

"Sorry, Xavier's not at home right now, can I take a message?" Lucifer laughed at his own joke.

"He can't hear me," I murmured under my breath.

"Oh, he can hear you," Lucifer replied pleasantly. "He just can't answer. Remember, it's still his body. He feels everything . . . acutely."

I searched Xavier's face for a hint of recognition but found none.

"What are you doing to him?" I asked.

"Just pulling the strings."

I balled my hands into fists. There were no words that could do justice to the depth of loathing I felt for him but at least I knew I wouldn't be doing Xavier any favors by vocalizing that. I had to think smart.

"I know you're angry with me," I said imploringly. "So take your anger out on me. Get revenge on *me*. Don't do this to him. This isn't his fault."

"Oh, you dear, sweet girl," Lucifer crowed. "I am taking revenge on you. What better way than this? To make you watch the one you love die before your eyes . . . and in such a slow and painful manner?" He shook his head. "It's almost too cruel."

"Don't do it," I hissed. "Get out of him, leave him alone!"

His eyes lighted on my ringed finger. "Oh, my, what have we here? Are you to be a widow, little angel? How tragic, losing your young husband so soon after the big day."

"If you kill him, my brother will hunt you down," I said. "We all will. You can be sure of that."

Lucifer ignored me and continued on his own tangent. "Married life seems to agree with you. You've lost that startled rabbit look. You're turning into a beautiful young woman." He looked at me appraisingly, and even though it was Xavier's face, I saw that the expression was so slimy it made me shudder.

"You know what?" I said suddenly, flopping down on the bed beside him. Lucifer raised an eyebrow. "A few minutes ago I was thinking about how much I hate you but I don't think it's hate I feel—it's pity."

"That very magnanimous of you, but the one you ought to pity is yourself. It's been a hard road, hasn't it? Choosing to love a mortal. Your little boyfriend has already died once, your brother and sister resent you, and Daddy set his trained monkeys on you."

"My Father had no part in that," I said hotly. "Don't you dare bring Him into this."

"Believe what you like." Lucifer shrugged. "But I thought He knew everything . . . isn't He supposed to be omnipotent and all that jazz?"

"He has a lot to deal with," I snarled. "Cleaning up the messes you and your vermin have left all over the planet."

"Isn't the cycle fun?" Lucifer grinned at me. "Shame you're in Daddy's bad books now."

"You really don't understand Him at all, do you?" I asked suddenly. "God is love and His mercy is great. Just because He threw you out, doesn't mean He'll abandon the rest of us. That's what it all comes down to, isn't it? A little boy who feels abandoned by his Dad."

Lucifer stared at me for a moment and his eyes became icy.

"Don't talk about what you don't understand," he said in a dangerous voice.

"I understand more than you think," I replied. "And I know you weren't always like this, were you?"

"Excuse me?"

"We've all heard the stories. You used to be one of Heaven's brightest stars. Our Father loved you; He had big plans for you. But you messed up. You blame Him for it, but it was you who made the mistakes."

Lucifer bared his teeth at me. "You should quit while you're ahead, little girl. You don't want to make me mad."

"Do you ever wish you'd done things differently?" I persisted. "I bet you do, every day. You must have known love once."

"And you must want to see Frat Boy develop internal bleeding."

"No!" I cried. "I'm sorry! Don't hurt him!"

Lucifer, who had lifted his body and was leaning forward as much as the chains would allow, settled back. He seemed to be breathing more heavily. Obviously, something I'd said struck close to home.

"We have more in common than you realize," he said eventually, licking his cracked lips.

"I seriously doubt that," I retorted.

"You don't think you suffer from the sin of pride?" he asked. "I don't see you bowing to the will of Heaven."

The comment stopped me in my tracks and I felt the blood rush to my cheeks. I hoped he wouldn't notice in the gloom. "Oh, yes," he continued. "I know a hell of a lot more about you than you think."

"You don't know anything about me."

"I know I've never seen anyone so small and harmless collect so many enemies."

"Why are you even wasting your time on us?" I burst out. "We're not worth it, you have nothing to gain here."

"It's hardly a waste of time when I'm enjoying myself so much."

"What do you want?" I leaned over him, demanding an answer.

"Just to be part of the family," he replied innocently.

"I know you have an agenda," I told him. "And it's not just to make my life miserable. But believe me when I say you won't succeed. I'll never let you." My eyes flickered over Xavier's face, remembering it the way it used to be. "You've gone after the wrong guy. When it comes to him, there's nothing I won't do."

"It will be interesting to see how this plays out then." Lucifer smiled pleasantly. "I'm just here to see it through . . . right till the bitter end."

19

Old Wounds

AS if on cue, a thunderous rumbling sounded and the washer and dryer began to shake so violently, they bounced on the concrete floor. I looked around uneasily, knowing for a fact that the power switch was turned off. The sound of scampering started up in the walls, and the old record player let out a scratchy tune of it's own volition, filling the room with hoarse noise. Finally, the naked lightbulb overhead sizzled and then went out, plunging us into total darkness.

I stopped my ears and closed my eyes but refused to budge. Lucifer could pull all the tricks in the book, but he wouldn't drive me from Xavier's side. I sat rigid; my limbs felt leaden and my brain numb from the clamor that was threatening to drive me mad. Suddenly everything went quiet and when I opened my eyes, I knew why. Gabriel and Ivy stood at the top of the stairs and their presence had changed the mood completely. They had the ability to drive away even the most penetrating darkness with their bright auras.

Seeing them lifted my sprits instantly. Showered and rested they looked more like their old selves, formidable and ready to face anything. I wasn't sure if they'd dressed deliberately, but they were both resplendent in white: Ivy in a crisp dress pinched at the waist and cowboy boots and Gabriel in a soft white shirt with his customary faded jeans.

They both descended the stairs slowly, as if tuned into some secret messages encrypted in the air that no one but they could hear.

"How long have you been down here?" Gabriel asked casually. There was no censure in his voice, as if he knew full well he'd find me here.

"A few hours," I said, trying to sound vague.

"Get any sleep?"

"Not much," I admitted.

"Why don't you go up into the house," he said with surprising kindness. "We'll take it from here."

I wanted to go, to run upstairs and bury my head under a pillow and hope that when I woke up, everything would be better. But I couldn't leave, I'd promised Xavier and myself. Besides, if Lucifer was going to see this through to the end then so was I. I was shaken and exhausted but nothing could convince me to leave . . . not until I knew Xavier was safe. I realized then that my siblings were alone. Had the angels refused to come to our aid?

"We're going to try this on our own first," Ivy said, and I instinctively shook my head, thinking she was probing through my thoughts. But she wasn't, she was just my sister who could read me like a book. Gabriel was too focused on the task at hand to pay me much attention. He gave me a fleeting glance that seemed to say, *If you must stay then be quiet.* I nodded to show I understood and accepted their terms.

As they approached, I saw Xavier stiffen slightly. He kept his eyes averted, refusing to acknowledge their presence. When they fanned their hands over him, he was bathed in a hazy yellow light. Xavier squirmed at first then struggled violently against the restraints that held him.

Ivy filled a gray plastic bucket with water at the sink and placed it at Gabriel's feet. Xavier seemed to be growing more and more alarmed as Gabriel uttered a prayer of renewal—blessing the water and turning it holy with his words. When Ivy cupped it in her pale hands and approached, she might have been carrying a lethal weapon by the way Xavier was looking at her. But Ivy didn't flinch, even when he bared his teeth and snarled like a feral animal. Instead she calmly sprinkled the water over Xavier's bare chest. Every droplet sizzled as if it were landing on a hot plate rather than on smooth skin. Xavier bellowed in pain, a sound so unbearable that I ran forward to help him but Ivy held me back.

"He's not hurt," she said firmly.

"He is!"

"It's part of the cleansing ritual."

Gabriel tossed me a bottle of water and I gulped half of it down without stopping for air. I needed to steel my nerves before I could get through this. A moment later, manic laughter filled the basement and the tortured expression was gone from Xavier's face. He was grinning now from ear to ear.

"Really?" he said in between bursts of laughter that wracked his chest. "Holy water? On me? What is this, a B-grade movie?"

"He was faking!" I cried, forgetting my promise to be quiet. "He didn't feel anything!"

"Laugh if you like," Gabriel said calmly. "But we're just getting started."

As if in retaliation, the shadow of a serpent appeared on the wall above Xavier's head. It proceeded to perform a macabre dance around the room, coiling itself around the bed, slithering over the floor and twisting in and out of the ventilation grate, causing clouds of dust to be coughed out into the air. Finally it came to rest at my feet where it formed a swirling hoop of black mist around my ankles. Each time I tried to kick it away, it dispersed for a few seconds but then re-formed. It seemed to be sending a clear message: *You can't catch me*.

My siblings remained unfazed. Ivy lit candles and arranged them in a triangle on the concrete floor so they cast elongated shadows around the room. From nowhere a gust of wind blew in to extinguish them. No sooner did that happen than Ivy waved her finger and the tapers sizzled back to life. This seemed to go on for some time in a tedious game of cat and mouse. Finally the gusts of wind stopped and the candles stayed alight. A tiny smile twisted the corners of Ivy's mouth. Had we achieved some small victory? Or was Lucifer just bored and ready to see the next trick we had up our sleeves? I didn't know. All I knew was that this was taking way too long. I had expected a long, protracted battle, but I was losing patience.

Gabriel finally approached the bed and drummed his fingers against the cast-iron frame.

"Who are you? Tell us your name," he began.

"She knows," Xavier's head jerked in my direction. "Why don't you ask her?"

"Because I'm asking you," Gabriel replied. It was no secret who the demon was inhabiting Xavier's body but a vital part of an exorcism was getting him to admit his identity. I knew Gabriel couldn't begin until that happened.

"Who are you?" he repeated dourly.

Suddenly, the doors of the chipped cabinet's lining the far wall of the basement flew open and various implements—screwdrivers, hammers, and jars of nails—went hurtling across the room. I had to fold myself over and cover my head with my arms to avoid the line of fire. I caught sight of a hammer heading straight for Gabriel and gasped. But when it collided with his shoulder, it bounced off as if it were made of rubber and clattered to the floor without leaving any mark. Gabriel strode across to the bed and grabbed Xavier's chin, turning his face toward him but Xavier refused to meet his gaze.

"Give us your name," Gabriel said more forcefully.

A subhuman tongue answered him, bearing no resemblance to Xavier's gentle voice.

"Do not toy with me, Archangel. You know who I am. Look deep inside and you will find me."

"Your name," Gabriel insisted, upon which the creature began irreverently humming a tune. "Unless you do not answer because you fear me."

If this was a calculated move on Gabriel's part, it worked. The expression on Xavier's face changed from amusement to superiority. Finally, he locked his startling blue eyes on Gabriel.

"I go by many names but know that I am your adversary, the one you helped cast into the abyss."

It wasn't new information but it still made me break out in goose bumps. When Ivy spoke for the first time, it was in her Seraph's voice, all the sweetness gone from it.

"What is your business here?"

"I'm putting my affairs in order," the creature replied cryptically.

"Speak plainly," she commanded.

"All right." Xavier's head twisted at an unnatural angle to look at her. "I'm here for revenge. Did you think I would let my loss go uncompensated? What's the expression humans like to use? Oh, yes, *The Devil must be paid his dues.*"

"We owe you nothing," Gabriel countered.

"You killed my son."

"He was a monster."

"With all your big talk about a father's love, you of all people should understand how I feel," Lucifer snarled. "Speaking of which, where are your brothers? Have they abandoned you in your hour of need—oh, dear." It was disconcerting to hear the voice morph and take on the melodic quality of a child.

Gabriel rolled his eyes. "Don't take out your inferiority complex on me. Did you really expect us to defend you?"

I was momentarily confused until I realized they were no longer talking about the present. They had both traveled back in their minds, back to the very beginning where it all began.

"I expected a little backup from my brothers," Lucifer replied. "But you were all more than willing to watch me burn."

"You wanted to be served," Gabriel said coldly. "We only serve one master. You never did understand His sovereignty."

"He should never have favored men above us," Lucifer said. "Men in all their pitiful weakness."

"Perhaps that is exactly why he chose them," Gabriel answered. "Because every day brings with it a new struggle for them that we cannot understand. Faith from men is more powerful than faith from angels, because they suffer more in choosing to walk with Him. Besides . . ." He folded his arms. "It is not for you to question who finds favor in the eyes of the Lord."

"I wondered if experience might have changed you," Lucifer said. "But I see you're the same righteous jackass you always were, singing His praises like a blind fool."

"Spare me," Gabriel muttered. "Nothing you say has any effect on me. I'm only here to return you to the bowels of the earth where all things foul belong."

"Give it your best shot!" the twang-filled voice replied.

Gabriel drew a deep breath and closed his eyes. "In the name of all that is holy I command you, quit this vessel!"

Xavier's body jerked briefly on the bed. We waited with baited breath but nothing happened. The low throaty chuckle that followed seemed to go on forever.

"That's all you've got? I'm afraid that's not gonna cut it, Brother. He's still mine."

I watched as Xavier writhed with pain, clenching and

unclenching his jaw. From the corner of his mouth came a trickle of dark blood. He must have bitten down hard on his tongue. I was desperate to help. This must be taking its toll on his body. Yesterday, he had been clinically dead and bringing him back once had been a major struggle. How much more could his body handle before it gave out altogether?

I knew I should silently stay in the shadows, but the words spilled out before I could help myself.

"I'm sorry about what happened to Jake!" I blurted out. Gabriel threw me a look like thunder but I pretended not to notice. "It wasn't my fault. It wasn't anybody's fault but his. I wish things had turned out different, I wanted to help him . . . I tried but I couldn't. I'm sorry he's gone, but don't take it out on Xavier."

"You're *sorry*?" echoed the sardonic voice. "Well, I guess that makes everything better."

"Hurting Xavier isn't going to bring your son back."

"That's true." There was a long pause. "Only you can bring him back."

"Excuse me?" I almost fell over in shock.

"He'll come back for you," wheedled the voice, "if you call him by his given name."

"What . . ." I stammered. "Why would I do that? How does that help? He'd still be dead . . ."

"I never got a chance to say good-bye." Lucifer sounded almost sincere. "I want to give him a chance to settle the score, to set his soul at rest."

"What soul?" Gabriel muttered.

"Don't even think about it, Bethany," my sister warned.

Xavier's body shook its head in disappointment. "His only crime was to love you and you repaid him by sending him to his death."

"That's not what happened!"

"Beth, don't listen to him. He's baiting you." Gabriel looked at Ivy with deep concern. "We should get her out of here."

"What do you mean settle the score?" I demanded, ignoring the nervous hovering of my siblings behind me.

"Here's my proposal," Lucifer said. "You're the only one connected enough to summon his spirit. Why don't you call him and we'll let him decide what's fair?"

His voice was like a cocoon, drawing me in and compelling me to listen. In a bizarre way it made sense. Perhaps summoning Jake was the only thing that would appease Lucifer.

"That is the worst idea I've ever heard," Gabriel declared. "How stupid do you think she is?"

But I was drawing closer to the bedside. "You want us to let Jake decide whether Xavier lives or dies?"

"No," Lucifer said in a scolding voice. "We all know how that would turn out. I want you to give Jake something he wants . . . and in return I'll give you your husband back."

I lifted my chin defiantly. "What if his terms are unreasonable?"

"Then feel free to disregard them," Lucifer said as if it were the most simple thing in the world. "Let's just bring him here and see what he has to say."

I felt Gabriel's ringed fingers grip my shoulder. Did he know how this was going to play out?

"Don't be a fool," he leaned down and spoke into my ear. "Trust *me*."

"Trust him all you like," persisted Lucifer. "But he hasn't helped Xavier so far. I'm the only one who can set him free."

I knew the idea was risky and part of me couldn't believe I was even considering it. And I wouldn't have if Gabriel and Ivy had the situation under control. But they seemed powerless, with no guidance from above. Could bargaining with the devil ever turn out well? It didn't really matter because I didn't have a choice. It was a hard thing to contemplate, bringing back someone I'd spent so long trying to purge from my life. Jake Thorn had tormented me, driven me mad, and almost killed me. I never wanted to see his face again as long as I lived. But if I didn't, I might never see Xavier's again. And I knew the gain outweighed the risk in my mind. A desperate action was better than no action at all.

"Bethany . . . please." Gabriel was almost begging me, but I was transfixed, staring into the blue eyes that were so familiar and so foreign at the same time.

"Do it, Bethany." The voice curled around me like wisps of smoke. "Listen to your heart. Call him. What harm can it do?"

"*Arakiel.*" It was a whisper and barely audible but I felt the word hanging in the air like an entity. I knew something was about to happen by the change in Gabriel's face and the way Ivy was bracing herself as if for bad weather.

The wind that howled outside was so ferocious we could hear it even from the basement. The moment it subsided, smoke began to pour through the bars of the ventilation grate, spilling onto the ground, gradually taking shape until the figure of Jake Thorn stood before us as a wraith. Although I could almost see through him, he looked just the same as he had the day we first met. There was the same pallid complexion, the same sharp cheekbones and eyes like a cat, their greenness sharply highlighted by the fall of dark hair. There was the same shapely mouth, almost effeminate in its rosiness, and the pinched, narrow nose. He was dressed as he had been in death—in a white shirt and tailcoat. His expression too was familiar—an odd mixture of beauty and cruelty.

"Bethany," he said in a voice that sounded older. "Nice to see you again."

The casual manner in which he spoke floored me. It was hard to pretend I wasn't amazed and terrified by what was happening. I was standing there talking to the ghost of a dead demon that I myself had a hand in killing.

"Jake? Is that really you?" I hesitated. "Uh . . . how are you doing?"

"Well, technically, I'm dead." He folded his arms and flashed a bitter smirk in Gabriel's direction. "So I've been better."

Lucifer, mesmerized, watched the phantasm through Xavier's eyes. Jake floated across to the bed and raised an eyebrow when he saw Xavier's condition.

"Oh, good, Dad's here."

"Arakiel, welcome back."

"I must say"—Jake waved a hand at Xavier's bruised body chained to the bed—"I like your thinking."

"Indeed," Lucifer replied, but a frown soon replaced his expression of pleasure. "It grieves me to see you reduced to this." The words sounded wrong coming out of Xavier's mouth, too scratchy, like it was filled with splinters of broken glass.

"Oh, you know me," Jake replied. "Rolling with the punches . . . like you taught me."

"We called you here for a reason," Lucifer said indulgently. "To bring you some kind of recompense."

"Oh?" Jake cocked his head.

"We want you to help settle a score." Xavier's lips stretched in a smile.

Jake gave a slight bow. "Always happy to be of service." He propped his chin in his hand mockingly, like a doctor. "What seems to be the problem?"

"They want this mortal released from my hold and I will be more than happy to oblige . . . but not without a price. It is up to you to determine the price, my son."

As if that was his cue, Gabriel emerged from the shadows.

"What do you want in exchange for the boy's life?" he said. A sudden sick feeling gripped me that I couldn't explain. My brother and sister seemed to be coming forward like sacrificial lambs and I didn't like the smug expression on Jake's face.

"Well, well, so now the Arch is prepared to bargain?"

"Just name your terms," Gabriel said tonelessly.

Lucifer turned his head invitingly toward Jake's ghost.

"Go ahead."

Ghost or not, Jake wasn't about to let this moment pass without milking it.

"Hmm . . . Let me see," he said theatrically, drumming his fingers together and enjoying this momentary return to glory. "What shall I ask for?"

"Make it quick," Ivy said, almost growling at him. "Before we change our minds."

"I'm in no rush."

"Jake . . ." I said warningly.

"All right." He held up his hand and laughed. "I propose a trade."

"What kind of trade?" I asked.

"Not with you," Jake replied dismissively. "For once, this isn't about you, Bethany. Besides, it wasn't your hand that killed me."

I felt as if someone had kicked me in the chest as I watched his eyes fall on Gabriel. Was he going to ask me to give my brother in exchange for my husband? I opened my mouth to tell him it was never going to happen, when Gabriel stepped in front of me.

"Let me handle this," he said. "His vendetta is against me."

"But Gabe . . ." I caught hold of his hand, my voice becoming suddenly soft and child-like. "You're my brother."

"Yes." Gabriel touched his forehead to mine and a lock of blond hair fell across his eyes. "I'm your brother, so let me do this for you."

From the bed, Lucifer let out a cracking laugh and Jake smiled.

"If we're all done with the sentimental moment, I'm ready to name my terms."

"Go on," Gabriel replied in a somber tone.

"His life . . ." Jake smiled haughtily. "In exchange for your wings."

AT first I thought I hadn't heard him right. The demand was too preposterous to be taken seriously. I almost laughed except Lucifer beat me to it.

"Oh, Arakiel," he said in between peals of laughter that reverberated around the room. "It's times like these I'm proud to call you my son."

"What did you say?" Ivy asked, her eyes wide with a mixture of rage and surprise. Lucifer tried to adjust his features to look consoling.

"Don't worry, they'll grow back in a few centuries. It just means your brother might be earthbound for a while."

Any hopes I'd harbored of a compromise crumbled. They must have known what they were asking of Gabriel was tantamount to extinguishing his existence. Without his wings Gabriel would be forced to live a half-life, devoid of purpose or meaning. Jake knew full well what he was doing—his request had seemed offhanded, but I knew he had given it careful consideration and chosen so as to hurt us all the most. With Gabriel powerless, Ivy would lose her partner and Xavier and I would be minus our protector, our mentor, and our guide. Not to mention, it would throw Heaven into turmoil. If an Arch willingly surrendered his wings to a demon, it was like giving his divinity as a gift—the ultimate sacrifice. It would signify more than I understood and prevent Gabriel's return to Heaven. He would be doomed.

"You're such an ass!" I yelled at Jake. I would have taken

a swing at him, but there was nothing for my fist to collide with.

"Now, now, language." He wagged a flimsy finger at me. "I think it's a fair price, seeing as he cost me my life."

"You are the only one to blame for your death," I snapped. "For being so selfish and destructive."

"Sticks and stones," Jake replied with a casual shrug.

"Why do you want his wings?" I asked, even though I already knew the answer. "What do you get out of it?"

"Victory," Jake said. "Satisfaction."

"He gets the great pleasure of seeing one of God's mightiest cut down," Ivy answered for him.

"You know me well," Jake said, winking. "So, deal or no deal? Let's move this along, I have places to go, people to haunt."

"Absolutely not," I said emphatically. "You're out of your mind."

"This is a travesty," Ivy added. "He will never allow it."

"I accept," said Gabriel.

I stopped dead, not believing my ears. I felt like he was speaking some foreign language and his words made no sense. Gabriel turned away, keeping his face hidden, like he didn't trust his resolve if he allowed himself to look at us. Anguish was written all over his features.

"Gabriel," Ivy whispered, edging closer to him. "Please, Gabriel, don't do this."

But he merely held up a hand to stop her. Their eyes locked for a moment and I saw desperation in my sister's face and a sort of tragic acceptance in my brother's.

"Don't be a martyr!" Ivy cried. "You don't even know if he's telling the truth!"

"A deal's a deal," said Gabriel in a voice so flat I almost didn't recognize it. "He'll keep his word."

"Demons lie!" my sister protested. "You're too noble for this! You cannot bow to Lucifer!"

"I'm not bowing to him," Gabriel murmured. "I'm protecting man, like Our Father would want." He walked over to the bed and placed his ringed hand on the pillow beside Xavier's head. "Our love for mankind has long tortured you, hasn't it, little brother? But I will defend my Father's creation unto the end."

Then I watched him, my brother, the Archangel and warrior, revered by Heaven and earth, fall to his knees. He bowed his head in a gesture of submission that on him looked like an aberration in nature. He slowly unbuttoned his shirt and let it slip to the floor. In the gloom, his magnificent body glowed softly. The room filled with the scent of rain when he unfurled his splendorous wings. They filled the space, feathered and tipped with silver. They looked as heavy as concrete, but I knew they weighed next to nothing. They were as light as gossamer and yet as protective as an arbor in a storm. Daylight began to filter down through an aperture in the wall above him, mingling with his hair like moonlight on the sand.

"Gabriel, please!" Ivy cried. "We'll find another way."

But her protest went unheeded. I wanted to speak, but couldn't find the words. I wanted to throw my body over his and shield him, but I knew it would do no good. So I did nothing, but cover my eyes and sob like a child. That was when they came, a crawling mass of fiendish ghouls was unleashed in the basement. Their faces were waxy and the color of cooked crab. They seemed to spring from below us but I couldn't be sure. They had teeth like carving knives and darting tongues. I noticed they couldn't stand upright but scuttled across the floor in crouching positions, like huge, monstrous insects. Behind them, stunted wings fanned out like wrinkled parchment.

Hideous as they were, what they carried terrified me most. In their knotted claw-like hands each gleefully wielded a cutting implement in the form of rusty handsaws.

20

Raphael

GABRIEL didn't even put up a fight. It was horrifying and heartbreaking to watch. My brother, who was a pillar of strength in my mind, was on his knees succumbing to the will of the demons. They clambered over him, their claws scratching the skin of his back and chest, until all that could be seen of him was his mussed blond hair and the flashes of silver that were his wings.

The creatures enjoyed the mutilation—that much was clear. They clipped his wings first, sending silver tips floating into the air. Then they began to hack into them and blood the color of liquid amber ran in rivulets, pooling on the dirty floor where it glowed like precious myrrh. The spilling of his blood seemed to incite fervor. The blood of an archangel was reputed to have life-giving properties; one drop could bestow immortality upon the one who consumed it. The vile creatures began to dip their hands in it and used it to anoint their faces. They slurped it up noisily with their darting tongues. All the while they waved their gruesome weapons in the air, reveling in their victory, while in Xavier's body Lucifer looked on in approval.

Through it all, Gabriel remained motionless, his head bowed and his eyes closed. The only changes were the color draining from his face, and the dark circles now ringing his rain gray eyes. It must have been painful, excruciating and drawn out, but he refused to give them the satisfaction of making a sound. His lips moved silently and I knew he must be praying for strength.

Ivy stood paralyzed, tears pouring down her soft cheeks. Gabriel had been her partner for thousands of years. Their bond ran deep and unbreakable. I didn't know how she could stand it. I moved forward and took her hand, which seemed to shock her out of her trance. I didn't say anything; I just followed Gabriel's example, bowed my head and began to pray. In a situation such as this, there was nothing we could do but rely on higher powers. Ivy stared at me for a moment, her eyes full of devastation. But then I felt her fingers tighten around mine and her eyelids fluttered shut. I could feel the combined energy of our prayers passing between our bodies. I felt myself fill up with it, like it was pushing against my walls from the inside, wanting to burst free. Prayer was a powerful force and ours was answered almost immediately.

Above the cacophony, I heard the sound of screeching tires as a car pulled up outside. The front door slammed and there were footsteps in the hall. The man that appeared in the basement looked nothing like an angel, although I knew he was one. In my mind I always pictured angels to be a variation of my brother, but this one was smaller in stature, with flaming red hair and an open face—much less severe than

Gabriel's. The biggest difference was how surprisingly human he looked.

I took him in as he came tripping down the stairs and I noticed the dusting of freckles across his nose, the vibrant emerald green cashmere scarf draped around his neck. I caught a whiff of expensive cologne.

"Raphael," Ivy whispered. Although it was out of character, she ran and buried her face in his chest. "Thank goodness you're here."

"Well, this party sucks," said Raphael, extricating himself from her embrace to appraise the damage. "I can't believe I left a river cruise on the Nile for this."

I couldn't tell whether he was joking until he winked at me. The devils in the meantime had ceased their work and stood frozen and bemused. Raphael gave them a congenial smile before pointing a finger at them and reciting a few words by rote. The bolts shooting from his finger caused them to disintegrate violently before our eyes, leaving behind only little mounds of gray ash. With the devils dispatched, Ivy rushed to Gabriel, who looked on the verge of passing out. Her hands went to work, making crackling sounds as healing currents passed over the ragged parts of his wings. Where she touched I saw skin knit over and wounds close, stopping further blood loss, but the broken quills didn't grow back. Xavier was lying motionless on the bed. Had Lucifer left him?

Raphael came toward me with an extended hand. I noticed his tie was patterned with tiny yellow fish.

"Good to finally meet you, Bethany."

"Likewise," I said, shaking his hand and wondering both how he knew me and what made him think there was time for niceties.

"Rumor has it that you're a bit of a rebel." The way he said it made notoriety sound like a good thing.

"I guess that's true," I mumbled. It was awkward making small talk with this stranger while the lives of my brother and husband hung in the balance.

"You're prettier than I imagined you," Raphael said.

"Uh . . . thank you," I said. "But I don't really . . ."

"Wait, wait, I've got one," he interrupted. "Somebody better call God. Because Heaven's missing an angel!"

He burst out laughing and slapped his thigh.

"What?" I demanded.

"I found a book," Raphael explained. "One hundred best pickup lines."

"You do know Xavier and I are married?" I narrowed my eyes.

"How's that working out for you?"

"Can we please try to concentrate?" I said. "Xavier's possessed . . . if you hadn't noticed."

Raphael continued to stare at me, in no hurry to get started. "You know the best way to get rid of a demon, right?" he asked with a serious face. I caught Ivy rolling her eyes as I shook my head.

"Exorcise a lot!"

Ivy caught my expression of dismay. "It's okay, Beth.

He's famous for his bad jokes. We're still waiting for him to grow up."

"And like Peter Pan I hope to avoid that at all costs," Raphael declared.

The idea of an archangel with a sense of humor didn't gel in my mind. I was hardly in the mood for jokes.

"Can you help us or not?"

" 'Course I can," Raphael said. "I've got swag."

"Great," I muttered. "Whatever that means."

"What it means"—he strode across to me—"is that your brother and sister have been running on reserve power. But don't worry, I'm fully charged."

"And you're sure you know what you're doing?" I asked.

"Trust me." He winked. "I'm a doctor."

Under different circumstances I might have mistaken him for a college kid trying too hard to impress. Finally Raphael focused his attention on the task at hand and gravitated with mild interest toward the bed.

"Lucifer, what's up, bro?"

I blinked in surprise, not quite believing the casual manner in which Raphael was addressing him.

Xavier's eyes snapped open and he gave a tight smile.

"Don't tell me you're the backup?"

"Surprised?"

"A little," he admitted. "Aren't you taking a risk getting involved in this?"

"Ah, well." Raphael sighed. "What's life without a few risks?"

"No need to tell me," Lucifer rasped.

"Anyway"—Raphael clapped his hands together—"I'd love to stay and chat, catch up on old times, but I think we better cut to the chase."

Lucifer raised an inquisitive eyebrow. "Go on."

Jake's ghost looked on wordlessly. It was strange to see him present and yet so inactive. He watched, wide-eyed, like a little boy at a pantomime.

"I'm gonna need the kid back," Raphael said simply.

"Sorry, can't help you."

"Let's not play games. It's insulting to both of us."

"No games. We had a deal and it fell through. Ask Beth."

"Look." Raphael adjusted his cashmere scarf. "We can make this clean and simple or we can make it messy and complicated."

"I have no pressing engagements, so let's go with messy and complicated."

Raphael looked nonplussed. "Fine by me but you're wasting your time."

"Am I?"

"There's something you don't know." Raphael's tone was slightly teasing.

"Please do enlighten me."

"It's nothing earth-shattering." Raphael smiled cheekily. "It's just that, well, I'm stronger than you."

"Are you indeed?"

Lucifer's words hung in the air for a moment and then Xavier began to retch. The veins in his neck pulsed and strained as he was gripped by a paroxysm of coughing. We waited for the fit to pass but it showed no sign of abating. Xavier's eyes rolled back and he gripped the bed rail. A bluish tinge appeared on his lips. Despite his medium stature, when Raphael spoke in his angelic voice, it was as intimidating as thunder.

"Depart this temple of the Lord! Show your face no more."

"He's choking!" I yelled. "Do something!"

Raphael ran to break the fetters around Xavier's wrists and together we helped him sit up. Raphael brought the palm of his hand down hard between Xavier's shoulder blades, again and again, until the source of the obstruction flew forward. The coughing changed to rasping breaths and Xavier fell back onto the bed. I knew how exhausted he was when his head lolled to one side as if it were made of stuffing. Beside him on the mattress I saw the problem: a handful of grisly talons, blood-stained from where they'd torn his throat. I picked one up to examine it. It was a grayish color and curved with sharp tips as if designed for clutching prey. It looked like it belonged to some predatory bird.

Raphael seized this hiatus to perform the exorcism rite, speaking in a measured voice but without stopping to draw breath, as if pausing might interfere with the results.

"I adjure you in the name of your Creator to depart this child of God. Depart, Seducer of Men, Corruptor of Nations, Prince of Darkness. You must bow to a power far greater than yours."

"There is no greater." Lucifer's voice was already fainter, crackling as though it were reaching us through a bad phone connection.

"Do not resist. Your plans will come to nothing. Depart now this holy vessel. Stubborn dragon, the longer you delay the harsher your punishment shall be. We repel your power. Yield. *Yield!*" He repeated the last word like a powerful mantra.

My heart sank hearing Xavier's coughing resume. Did this mean defeat? But then I noticed the coughing was different this time. Xavier wasn't choking; he was trying to expel something. From his open mouth something long, dark, and reptilian emerged. It was black and scaly apart from a white pulsating throat like a frog. It took me a moment to realize it was a snake, as it forced its way out of Xavier's body, where it must have been coiled deep inside him. It slithered off the bed onto the concrete floor where it writhed and turned, navigating its way along until it found what it was looking for. It settled over a crack that began to widen immediately with a jarring sound. When it was large enough, it swallowed the snake whole with a sucking sound and the crack closed over, leaving only a putrid smell and a black oil stain where it had passed. Jake's ghost vanished with it.

"Beth?" The voice that broke the silence was raspy but there was no doubt it belonged to Xavier.

I sank to my knees by his side and pressed my face into his neck. "I'm here, baby. It's over. It's over."

"We made it?"

"I told you we would." My tears and laughter mingled freely, triggered by relief. Ivy brought him a glass of water. He thanked her and drank so shakily that half of it spilled down his front. Then he took my hands and pressed them over his heart, lying back down on the tattered pillow, pushed to a point beyond exhaustion, but finally free. Seeing his vivid blue eyes belonging to him once more, I was almost euphoric. I couldn't hold him any tighter. I wanted to absorb him inside my own body so nobody could ever hurt him again.

Raphael cleared his throat politely to remind us of his presence. He looked embarrassed to be intruding on our private moment.

"This is Raphael," I told him. "He saved our lives." There was no longer my life and his. They were completely entwined; when one of us hurt, so did the other and if one of us died . . . I shuddered to think what would become of the one left behind.

"Thank you," Xavier mouthed. Talking must have been painful because he brought his hand up to his throat.

"Don't mention it."

"Wait." He propped himself up. "Raphael—as in the archangel? Patron saint of travelers?"

"You know your angelology." Raphael looked impressed.

"Ex-altar boy," Xavier rasped.

My eyes fell on Xavier's bruised wrists. They looked chafed and swollen where the iron had cut into his flesh. I hadn't done any healing in a while. Did I still have it in me? Or had that power been confiscated as punishment? Xavier flinched when I touched the raw flesh but didn't pull away. I focused hard on sending healing vibrations and soon my hand was tingling. As I continued to lay my hands on him, the swelling reduced and then the rawness faded slowly, leaving only unblemished skin in place of the injuries.

"You've still got it," said Xavier, and I beamed at him,

pleased with my achievement. I chose to read the fact that my ability hadn't deserted me as a sign that there was still hope.

Movement from the other side of the room drew my attention. Ivy was helping Gabriel to his feet. He still seemed unsteady. I saw him wince as he retracted his wings quickly before any of us could see their mangled state. His face was still pale and he kept his arm around Ivy's shoulders for support. Still, I watched him swallow hard and lift his chin to address his brother.

"What made you decide to come?" he asked Raphael.

"I guess I'm just a sucker for a lost cause."

"So you don't think we can win this one?" Gabriel stumbled slightly from light-headedness, but Ivy caught him.

"Doubtful." Raphael gave a cheerful smile. "But you can have fun trying."

Gabriel pursed his lips and without saying another word, headed upstairs, his arm still draped around Ivy's shoulders. I helped Xavier off the bed and Raphael watched, a smile on his lips, but sadness in his eyes. And we all trudged up the stairs back to the house, a sick and sorry procession.

21

We'll Make It, Y'all

IN the kitchen Ivy's brewed coffee and homemade brownies revived us. I still felt like I'd been run over by a bus, so Xavier and Gabriel must have felt ten times worse. I knew I'd recover from the physical exhaustion but the trauma of nearly losing Xavier twice in the same week was going to haunt me forever. We ate glumly, shoulders slumped and faces withdrawn. Gabriel didn't eat anything; he just sat with his face pressed into his hands. Only Raphael was in high spirits. He looked appraisingly at Ivy's figure when she went to the fridge for milk.

"Still the hottest angel I know," he murmured.

"It's beyond me how you're still on staff," Ivy replied.

"Must be because He appreciates my sense of humor. Can't have everyone being criminally serious." He glanced around at us. "We've got enough of that."

Despite our moods, Raphael's cheer was infectious. Even Ivy couldn't help smiling.

"You ought to smile more often," he told her. "Makes your whole face light up."

"Will you stop flirting?" Gabriel protested, without lifting his face. "It's unbecoming."

"Anyway, aren't you all, like related?" Xavier asked.

"The brother-sister thing is really more symbolic than genetic." Raphael gave a toothy smile.

"But angels don't normally feel . . ." Xavier scratched his head, uncomprehending. "They're not supposed to . . . have those feelings . . . for each other?"

"No," Ivy answered firmly. "But once in a while we throw out a deviant." I knew she was joking but I couldn't help thinking that was how she and Gabriel thought of me.

"Usually as a result of fraternizing with humans too much," added Gabriel drily.

"I happen to find humans good company. Beth and I have that in common."

"Is that why you travel with them?" Xavier asked.

"That plus the fact that I'm easily bored." He sipped his coffee calmly. "Humans might cause a lot of trouble and drive us crazy." He looked at me over the rim of his mug, a smile in his eyes. "But they're so worth it."

A pensive silence followed as everyone considered these words. Raphael broke the mood by leaping to his feet and searching his pockets.

"Does anyone have the time?" he asked. "I can't find my cell."

"It's just after six," Ivy replied, without needing to check. "Party to get to?"

Raphael ignored the jibe. "Tell me there's a TV here."

"Yes."

"And . . ." He waved his hands impatiently. "Where is it located?"

"The living room."

We followed Raphael as he bounded to the front of the house and made a beeline for the couch. He didn't even bother trying to find the remote; with a snap of his fingers he switched the TV on.

"Football?" Ivy asked. "Seriously?"

On the screen, kickoff was about to begin, the first game of the season, the Rebels against the Razorbacks. People had been talking about it all week.

"You're not a fan?" Raphael sounded surprised. "You're missing out."

"Good, it hasn't started yet," said Xavier, settling himself comfortably on the opposite end of the couch. "Don't forget to check the score of the Bama game."

I stared at Xavier, worried that this sudden return to normality might be a sign he was repressing dangerous emotions. He smiled when he saw my face.

"Relax," he told me. "The game will help take my mind off things." He patted the space beside him. "Come sit with me?"

I glanced at the screen and the bird's-eye view of the stadium with REBELS stamped into the ground in huge letters. I recognized some of the faces as the camera panned the sea of red-and-blue fans. I knew Molly would be among them somewhere. She hadn't stopped going on about tailgating in the Grove since she'd arrived. I watched the Rebelettes in their sequined outfits wave their pom-poms in the air. The words

ARE YOU READY? flashed on the Jumbo Tron and the crowd erupted into the "Hotty Toddy" chant.

WE were losing by the end of the first quarter. I left Xavier and Raphael to yell at the screen and went into the kitchen to join Ivy. Gabriel had disappeared to his room and locked the door. I wanted to go check on him but Ivy said he needed space to meditate and recover.

When the game ended, Raphael reappeared, stretching lazily. Xavier followed, looking more relaxed if a little sheepish about his protracted absence.

"Sorry, I wasn't planning to watch the whole thing."

"It's okay." I patted his arm. "You need your man time."

"Did we win?" Ivy asked.

"Nah . . . but made two touchdowns, which isn't bad."

"I better head out," Raphael said, grabbing his coat and sauntering toward the door. "Thank you for your hospitality, it's been a pleasure as always."

We walked Raphael out to his car. On the curb a metallic green Porsche was parked. It was a color I'd never seen on a car before, but I had to admit it suited the extravagant archangel.

"Nice wheels," said Xavier, circling the car appreciatively.

"Take it for a spin anytime."

"This guy"—Xavier pointed with his thumb—"is awesome."

"Are you two kidding?" Ivy asked, exasperated.

"Boys will be boys," Raphael declared. "Don't try and change us."

"Football and cars," I said with a grin. "Actually makes a nice change."

"This isn't just a car," Xavier said. "It's a thing of beauty."

"They don't get it." Raphael directed a wink at me. "Maybe we'll take her out some other time." He jumped into the driver's seat and revved the engine. He stuck his head out the window and yelled out, "By the way, Xavier, medicine is still your calling. Don't forget that."

Then he took off down the street so fast the tires screeched and the exhaust released a billow of smoke into the air.

"Such an attention-seeker," Ivy muttered, and Raphael sounded the horn at the end of the street as if to say, "*I heard that!*"

When he was gone, Xavier and I were both beyond ready for bed. Ivy showed us upstairs to the guest room that we hadn't even had a chance to see yet. It was quaint with polished furniture and a king-sized bed full of plump cushions. The window was circular and looked onto the tangled Mississippi woods. As I sat lightly on the bed, it occurred to me that Xavier and I hadn't had the privilege of sharing a bed for a while. I hoped nothing had changed between us.

While Xavier flopped down on the bed, I excused myself to take a shower, letting the hot water pour over my body and steam up the glass. It felt like a sort of cleansing ritual, like I was letting all my troubles sink down the drain. I used up half a bottle of shower gel, soaping and resoaping my muscles, kneading them gently with my fingers and feeling the tension ebb away. I finally emerged with my hair toweled dry and my whole body tingling and smelling of lavender.

Xavier was sleeping, the exhaustion of the day visible on his face. He stirred when I came in and reached out to pull me onto the bed.

"You smell good." He pressed his mouth into my neck, inhaling deeply.

I giggled as his stubble tickled my skin. "You don't."

"How rude," he replied with a laugh. "But probably true." He slid out of bed. "My turn in the shower. Don't go anywhere."

He peeled off his clothes and dropped them in the laundry hamper before disappearing into the bathroom. I dove eagerly under the covers and scrunched the crisp sheets with my toes. I buried my face in the clean pillow that smelled faintly of baby powder and stretched like a cat. Almost immediately my body was ready to surrender to fatigue. I was struggling to keep my eyes open when Xavier emerged from his shower wearing only a towel wrapped loosely around his hips. Every time I saw his physical form, it floored me completely. Droplets of water still clung to his shoulders and the light coming from behind lent a polished golden hue to his skin. He was so well proportioned he reminded me of a statue on a pedestal in a museum.

"That was fast," I said, trying not to stare.

"You learn not to linger in the bathroom when you have sisters." His smile faded a little.

"You miss them, don't you?"

"More than I thought I would," he said. "But mostly I hate

the thought of them worrying about me. I know Claire is probably sick over it and I'm sure Nic hates me for taking off like this."

"You can make it up to them," I promised. "When all this is over."

"Do you really think it'll ever be over?" Xavier asked distantly.

"Yes," I said as firmly as I could manage. "This is not going to last forever. I promise you that."

"Hey," Xavier said, suddenly looking down at himself. "I just realized I don't have any clean clothes."

I flipped the cover off his side of the bed. Now was not the time for heavy discussion, we'd had enough of that. Now was the time for loving my husband. "You don't need them," I said.

"Oh, really?" Xavier's mouth twisted in a smile. "Does that door have a lock?"

"Do you care?" I challenged.

Xavier raised an eyebrow, but dropped his towel and slid into bed beside me. I felt his presence envelop me, his skin still warm from the shower. His lips were reverential as he kissed me lightly, working his way down from the tip of my chin to my collarbone.

I traced the scratches on his body from the ordeal he'd endured and instinctively held him tighter, my fingers digging into his warm flesh. The memory of him bound to the bed sprang up in my mind, the way his ocean eyes had filled with cruelty that didn't belong to him. I felt my mouth go dry at the thought.

"Are you okay?" he murmured into my chest.

"Uh-huh." I bit my lip and tried to shove the unpleasant memories out of my head.

Xavier sensed my tension and looked up. "You sure you're not too tired for this?"

His consideration was stirring. It was the old Xavier resurfacing, the one who put my needs above all else. "Me?" I smiled. "I think I should be asking you that question."

"I'm actually okay," he said, sounding surprised. "I just can't shake the feeling my body is being controlled by someone else."

"Well it was," I said, letting my fingers lightly caress his chest. "But they're gone. It's just you and me now."

Xavier lifted me up easily so I was lying on top of him. The firmness of his body beneath me felt like a safe harbor.

"You want to hear something funny?" he asked as I buried my face in his neck, letting the wooden cross he wore leave an imprint on my cheek. "What happened today was really hard, one of the hardest things I've ever had to do. Lucifer was inside me. And even after he went, I felt like he left a mark behind, a stain on my soul."

"That's not funny," I told him.

"Wait, you didn't let me finish. Every time you touch me it feels like you're washing me clean, washing away the darkness. You're healing my body with your body and renewing my soul with your soul."

"I don't have a soul," I murmured.

"Yes, you do," Xavier insisted, cupping my chin in his hand. "Maybe it isn't the same as mine, but it's there. You have so much light; I feel it every time I look at you. That's the way God made you."

"Do you know what I think?" I said. "I think everything we've been through so far might feel like a curse, but really it's a blessing. Our Father set us on this path because He meant for it to lead somewhere . . . somewhere amazing. And He equipped us with everything we need for the journey . . . each other."

Xavier gazed at me for a moment, then brought his lips to meet mine. His kiss this time was long and deep. It felt like tiny internal flames had appeared from somewhere inside me and were now igniting every particle of my body. This time was different from our first encounter in the woods. The mood was more leisurely, less urgent. There was no fear of discovery and more time to explore. This was how I'd imagined the easy intimacy of marriage. I felt safe and protected and warm from head to toe.

THE muted morning sun seeping through the open shutters was conflicted, duty bound to wake us but hesitant to disturb our rest. I crept out of bed, trying not to disturb Xavier, who was sprawled on his belly. I wanted him to sleep for as long as possible before having to face any challenges the new day might bring.

I wrapped myself in a pink robe and trotted downstairs to the kitchen where I found Ivy preparing a breakfast for giants. There were muffins bursting with blueberries, eggs and sausage and grits warming on the stove, and granola-topped glasses of yogurt parfait. Ivy was expertly flipping pancakes and stacking them on a plate. The smell of ground coffee filled the room. Gabriel was nowhere to be seen.

"I hope you're hungry," Ivy said. I could see she was trying to ease the stress of the last few days and I appreciated her efforts.

"Smells good," I replied.

"Where's Xavier? Still sleeping?"

"Yeah. Where's Gabriel?"

Ivy gave a resigned shrug. "He was gone when I woke up this morning."

"How's he doing?" I asked awkwardly.

"I don't know," Ivy said. "He won't talk about it."

"Okay," I said, trying to keep my anxiety under wraps. "I guess he just needs time."

Back in the bedroom, the covers had been thrown off, telling me Xavier was already up. I peeked in the bathroom and thought nothing of it when I found it empty. But when there was no sign of him on the balcony or out in the hall, my heart was already thudding. I breathed a sigh of relief seeing light coming from under a door across from our bedroom. I pushed it open gently and found him in the study. He was sitting at a broad desk poring over the contents of a book he'd pulled from the shelves. When the door creaked, he glanced up.

"Morning."

"Am I disturbing you?"

"Of course not, come in."

I walked over to him and peeked over his shoulder. The

book he was reading was an Atlas of Human Anatomy open to a labeled color plate of the foot's skeletal system.

"Do you know how many bones make up a foot?"

I probably should have known but my mind was still full of morning fog.

"How many?"

"Twenty-six. Amazing when you stop to think about it."

"Yes, it is. Um . . . are you okay?"

"I'm fine." Xavier smiled. "It's just what Raphael said earlier got me thinking, that's all."

I frowned. "What did he say?"

"That medicine was still my calling. And I think he's right, it's my way of making a contribution. When all this is settled down, I want to go back to college. I want to be a doctor."

"You've always wanted that."

"No." He shook his head. "Before it was my parents choosing for me. Now, it feels right."

"Good," I said. "Because you're going to make a great doctor."

"One day."

{ 22 }

Speak Now or Forever Hold Your Peace

WE decided not to return to Ole Miss for a few days. Xavier needed time to recover physically and I was emotionally drained from the stress. We hid out in the house, mostly sleeping and only wandering downstairs to eat and interact briefly with my siblings. Ivy seemed to have bounced back as usual, but I didn't see much of Gabriel. He stayed locked away in his room and hardly spoke to any of us. I was still amazed at the sacrifice he'd been willing to make for us. I prayed every night for him and thanked my Father for sparing Xavier's life. When I finally thought to check my phone, I found a barrage of missed calls from Molly, Mary Ellen, and even some of Xavier's friends all wanting to know what had happened to us. I recalled Molly's announcement about her engagement to Wade, but I didn't have the space in my brain to worry about it just yet.

I lay down against Xavier, curling up against his warm gray T-shirt and feeling his soft hair tickle my nose.

"I'm sorry," I told him for the hundredth time since we'd woken up.

"Beth, please." He rolled over and stared at the ceiling. "It wasn't your fault. I'm the one who's sorry you had to see me like that."

"It wasn't you," I replied. "None of it was."

"But I let him in."

"You were dead. He invaded your body. You couldn't help that."

"It's so weird to think I was dead," Xavier murmured. "I wish I could say I saw a bright light or something, but all I saw was you."

"Me?"

"Yeah." He nodded. "Just different variations of you: you on the porch swing, you and Phantom asleep on the couch at Byron, you in your dress on prom night. It's like I was supposed to be seeing Heaven, but all I wanted to see was your face. I guess my Heaven is you."

"I was so scared." I turned my cheek across the pillow to face him. "Thinking you were going to die. It made me realize there isn't anywhere I wouldn't follow you to."

The corners of Xavier's mouth turned up in a smile. "You know something? Heaven is supposed to be so pissed at us right now . . . but you and I both should have died over and over again. But we're still here. Do you know what that means?"

"We're like cats?" I asked. "We've got nine lives."

"Maybe." He laughed. "But I think it means someone is looking out for us."

"I hope so," I said, kicking my foot out from under the covers and letting the sunlight through the window warm my toes. "I'd like to believe that."

When my phone went off for the fifth time in under twenty minutes, I sighed and leaned out of bed to retrieve it. It was no surprise the missed call was from Molly. I called out to my sister in the next room and she poked her head through the door.

"What am I supposed to do about Molly?" I asked. "She's freaking out."

"Let her come over," Ivy said. "Shutting her out usually does more damage than good."

That much was true. Molly hated to be ignored or excluded and if she got worried, she was capable of putting up missing-person posters all around campus. Xavier hid his face beneath the cover.

"Don't be like that," I said, nudging him. "She's our friend. We should be excited to see her."

"Yay," he replied flatly.

WHEN Molly turned up, she seemed calmer than usual, less hyperactive and excitable.

"I've been worried," she said, sitting down at the kitchen table while Ivy poured her some tea and set a plate of cookies down. "Is everything okay?"

"No," I said truthfully. "But it will be. We're working on it."

Molly nodded and looked at her hands. "Is there anything I can do?"

"Have a cookie," I told her.

"Beth, be serious."

"We appreciate your support," Ivy cut in. "But there really isn't anything you can help us with. The situation is messy enough already."

"Messy how?" Molly wanted to know.

"I'd rather not discuss it," Ivy said delicately. "I would hate to implicate you."

"But you're all going to be okay, right?" Molly jerked her thumb at Xavier. "He doesn't look so hot. And no offense, Beth, but neither do you."

"They're going to be fine," Ivy replied. "They're just tired."

Ordinarily, we might have let Molly in on what was happening. After all, she already knew our identities. But I understood the reason behind my sister's silence was not mistrust. The less Molly knew, the safer she would be. We didn't want any more blood on our hands.

"Don't worry." I gave her my most convincing grin. "We'll be back to normal in no time."

"Okay," Molly said, sounding surprisingly mature. "I don't want to make things worse."

"So tell us about Wade," I said, eager to change the subject. At the mention of his name, Molly's eyes seemed to grow misty.

"He's so great," she said with a sigh. "I've just wanted to tell everyone, but of course I can't."

"Why's that?" Xavier asked.

"Well, I can't tell people who aren't invited to the wedding. Wade doesn't want to invite anyone outside the faith."

Xavier and I exchanged puzzled glances. As far as we knew you didn't have to be a particular denomination to attend a wedding.

"Isn't Wade Christian?" I asked.

"Yes," Molly said. "Well, sort of. His family started their own church. It's still pretty small but it's growing. They don't really like to associate with outsiders, they think it's dangerous."

"Dangerous?" Xavier repeated. "How?"

"You know, corrupting influences and all that," Molly said dismissively. "Wade says television is the devil's mouthpiece and that negative messages can be transmitted through social groups as well."

"Exactly what kind of negative messages is he afraid of?" I asked. This wasn't sounding healthy to me. "Don't you think faith needs to be tested for it to be proven?"

"I don't know," Molly said. "But Wade says isolating myself from bad things will bring me closer to God." She sounded like she was quoting from a rule book.

"It sounds like a cult to me," Xavier said bluntly, voicing what the rest of us were thinking.

"It isn't," Molly snapped. "They might not be mainstream, but they really know what they're talking about."

"What denomination do they classify themselves as?" I asked.

"Huh?" Molly asked.

"You know," Xavier said impatiently. "Are they Baptist, Methodist, Presbyterian?"

"I told you," Molly repeated emphatically. "It's a family religion."

"So it's made-up?"

"No," she insisted angrily. "It's just one of the many versions of Christianity."

"You can't alter Christianity!" I exclaimed. "Only the Bible is gospel—you can't just invent your own rules!"

"Look." Molly laid her hands flat on the tabletop. "I don't care what you say. Wade and his family have taught me a lot. They showed me everything I was doing wrong in life."

I didn't like the sound of this. Anyone who took the word of God and manipulated it to form their own religion was trying to play by their own rules and pass it off as faith.

"What did they tell you?" Ivy asked.

"Oh, just little things," she replied. "Like how I should dress and how I shouldn't speak to men who aren't my husband." She waved her hands at Xavier. "Don't worry, you have a wife so you don't count."

"Molly . . ." Xavier said slowly. "You don't have to believe everything they say."

"Well, actually, Wade is my fiancé," Molly replied. "And I have to be obedient to him."

"Obedient?" Xavier repeated. "What, like a dog?"

The old Molly might have gotten angry, but she just shook her head sadly. "You clearly don't understand. Wade is trying to save my soul from Hell. He says your husband should be your earthly God."

"What?" My eyes almost bugged out of my head. "That's completely sacrilegious."

"It is not," Molly said. "It makes sense."

"It's breaking a commandment," Ivy said gently. "*You shall have no other God's before me.*"

"He didn't say he *was* God, he just believes that . . . look, whatever, Wade knows what he's talking about."

"I don't think he does." The voice came from the doorway and we all turned to see Gabriel standing there. His white blond hair was pulled back into a ponytail and his cheekbones looked sharper from the ordeal he'd been through. But he was just as painfully handsome as ever. I could hear Molly's heart begin to beat faster when she laid eyes on him.

"What did you say?" she asked defiantly.

Gabriel didn't move from the doorway, where he leaned with his arms folded. His silver-blue eyes stared unblinking. "I think you're making a big mistake."

Molly let out a sharp breath. "Well, this has nothing to do with you, does it?"

"No, but your fiancé sounds like a raging idiot."

I saw Ivy's head jerk up. Gabriel never spoke that way, not to anyone. He was always distant and detached, laying out arguments in clear, rational points. Now he actually sounded like he was emotionally involved. Was that even possible?

"How dare you!" Molly stood up, her chair screeching across the floor. "You have no right to judge him."

"I don't want to see you miserable," Gabriel said. "Living out the rest of your life in a loveless marriage."

"How do you know it would be loveless?"

"I can see it in your eyes. You're pretending, trying to convince yourself to be happy. You think if Wade gives you something to believe in, your life will have meaning. But Wade and his rules can't fill the gaping hole you feel, Molly."

"You don't get to care about me!" Molly yelled suddenly. "You didn't want me, remember? I'm too human, too flawed for you to ever give a damn about so why don't you leave me alone?"

"Maybe I was wrong," Gabriel said softly.

All three of us simultaneously looked up to gape at him.

"You . . ." Molly was stammering to get the words out. "You what?"

"I didn't think it would end up like this," Gabriel murmured. "Things were not supposed to happen this way."

"What are you talking about?" Molly looked frantically up at Ivy and me. "What's he talking about?"

"Gabe?" Ivy asked slowly. "What's going on?"

"I'm sick of fighting." Gabriel gave a heavy shrug. "I'm sick of this endless war between angels and demons and seeing nothing but pain and death all around us. There has to be something better. There has to be some other way. When will there be peace, Ivy? The battle has been raging for centuries. When will it be over?"

"I don't know," my sister admitted. "But that is how our lives have always been, since the beginning of time."

"Then maybe Bethany has been right all along. Maybe it's better to be human or at least allow ourselves to love them."

"What are you saying?" Molly's blue eyes were wide.

"I'm saying that yes, you are flawed," Gabriel said. "You are impulsive and short-tempered, brash and foolish. Your heart is fickle and your mood changes faster than the wind. But *that* is what makes you human and that is what makes you beautiful."

"You think I'm beautiful?" Molly could barely get the words out.

Gabriel crossed the room in two strides and Molly stood up to face him. He placed his ringed hands on her slender shoulders.

"You belong to no one," he told her intently. "Unlike me, you are not owned. You were created to be free, to live and love and find happiness. I was not built for happiness; I was built for nothing but servitude. But you . . . you feel so much and so passionately and I think it is beautiful."

"This is bad," I whispered to Xavier. "This is very, very bad."

"What the heck is going on?" he hissed.

"A moment of doubt," I said. "With his wings injured even Gabriel isn't infallible. He's questioning his faith . . . just like a human would."

"I don't like it," Xavier said uncomfortably. Molly and Gabriel remained transfixed, their eyes locked on one another.

"My life is governed by rules," Gabriel said, almost to himself.

Before any of us knew what was happening, Gabriel took Molly's face in his hands, leaned down, and kissed her. It was like watching a scene from ancient mythology, the legendary hero and the fair maiden united. Although it couldn't have lasted more than ten seconds, I felt as if time stood still as they were locked in their embrace. Gabriel's powerful form, curved around her as their bodies pressed together, his fingers caught in a mess of titian curls. It was so sudden I almost didn't believe it happened. It seemed Molly was struggling to wrap her head around it as well. When he released her, she was so intoxicated she fell back into her chair without saying a word.

"Wow" was all she could say when she finally mustered enough breath to speak.

"Wow," Xavier echoed.

Ivy ran forward and shook Gabriel's arm. "Stop! I know things have been hard lately, but this is too much."

"No," Gabriel replied with a short laugh. "Having my wings sawed from my back and Lucifer as a house guest . . . that was too much. This is a release."

"Please," Ivy said pressingly. "You're going to regret this later. I know it."

"I won't regret it," Gabriel said. "Because this is the first thing I've ever done for myself."

Listening to them, a strange expression came over Molly's face. As they continued to argue, she moved so she was standing behind my brother. Then slowly, she reached out and lifted the tail of his shirt. Everyone fell silent as she slid her hands up his back and rested them on his broken wings. I saw Gabriel shiver and drop his head. He didn't speak and it was impossible to tell what emotion he was feeling, but he didn't move or push her away. Neither of them seemed to notice they had an audience. Or maybe they just didn't care. They were too caught up in their own private moment.

"It's okay," Molly told him, her fingertips stroking his wings beneath the shirt. "It's going to be okay."

"I'm sorry," Gabriel said without looking up.

"Don't be," Molly replied. "You don't have to take responsibility for everything and everyone. You can make mistakes, you know?"

Ivy, Xavier, and I all looked at one another. It was clear this moment was intensely personal and we all felt as if we shouldn't be there. Molly's phone vibrated on the kitchen table and she seemed to jump out of her trance. Wade's name flashed on the screen. She quickly dropped her hands and gathered up her belongings.

"I should go. . . ." She stumbled over her words. "I really don't . . . I just wanted to . . . I should go."

A moment later we heard the front door slam behind her. We all turned to stare at Gabriel.

"What?" he asked irritably.

"Do you . . . um . . . want to talk about this?"

"No, thank you, Bethany," he said almost sarcastically. "I don't need relationship advice from the couple of the year."

He regarded us all with hostility for a moment, before disappearing onto the back porch.

Xavier turned to Ivy, lost for words. "Do you . . . does he need to see a therapist?"

"Gabriel has seen every human atrocity since the dawn of time," my sister replied. "It'd be a long session."

"This is temporary, right?" I asked worriedly. "Once his wings are healed he'll be back to normal?"

"Fortunately, yes," Ivy said. "We should be grateful it wasn't worse. The destruction of an angel's wings can cause injury beyond repair. But Gabriel will heal."

"I don't understand how damage to his wings can make him behave this way," Xavier said. "I mean, Molly . . . seriously?"

"Our essence is contained within our wings," Ivy replied. "They are the source of all our power, like the roots of a tree. When the roots are poisoned, the whole tree suffers. He has been weakened, made susceptible to doubt and worry and a multitude of emotions he has never been exposed to before."

"So what should we do?"

"Nothing," my sister replied. "He just needs time."

"And what about Molly?" I asked.

"His new feelings for her will disappear and he will return to being the Archangel Gabriel," Ivy said.

"Great," Xavier said. "That should go down well."

I left Xavier and Ivy to talk and pushed open the screen door to find my brother sitting on the creaking porch steps, looking out at the tangled yard. He was staring at the dead leaves beneath his shoes, his forehead creased with what looked like confusion. Anybody could see he was not himself.

"You know this isn't you," I said, settling down beside him. "All of this is only temporary, it's going to pass."

It felt strange, me being the one to give him advice. It had always been the other way around.

"How do you stand it?" Gabriel asked softly. "The instability of human life. Why would you want to feel as they do? It's chaos. I cannot find space inside my head to think."

I smiled. "It's not for all of us."

When Gabriel looked at me, I noticed his eyes were darker,

like an internal storm was raging. For the first time he looked like he understood me, like he perhaps even identified with me a little.

"I know my actions were reckless," he said. "I hate myself for it."

"Don't." I put my hand on his broad shoulder. "You made a huge sacrifice for me. I wish you weren't suffering for it now, but you saved Xavier's life . . . and mine. Nobody is angry with you. We're here to help you get through this."

"Thank you," Gabriel murmured. "I hope it's a swift recovery. I feel as if I don't recognize myself."

"You know yourself, Gabe," I replied. "You've always known exactly who you are and what your purpose is." I squeezed his hand. "He might be buried right now, but the Gabriel we know and love is still in there. And don't you worry, he'll be back."

23

I Know Something You Don't

"YOU can't go back to school," Ivy told us.

Even though I knew it'd been coming, it still stung like a slap in the face. Ole Miss represented everything that had been remotely normal about our lives. Now I felt like Peter Pan, with my nose pressed up against the nursery window, looking in on the life I was forever barred from and the people that would soon forget me. Only Peter Pan got to stay young forever. I felt like Xavier and I were a hundred years old, world-weary with no will to fight anymore.

I longed to go back to school and start over with a clean slate. I wanted to go to class and football games and be surrounded by the buzz of human activity. But here was only the lonely ring of silence and the heavy weight of conversations yet to be had, hanging in the air. Xavier and I would always have each other but I didn't know anymore if that meant we shared the burden or doubled it. There was just too much destruction around us to comprehend. I wanted to make it all go away. I even missed Mary Ellen and longed to have a tedious conversation with her about nail polish or sorority rankings—anything that didn't revolve around the mess our lives had become.

Gabriel had disappeared somewhere in the woods without telling us where he was going. Ivy said he needed time to come to terms with what had happened.

"He might not be the same until his wings are fully restored," she said.

"Really?" I asked. "It's going to take that long?"

"Our wings are like our soul," she said drily. "Imagine if someone took a knife to your soul. It takes awhile to repair."

"I wish I could help him."

"You can't," my sister said, and I thought I detected a note of bitterness in her voice. I wouldn't be surprised if she blamed everything on me. I had set the ball in motion the moment I'd slipped that ring on my finger. But it was too late to change things now. Ivy gave a heavy sigh. "Just go and get your things from campus and come straight back. Don't talk to anyone if you can help it."

"Okay." I nodded. I'd caused enough trouble; the least I could do was obey this one request.

BACK on campus, I crept up to my dorm, praying Mary Ellen wouldn't be there and for the first time all week, I was in luck. I grabbed my bag out of the closet and started yanking clothes off the hangers, dumping them inside. It was a good thing I didn't have too many possessions and ten minutes later I was done. I decided I better leave Mary Ellen a note, in case she reported me missing to the school. I wracked my brains for what might seem an acceptable excuse for taking off a month into the semester. In the end I couldn't think of anything so I scrawled: "*Family emergency. Had to leave. Good luck for rush!*" I knew it wasn't even halfway plausible, but I hoped it might be enough to stop her from reporting anything.

I met Xavier outside and together we headed straight for the parking lot. He had been to his apartment, clearing out his room and like me, only had one bag crammed full of possessions. I knew why: Anything that wasn't a necessity had to be left behind. That was life on the run.

"What did you tell the boys?" I asked.

"Nothing," he said. "They weren't there."

I knew it hurt him to leave his friends in the lurch with no explanation. He had lived with them in close quarters and gotten to know them well. I knew they took the bond of brotherhood seriously. But what explanation could he possibly offer? Nobody would understand our sudden departure, not even the closest of friends.

As we loaded the car, I threw a last glance over my shoulder, trying to absorb as much of Ole Miss as possible and cement it in my memory. I wondered if I would ever see the leafy campus again, with its old buildings and fun-loving students—the perfect blend of the past and the present. I looked over the hill to where people were making their way to class in the sunshine, backpacks slung over their shoulders and textbooks bundled under their arms. They stopped to talk to one another and texted rapidly on their cell phones. It was so wonderfully normal. But I forced myself to tear my eyes away.

We were just slamming the trunk shut when a voice called out behind us.

"Hey! Where are y'all going?"

It was Clay, Xavier's former roommate. I spun around apologetically. Clay had been such a good friend to us both, he'd made us feel welcome and we both genuinely liked him.

"Hey, man," Xavier bit his lip. "We're taking a trip."

"Where?" Clay asked. "And where have you been?"

"I wish I could tell you," Xavier replied. "But I can't. You gotta trust me on this."

"Dude," Clay said in disbelief. "You can't just take off."

"There's no time to explain right now," I said. "But we have to go."

His gaze fell on my packed bag through the rear window. I'd been in such a hurry to leave that I hadn't even bothered to zip it up properly and my clothes were spilling out.

"You're not coming back, are you?" Clay looked wounded. "And you weren't going to tell us?"

"We wanted to," I told him. "But the less you know about us the better. We don't want to drag you into our mess."

Clay's eyes widened. "What have you done?" he asked.

Before I could respond, I felt Xavier grab my wrist. I diverted my attention from Clay for a moment and saw it. The Seven was standing just a few meters to the right. It was dressed in the same long black coat, its hands buried deep in the pockets. Its hideous empty eye sockets seemed to be staring right at us. I couldn't help myself—I gasped aloud and Clay spun around.

"What?" he asked nervously. "What's the matter?"

I realized with a start that he couldn't see it. It was standing right behind him and he was completely oblivious to its presence. After the last debacle, the Seven was making itself visible only to those it hunted. Was that an edict handed down by the Covenant? Or were they just playing it safe?

"Get in the car!" Xavier shouted as he flung open his door and twisted the key in the ignition.

"Go home, Clay!" I yelled as I jumped in the passenger seat. "You need to leave now!"

"What the heck!" Clay cried as Xavier reversed out of his space and hit the gas, pulling out of the parking lot at breakneck speed. The Seven didn't give chase—it never did. It just watched and waited. I knew it would come after us, in its own sweet time.

Xavier didn't slow down until we were outside of Oxford, on the open road. Even then, the tension didn't let up. We were so sick of being pursued and yet we couldn't give in; we knew what the consequences of that would be.

"You should pull over," I told him once the town was a safe distance behind us. "We need to call Gabriel and Ivy, let them know what happened."

Ordinarily, we would have gone home, but we didn't want to lead the Seven straight to our hiding place. It was safer to make a break for it and let my siblings deal with the rest. I hoped the added stress wouldn't worsen Gabriel's condition.

"I can't stop here," Xavier said. "This road is too exposed."

"Good thinking." I pointed to a disused barn up ahead. "See there? Pull up around back and I'll call from inside so we're out of view."

Xavier swung the car off the road and parked it close to the weathered old barn. Graying bales of hay were stacked inside and I could see rusted machinery that looked like it hadn't been used for years.

"I'll make it quick," I promised as I ducked inside. Xavier paced agitatedly while I punched numbers into my cell.

"What's happened?" Ivy's voice was tense with worry when she picked up. They must have already sensed we had a situation on our hands.

"A Seven," I said breathlessly. "One turned up just as we were leaving."

"I told you to make it quick!" Ivy burst out.

"Don't yell at me," I countered. "We were only there half an hour!"

"Okay." I heard her exhale loudly. "Where are you now?"

"Just off the highway outside of Oxford. We're still in Lafayette County."

"Stay right where you are," she instructed. "We're coming to get you."

"Okay," I lowered my voice. "Is Gabriel . . . will he come with you?"

"Maybe this is just what he needs," Ivy replied. "To snap him out of it. You stay low and stay hidden. Don't go out in the open. We'll see you soon."

The line went dead as she hung up and I turned to face Xavier.

"They're coming," I said, forcing a tight-lipped smile. "We shouldn't worry."

Xavier crossed the barn, loose straw crunching under his shoes, and kicked at a haystack. In his checked shirt and worn leather boots, he looked comfortable in this environment. A piece of machinery hanging overhead groaned and swayed. Xavier glanced up and knitted his brows together above his vibrant blue eyes. I tried to walk across to him, but tripped myself up on a bucket full of muddy water.

"This place is a death trap," he said with a smile as he helped me up and brushed off my clothes.

"We won't be here long," I replied.

"I almost wish they would find us." He sighed. "So we can get this over with."

"They're not going to get us," I said forcefully. "I won't let it happen."

"We're going to have to face them eventually," he said. "We can't run forever."

"We don't know what will happen if they find us," I argued. "We can't risk it."

"Yeah, well, this game of cat and mouse is getting old."

"I agree," said a rasping voice.

We both looked up to see the Seven standing before us in his long black overcoat, blocking the entrance to the barn. I glanced around but there was no feasible point of escape. I grabbed Xavier's arm and held on tight as if that would keep us from being torn apart.

"At last," the Seven said. "You two have been eluding us for quite a while."

"Take a hint," Xavier said boldly. "We don't want to be friends."

"How amusing," the Seven said drily.

"Why can't you leave us alone?" I positioned myself in front of Xavier even though he was a good head and shoulders taller than me.

"I'm afraid that is impossible."

"What exactly do you want from us?" Xavier asked, lifting me up easily and pushing me behind him.

"We want to restore order," the Seven answered in his sandpaper monotone. "It is our job to keep the peace."

"Good job on that so far." Xavier gave him a sarcastic thumbs-up.

"Look, I get it," I said, suddenly exhausted. "I know it's against all our rules to be in love with a human but it's done now. There's nothing I can do to change it."

"Human." The Seven smiled. "Is that what you think he is?"

"Excuse me?" I demanded.

"Hey." Xavier straightened, slightly offended. "What the heck is that supposed to mean?"

"You really don't know, do you?" the Seven mused, like he found this information greatly satisfying.

"No, so why don't you fill in the gaps?" I replied.

"There are forces surrounding this boy."

"Care to elaborate?" Xavier snapped. The Seven's smug attitude was getting on his nerves.

"We lost track of you, all those years ago," the Seven said. "You disappeared in a sea of human chaos. But we always knew one day you would find your way back. And so you have."

"What are you talking about?" I insisted. "I thought you were looking for me."

"We were," the angel replied. "Until we discovered his true identity. Now he must serve us."

"Hey, he's not your property," I said, overcome with indignation.

Xavier moved closer to me so our shoulders were touching. "And I'm not your servant."

I felt my heart drop to my shoes as the realization sank in. They were no longer after me, coming to dole out my punishment and drag me back to my former home. It was worse—they wanted Xavier.

"What do you want from him?" I choked out.

"We have plans for him," the Seven said, twisting his smooth bald head and pointing a crooked finger at Xavier. "Heaven needs you."

"What are you, Uncle Sam?" Xavier said gruffly. "Earth needs me. I have a life; I have a family. And I'm not leaving Beth."

"I anticipated as much," the Seven said, and he thrust out a palm toward us.

But before his power could touch us, I reached out and grabbed Xavier's hand, letting all the anger and regret that had welled up inside me surge through my body.

"It's just us," I told him. "Us against the world."

Xavier's hand tightened around mine and then, for the first time, I felt a different power mingling with my own and realized it was coming from him. It wasn't angelic like Ivy or Gabriel might produce but it certainly wasn't human. It tasted like sunshine and my mind flooded with a beautiful aqua blue that made my worry wash away like a receding tide. It rippled and danced and I realized it was water, cool, refreshing life-giving water. I felt a breeze rush through my body, followed by a pulsing heat and then a solidness that seemed to plant my feet firmly on the ground, like not even a tornado could move me.

And then, slowly, it dawned on me; air, water, fire, earth. I was experiencing all the elements in a single rush. But I wasn't producing the sensations—my power felt like light; bright, blazing white light that made you feel as though you were floating. This power was coming from Xavier. He was an embodiment of the earth and that's what I could feel surging from his fingertips. Everything magnificent the earth could produce, the strongest forces of nature, seemed to be flowing from his body. What did that mean? Were the elements under his control? All I knew was that Xavier seemed to have Mother Nature on his side, as if Our Father were commanding the very earth itself to rise up and stand by him. Xavier's eyes were shut and I knew I couldn't disturb him. Instead, I focused on contributing every scrap of energy I had on letting our abilities feed one another.

So when the Seven's power reached us, it seemed to hit an invisible shield and shattered into a thousand pieces of clay on the ground. He conjured a shimmering, opal-colored orb in his hands and hurled it at us, like a shot put. This time, it burst into flame a foot away from us and the cinders floated down like glowing confetti. The next orb exploded in a dazzling arc of water, drenching the Seven from head to foot.

"What trickery is this?" the Seven hissed.

"Walk away," Xavier said darkly. "You can't touch us."

"My power usurps yours," the Seven said, although he didn't sound so confident anymore.

"Yeah?" Xavier asked. "Prove it."

"Arrogant boy." The Seven made a low growling noise in the back of his throat.

"Yep, that's me." Xavier shrugged.

The Seven dropped back a few paces. "You should know that surrender is imminent," he said. "You cannot fight us indefinitely."

"Oh, well, we'll do our best."

"Very well," the creature said. "But you are only delaying the inevitable."

And then with a sound like flapping wings, he was gone.

Xavier dropped my hand and bent over, bracing his hands on his knees. A slight sheen of sweat had broken out across his brow.

"Crap," he exhaled. "What was that?"

"I . . . I don't know," I replied. "I think it was you."

"No." He shook his head, still breathing heavily. "It was us."

"We took on a Seven?" I almost laughed at the absurdity of it. "Without help? We really made it leave."

"Yeah, we did." Xavier's brilliant azure eyes fell on me and he smiled. "I guess we're stronger than we thought."

And it seemed we were. When Gabriel and Ivy turned up a few moments later, the crisis had passed. There was nothing left for them to do. We had saved ourselves.

24

The Best-Kept Secret

THERE was a conversation waiting to be had. Xavier and I both knew it as we followed my siblings back to the house. We may have been reveling in our single-handed defeat of one of Heaven's most notorious hunters, but we couldn't ignore what he'd said. "*Human? Is that what you think he is?*" The words kept ringing in my head. What was that supposed to mean? Of course Xavier was human. I'd seen him bleed. I'd seen him nearly die. That classified him as human, right? I concluded the Seven had just been trying to rattle us. Ivy and Gabriel would clear everything up when we got home.

Back in the kitchen, Xavier hesitated in the doorway.

"All right, out with it," Gabriel said. "What did he tell you?"

My brother seemed better than he was a few days ago, but still not quite himself. He was more impatient and unwilling to skirt around the truth. The old Gabriel might have worded things more tactfully, tried to steer the conversation naturally in the direction he wanted. But he wasn't wasting time and cut straight to the point. It was sort of refreshing.

"He said I wasn't human." Xavier folded his arms. "And

that Heaven needs me, they have plans for me or something. That's crazy, right?"

"Xavier, there's something you have to understand," Ivy began.

"Oh, for goodness sake," Gabriel interjected. "Just tell them. It's time they knew anyway."

"Time we knew what?" I asked warily. I didn't like the sound of this. "What have you been hiding?"

Ivy pressed her slender fingers against her temples. "Maybe you should sit down. This isn't going to be easy on any of us."

"Okay." Xavier gave an uneasy laugh. "You're really starting to freak me out. What's going on?"

"Just sit?" Ivy implored. "Please?"

I tugged Xavier down onto the couch beside me and knotted the patchwork quilt beneath my fingers. Gabriel was staring solemnly out the window, waiting for Ivy to begin. I noticed she couldn't keep her hands still and it took a lot to rattle her that way.

"I suppose I should start at the beginning," she said absently.

"Is this gonna be a long story?" Xavier said. "Because I'd rather cut to the chase."

"Just listen," my sister said heavily. "It won't make sense otherwise." She cast a loaded look at Gabriel, who nodded encouragingly. "The last time I was on earth was almost twenty years ago. I was headed to Charlotte but I miscalculated and landed in Birmingham. I didn't plan to speak to anyone, but I met a couple whose car had broken down and they asked to borrow my cell phone. We got to talking and they told me they were there visiting a fertility clinic. But it wasn't working. They couldn't conceive."

"That's very interesting," I said. "But I don't see how it relates to us."

Gabriel held up his hand. "Let her finish. You have to hear the full story."

"I shouldn't have gotten involved." My sister shook her head. "But the woman told me they'd been praying for a miracle. I couldn't walk away when I had the power to help them."

"What did you do?" I asked.

"I gave them a child," Ivy murmured. "When the woman left me that day, she was pregnant although she didn't know it. I restored her body to full health so she would be able to conceive in the future."

"You acted without consent?" I said. "Did Heaven try to punish you?"

"I brought punishment upon myself."

"What does that mean?"

"Nothing happened for a long time." Ivy sighed. "But I eventually found out the couple had given birth to a son and have since had five more healthy children."

I saw Xavier shift uncomfortably beside me. "What happened to the kid?"

"My involvement went no further than his conception," Ivy said. "I left him alone to live a normal life. I never expected to see him again."

"I don't believe it," I whispered. "How come you never told us?"

"I was ashamed of myself," Ivy said. "And after I berated

you for getting too involved in human life, how could I reveal what I had done? I was a hypocrite."

"Oh, Ivy," I said. "You could have trusted me of all people. I would have understood."

"Bethany, I'm not finished," my sister cut in. "There's more. Heaven told me I would see the boy again, that one way or another he would come back and merge with the world of angels."

"You mean we're going to meet him?"

Gabriel turned to look me straight in the eye. "Bethany, you already have."

My mind struggled to grasp the information being thrown at me. "I don't understand. . . ." I said.

"I do," Xavier spoke in a hoarse voice. "Whatever you're trying to say just spit it out."

My sister lifted her gaze slowly. "The couple I met all those years ago—their names were Peter and Bernadette Woods. The child is you. I'm so sorry, Xavier."

There was a long silence. It felt as though the earth itself were at a standstill. Xavier didn't move. He sat very quietly, staring at his hands. We all waited for him to speak. Gabriel sat down and put a tentative hand on his shoulder. Xavier shook him off and jumped up.

"Xavier, please try and stay calm," said my sister.

"Calm?" Xavier let out a short laugh. "You just told me that I'm some kind of Immaculate Conception miracle child and I'm supposed to stay calm?"

"You are still human," said Ivy urgently. "You are flesh and blood, just not quite the same as everybody else."

"How long have you known about this?" Xavier asked suddenly.

"Since I first met you." Ivy couldn't quite meet his gaze. "We weren't sure initially but it soon became clear. That's part of the reason we tried so hard to keep you and Bethany apart. Any ordinary human would not have been able to handle the reality of our world—we would have wiped their memory and moved on. But you . . . you were different."

"You've known all this time?" Xavier looked genuinely devastated. "And you waited till now to tell me?"

"You had other things on your mind," Ivy said pleadingly. "Your journey has not been easy; I didn't want to add to your burden."

"My brothers and sisters?" Xavier asked in a tight voice. "Are they . . . ?"

"They were all naturally conceived. I only took part in *your* creation."

"So . . ." Xavier sounded a little bit sick. "Are you . . . does that make you . . . like . . . are you my mother?"

The alarm that surged through me was uncontainable.

"Oh God," I moaned. "Please no."

"I am not your mother," Ivy said firmly. "I do not have DNA that can be transferred. You are Bernadette's child. But I gave you our essence, our spirit. The blood of angels runs in your veins, but so does the blood of your human parents."

"So what the hell am I then? Angel or human?"

"I suppose you are both," Ivy replied.

"Great. This is so messed up."

"I didn't want you to find out this way."

"There isn't really a good time to find out you're some kind of freaky half-breed," Xavier said scathingly.

"Don't say that," I told him. "You're the same person you've always been."

"How do you figure, Beth?" he asked.

"You've always known you were extraordinary," I said. "Fate wouldn't have brought us together otherwise. You've survived so much, you've got so much strength, and now you know why."

"What do the Sevens want with me?" Xavier asked. "What do they think I can do for them?"

"Halflings have powers," Gabriel said. "Powers we don't quite understand. I'm guessing they want to find out what they are."

"So they want to use me?" Xavier asked in a hard voice. "Like some kind of lab rat?"

"Probably." Gabriel didn't bat an eyelid.

"Surely I'm not the first . . ." Xavier rolled his eyes at the word. "Halfling."

"You're the first one they've found," Gabriel answered. "There have been others over time, but the angels that created them were not forthcoming about their whereabouts and for the most part, they live out normal human lives. That doesn't make them easy to track."

"And now that they've found me . . ." Xavier trailed off.

"Now that they know your identity they will not relent," Ivy said. "But we will do everything in our power to protect you."

"They want you and Bethany separated," Gabriel said.

"Especially after what happened today. Your combined powers are too strong, they feel threatened."

"Are you saying if we weren't together they'd leave us alone?" I asked in disbelief.

"They would continue to monitor Xavier and watch him from afar," Gabriel replied. "But he wouldn't pose such an immediate threat."

"He's not a threat now!" I cried. "He hasn't done anything!"

"The Sevens are competitive creatures," Ivy said glumly. "They know your alliance overpowers them and they can't deal with that."

"What if we promise to keep to ourselves?"

"That would hardly make a difference," Gabriel said. "You must understand how they work by now."

"Okay." I bit my lip and tried to keep my hands from fidgeting. "What do we do now?"

"They'll be back," Ivy said. "And this time we'll be ready for them."

WHEN Ivy and Gabriel left us alone, I waited for Xavier to speak. This was a lot to take in and he must have a hundred things on his mind right now, unanswered questions and accusations of blame.

"So this is . . ." He lifted his hands and let them fall limply on the couch. "I don't know what to say."

"Xavier . . ." I began, but he cut me off.

"How could I not know? There must have been signs. Did I just miss them?"

"There *were* signs," I insisted. "Just nothing you took notice of. I mean think about everything that's happened since you and I first met. How many people could watch their friends die in front of their eyes, how many people could witness a full-blown exorcism and not be traumatized? How many people could break into Hell to save someone they love? And how many people could be possessed by Lucifer, literally have him inside them, and survive? You're special, Xavier. The angels chose you."

He stared into space. "I just feel like I don't know who I am anymore."

"No," I said, shaking my head vigorously. "No, it's the exact opposite. *Now* you know who you are. You're blessed and you're on a path that will lead to great things. God is looking out for you."

"It seems like I'm just pissing Him off," Xavier answered in a dull voice.

"The Sevens," I corrected. "You're pissing the Sevens off. But God loves you. He's marked you as one of His own."

"Then why is everything so hard?" Xavier looked at me intently, needing my answer to make sense. "Why does it seem like we're being punished?"

"Because the path of the righteous man was never supposed to be easy," I whispered. "Those who are chosen by the Lord are given a hard journey. The rewards will come later. And if He is the merciful Father I know, we'll have eternal peace together. You just have to believe in Him. Believe in His plan and trust Him with your whole heart. I know it's hard but look at the proof you've been given through my siblings and me. Most people have to go on blind faith, but not you. You've been given proof."

"Okay." Xavier looked at me, a pensive expression in his turquoise eyes. "Okay . . ." he repeated. I knew it must be a lot to take in and we couldn't rush him.

"Wait . . ." A sudden thought occurred to me. "You two were always talking about how I'm different, how I *feel things* I shouldn't for a human. Could this be why? Because Xavier isn't"—I caught myself just in time—"entirely human?"

"It's the most likely explanation," Gabriel replied. "The bond you share surpasses the human experience. Otherwise, it's unlikely your relationship would have survived so many hurdles."

"Are you saying I wouldn't love her if I were normal?" Xavier asked sharply.

"No," Gabriel's voice was steady. "I'm saying you may not have had the resources to cope with the things you've seen and the truths that have been revealed to you."

"Xavier." Ivy put her hand on his shoulder. "The blood of angels flows in your veins. It means angels will always be with you. It means you are protected and you are destined to be a protector of men. But the choice is yours. You can take this knowledge and do something with it or you can pretend you never found out."

"I don't think that's an option," Xavier replied. "I guess I just need time to process."

I didn't know why the new information wasn't rocking my world. I supposed it was because Xavier already rocked my world and the idea that his creation was extraordinary seemed natural to me. In my mind, he had never been an average human; his presence was like fireworks and even just hearing his name made my knees weaken. Of course he was special, how could he not be? I supposed the fact that my sister had a hand in his conception was a little weird but I had to keep reminding myself that Ivy was not my biological sister. We were connected to a greater heavenly family but there was no shared DNA. That was uniquely human.

And so I accepted the fact that Xavier was a Halfling with little question. If anything, I was a little proud.

{ 25 }

Watch Me Burn

WE all agreed there was no point in trying to calculate when the Sevens might attack next. We were through with schemes and strategies. We knew what we could do now and we were not afraid. Of course, the fight wasn't over, but I doubted the Sevens had much more up their sleeves that could rattle us.

Xavier was still trying to wrap his head around the concept that angelic blood flowed in his veins and didn't seem to want to talk about it further with anyone. I didn't press the issue, knowing he would need time to come to terms with such staggering information. So instead, I decided to worry about Molly.

The next afternoon, I dragged Xavier out of the house to come and look for her. She'd been avoiding us since the spectacle with Gabriel in the kitchen and I was worried about her. Oxford was a small town, there weren't too many places to hide and we eventually found her, sitting in a corner of Starbucks frowning at her phone, a crumbled scone on a plate beside her. Xavier and I decided to act as if nothing had happened.

"Bad news?" asked Xavier sneaking up behind her.

"No," she said, quickly putting her phone facedown. Molly had never been a good liar.

"Why the long face then? Your manicurist out of town?"

"Ha ha. Very funny." Her smile froze on her lips.

I noticed Molly looked different. Her unruly curls had been tamed into a long braid that hung over one shoulder like a flame-colored rope. She'd abandoned her customary Nike shorts and T-shirt for a high-collared floral blouse and faded jeans, which she'd teamed with tennis shoes. The old Molly wouldn't have been caught dead wearing jeans and tennis shoes.

It was definitely a new look for her and I figured it must have been an attempt to win favor with Wade. Her wide blue eyes lacked their usual luster but seemed to brighten when she saw us. She peered closely as we pulled up chairs to join her and the Molly I knew seemed to surface for a moment. "You two look like crap!"

"Gee, thanks!" said Xavier.

"Sorry, but you seriously need more sleep and less sex."

Xavier gave her a forced smile. "It's nothing like that."

There was a pause, neither party wanting to bring up the scene with Gabriel when we'd last seen her. But Molly seemed happy to pretend it never happened. Was she scared of getting hurt again?

"So what's up?" she asked. "How are things?"

"They've settled down a little," I answered carefully.

"There's always another crisis with y'all," Molly said, exasperated.

"Yeah." I nodded. "But listen, at the moment it looks like we won't be able to come back to school."

"No way! You are not disappearing on me again!"

"Of course not," I said quickly. "We'll still be in town, you just won't be seeing us on campus. We've told people there was a family emergency, so if anybody asks, that's the story. Tell them that's all you know."

"Okay." Molly traced the rim of her cup with her fingertip. "I guess I'll pray for you."

Xavier raised his eyebrows. It wasn't the idea that surprised him; it was just hearing those words coming from Molly. She kept her eyes downcast as she spoke, as if she was simply repeating what she knew Wade wanted her to say.

"Thanks," Xavier replied lightly, letting the moment pass.

"So will I be able to come see you?" Molly asked.

"Sure," I said encouragingly. "Anytime you want. Just call ahead."

Molly nodded, but she seemed a little unsettled, sneaking furtive looks at the entrance. I had the feeling it was more than our nomadic lives that was causing her jumpiness.

"But you can't tell anyone where we are," Xavier added. "Not even Wade."

"Don't worry; I can keep my mouth shut."

"Good," said Xavier. "We trust you."

It was warm in the confined space of the café. When Molly unthinkingly pushed up the sleeves of her sweater I saw bruising that wrapped around one of her wrists, like someone had grabbed her with extreme force. It was already fading, tinged with yellowish green at the edges.

"Molly, what happened to your arm?"

She pulled down her sleeve, suddenly self-conscious. "I'm such a klutz. I fell down some steps wearing high heels."

"Where were you?"

"At a frat party."

"With Wade?"

"No! He doesn't know so please don't tell him. He wouldn't approve."

"He sounds a bit controlling," Xavier ventured. "If you can't even be honest with him."

"No, no, he isn't," Molly insisted. "Wade's good for me. I just need some time to catch up to where he is spiritually."

"How are you going to do that?"

"Well . . ." Molly frowned. "I'm not exactly sure. But Wade has a plan."

"Sure he does," Xavier muttered, and glanced up. "Speak of the devil."

We all looked up then to see Wade walking through the door in a crisp polo buttoned up to the neck.

"Oh, no." Molly grabbed my hand under the table. "You won't tell him anything, will you?"

It was the first time she'd mentioned it. I knew she must be repressing a whole lot of emotions and it wasn't healthy. But we would deal with that later.

"I would never," I said, almost offended. "What kind of friend do you take me for?"

"Thanks." Molly bit her lip and slipped her phone into her bag as Wade approached. She couldn't wipe the guilty look off her face and Wade, of course, picked up on it. But he greeted us with a gracious smile.

"Hi. What are y'all gossiping about?"

"Girl stuff," said Molly.

"With Xavier here?"

"We think of him as one of the girls."

"I usually tune out," Xavier corrected, eliciting a sympathetic chuckle from the usually poker-faced Wade as he bent to plant a dutiful peck on Molly's cheek. Wade frowned and pulled away suddenly.

"Molly, is that lip gloss I smell?"

"You noticed! It's new. It's called Strawberry Fields, or Strawberry Kiss, or something like that."

"I thought we agreed you weren't going to wear makeup anymore." His reproving look made Molly's cheeks color.

"Wade, I wouldn't exactly call lip gloss *makeup*."

She flicked glances at us for support, but Xavier and I were too surprised to say anything.

"Does it enhance the natural appearance of your lips?"

"Um . . . I guess so. Yeah."

"Then, Molly, you don't need it. You're perfect the way God made you. Why would you tamper with His work?"

"I'm sorry." She hung her head. "I never thought of it that way."

"That's because it's so easy to be sucked in by the lies cosmetic companies feed women. But it's the Devil's work, don't you agree, Xavier?"

"Uh . . . yeah." Xavier and I exchanged awkward looks. "But it's not that big of a deal. Molly's always worn it."

"And now she's trying to better herself," Wade interrupted. "Is it in your handbag?"

"What?"

"The lip gloss." The way he said it, the offending item might as well have been illicit drugs she'd stashed in there. Molly fished out a pink-tinged cylinder with a gold tip. I couldn't see the label but I could tell it was from a higher-end cosmetic line. It had probably taken her ages to pick out. Wade held out his hand.

"Hand it over. It'll be easier if I dispose of it for you."

I looked expectantly at Molly, waiting for a burst of outrage or at least a snide remark, but neither was forthcoming. She just kept her eyes lowered as Wade pocketed the item in question.

"But Molly likes makeup," I proclaimed. It was a challenge rather than an observation. "Why should she give it up?"

"Beth, leave it," Molly said.

"It's okay, honey." Wade looked at me with his flat eyes. "Beth is entitled to her opinions. She's probably too naïve to realize the damaging messages behind advertising."

"It's just lip gloss," I said helplessly. There was a barely perceptible headshake from Xavier hinting that now might not be the time to engage in a heated debate.

"Cosmetics by their very nature objectify women," Wade said. "How can you justify their use?"

Xavier got up suddenly and looked around at us all.

"I'm getting a frappe. Anyone want anything?"

"I'll have a vanilla latte," I said.

Wade shook his head to indicate he wouldn't be joining us. "I think we'd better get going." He began to help Molly gather up her things but she seemed reluctant to part company with us. "Do you want to get an early dinner or something?" she suggested. "Do y'all have time?"

"Sure," Xavier answered. "Beth, you up for it?"

Wade coughed conspicuously to get Molly's attention. "Um, sweetie, we've got a Bible Study to get to. Don't tell me you forgot?"

"Oh, dang." Molly looked torn for a moment. "It's just that I haven't spent time with my friends in ages."

"Don't worry," Wade said. "I can go without you. You go ahead and catch up with your friends." His words said one thing but his domineering body language told a different story. The folded arms and tapping foot told us he wouldn't be happy if Molly bailed on him. She squirmed indecisively.

"Don't worry," I reassured her. "We'll do dinner another time."

"Okay." Molly hurried to Wade's side but looked back at me longingly over her shoulder. "Don't forget."

"Not a chance."

"Okay. I'll text you tomorrow."

"Molly . . ." Wade cut in. The sound of his voice was really starting to get on my nerves. "We really have to leave if we're not going to be late. You know how much I hate being the last to arrive."

"Coming!"

Wade threw an arm around Molly and steered her out of the café. I watched them leave, thinking his grip on her shoulder was too tight. Xavier came back with our drinks.

"Boy, that dude is weird," he said, setting my coffee down in front of me.

"Definitely," I confirmed. "Should we be worried?"

"I don't know. Molly's not a kid. She's makes her own decisions."

"Do you get the feeling she was reaching out to us . . . like, for help?"

Xavier frowned. "She knows we're here if she needs us, right?"

"Yeah, but what if she's in over her head?" I persisted.

"I guess we'll find out," Xavier said. "But you'll never get anywhere with Molly by confronting her. She has to come to you herself."

I didn't get the nature of Molly's relationship with Wade, but I'd seen enough of it to know it couldn't be healthy. The fact that they were together at all didn't sit right with me. He wasn't her type and it was obvious she had trouble asserting herself with him. I couldn't help thinking she had thrown herself into this relationship as a way of trying to get over Gabriel. And now she was engaged. It must be confusing to say the least. I silently admonished myself for being so preoccupied by my own problems that I'd hardly noticed what was going on in the life of my best friend. But I wasn't going to let Molly make a huge mistake. One way or another, I had to get her out of this.

Later at the house, I brought it up at the dinner table,

relaying the exchange in the café while Ivy was heaping my plate with barbecue and salad.

"I have a bad feeling about Molly being with Wade."

"What makes you say that?" my sister asked. Gabriel, who was standing at the bench, didn't even look up.

"Can you believe he objects to her wearing lip gloss?"

"That makes him controlling, not a serial killer," said my sister. "Don't be too quick to judge."

"What should we do about it?"

"Nothing; it's not for us to interfere in other people's relationships. Molly will let us know if she needs us."

"That's what I said," Xavier added, cracking open a can of Coke and throwing me a look to say *I told you so.*

"What if she's too scared?"

"Do you have any evidence that she's in danger?" asked Ivy.

"No."

"Then I think you should stay out of it."

"She did have these bruises," I said. For some strange reason bringing that up felt like betraying Molly's confidence.

Gabriel finally lifted his head. "Bruises?" he echoed.

He'd refrained from commenting until now. In fact, I'd hardly spoken to him since that night in the basement. A few times I'd woken up in the middle of the night, gone downstairs to get water, and found his bedroom empty. He'd been keeping to himself as he tried to heal and like Molly, he hadn't mentioned their encounter again. I didn't think they'd even spoken to one another, both opting to pretend like it never happened. But Gabriel seemed to bristle at the idea of someone hurting her.

"On the inside of her arm. When I asked about it, she said she'd fallen over from wearing high heels."

"Sounds plausible," said Ivy.

But Gabriel had straightened up and was shaking his head.

"Not for Molly," he muttered.

"Huh?" Xavier wasn't following.

"Molly's been wearing heels since the fifth grade," I said. "I've never seen her even stumble. And besides, how do you fall so you manage to bruise only your wrist?"

"I don't know." Xavier twisted his hand at different angles, trying to work it out. "I guess it could happen."

"Maybe we should go and check on her," Gabriel suggested. "Just to make sure."

"But I just made dinner." Ivy looked put out.

"Hold on," Xavier interrupted. "How are you going to explain just turning up? It's kind of weird, don't you think?"

"We don't have to speak to her," I countered. "I just want to check up on things, make sure she's okay. Then we can leave."

"Where are they right now?" asked Gabe.

"Bible study."

"Okay. Let's head out there."

IN the fading sunlight, the campus chapel was beautiful with its bell tower and archways. It operated as a sanctuary in the heart of the bustling campus. Stepping through its doors was always like entering another, quieter dimension where worldly cares could no longer reach you. I wondered if Wade had permission to use this place for his meetings.

The door was open and a strange hypnotic voice reached us. It didn't sound like any kind of Bible study to me and I guessed that was simply the excuse Wade had given the school in order to use the facility.

"The only way to conquer the flesh it to mortify it," the voice was saying. "To crush it, to tear it down."

Gabriel and Xavier looked at one another and my brother scowled. I tiptoed forward to peer around the door, far enough to see what was going on inside without disclosing our presence. Inside, I could see a group of about ten people gathered. Wade was the speaker and three other men stood by him. The rest were girls and they were kneeling in the pews. But Molly was before the altar and for some unbeknownst reason she was stripped of her clothes, right down to a silk undergarment, which looked like it belonged in a different century. Even from my distance I could see she had goose bumps along her arms and her alabaster skin was mottled pink from the chill inside the chapel. Wade's eyes were burning with intensity and he was so engrossed in what he was saying he barely looked in our direction. He seemed to be speaking only to Molly.

"You must acknowledge your weakness before the Lord. You must reject those who will lead you astray and commit to a life of contemplation."

"I know," Molly murmured. She nodded but looked less sure of herself than she actually sounded.

"I want to help you but you have to work with me, Molly," Wade said. "Are you ready to commit your life to this church?"

"I'm ready."

"Are you ready to make the sacrifices required to serve as you should?"

Was this some kind of weird initiation?

"I am," Molly whispered, but Wade wasn't finished yet.

"To cast aside worldly vanity as a sign of your devotion?"

"Yes." Her voice was muffled now as if close to tears.

Wade strode across to where Molly was kneeling, looming over her like the figure of an executioner. He had something in his hand that I couldn't make out until he lifted his arm above his head. Then the light coming from the stained glass windows hit the metal and I realized it was a pair of scissors.

"Only when we master the weaknesses of the flesh can we be truly free." He picked up the rope of hair with his free hand as if weighing it. Was Molly really going to let him do that to her? With her face scrubbed free of makeup, her freckles were highlighted and she looked like a child. I glanced across at Gabriel, whose features had turned to stone and his silver eyes narrowed into angry slits.

"Step away from her." His voice seemed to bounce off the walls of the chapel. Wade, caught by surprise, lowered his arm and looked around for the intruder. When he saw me, he recovered his composure a little, although Gabriel's presence had clearly thrown him.

"Who are you?" he demanded. He glared at Molly. "Did you ask them to come?"

"No," she stammered, getting shakily to her feet. "I . . . I . . ." She looked around uncertainly, from Wade to Gabriel and back again. Then Gabriel said her name, not like he was calling her or commanding her to do anything. He just said it softly to himself like he was truly saddened seeing her like this. And then Molly broke. She twisted herself free of Wade's grasp and stumbled forward, running straight into Gabriel's arms, where she collapsed, sobbing.

Wade lifted his hands helplessly, like he didn't know what to do. Molly still had her face buried in Gabriel's chest and his hand rested protectively on the back of her head.

"What crazy notions has he filled your head with?" he murmured.

"Prayer and fasting bring us closer to God," Wade shouted defensively. "Only then does He reveal his true purpose to us as he did to Daniel."

"Daniel was a prophet, you moron," I replied.

"Beth, that's enough. Insults serve no purpose."

"But he's crazy."

"He is just very misguided," Gabriel said. "The path to God is a personal journey. Wade, you cannot force it upon someone by locking them up and cutting off their hair."

Molly raised her head to look at him, the tip of her nose red from crying. "I was trying to atone for my past sins, because I realized that's why you couldn't love me back."

Gabriel closed his eyes for a moment. "Molly, you atone through changing your life, not having someone change it for you."

"Going to church doesn't make you a Christian any more than sitting in a garage makes you a car," I said, quoting a book I'd read awhile back. "It's about how you feel inside, Molly, and you're just miserable right now."

"Molly, don't listen to them. You're a sinner," Wade said. "You're evil and I'm the only one who can redeem you."

"Christ is the only one who can redeem anyone," I yelled at him. "You have one massive God-complex, buddy!"

"Who are you to judge her?" Gabriel asked, fixing his gaze on Wade. "You are just as much a sinner as anyone else."

"She's a woman." Wade shook his head. "That makes her corrupt and lustful by nature. It was Eve who introduced man to sin. That makes me more righteous than she'll ever be."

"Really?" Gabriel said. "What an interesting interpretation."

"Molly, you're making a big mistake," Wade said, ignoring my brother. "I'm trying to help you because I love you."

"Don't make me laugh," I snorted.

"You—" Gabriel pointed a finger at Wade. "If I see you speaking to her again you'll have me to answer to. Got it?"

"And who do you think you are?" Wade's confidence had returned. He wasn't about to give Molly up to a stranger without a fight.

Gabriel gave a slight smile as the lights began to flicker and the windowpanes rattled. The door of the chapel burst open and a powerful wind swirled around him. "You have no idea."

Wade took several steps back in alarm and his little congregation gasped. They may not have known exactly who Gabriel was, but it was clear they were in the presence of greatness. Gabriel took hold of the metal clasp that held Molly's braid in place and removed it. She remained perfectly still while he shook her hair free so that it fell like a mahogany waterfall. Then without saying another word, we ushered her outside.

"We were going to get married," said Molly forlornly once we were back in Gabriel's car.

"That wasn't about love," said Gabriel. "It's always been about power."

"I sure know how to choose guys. What is wrong with me?"

"Everyone makes bad decisions sometimes," Gabriel replied.

It was strange the way he included himself in the observation. The old Gabriel might have commented that to err was the nature of humans, but this time it seemed he was right there with us, rather than watching from afar.

"Really?" Molly wiped her nose with a tissue Xavier had handed her. "So you're not all judging me?"

"No, that was Wade," Xavier replied. "Not us."

She sniffed and stared out the car window. "I just feel like such a failure at everything."

"You're not," Gabriel replied from the driver's seat. "You're just young and confused. It's normal."

"How long did it take you to get so wise?"

My brother looked at her through the rearview mirror. "Give or take two thousand years."

Even through her tears, Molly had to smile. "One day you'll find your place in the world," Gabriel said. "And all this will be nothing but a distant memory."

I couldn't help but wonder if he included himself in that statement. Years from now would he too be nothing but a fading image in Molly's mind? All I knew was that my brother wasn't easy to forget and I could tell from the look on her face that Molly knew it too.

26

Take Me Home

MOLLY was still rattled from the scene in the chapel, and even Gabriel's reassuring presence couldn't stop her from shivering.

"It's okay, Molly," Gabriel leaned in to whisper. "It's over. Wade won't hurt you anymore."

"Molly should probably stay with us for a while," I suggested. "Just until things settle down."

"Good idea," Gabriel agreed. "I don't like the idea of her being alone right now."

"Thanks," Molly said in a small, plaintive voice. "I'm sorry I've been so stupid about everything."

"It's not your fault," Xavier said. "We all misjudge people sometimes."

"I've messed up worse than you," I added. "I once thought Jake Thorn just needed a friend."

Xavier wrapped a comforting arm around my shoulder, as if he would have liked to erase those bad memories from my past.

EVEN before we pulled up outside the house, we knew something was wrong. The trash can lay on the sidewalk, its contents spilled onto the path like someone had violently kicked it over. Gabriel slowed the car. As we drew up to the house, we saw something even stranger. The front door was wide open and half hanging off its hinges. Xavier's grip on me tightened when we saw the porch strewn with shattered glass from smashed windows.

As we got out of the car, Gabriel scanned the street, his silver eyes taking in everything in a heartbeat. We followed him up the steps and into the house. The sofa had been overturned and all the cabinets ransacked. The majority of Gabe and Ivy's possessions now lay bent and broken on the floor. Spilled wine from an overturned decanter created an abstract stain on the white rug in the front room.

"I don't believe this," Molly cried. "You've been robbed! As if this night could get any worse!" She groped frantically in her pocket for her cell phone. "I'm calling the cops."

"Molly, wait." Gabriel reached out and grasped both her hands to calm her. "This doesn't look like a robbery."

Xavier and I followed my brother's gaze across the living room, where one word had been scrawled across the wall in an angry red marker: WHORE.

"Oh, no," I groaned.

Molly's hands flew to her mouth and her eyes filled with tears.

"Molly, he's psycho." Xavier tried to sound reassuring. "You can't take this seriously."

"Oh, my God." Her hands started to flap at her sides. "He's going to *kill* me!"

"Nobody's killing anyone," Xavier said.

"This isn't exactly a surprise," Gabriel said. "We've always known Wade was unstable."

"What do we do now?" Molly cried.

"We get out of here," I replied.

Just then, a door slammed upstairs and a shadowy figure moved across the landing. Wade stood motionless when he saw us—a crowbar in one hand and a demented look in his eyes.

"Yep," Xavier muttered. "I'd say it's definitely time to go."

Molly screamed when Wade came bolting down the stairs toward us. With a flick of his wrist, Gabriel brought down the banister, tripping him up and blocking his path.

"Let's move," my brother instructed, herding us out.

As we ran down the path and leapt into the car, I wondered why Gabriel, a powerful archangel, was running from a human, even if it was a crazy one. Just as he slammed his foot on the accelerator, an even-more worrying thought crossed my mind.

"Wait! Where's Ivy?"

Xavier craned his head back in alarm. "She was in the house when we left!"

"Ivy can take care of herself," Gabe answered. He sounded so certain, I didn't doubt him for a second.

As we veered off the main road, it wasn't long before we left the twinkling lights of Oxford behind. As the dark and endless highway swallowed up the car, the misery of being back on the run hit me full pelt.

"Where to now?" I groaned, not bothering to hide my weariness. "I'm not sure I can do this anymore."

"Yes, you can," Xavier said firmly. "We've done it before and we can do it again."

"Why are we running anyway?" Molly protested, looking more confused than alarmed. "Why can't we just call the police?"

"Wade isn't the only threat in this town," Gabriel said. "Something tells me he didn't do all that damage on his own. Trust me. Right now, it's safer if we just clear out."

"Where to this time?" I asked softly, understanding now the reason behind his decision to run. "Is there anywhere left to go?"

When Gabriel caught my eye through the rearview mirror, it was as if I could read his thoughts.

"Maybe, it's time we headed home," he said.

At that moment, there was nothing that could have lifted my spirits more. Home. It felt so far away, like a distant memory or a place I'd only read about in stories. I knew the battle with the Sevens was far from over, but I had a feeling we could use the advantage of being on our home turf.

I could smell I was home even before the tiny town of Venus Cove came into view. The scent of the sea found its way to us. It flowed in through the open windows, wrapping around us like the arms of an old friend. When we drove through the town, I saw that nothing had changed. It was as sleepy and untroubled as when I'd first seen it. The quaint storefronts and the white courthouse with its columns and clock tower seemed to magically erase the uncertainty of the past few months.

It was late in the evening by the time we pulled onto Main Street, looking for a place to eat. I wanted to go to Sweethearts, but Gabriel said too many people would recognize us there and we needed to lay low for a while. So, we chose a local steakhouse where the waitresses didn't know us. But the patrons still glanced up with curiosity when we walked in. They looked Gabriel and me up and down suspiciously, like they recognized us from somewhere.

"Reckon they're vampires?" I heard one whisper as she wiped down the bar.

"Girl, you have got to stop watching *True Blood*," her friend said, shaking her head in mock concern.

Molly and Xavier shared a chuckle while Gabriel and I looked on blankly.

Xavier patted my knee. "I'll explain later."

AFTER dinner, I was looking forward to spending the night in my old room at Byron, but Gabriel had other ideas.

"I'm afraid it's too dangerous right now. It's the first place they'd look."

"Who's looking for us?" asked a puzzled Molly.

"I'll tell you everything later," said Gabriel with a stern look.

"Where will we stay then?" I asked.

"We'll check into a hotel. At least until we can work out our next move."

Much as I didn't like it, Gabriel's plan made sense. We really couldn't risk going anywhere near Byron. Besides, what was the point of going back to our old home only to be uprooted again when the next attack hit? I couldn't go through that again; I already felt like I didn't belong anywhere anymore.

Before we headed to the hotel, Xavier and I offered to stop at a drugstore to pick up some toothbrushes and other essentials we'd neglected to bring after leaving in such a hurry. Gabriel and Molly went off on foot to check us into the Fairhaven on the esplanade, and then try and work out what had happened to Ivy. Gabriel didn't seem overly concerned, but I knew he'd feel better once our sister was back with us.

We made the trip to Walgreens short and sweet, hardly even checking what we threw into our basket. When we were done, Xavier surprised me by making a detour and veering back onto Main Street. I guessed what he was thinking as soon as he pulled up outside our old haunt, Sweethearts.

"Feel like taking a trip down memory lane?" he asked. Looking at him, with one hand on the wheel, the other slung lazily behind my headrest, I felt catapulted back to our first date. Nothing had changed. I could see the backdrop of the Mercury Cinema through the car window, so old-fashioned it seemed like a theater set. The boy in front of me hadn't changed, either. He still had the same soft, honey-colored hair that swooped gently across his forehead, he still wore the same cross that sat just in the hollow at the base of his neck, and his eyes were still the same glittering turquoise that seemed to reflect all the colors of the ocean. Only now, there was something different about his eyes. His expression was wiser, perhaps darker than it had been before. He had seen things, and fought for his life and for the lives of those he loved. I wondered if others would see it too.

"Do you think it's a good idea?" I asked cautiously.

"We won't be long."

Sweethearts hadn't changed a bit. But we had. It was strange to see new faces at the tables sharing sodas and fries. So much time had passed since I first came to Venus Cove. The days of Molly and her gang were over. The jukebox still played old-time rock and roll and the waitresses still wore roller skates, but there wasn't a single face in there we recognized. Our school peers had moved on to colleges around the country. We didn't belong here anymore.

"Is it just me or . . . ?" Xavier began.

"Nope." I took his hand. "This is weird. I feel old."

We gravitated toward our old booth, but found it already occupied. We stood uncertainly for a moment before a voice interrupted us.

"Hey, honey, long time!" It was one of the older waitresses, recognizing Xavier. "Always nice when the high school studs come back to visit."

"Hey." Xavier flashed her his best lazy smile. "I've missed this place."

"And it's missed you." She winked playfully at him. "If you're looking for your sister, she's out back." She jerked her thumb toward the exit and waggled her eyebrows meaningfully. Xavier frowned.

"Nikki's here?" He checked his watch. "It's after eleven."

I recognized his sister Nicola's voice as soon as we walked

through the café's back kitchen and out into the alleyway. It was lilting, high-pitched, and overly confident. We emerged to see a bunch of tenth-graders sitting in the back of a dusty pickup truck parked between the Dumpsters. They were all talking and texting at once. A few of them were swigging from beer cans and passing around cigarettes. The freckled boy at the wheel looked barely old enough to drive, despite the tattoos on his biceps and the toothpick twirling in his mouth.

Xavier folded his arms and scowled at the scene in front of us. "No way," he muttered.

If I'd been expecting an emotional reunion, I couldn't have been more wrong. Nikki froze when she saw her brother and a range of emotions crossed her face—from surprise to relief to sheer rage. She'd changed in the time we'd been gone. She'd lost weight and looked leggier. Her curly hair hung down her back and her bitten nails were painted with black polish. Her skirt was too short and the laces of her Doc Martens were undone. Her sassiness had morphed into real attitude. She eyed Xavier coolly as she sat smoking and swinging her legs over the side of the truck.

Xavier strode calmly up to her without unfolding his arms. They stared at each other for several long moments. I would have crumbled under his intense gaze, but Nikki just took a long, deliberate drag of her cigarette and blew the smoke nonchalantly into his face.

"Look who's back."

Xavier didn't react. I had to hand it to him. He seemed to know instinctively how to deal with his rebellious younger sister. He plucked the cigarette casually from her mouth before she had time to protest, and put it out under the heel of his boot.

"Did you miss me?" he asked with a smirk.

Nikki's expression darkened. "You can't just show up here and pull the big-brother act. Where the hell have you been?"

"Beth and I had some things to take care of."

"*Things to take care of*? You've been gone six months. Mom's been going crazy."

"I couldn't contact her. I couldn't contact any of you."

"What a load of crap! That's the lamest excuse I've ever heard!"

Xavier sighed as the other kids sniggered, enjoying the show. "Nikki, it's complicated."

She rolled her eyes. "'Course, it is. You're so unbelievably selfish."

"Don't talk about what you don't know," Xavier snapped. "You have no idea where I've been or why I had to leave."

"So explain . . . I'm listening," she said with biting sarcasm. Xavier's face fell. It was not going to be possible to offer Nikki any explanation that would have made sense.

"I can't get into it."

"Then just *piss off!*"

"I think I better get you home."

"I'm not done here."

"Yeah. You are."

The driver of the truck spat his toothpick onto the ground and turned to Nikki in a show of solidarity.

"I can give you a ride home," he offered.

Xavier gave him a withering look. "She's got one."

The boy shrank into his seat. Knowing her brother wasn't about to back down and wanting to avoid a public confrontation, Nikki jumped from the truck with an exaggerated groan.

"This isn't over," she muttered with a sidelong glance at Xavier. But she followed us back to our car.

"Sorry if I embarrassed you," Xavier said. It was clear he didn't want to fight with his sister so soon after his return. "But Mom and Dad are bound to be worried about you."

"That's real funny," Nikki snorted. "I don't think breaking curfew even comes close to skipping town *without telling anyone*."

"Touché."

"And you!" she said, turning to me. "I don't know if you want to be showing your face around our place. My mom isn't your biggest fan right now."

I looked at Xavier anxiously.

"Don't worry," he said. "I'll talk to her."

"Are you sure?" I whispered.

"She probably won't even notice you," Nikki said. "Not after the prodigal son returns."

"Okay, Nikki. That's enough."

I remembered the two-storied house with its wide front lawn and windows that glowed like lamps. Two SUVs were parked side by side in the driveway. It struck me as odd how normal it felt being there.

When Bernadette Woods opened her shiny black front door, the dishcloth she was holding slipped from her grasp. She stood rigid, her eyes fixed on Xavier.

"Mom?" he said, trying to gauge her reaction.

She reached out and gripped her son's arm, still speechless. Nikki stormed past us, stomping noisily upstairs to her room. We heard her bedroom door slam shut. Even then, Bernie didn't react. She looked as if she didn't quite trust what her eyes were telling her. Nikki was right; it was as though I didn't exist at all. And I was grateful. It was a relief when Xavier's father walked out of the kitchen to see what all the commotion was about. There was a sharp intake of breath when Peter first saw us, then his face broke into a smile. He seemed to absorb the situation in an instant.

"Don't mind your mom," he said, gently shuffling her aside. "Come on in. Honey, why don't we fix them some tea?"

Still staring, Bernie stepped mechanically aside to let us in.

"So Nikki hasn't changed much," Xavier said casually.

"She's in a hurry to grow up," his dad replied. It was as if they'd spoken yesterday.

Things should have been strained, but they weren't. The bonds in this family were too deep to be erased by time. Just like my love for Xavier would outlast eternity.

We sat facing each other on the overstuffed sofas in the formal living room. I was too nervous to make eye contact with anyone, so I just stared at the toys that Madeline and Michael had left on the floor. An oversized ginger cat was asleep in a basket just as it was the first time I'd come over. That seemed like centuries ago now.

"We thought we were never going to see you again." Bernie choked on her words and her eyes had misted over.

I had to bite down hard on my lip to keep my own emotions in order. I didn't dare speak. Xavier had to handle this one.

Bernie wiped her eyes with the back of her hand. "I've been praying for you every day. Praying you were safe and that you'd come home."

"I know, Mom. I'm really sorry."

"Where exactly have you—" she began, but Peter raised a cautionary hand, as if to say, *now is not the time*. The relief of seeing his son alive and well outweighed any need for explanations. Bernie picked up on her husband's signal, coughed, and changed her tone.

"All that matters is that you're here now. Have you eaten? Can I fix you something?"

"We're okay."

"And you're safe?" Peter asked.

"Yes," Xavier nodded. "And I want you to know, I never meant to hurt you . . . or our family."

I waited for Bernie to respond, but she had gone silent again. Xavier followed her gaze as it fell on the soft sheen of the diamond I wore on my ring finger—her mother's antique ring. Bernie's face seemed to cloud over, and I squirmed in my seat and tried tucking my hand underneath my knees.

"Mom, Dad, there's something you need to know," Xavier said, even though there was little he could do now to minimize the shock.

"Oh my God." His mother covered her mouth with her hands. "No, it can't be true."

"Don't freak out," Xavier said. "I know you weren't expecting this."

"You're married?" Bernie sounded heartbroken. "My son is married?"

"We wanted to tell you," Xavier said. "But there wasn't time."

Bernie suddenly jerked in my direction, addressing me for the first time that night. "Are you pregnant? Is that what's going on here?"

"No!" I exclaimed, feeling myself flush deeply. "Nothing like that."

"Then why?" She waved a hand at the ring. "And why didn't you tell us?"

"I'm sure they had their reasons," Peter said softly.

I was impressed with the way Xavier's dad was handling things. He must have had a million questions of his own, but he was making a real effort to be our ally and make this reunion go as smoothly as possible. He stood up and pumped Xavier's hand. "Congratulations, son," he said, before pulling me to my feet and enfolding me in a vigorous embrace. "Welcome to the family, Beth. We're proud to call you one of the Woods."

"Um . . . thanks," I said, taken aback. Surely, they must have blamed me for taking their son away from them. But I couldn't see any anger or accusation in Peter's face, only openness and genuine happiness. The warmth of Xavier's hand reaching for mine was all the reassurance I needed. I was Xavier's wife, part of him now, part of his family. I finally felt like I belonged somewhere, and nothing was ever going to change that.

"We need to celebrate with some champagne," Peter declared, rubbing his hands together.

"Dad, we can't stay."

Bernie looked distressed. "But you just got here!"

"We'll be back as soon as we can."

"I don't like this," Bernie said. "I don't like all these secrets. What's going on? Why won't you let us help you?"

"You both mean the world to me," Xavier said earnestly. "And there isn't anything I wouldn't trust you with. But Beth and I have to handle this on our own. And I need you to trust me. I've never lied to you before; I've never let you down. Just trust me, okay?"

His mom nodded mutely. I could see in her eyes that she would never understand what had caused her son to abandon his home, but she knew she couldn't argue with him.

"You'll be in town?" she asked anxiously.

"For now, yes."

"Is there anything your father and I can do? If you're in trouble, we know people. . . ."

"It's not that kind of trouble, Mom."

"There must be something! I feel so useless."

"There is," he said, standing to kiss the top of her head. "You can stay safe."

Aside from me, there was nothing Xavier cared more about in the world than his family. It was one of the reasons I loved him. So in that moment, I didn't care that the Sevens could be zoning in on our location. I didn't care that our future was uncertain and everything could slip away in a heartbeat. Right now, nothing was more important than this reunion, and what it meant to this family. It was worth the risk.

Back in the car, Xavier and I sat for a moment, looking down the familiar street. For the first time in a while, we both felt utterly at ease. I didn't know how long the feeling would last, but I knew I wanted to savor it. Chances were, Xavier and I would never truly be free of our persecutors. Our union had disturbed too many in both Heaven and Hell. Maybe there would never come a time when we could rest easy. I didn't know. All I knew was that every day we woke up in each other's arms was a blessing. So, if fate was offering us even a fleeting moment of happiness, we should grab it.

And for the first time in months, the lines of guilt I'd seen etched in Xavier's forehead disappeared. At least for now, he looked happy.

27

Hostage

THE night sky was like velvet and studded with stars. A full crater-faced moon lit up the streets in a soft glow. It was good to be home, where everything felt so familiar, where every place had a memory attached to it. Xavier and I walked hand in hand until we reached the pier where I'd first seen him fishing and my siblings had hurried me away. Had they known who he was even then? Had they sensed something? I wondered if they'd had any inkling of how our lives would unfold, the saga we would be drawn into.

Neither of us wanted to go back to the hotel yet. This was our town and we'd been away too long. We needed time to rediscover it, to visit our old favorite haunts, but mostly just to be reassured that it hadn't changed too much in our absence.

"It's just as sleepy as it ever was," I murmured. "Good old Venus Cove."

"Nothing to do and nowhere to go," Xavier replied. "Until you came along."

"Right." I rolled my eyes. "Sorry about that."

"Don't be." He wrapped an arm around me and pulled me close. "Wouldn't trade it for anything."

When we reached the shore, I slipped off my shoes and let my toes sink into the sand. It had been awhile since we'd just been able to take a break from everything. The beach was more surreal than my daytime memories of it. The black waves encroached territorially onto the shore. We sat on the cool sand in silence for a while. The horizon and the water had long merged into a mass of undulating darkness. A few white yachts moored to the pier swayed gracefully on the surface.

Xavier suddenly stood up.

"C'mon. Let's walk to the Crags."

"Really?" I asked hesitantly. "Are you sure? We haven't been there in forever."

"Exactly," he replied. "And so much happened there. I feel like we need . . . closure or something. We go one last time and then we never go back."

"Alright." I stood up to join him. "Deal."

We walked along a flat stretch of beach until we reached the rock pools, which were like tiny aquariums left behind by the sea. Even in the dark, I could still catch the darting of tails in the shallow water and see the twisted braches of dead coral like pretty skeletons on the sand.

We rounded a bend and then there they were. We'd reached them. Towering, black monoliths washed in moonlight. I felt like I was standing side by side with the Bethany of two years ago. I could almost picture us—we seemed so much younger then, so carefree with no idea what lay in store for us. We were a mixture of excitement and nervous anticipation. We couldn't wait to see how our story unfolded. We thought there was so much in store for us. And there was, just not what we'd been expecting. And now, we felt so much older, heavier, weighed down by too many cares.

The Crags were deserted as usual. No one came here except people who wanted a break from the world or a place to think uninterrupted. All noise was wiped out by the waves smashing against the rocks and the wind howling as it danced in and out of the caves around us. Despite the warm weather, it was chilly under the looming shadow of the Crags, in a place where the sunlight never could reach. I backed up, pressing myself against Xavier and absorbing his heat. His arms closed around me from behind.

Somewhere far above us, we heard church bells chiming the hour. Was it really midnight already?

"Gabriel and Ivy are gonna be mad," I groaned.

Xavier laughed softly as he rubbed my shoulders. "You still think like you're in high school," he said. "You're in college now and we're married. You can do what you want."

"Hmm." I paused to consider that thought. "I guess so."

"It's funny how you've got no problems taking on a Seven, but your brother and sister still make you nervous."

"They're scary!" I protested. "Have you ever seen Ivy get mad? She can spit fire with her tongue."

"That's not scary," Xavier said. "It's kind of cool."

"You used to think I was cool," I said teasingly. "Sorry I don't have any celestial tricks to show you."

"Yeah." Xavier shook his head. "It's pretty disappointing. You really need to pick up your game."

"Oh, really." I folded my arms. "In that case there's no lovin' for you tonight."

"Using sex as a weapon already," Xavier replied. "Two can play at that game."

"You can't withhold sex, you're a guy," I told him.

"With a lot of willpower." He smirked. "I bet you'd break first."

"Please," I snorted. "I'm an angel."

Xavier winked at me. "Turns out so am I."

We were both quiet for a while, watching the clouds drift across the moon.

"COME on." I grabbed Xavier's hand. "It's past midnight, we really should be getting back."

Xavier agreed and stood up to dust off his jeans. We were just gathering up our things when a crackling sound like a dozen electrical appliances going haywire filled the air. Instantly the whole beach lit up, as if someone were setting off fireworks. As it dulled slightly, I saw a now all-too familiar sight. Sevens. They were all around us on the shore, perched on the rock like statues, even waiting in the water. This time they were all dressed in starched black suits like some bizarre parody of FBI agents. Some stood alone and others in pairs. As usual Hamiel occupied the highest position on the rocky pinnacle that was the peak of the Crags, allowing him a clear view of what was happening around him. He leapt down, landing on his feet like a cat. Xavier and I were both beyond reacting defensively. This time we just stood and waited. I wondered if I should try using the same powers I'd called upon during the last attack, but there were too many of them now; we were surely outnumbered. I thought of trying to reach Ivy and Gabriel, but I'd led them into enough battles and Gabriel had already lost his wings because of me. Did he even have enough strength to overpower an army like this? I didn't want to take any chances.

"Hello, again." Hamiel folded his hands pleasantly in front of him.

"You're back?" I asked. "Really? We thought you'd be tired of playing cat and mouse by now."

"Actually, I believe this is check and mate," Hamiel replied.

I was no longer capable of feeling any fear toward him. I only felt unadulterated hatred. I was looking at the man who had killed Xavier just to prove a point. I knew it went against my nature, but the only thing I wanted was revenge.

"And how do you figure?" I hissed.

"Well"—Hamiel seemed to be taking his time—"we realized there was little point trying to fight you."

"Yeah, because we'd win," I replied. "And you know it."

Hamiel chuckled. "Because the collateral would not have been worth it. So we decided to bargain instead."

"You have nothing we want," Xavier told him in disgust.

"Think again." Hamiel motioned to someone standing, hidden by the gloom of a cave. Two Sevens glided forward, tugging between them a young girl. She was barefoot and a burlap sack covered her face.

"What the . . ." Xavier said. "You can't just bring strangers into this! Let her go."

"Oh, but she's not a stranger," Hamiel replied, and he walked across to the struggling figure, his heavy boots leaving deep imprints in the sand. He reached out and yanked away the sack, revealing the face beneath.

At first I didn't recognize her. She was a mess of curly brown hair and a bloodied nose. But it was the same lanky figure and thin shoulders we'd seen earlier at Sweethearts. It was Nicola Woods. Xavier's little sister.

My sudden intake of cold air hurt my lungs. Nikki was still squirming and wearing her pajamas: little cotton shorts and a tank. Minus the heavy eye makeup and Doc Marten boots, she looked much more her age. And she looked scared.

"Nikki?" Xavier's face drained of color and he started forward, until one of the Sevens took Nikki by the throat.

"Don't move," Hamiel commanded.

Xavier darted forward and then caught himself just in time. He stopped, holding up his hands in defeat. It was as if he realized the madness of making any move under the circumstances.

"Okay," he whispered. "Just don't hurt her."

"Xav," Nikki called out. "What's going on?" I could see she was trying to be brave, but her voice was quivering.

"It's okay Nic," Xavier replied. His whole body was braced

forward. I knew he desperately wanted to go to her aid, every fraternal instinct in his body was screaming at him to do something. "It's going to be okay, I promise."

Nikki turned her face up toward her assailant and twisted her body violently. "Let go of me!"

"Be quiet, Nikki," I heard Xavier mutter under his breath. "Be smart."

"Xavier, what's happening?" she screamed. The Sevens had her by the arms; she tried to kick her way free but any blow she landed might as well have landed on iron for all the impact it made. The Sevens hardly seemed to notice. "You're hurting me!" Nikki cried, and Xavier winced as a ripple of frustration ran through his shoulders.

"What do you want?" he yelled. "Tell me what you want!"

"We want the two of you separated," Hamiel replied. "That's what we've always wanted."

"So you're asking us never to see each other again?" Xavier said, like it was the stupidest thing he'd ever heard.

"No." Hamiel shook his head slowly. "You must come with us."

"Fine." Xavier didn't hesitate, and I felt my heart drop like a stone. "I'll come with you. Just let my sister go."

"Not you." Hamiel clicked his tongue and pointed a thick finger in my direction. "Her."

"No." Xavier gritted his teeth. "You leave her alone."

I could see him wracking his brains, desperately searching for a solution. It was an impossible situation, his sister or his wife. But I wasn't about to make him choose. And I couldn't let his sister get hurt. Xavier had already lost one girlfriend, his best friend, his childhood priest, and his roommate. He'd seen more death than anyone should have to and he was only nineteen years old.

Nikki was still struggling and in order to subdue her, the Seven twisted her arm up behind her back, making her face crumple in pain. I felt Xavier's body tense with anger and twitch forward instinctively. It seemed to be taking all his self-control not to run headlong into a fight.

Up until now, the threat had always been directed at us; someone had always been trying to harm *us*. But this was different. I had thought there was nothing Xavier and I couldn't handle, it was us against the world, us against what seemed like insurmountable odds. We always opted to fight, to take our chances, because being together surpassed everything. But not this. We had been prepared for every eventuality except this one.

"No!" Xavier repeated. "Not her. Take me instead. Please?"

"We cannot," Hamiel said evenly.

"Why?"

"Because you are one of the Elect. Our Father has big plans for you. We cannot interfere. If we did, the consequences would be severe." His dark eyes fell on me.

Xavier stepped forward. "She's my wife. You can't take her."

In response, Hamiel drew a gleaming silver blade from

inside his coat and rested the tip at Nikki's throat. She let out a scream that turned into a gurgle as one of the Sevens clamped a hand over her mouth. But her eyes were wide and wild with panic. Xavier covered his mouth like he might be about to throw up. There was so much anguish in his eyes I couldn't stand it. I knew he would never surrender me to Hamiel, but at the same time he couldn't let his sister die.

"Enough." It was me that stepped forward this time, feeling as hollow as a drum inside. "That's enough."

If there was ever going to be a final straw in our story, this was it. I had seen enough destruction to last a lifetime. Nobody else was going to die on our account. If one thing existed that was going to break my resolve the Sevens just found it. And they knew it. Besides, we couldn't keep running and fighting for the rest of our lives, letting the bodies pile up around us. Who would be next? Someone had to put an end to it all. And I had the chance to do it. I looked at Xavier's face and all the grief he'd suffered was somehow reflected in his eyes. I only hoped this would be the end of it.

"I'm yours," I said to Hamiel. "I surrender."

Behind me, I heard Xavier let out a heartbreaking sound somewhere between a groan and a cry.

"No," he whispered. "Beth, no."

But I forced myself to block him out. "Let the girl go first," I said, trying to keep my calm. "Let her go and I'll come with you."

"What, don't trust me?" Hamiel sounded amused.

"Not at all," I replied.

"We live by an honor code," Hamiel said. "The soldiers of Heaven will stand by a deal. However, we don't know if the same can be said of you. How can we be sure you're not lying?"

"Because I know you could kill her in a heartbeat," I said. "So you win. Just let her go, okay? I'm not going to try anything."

Hamiel considered this for a moment and then nodded at the Sevens that held Nikki. They released her and she ran to Xavier, collapsing in his arms. He caught her halfway to the ground and hugged her tight to his chest, but his eyes were still fixed on me. It was Xavier's job to look after his younger sister and his wife. I read the failure in his eyes. I walked across to him.

"What do you think you're doing?" Hamiel snarled.

"Just give me a minute to say good-bye," I said. "Just one minute."

"Make it quick."

It was the hardest minute of my entire life. Standing there at the Crags, looking at Xavier, I truly felt like the world had come to an end. At least my world had. This was the place where it all began, it was only fitting that this was where it should end. I took his hand, trying to memorize the feel of his skin against mine and bent my head to gently kiss the cool metal of his wedding band.

"Beth . . ." he began.

"Shh . . ." I pressed my finger against his lips. "Don't say anything. Just know that I love you." I let my hands run through his hair one last time. I never noticed how many shades of blue there were in his eyes. His tears looked like droplets of crystal on his cheeks.

"I can't lose you again," Xavier said.

"I won't be lost," I told him. "I'll always be watching. I'll be your guardian angel."

"No." His voice was thick and choked with tears. "This isn't the way it was supposed to end."

"We always knew I couldn't stay forever." I could hear my heart thumping so loud it almost drowned out his voice. But I couldn't let Xavier know how much this cost me. He was already in enough pain.

"We were going to find a way," Xavier said. "We were going to fight."

"We did," I said softly, glancing across at Hamiel. "We just didn't win this one."

"Please," he said, closing his eyes. "Don't do this to me. I can't go on without you."

"If you ever need me just close your eyes," I whispered. I felt like my chest was being torn in two and I could barely hold myself together. "You'll find me in the white place."

Xavier's eyes suddenly flew open and he grabbed my shoulders so hard it hurt. "You have to find a way back."

"I will," I said, trying to look as though I meant it. How was I supposed to stage a jailbreak from Heaven?

"Promise," he said. "Promise you'll find your way back to me."

"I promise," I whispered. "If there's a way back I'll find it."

Hamiel's voice cut through like steel. "Time's up," he said coldly.

PICTURES from the past began to flash through my mind. I saw our descent into Venus Cove, my old room at Byron, Molly crying, Jake laughing, Phantom sleeping on my bed. I saw my brother and sister in a blur of golden glory. I saw the flames of Hell and the bodies of the damned. And then I saw Xavier: Xavier on the pier, Xavier sitting at the wheel of the Chevy, Xavier in French class with a half-smile on his lips. I saw him on the beach and on the porch swing and standing at the altar waiting for me. I thought I was drowning in the blue of his eyes.

My reality was starting to crumble. I knew I was still holding on to Xavier's hands, but all of a sudden they weren't there anymore and my hands were hooked around thin air. The sand beneath my feet began to shift like it was sinking and I saw a light in the distance, growing brighter. Everything around me became blurry and washed out like a photograph that had been overexposed. The faces around me lost their definition, the voices merged together so they all sounded like nothing but a high-pitched whine in my ears. The light was growing brighter, absorbing everything around it. Soon it would absorb me. And then I could no longer feel my feet on the ground. I could no longer feel or see or hear anything other than a rushing, roaring wind and my hair streaming across my face.

I knew instinctively the earth was far behind me and the heavens were opening up to take me in. This was it. The moment I'd been dreading since I first set foot on dry ground. I was going home.

28

They Tried to Make Me Go to Rehab

THINGS were all wrong from the moment I got back. Although I never expected I'd be happy to return, I never realized how much it would feel like exile.

When I finally opened my eyes, I was inside the gates of Heaven. They stretched up endlessly above my head disappearing into the swirling whiteness. I turned around and clung to the golden bars, looking down at the world I'd left behind. Earth was a long way away from here. From the vantage point where I stood, it resembled a dark blue, textured marble suspended in space and covered in a white veil. It looked so beautiful it was hard to imagine its continents ever being ravaged by war or famine or natural disaster. It looked peaceful and protected, like it fit snugly in Our Father's spiderweb of life. Every part of me longed to go back. But there was no way back.

I turned again, this time to face the white wonderland before me, the air rippling with the color of opals, pale pinks, and the lightest shades of green like foam on the ocean. But I didn't know what to do with myself anymore. I could see other angels around me, appearing as globes of light in the mist, darting here and there as they guided souls and passed messages through the chain of communication in the Kingdom. Everybody seemed to have a purpose . . . except me. The only place I wanted to go was backward.

I wasn't even sure if I was in trouble. I had expected some kind of reaction, fury or punishment or condemnation but everybody was acting as if I didn't exist. So I stood there helplessly, dithering, unsure what to do until a voice spoke to me.

"Bethany," it said. "There you are. Welcome home."

I looked up to see a woman standing before me. She was wearing a crisp white suit and her hair had been wound into a neat French bun. Her fingers were manicured and she had gold-framed glasses resting on the tip of her nose.

"Who are you?" I asked without stopping to consider whether I might sound rude.

"I'm Eve," said the woman, pulling out a clipboard and making notes as she peered at me over the rim of her glasses. "Come with me."

I followed Eve because I had no other choice. I couldn't stand there at the gates indefinitely and I didn't know which division I belonged to. Was I still a transition angel? I doubted they'd credit me mentally stable enough to deal with the souls. So what was I supposed to do? That was the only life I'd ever known . . . and my life on earth. So I followed Eve into what looked surprisingly like an office. A very clinical office.

One moment I had been in Heaven's marble foyer and the next I was sitting on a plump white couch with a white fur rug at my feet and a fat, purring cat in Eve's lap. She was sitting opposite me in a leather-backed chair, still silently inspecting me.

"So . . ." she said with a small, knowing smile, like it was a prelude to a conversation we were supposed to have. Did she expect me to say something in reply?

"So," I repeated stubbornly.

"It's been a very interesting turn of events, hasn't it?" Eve asked, nodding her head as if she could completely empathize with the situation. "Tell me, how do you feel about everything right now?"

"Is that a trick question?" I said. "How do you think I feel?"

"I see." Eve smiled again and scribbled some notes on her pad. "Well, I think we have some issues to tackle!"

She sounded like a camp leader trying to motivate her students.

"I want to go home," I said loudly, as if that might get through to her.

"Don't be silly." Eve tapped the end of her pencil against her clipboard. "You are home."

"Who are you?" I asked again. "Why am I here, talking to you? If you're going to excommunicate me, just do it already."

"Excommunicate?" she repeated, writing it down on her pad for good measure. "Nobody's being excommunicated today. I'm here to help you."

"Really?" I asked skeptically. "And how exactly are you going to do that?"

"In our sessions," Eve replied, opening a drawer that seemed invisible in the white wood of the coffee table and offering me a bowl of striped candy. "Would you like one?"

"Did you say sessions?" I asked, ignoring her offer and pushing the bowl away. "We're going to be doing this regularly?"

"Oh, yes, everyday," Eve replied. "Think of me as your mentor."

"You're a shrink, aren't you?" I asked angrily. "Heaven's version of a head doctor?"

"I prefer the term mentor," Eve replied pleasantly.

It was clear they didn't know quite what to do with me. There was no precedence for my case and no experience to draw upon. I was an anomaly and so they had decided to put me into therapy with Eve, who was growing more irritating every minute. She refused to answer any of my questions and expected that I'd answer all of hers. She claimed her job was to help me *reacclimatize* until I felt ready to resume my old responsibilities. She made it sound so clear and simple. Soon everything would go back to the way it was. Except for one major problem. I didn't want to go back to the way things used to be. I wanted to go back to earth, back to Xavier. That was my sole focus and my sole ambition.

"I understand you were living with a seraph and an Arch, is that correct?" Eve asked.

"Don't pretend like you don't already know," I snapped, and she raised her pencil-thin eyebrows at me.

"Try to answer the question, please."

"Yes," I replied sarcastically. "I lived with them and my husband. Remember him?"

"Hmmm," Eve said thoughtfully, and conveyed the information to her trusty notepad.

"Will you stop that?" I demanded.

"I'm just making observations," she replied pleasantly.

And our conversation went on like that, round and round in circles, with Eve divulging nothing and me having periodic outbursts. After what seemed like hours she finally dismissed me and said she'd collect me for our next session tomorrow. If there had been a cliff in Heaven for me to jump off of, I would have headed straight for it. But I was back in my true form now and of course, I couldn't die. I couldn't sleep either, so there was literally no form of escape. I didn't eat. I didn't do anything. I just existed. And being an angel in Heaven with nothing to occupy your time was a pretty good way to lose your mind. Our existence was to serve and protect the Kingdom and Our Father's creations. We were always busy because there was always another human in need. But I was barred from interaction with anybody other than my mentor until I was deemed in a fit condition to work.

And so there was nothing to fill the endless space of time that stretched before me. I wanted to scratch at the walls of my mind. The tedium was insufferable. I wanted to scream, to run, to cry, or to fight, but I couldn't do any of those things. I wanted to stop existing. Besides the gaping chasm in my chest that ached for Xavier, I missed everything about earth: the smell of coffee or freshly cut grass, the romantic flush of light between dusk and sunset, the touch of another body or the sensation of water on my skin. I sensed other angels around me, going about their business, but none approached or made any effort to speak to me. Were they afraid of me? Or had they been instructed to stay away? I knew I came across as a loose cannon, drifting around, talking to myself or completely zoned out, remembering my past life. They all thought I was falling apart and it was true, I was. Only I didn't care. There was nothing and no one I needed to stay together for now. And so I was Heaven's resident screwball. I was pretty sure that if Eve got her way (and she struck me as the persistent type) in successfully rehabilitating me there would be no trace of the human me left. But in my mind I was still the girl from Venus Cove. I wasn't ready to let go of her and I didn't think I ever would be.

"I wonder if Xavier's been to see his parents," I said one day in a session with Eve. I'd quickly learned to throw out random thoughts because I knew they bothered her.

She had asked me a question that I hadn't even heard. She was irritating me without even doing anything. I hated how groomed she always looked with her caramel hair, slick as glass, coiled in a swoop at the nape of her neck. Her white suit was always perfectly pressed and her face was bland with flat planes and level benevolent eyes. Of course, Eve wasn't her angelic name, it was what they wanted me to call her so we might establish a "connection." In human years she looked around forty, with the kind of face you'd expect to see on a headmistress.

"There's no point discussing your time on earth," Eve said firmly. "It's all in the past now."

I looked at her, sitting there with her cool Nordic beauty. To her credit Eve did seem to have an answer for everything and I imagined I could ask the same question twenty times over and still get the same, calm, collected response. But there was a schoolmarm air about her that made me not trust her. I didn't believe she was really on my side and I didn't like her unblinking little eyes. She was on the side of order and I represented chaos in her book.

"Your memories are millstones. You must let go of them."

"Shut up," I told her, and she pursed her lips together and wrote something decisively down in her little book. "I almost think Hell was better," I said to myself.

"What's that?" Eve asked. "What did you say?"

"I said I think I miss Hell," I replied chattily. "At least there was always something to do there."

"I don't think you know quite what you're saying."

"I don't think you know quite how boring you are," I shot back.

"It isn't boring to be at peace," Eve informed me. "To be at one with a collective cosmic energy that is greater than anything you can understand."

"Whatever," I muttered. "I don't want to be part of your cosmic mosh-pit. Haven't you seen *Lord of the Rings*? *I choose a mortal life.*"

"Who's offering you a choice?" Eve asked and changed her tactic when I glared daggers at her. "Sometimes you must trust that others know what's best for you. We're trying to help."

"Why do I still have a body?" I asked. "And why do you? That's not how I remember Heaven."

"We're making allowances," Eve replied. "Trying to ease

you slowly back into this life. We thought giving you a body for years and then taking it away might be damaging."

"How considerate," I said. "Are you married?"

Eve furrowed her brow, trying to keep up as I jumped from topic to topic. "Of course not. We're not permitted to marry. You know that."

"You can't hold me forever," I told her. "I'm going to find a way out of here. Even if I have to blow myself up with cosmic kryptonite."

"Is that so?" Eve asked, puzzled.

"Yep," I said. "And if I can't get out, I'll stir up so much trouble you'll wish you never dragged my ass back up here."

"I can see we still have a fair bit of work to do." Her use of the royal pronoun annoyed me; it just made her sound condescending.

"Until what?" I asked in a snarky tone.

"Until you understand that earthly pleasures are nothing compared to the eternal riches of Heaven."

"Well, you better up your game in that case," I said. "Because earthly pleasures are winning right now."

"You won't always feel that way," Eve replied.

"Why are you doing this?" I asked. "Why don't you just punish me? Throw me into the pit with Lucifer? It'd be easier."

"We're trying to fix you," Eve answered. "I doubt Lucifer would be much help."

"What if I don't want to be fixed?"

"You can't live like this forever."

"No," I agreed. "And I don't plan to."

Eve and I clearly had different solutions in mind. But I

had one thing over them—complete indifference to what happened to me. There was nothing they could use to scare me anymore. I'd heard the Sevens; Xavier's life was valuable, they couldn't hurt him. And so I could afford to be as difficult as I wanted. And I planned to give them hell. I just hadn't figured out how.

I thought I'd start with a few mind games.

"The demons told me things, you know," I said to Eve, leaning back and letting myself sink into the embroidered silk cushions. "All sorts of things."

"Like what?" she asked, twitching her nose like she had an itch. Her look told me that if in Heaven everyone had been assigned a cross to bear then I was hers.

"Like how to let them into Heaven." I gave her my most angelic smile. "How to open a portal for them."

"That's preposterous," Eve snorted. "I've never heard anything so ridiculous."

"How would you know?" I asked her. "I was in Hell. I lived there for months. Do you think I didn't learn a thing or two? They really have it in for you guys. All they need is someone on the inside."

"Don't tell lies," Eve said. "Demons can't get into Heaven."

"I was an angel and I got into Hell," I replied, casually inspecting my fingernails. I saw Eve shift in her seat and tug at her collar. Of course I was completely bluffing. I'd never stoop so low as to call on demons for help, to put my Father's Kingdom at risk. Even if I didn't belong there anymore, it was still the sacred Promised Land. But if I could convince Eve I was crazy enough to do it, she might start taking me seriously.

"Well . . ." Eve said. "Then you really would be exiled to Hell."

"Do it," I said. "Gabriel will find a way to get me out. He might not be able to question Heaven, but Hell's got no hold over him."

"This is all very disappointing, Beth," said Eve, like she was scolding a naughty child. "Very disappointing indeed."

Who was she to judge me? How dare she sit there in her pristine suit and presume to understand anything about my life. Before I knew what was happening, I was on my feet, screaming at her, every profanity I could think of, cursing her to Hell and making up all sorts of wild threats. All I could think about was the red-hot anger surging through me. The rage could literally not be contained. My life had been so messed up by these people. We'd fought so hard only to be grabbed by the scruff of the neck and torn apart.

Eve stood up and walked over to me. She didn't even seem alarmed. I had to admit she was pretty unflappable since I was throwing a major tantrum. But when she reached out to touch me, something happened. Upon making contact with my skin, blue sparks seemed to fly and the tips of her hair sizzled. She made a strange yelping noise and jerked away. I was so surprised that I stopped shouting midsentence. Before I could say anything in my defense, two men who looked like bodyguards appeared in the room and sandwiched me between their muscled arms. Seconds later I found myself alone and imprisoned in a white room.

There was nothing to do but lie down on the floor and wait. The whiteness felt like a physical weight, suffocating me. This was not the Heaven I remembered. I remembered a glittering pyramid of colors, space, freedom, and the feeling that earth, sky, and water were all coming together in perfect synchronization. But now I only felt like someone had tried to cram me into a box that was too small. For all the vastness of Heaven, I might as well have been in a prison cell.

I heard Eve's voice speaking to me through the walls, like Big Brother.

"I thought we were getting along so well. It isn't nice to electrocute people who are trying to help you."

"I didn't do it on purpose," I said flatly, without lifting my cheek from the floor.

"Well, I'm not angry," Eve said. "I'm just giving you some time to cool off."

"Super. Thanks."

"You don't have to punish yourself, you know?" she said.

"Actually, I think I was trying to punish you."

I heard Eve give a sigh, before her demeanor returned to her subzero cheer.

"We'll get you on track soon enough."

"What are you, a motivational speaker? Go away."

"Fine," she said. "I'll be back later."

"Save us both the trouble," I replied.

I heard Eve's shoes clack on the floor outside as she walked away. Then suddenly, they stopped. "What are you doing here?" her voice demanded of an imposter I couldn't see. "You're not supposed to be here. Do you have clearance?"

"Where is she?" The mellow voice belonged to my brother, Gabriel.

29

I See Dead People

I sat up so fast it made my head spin. Could Gabriel really be here? Had he come to get me out? I heard Eve's voice again, sounding flustered now.

"You're not authorized! Stop, you can't go in there!"

There were no doors in my isolation room. Gabriel materialized through the wall, more luminous than in his earthly form. I'd never been happier to see anyone. I scrambled to my feet and clung to him, drinking in his presence. I was scared he might disappear if I let go.

"They really have you in lockdown," he observed.

"It's awful," I said into his chest. "There's just nothingness. I'm going out of my mind. You have to get me out of here."

"I can't," Gabriel said.

"What?" I pulled away from him, blinking in shock, feeling the pain in my chest that had receded for a few moments flare up again, more acute than ever. "Then what are you doing here?"

"I can't just take you with me," he said in a low voice, speaking rapidly, as if he knew we didn't have much time. "But I came to tell you there are people who can help."

"Who? Like Eve?"

"Bethany, it's obvious you don't belong here anymore. There are people who understand. You have to find them."

"Where?" I asked desperately. "Where are they?"

"Think," Gabriel pressed. "Allies come in all shapes and sizes." My mind was too fuzzy to work out what Gabriel was trying to communicate.

"Can't you just tell me?"

"I just want you to get well."

He cast his silver penetrating eyes around the room and I understood the message. He didn't know who might be listening.

"So what should I do now?"

"Play the game," he murmured. "Just play smart."

"What does that mean?" I pressed.

"You're doing a pretty good job of acting like a head case," Gabriel said. "Sudden changes make people nervous. I'm sure you understand."

It took me a moment, but I worked it out. I had to keep acting crazy so they wouldn't suspect anything.

I nodded. "How's Xavier doing? Is he okay?"

Gabriel cast his eyes toward the ceiling. "He's coping."

"What does that mean?"

"He's coping about as well as you are."

"Tell him I love him so much," I said. "Tell him I never stop thinking about him."

"If you really think that's going to help . . ."

Before I could ask any further questions, a brilliant iridescent corridor materialized in the wall and Eve burst through, followed by a posse of bodyguards. Gabriel's lip curled in a smile.

"We both know you can't arrest me, Eve," he said. "Let's drop the pretense."

I liked the way he treated her as if she was as inconsequential as a cloud. I could tell it really got on her nerves.

"Maybe not." Eve puffed herself up like a blowfish. "But I can report you."

"You do that," Gabriel said dismissively. "I'm leaving anyway."

"What did you want?" Eve asked, looking at me suspiciously.

"I wanted to make sure she was all right," Gabriel said, as if it should be perfectly obvious. "Which she isn't, which means you're not doing your job properly."

Eve had no idea that Gabriel was playing her. "I'm doing my best," she said. "It isn't easy."

"Well, try harder," Gabriel said. "She's a mess. And it's your job on the line." He turned to me. "I'm sorry I can't help you more, Beth."

He raised an eyebrow indicating it was my cue, time to test out my skills as an actor. I hesitated for a moment, trying to work out the best response. Then I fell to the ground at Gabriel's feet and grabbed hold of his ankles.

"Don't leave," I cried. "Please don't leave me here."

I was grateful that my hair fell in a curtain, covering my face. I wasn't sure I could quite twist my features into a mask of distress when Gabriel had just given me hope.

"You see?" he said to Eve. "You need to fix this."

He disentangled himself from my grasp and took a few steps back. "Take care of yourself, Bethany," he said. "And remember who your friends are."

"She isn't my friend," I said, glaring at Eve and pretending I thought that's who Gabriel was referring to. I only wished I knew who he *was* referring to.

"God's wisdom is infinite, Bethany. Trust His judgment."

Gabriel gave me a small smile and then he was gone. Eve dismissed the bodyguards and regarded me carefully with her squinty eyes.

"Did it help to see him?"

"No. He's going back to earth and I'm not."

"Which puts you in the better position," Eve said.

"Will you go away? I've had enough of your crap for one day."

"Well, that's honest if nothing else," she replied. I wondered if there was anything she couldn't put a positive spin on.

"You might as well quit now," I said bitterly. "I'm never going to like you."

Eve raised her eyebrows before walking off haughtily down the shimmering corridor. It sealed shut behind her.

I thought over what Gabriel had said. *Allies come in all shapes and sizes*. Did that mean I needed to think outside the box? Someone who I might not necessarily look to for help? But who in Heaven was on my side? It wasn't like I had any friends. Angels didn't exactly hang out in cliques. Of course there was Michael, but he was a poster child for playing by the rules. There was Raphael, but last I knew he was somewhere on earth overseeing business of his own. I didn't know how to summon him even if I wanted to. It required powerful magic to call upon an angel, you could always pray to them but millions of prayers were sent up every minute. Every angel had a list a mile long. And besides, the Archs didn't deal with prayers, that was a job for the lower-order angels—almost like working in a post office, sorting through the prayers and laying them out in order of priority. Like posting a letter via express, there was priority-prayer. I considered trying to reach Raphael that way, but somehow I didn't think that was what Gabriel meant. Whomever he was thinking of was already here.

Nobody in Heaven understood how I felt. Nobody had ever fallen so deeply in love with a mortal; no one empathized with our situation. But as I thought about who in Heaven might be able to relate to our plight, to the pain of our separation, it hit me. Emily.

Xavier's first girlfriend, the first person he ever made love to, ever felt a duty to protect. She had been with him at Bryce Hamilton long before I ever showed up. They had known each other since they were born, everybody in Venus Cove did. They'd thought they would end up married. And then she had burned alive in her bed, murdered by demons, though nobody knew it at the time. She had been separated from him against her will, just like me. But would she want to help us now? Could her soul still harbor feelings for him? Maybe she was glad we were finally torn apart.

There was only one way to find out.

Though it was difficult to summon another angel, I had

the ability to reach a soul in my mind. There were millions of them in the Kingdom and we weren't expected to sift through every one until we found the person we were looking for. But I had to focus; I was out of practice and it had been awhile since I'd tried this. I closed my eyes and let my mind reach outside my white prison and into the vastness of Heaven. I could feel the energy of souls swirling through my head. Of course, I couldn't see what they saw. Each soul lived in their own personal Heaven. They were side by side, but the Kingdom allowed them access to happy memories from their past or a favorite place they liked to visit as a child. I was told there were a lot of tranquil gardens and beaches, but everyone was different. There was one man whose Heaven was the inside of his closet. He used to hide in there as a child when things got too much and it had always remained his safe place. And so that's what his soul conjured. The angels thought it was a little strange, but it wasn't our place to judge anyone.

"Emily," I spoke her name so softly it was barely audible. "Emily, I need your help."

I repeated her name again and again. As my mind became sharper and more focused, the white room began to fall apart and the rainbow passageways opened before me. I traveled through them without moving, like I was being sucked into a beautiful whirlpool of color and when I came out the other end . . . I was in Xavier's bedroom.

At first I was confused and the emotion hit me harder than a speeding train. Then I saw the girl sitting cross-legged on the bed and realized . . . this was Emily's Heaven. Xavier's room looked different, sports gear was strewn across the floor and there was a box of Mike and Ike candy spilled across his desk. The photos on the shelves were different too—they showed the ninth-grade swim team and a group of friends I didn't recognize—Xavier and Emily were among them. At first I couldn't see him, until I spotted him sandwiched between a girl with braids and a boy wearing a backward baseball cap. I wasn't sure, but the boy looked like a younger version of his friend Wesley. As for Xavier, I'd almost missed him in the picture. His hair was lighter and cut short—not flopping over his forehead the way it did now. He wasn't as physically built, he was slender and more boyish looking. Were those braces on his teeth? He was still beautiful, but he looked like a child, so different from the man he'd become.

The whole scene was so surprising to me. I was standing in a room that belonged to a kid. But it was only four years ago. How much had changed in that short time? I stared at the faces in the picture—you could tell they had no worries in the world. They were good, wholesome kids who went to the movies and rode their bikes to each other's houses.

"I guess that's not how you remember him, huh?"

Even though I was the one who'd invaded her Heaven, I jumped when Emily addressed me and turned to look at her. I'd only ever seen faded photographs in old school pictures. Xavier had gotten rid of all the ones he had—or put them someplace where he wouldn't have to look at them. Emily was not what I expected, though I wasn't really sure what I'd been expecting. She was small with fine blond hair and brown eyes. Her nose was slightly upturned and her eyebrows were arched, which made her appear judgmental.

She wore an oversized black hoodie and jeans and was sitting in the middle of Xavier's bed, holding a stuffed teddy bear.

"Hey," I said, feeling suddenly awkward. "I'm . . ."

"I know who you are," Emily cut in.

"Right." I bit my lip. "And I bet you're not thrilled to see me."

"Yeah, I'm kind of pissed at you." She nodded and leaned back against the pillows.

"Okay," I said. "I realize nobody likes the new girl."

"It's not that." Emily frowned at me. "He was going to get a new girlfriend and get married eventually. I expected him to, I wanted him to."

"But?"

"But you really messed him up," she said, knitting her eyebrows together. I noticed her nails were bitten down into little stumps. "He was going to go to med school, he was supposed to meet a nice girl, get married, and have the whole white-picket-fence deal."

"I know" was all I could say. Everything she said was true.

"You dragged him into a mess he'll never get out of," she said, brushing away the strands of blond hair that fell into her eyes. "You don't know how much he did for me. He started looking after me when we were fourteen."

"He never told me much about it," I murmured. "He wouldn't really talk about you . . . not with me at least."

"He's a boy." Emily shrugged. "They repress their feelings."

"Why did Xavier need to look after you?" I asked.

"My dad took off when I was two," Emily said. "Then in ninth grade my mom lost her job and pretty much fell apart and my big sister started getting into drugs. I didn't have anything good in my life except Xavier. And after I died, I didn't want that for him anymore. He'd already played his part. He'd rescued the girl with all the crap to sort out. The next relationship was supposed to be different, it was supposed to be normal."

"Emily, I know I'm the farthest thing from normal," I said. "And maybe I was selfish for ever letting this happen, but I didn't know how far things would go. If I knew what I was signing him up for, I would have left him alone. But you have to understand that I love him too."

"I don't care how you feel," Emily said. "But I do care how he feels. And lucky for you, he loves you too. I'm still mad at you, but I don't want to see him lose someone else. He's lost enough, don't you think?"

"Are you saying you'll help me?"

"I'm saying I'll help *him*," she corrected. "And if that means helping you, then so be it."

"Thank you," I said. "And Emily?"

"Yeah?" She glanced up.

"I'm sorry about what happened to you. It wasn't fair. He's dead now . . . the demon who killed you. I don't know if that helps at all, but my brother killed him."

"Yeah." Emily looked down at her bitten fingers. "It's all part of the plan, right?"

"No," I shook my head. "That was never part of God's plan for you. The demons interfered because that's what they do. But your story wasn't supposed to end that way."

"It's okay," Emily said, sighing. "I'm not angry anymore. I was for a while but there was no point. It's just hard . . . not being able to talk to your family. And then you realize that life goes on without you."

"Life goes on, but people don't forget," I told her. "You haven't been forgotten, Emily."

"You're wrong," she told me, her wide eyes full of sadness. "People let go . . . they have to, it's the only way they can keep going. I hope you make it back . . . before Xavier lets go of you."

30

Zach

IT turned out Emily had an idea.

"You have to go and see Zach," she said with a smile, clearly pleased with herself.

"Zach?"

"That's right."

My mind flashed back to the angel I used to know, the one who guided children as they transitioned into the Kingdom. I'd thought I'd never see him again since his change of career path.

I frowned. "But Zach's a Seven."

"Not anymore," she said. "He quit when they started going after you."

"Seriously? He left his job because of me?"

"He was never cut out for that lifestyle. Zach's a guardian, he always has been."

"How do you know that?" I asked curiously.

"Because he's my guardian," Emily replied smugly. "They sent him back to work with the children. He helped me with my transition when I first got here."

"But you were sixteen," I said. "That's hardly a child."

"I had a difficult time adjusting," Emily said. "So they assigned him to help me out. And it worked. Zach made a big difference, until he signed up to the Sevens. Nobody thought it was a good idea. But he's back now."

"And you know where to find him?"

"Of course," she said like it was obvious. "I've got him on speed dial."

Emily was by my side in the time it took me to blink. She grabbed my hand and her fingers felt cool and fragile, as if they were made of glass as they closed around mine. I heard her whispering under her breath and a moment later, the bedroom began to dissolve. Xavier's bed with its dark blue duvet, his desk, and the football lying by the door all began to blur at the edges. I held on tight to Emily's hand—the whole thing made me feel a little motion sick. As the room continued to fall apart, with items vanishing into thin air, the same multicolored passageways Eve had used began to open around us, light reflecting from every angle. Emily seemed to know exactly where she was going and we drifted forward, letting the rainbow corridors swallow us up.

WHEN I opened my eyes, I was standing in a garden. I looked down to make sure I'd made it in one piece and found my arms and legs streaked with the colors of the rainbow.

"It washes off," Emily told me, dusting her hands over her thighs. They came away covered in colorful powder and she blew it into the wind.

As my dizziness cleared, I looked around to see a glittering lake stretching before us and rows of tall trees disappearing into the clouds. The air was warm and full of birdsong. I spotted Zach sitting a small distance from us, cross-legged on the ground among a circle of children. He looked just the same as I remembered, slight in build with dark hair and an olive complexion. His eyes were a sparkling shade of green and always had a mischievous glint, like he knew something you didn't. He had an upturned nose and a cheeky smile—he was essentially Heaven's version of the Pied Piper. It was what made children drawn to him. Why he ever wanted to join the Sevens was beyond me.

When he glanced up and caught my eye, he excused himself from the group. The children made mild noises of protest, unwilling to share their leader. A white cobbled path unfurled before him as he strolled barefoot up to where we stood.

"Lookin' good Emily." He winked at her. "Hello, Beth. It's been awhile."

"It has," I agreed. "Good to see nothing's changed."

"Oh, I wouldn't say that," Zach replied. "But everything always ends up back where it belongs."

"You really left the Sevens?" I asked. "I didn't even know you could do that. I thought it was a life sentence."

Zach looked around with an easy shrug. "I missed the children. The military wasn't my scene."

"Why did you ever join?"

He fixed me with his emerald stare. "Oh, you know, I was drunk, made a bad decision." Emily giggled, clearly impressed with anything that came out of Zach's mouth. "Call it a journey of self-discovery," he continued. "I needed to work out where I belonged. I had a moment of doubt, if you will."

"But he's back with us now." Emily hugged him.

Zach laughed and ruffled her hair. "She's special, this one. So . . ." Zach studied me. "I figure you didn't stop by just to chat?"

"We need your help," Emily said, before I could answer. "It was my idea."

She really did sound like a kid, gunning for approval. It wasn't her fault. She was an eternal child; her soul was only as wise as her sixteen earthly years had allowed.

"Hmmm . . ." Zach pressed his fingers together under his chin. "And how may I be of assistance?"

"Beth wants to go home," Emily told him.

"Does she now?" Zach raised an eyebrow at me. "I figured it was something like that. But what makes you think I have the power to zap you back?"

"I never thought you did," I replied. "But I hoped you might point me in the right direction. There has to be some way out of here."

"You know, most people don't want to leave Heaven," Zach said. "It's kind of a final destination."

"I'm not most people. Not anymore. I hate it here."

"No you don't, you hate being without Xavier," Zach corrected. "But he'll end up here too one day."

"I don't want to see Xavier again as a spirit," I said. "I want to have a life with him . . . on earth."

"Well, there's only one way to do that," Zach said simply. "You'd have to lose your divinity."

"Lose it?" I repeated. "You mean give it up?"

"Yes," Zach said. "Everything that makes you an angel will

have to go. If you want to live like a human, you have to become human."

"And how exactly do I lose my divinity?" I asked cautiously.

"There's only one way I know of. And you're not going to like it," Zach said gravely. "You have to tear out your wings."

My mind immediately thought back to Gabriel and how his ruined wings had brought out the human nature in him. But his wings had not been completely severed; Raphael had turned up and stopped the devils from completing their work. But I'd known it was extremely painful and caused great damage to my brother. It was like asking humans to cut off their own legs.

"Isn't there another option?" I asked. "Anything?"

"There might be," Zach rebuffed. "But I don't know what it is."

"Couldn't I run away?"

"Didn't you already try that?" He tutted. "It didn't work out well. You can't run from Heaven."

"I was doing a pretty good job," I said stoutly. "We were fighting the Sevens and we were winning. I'm only here because they played dirty."

"Yes, the little girl," Zach mused. "They broke a lot of rules getting her involved."

"They broke a lot of rules showing up in front of a room full of college kids," I said hotly, aggravated by the memory. "They killed our friend, Spencer!"

"I know," Zach murmured. "And I'm sorry. They were not authorized to do that."

"Can't we report them or something?"

"You would need to tell someone who could pass the message on to Our Father. And he's busy these days. People are losing faith, the world is falling into the wrong hands." He looked at me intently. "Are you sure you want to go back?"

"Yes," I said emphatically. "I'd rather live in an imperfect world with Xavier than spend an eternity here alone."

"It's your call. But you should think about it carefully. The decision is irreversible."

"Have you considered the other possibility?" Emily interjected. "I know you're trying to get back to Xavier . . . but have you thought that maybe he could come to you?"

"Excuse me?" I turned on her. "Are you implying what I think you're implying?"

"He's going to end up here anyway," she muttered.

"Xavier is *nineteen*," I said angrily. "He's got a whole life ahead of him."

"It's no use to him without you," Emily said. "The two of you are so codependent that one can't survive without the other."

"How would you know?" I snapped.

"I've got cable," she replied tartly. "I can see what goes on in the lives of the people I left behind."

"So you've been spying on us?"

"It's not spying, it's just observing."

"Yeah, well, it's creepy, so cut it out."

"Ladies . . ." Zach said calmly. "This isn't helping. And Bethany, Emily is right. Either you find some way to get back to Xavier or he'll find a way to get to you. It's only a matter of time."

"Do you really think he'd do something like that?" I asked.

Zach looked at me carefully. "Wouldn't you?"

"That's different!" I burst out.

"No, it isn't. Whatever you'd be willing to do, you can bet Xavier would do the same."

"Okay." I took a deep breath. "So you're saying I better get back quickly . . . before Xavier finds some way to die?"

"Yes," Zach replied. "That's exactly what I'm saying."

I didn't think there was anything left that could throw me, but this had come as a surprise. I'd been so caught up in my own depressive spiral I hadn't even considered that Xavier might be feeling the same thing. Of course he'd be trying to find a way to get back to me—it wasn't like him to sit on his thumbs and do nothing. He had been to Hell and back, why would he think Heaven was beyond reach? So now not only did I have to lose my divinity, but I had a time limit and I had to act fast.

"Wait," I said. "Surely Gabriel and Ivy will keep him safe."

"They can't watch him twenty-four hours a day," Zach replied. "And you of all people should know, if someone wants something badly enough, they'll find a way to get it."

Emily watched my forehead crumple as I tried to wrap my head around this new information. "Relax," she said, rolling her eyes. "We've still got time. Dang, I was never such a drama queen."

"Be quiet," I replied. "I'm sure you had issues of your own."

"Okay." Zach held up his hands. "Time out, both of you."

I turned my back on Emily and tried to compose myself.

Arguing with her wasn't going to get us anywhere. We needed to work together here.

"Tell me what I need to do," I said to Zach. "Just tell me and I'll do it."

"You need to find Joseph," Zach replied. "He can help."

He looked down as a young child came and tugged at his sleeve, trying to draw him back into the circle. All the children were waiting expectantly.

"I have to go," Zach said.

"Wait!" I cried. "Who's Joseph? And how do I find him, whoever he is?"

"You don't," Zach said. "He'll find you. I'll let him know you're looking."

"Has he . . ." I hesitated. "Has he tried this before . . . sending one of us back?"

"Yes."

"And succeeded?"

"I don't know."

"*You don't know?*" I repeated in exasperation. "Come on!"

"Sorry, Beth, I don't have any figures for you. All I know is that it's risky."

Zach averted his eyes and fell silent. There was a part of me that wanted to end the conversation then and there. The last thing I needed was some wild plan that could backfire at any minute. But I had no choice. It wasn't self-preservation that concerned me; I had one chance here, and if I blew it, I would never see Xavier again.

"So there's no other way?" I asked weakly.

"Not that I know of."

"Couldn't I just run away?"

"Beth, you can't jailbreak Heaven," Zach said. "And even if you somehow managed to get away, where would you go? You did a lot of running on earth and it got you nowhere.

"He's the one who's been around since the beginning," Zach called out as he allowed the children to take his hands and pull him back toward them.

"Since the beginning of what?" I was growing frustrated.

"Since the Word was made flesh. Have they still got you in a holding cell?"

I nodded, conscious of our time running out.

"Get out as fast as you can," he said in a low voice. "That place will screw with your head." He took a step back, allowing the children to pull him in. "Good luck, Beth. I'll pray for you."

"Wait!" I cried. "You haven't even told me who Joseph is."

"He's the leader of an underground group."

"Zach!" I exclaimed. "This is not the time to be messing around."

He was already leaving me, returning to the grassy banks, led by his wide-eyed companions.

"It's no joke," he called out. "They call themselves the Society of Dark Angels. There are more of them than you think." He held up a hand in farewell. "Remember, there's a lot that goes on up here that doesn't meet the eye."

And then he was gone.

31

Dark Angel

I didn't want to hear anymore. I felt my knees begin to tremble and my hands slicken with sweat. Any act of self-violation was an act against creation. It went against everything we were meant to believe in. It was true that humans could turn to self-destructive behavior when things overcame them—drinking to excess or losing themselves in the stupor of drugs. But they were imperfect, they were meant to stumble. Forgiveness was their prerogative. It was different for angels; we were meant to be infallible. There would be no turning back from the road Zach had suggested.

My mind flashed back to Gabriel in the basement of the house in Oxford. I remembered how his ruined wings had changed him, brought out the human qualities in him. Even though my head was spinning, I tried to keep my revulsion in check. I held onto the image of Xavier's face in my mind and felt the fear shrink back, like a vampire exposed to sunlight.

Joseph. For a moment I saw the name take form and shimmer in the air before me like a jewel. Zach had said the name with such authority I almost instantly believed help was on the way. Then frustration took over and I let out an angry sigh. Who the heck was Joseph? Where was I supposed to find him? This was sounding more and more like a wild-goose chase. First I'd had to find Emily, who led me to Zach, and now he was trying to palm me off onto someone I'd never even heard of. I was no closer to getting what I wanted and with every second that passed, Xavier seemed further and further out of reach.

I walked away from the meadow without looking back. I still felt confused and angry but now there was another feeling thrown into the mix: hope. I'd learned three things I didn't know before: It was possible for an angel to renounce his or her divinity, Zach knew someone who could help me do it, and I wasn't the only one pissed off at the system. For the first time since my return, my chest felt lighter and I felt a hint of a smile.

"Well, that was a lot to take in," Emily said, peering at me closely. "Are you okay?"

"I'm fine," I replied. "Now I know I can find a way back to him . . . to Xavier, I mean."

"You're not seriously thinking of going through with it, are you?" She gawked at me. "Ripping out your own wings?"

"I don't have a choice."

"You don't even know if you'll survive it."

"If I don't, then at least I'll have tired. Beats hanging around here waiting for a miracle."

Emily grabbed my arm. "There's no way Xavier would want you to do something like this."

"Then it's lucky he's not here to try and change my mind."

"Why are you not freaked out?" Emily demanded.

"You don't know where I've been," I told her. "I've seen things darker than your wildest nightmare and none of them are more frightening than the idea of living without him."

"Wow." Emily looked pensive. "You really love him, huh?"

"I do."

"Y'know, there were times I thought you were selfish, getting so close to him when you knew you'd have to leave one day. But you never planned to leave, did you?"

"No," I said softly. "From the day I met him I knew I was never going back."

We realized at the same time that we had drifted to the edge of the meadow, the spot where the corridors had opened in the air and delivered us to our destination. I lingered indecisively.

"So what now?"

"Zach said not to go back," Emily said thoughtfully.

"I have to. If I don't, Eve will come looking for me."

"So what?" Emily shrugged.

"You don't know her," I said. "She's a complete control freak."

"Okay." Emily nodded. "So go back and convince her you're okay. Ask for your old job back or something. You can pull it off."

Was this Emily's way of calling a truce between us?

"Okay," I said uncertainly. "I'll try."

No sooner had I spoken than the rainbow tunnels opened before us, throwing sparkling beams of light onto the grass. It was amazing how prompt they were, like someone had pushed a button on an elevator.

"Do you want me to come with you?" Emily asked. "In case the crazy cat lady is waiting at the other end?"

"Thanks." I laughed. "But I think I can handle her."

I moved to let the whirlpool passageway draw me in, but Emily's hand shot out and grabbed hold of my elbow.

"Wait!"

"What?"

"Do you hear that?" she hissed.

"I don't hear anything . . ." I began, then suddenly stopped. There was a peculiar humming that seemed to be building in the air, growing steadily louder. Was this Eve's doing? Had she sent an army after me already? Emily and I held on to one another as an opening appeared in the air as if it were made of fabric. And then it was rushing toward us or we were rushing toward it—I couldn't tell and it happened so fast there barely time to react. Then we both tumbled headlong onto a marble floor.

"What the—?" Emily struggled to sit up, her arms waving as she fought off invisible restraints.

"No need to be alarmed," said a voice, and we looked up to see three informally dressed figures hovering before us amid the vast pillars. The tallest of the men stepped forward and somehow I knew instinctually who he was. I felt suddenly awkward, like I had arrived for a job interview without bringing my résumé.

Joseph was different than any angel I'd ever seen. He had wavy brown hair, short and thick, and a sharp, intense stare that was more assertive than the misty gaze I was accustomed to seeing on angels. He failed to acknowledge Emily's presence but surveyed me from head to foot then looked decidedly unimpressed. I couldn't blame him given the state I was probably in.

"Hello, Bethany."

"You know me?"

"I know *of* you."

"So I guess Zach filled you in." I tried to sound casual but my hands were fidgety. "You sure don't waste any time."

"What would be the point of that?"

I could see that engaging him in small talk wasn't going to be an option. I noticed that his firm-set mouth barely moved when he talked. I noticed the heavy boots on his feet—this guy was really in the wrong place. He would have been more comfortable hunting game with a rifle slung over his shoulder. His stance was slightly defensive, as if he was prepared to fight at any moment.

I glanced quickly at the faces of the two men flanking him. They were both built strong and thick, made for battle. But I wasn't afraid of them—in fact, deep down I knew these were the angels I had been searching for.

"So what can I do for you?" Joseph asked.

It was a stupid question—he obviously knew why I was there. But maybe this was his way of testing me. I didn't want him to think I was wasting his time.

"Zach said you could help me," I said, deciding to be as direct as possible.

"Is that so?" He raised a single eyebrow.

"Is it true?" I blurted. "Do you really know how to send someone back to earth?"

"I do," Joseph replied stonily.

"Then why are you still here?"

He sighed, as if the question disappointed him.

"If I wasn't, then who would be left to advance the cause?"

"Maybe I could answer that question if I actually knew what the *cause* was," I said. Joseph gave a hard smile.

"You and I," he said. "We are the cause. There are angels out there who've had experiences just like ours."

"Really?" I was intrigued.

"Yes," Joseph replied. "It isn't right to give us humanity and then take it away. We should at least be offered the choice. That is what we're fighting for."

"That sounds . . . noble," I said, struggling to find the right word. I wanted to say *awesome*, but didn't want to come across as juvenile.

"It's not noble," Joseph retorted. "It's practical. Angels who have lived as mortals don't make decent angels anymore."

"So . . ." I began cautiously. "You must have been on earth once. How long ago was it?"

I felt like I was prying, but I needed to know more before entrusting him with my future.

"Several millennia ago."

He stared at me with his deep, dark eyes, not bothering to elaborate. I wondered if it was still a raw subject.

"What was your life there?" I pressed.

Joseph pursed his lips and exhaled heavily through his nose. "For a time it was happy. I did everything in my power to stay. I was married—just like you."

"You were?" I could hardly believe my ears. "What happened?"

"I didn't think about the consequences of embroiling her in a life of turmoil."

It could have been my story he was narrating with different dates and names.

"So your wife . . . she must be here now."

"She is. Only someplace I can never find her. That's my punishment." He winced as if the pain of the memory had not yet been dulled by time.

"That's so cruel."

He shrugged. "Heaven is just, if not always kind."

"So if I were to wait for Xavier to come here . . ."

"There's every chance the same thing would happen to him," Joseph said. "Heaven is like a labyrinth—there are many realms and some dimensions even the most powerful cannot access."

"Why didn't you go back when you had the chance?" I asked in confusion.

"Because I didn't know then what I know now. But we're not here to talk about my history. I presume you want my help getting back?"

"Yes," I said quickly. "Please, before it's too late."

"And you're aware of what is required?"

I nodded, an involuntary shudder running up my spine. I hoped Joseph hadn't picked up on it.

"And you're not scared?" I shook my head vehemently, holding my face in a perfect mask of composure. Joseph regarded me carefully. "Whatever experiences you've had have made you strong. Even so, I want you to think about this carefully. Come and see me again."

Was he trying to get rid of me? Had he deemed me unworthy? How had I failed to convince him of my sincerity? I almost panicked. I could feel tears welling up but I blinked them back and bit down hard on my lower lip. If Joseph was my only chance of being reunited with Xavier, I couldn't afford to blow it. I straightened my shoulders and lifted my chin.

"I don't need to think about it. I need you to help me *now*."

"I'm sorry—I don't help people who make rash decisions."

That got me riled. How he could pass judgments about someone he'd just met? I didn't care how finely tuned his instincts were, he knew nothing about Xavier and me.

"Don't help me then!" I said, spinning on my heels and starting to walk away. I couldn't remember a time where I'd felt more alone. Even in my darkest hours in Hades I'd had allies to guide me. "I'll take care of it myself. I'll take care of everything on my own!"

My outburst seemed to change something in Joseph.

"There will be terrible pain." His words stopped me in my tracks. "Unimaginable pain that the likes of us have no concept of."

I turned slowly to face him and this time didn't flinch from his grim, humorless stare. His manner was so blunt and businesslike.

"I'm prepared for that."

He looked intrigued by my blind determination. "And you have no questions?"

"Just one. Will it work?"

"What happens to you afterward is beyond my control."

"But this is my best shot?"

"Yes."

"And there are angels living as humans right now?"

"Only those who survived the transition." His directness was disconcerting. I almost wished he'd sugarcoat the truth. "If it doesn't work, it won't be pretty. The physical trauma alone can be fatal. If you don't transform you'll end up a mangled mess."

"Define *mess*."

"You'll be on earth but in a sort of paralytic state, not much use to anyone."

That was scarier than any punishment I could imagine. To be on earth and living only as a burden to those I loved . . . there couldn't be anything worse.

"Do you still want to proceed?"

I swallowed the lump in my throat.

"Let's get this show on the road."

"Prepare yourself," Joseph said. "We'll return to collect you."

"Where are we going?"

"The furthermost regions of Heaven where we will not be disturbed."

"You're trying to breach the gap between Heaven and earth. How can *that* go unnoticed?"

"We are very good at what we do," Joseph replied.

"I can't believe I didn't know about you sooner."

"You thought power struggles were confined to humans? Who do you think taught them about power in the first place?"

"I never considered that."

"We are working to close the gulf between Heaven and earth. You've heard of the Promised Land? We want to expand the Kingdom—let souls and angels mingle freely. Darkness will be exterminated. Whether you live to see that day or not, you have been chosen to play a part. Make your part count."

32

Torment

JOSEPH and his entourage departed moments later, promising they'd find me when the time was right. They didn't give any indication of exactly how much longer that would be. Emily was still beside me, although I was almost completely oblivious to her presence. She reminded me by clearing her throat. I glanced at her, trying to work out the most polite way of getting rid of her. I needed time alone to mentally prepare for what lay ahead. Emily seemed to read my mind.

"Is this my cue?" she asked.

I smiled sheepishly, not wanting to seem ungrateful for her help so far. "I'm sorry. I think I just need to be by myself."

"That's okay." She twisted her mouth in a half-smile. "Is there anything I can do?"

"Just keep Xavier safe until I get back."

"I'll do my best," Emily said.

"Thanks. And thanks for helping me out. I couldn't have done this without you."

"It was good to finally meet you," she conceded. "You're not as bad as I thought you'd be." Emily paused and held my gaze. "Do me one favor once you get home?"

I liked the way she just assumed I'd make it back in one piece. Her confidence made me feel stronger.

"Sure."

"Can you tell Xavier I'm okay?" I blinked in surprise as Emily continued. "All this time he's been blaming himself for what happened to me. I just want to put his mind at rest."

I nodded mutely. In that moment Xavier's past and his future seemed to merge together. Emily's death didn't mean she'd stopped loving him. It occurred to me that if things went according to plan, one day we'd all be reunited.

Emily gave me an awkward hug then turned to go. We both froze at the sound of heels clicking on marble. The passageway formed in the air before either of us could even think about running away.

When Eve appeared, she gave Emily a sidelong glance then brushed past her as if she was too insignificant to merit attention. Eve moved so decisively she seemed almost mechanical. Today she was wearing white pumps, a sage pantsuit, and pearl earrings. Her wispy blond hair was arranged so perfectly I wanted to reach out and mess it up.

She stood before us with her feet slightly apart and her arms folded while her pebble eyes bored suspiciously into mine. Her stance reminded me of a prison warden, which she pretty much was.

"Would you like to tell me what you've been up to today? Hmmm?" Her tone sounded like a teacher who regretted the removal of corporal punishment.

"Nothing in particular," I said. "I thought you'd be happy to see me out and about."

Eve colored slightly, the way she always did when anyone dared to criticize her. "You are in a very fragile state," she said. "And I happen to be responsible for you."

My mouth twitched as I fought to swallow back the snide remark on the tip of my tongue. Emily flashed me a warning look.

"Don't blame, Beth, ma'am," she piped up. "It was my fault."

Eve swiveled her neck to look at her, thawing a little at Emily's respectful tone. She automatically liked anybody who sucked up to her.

"Emily, isn't it?" she purred. "Perhaps you might tell me what's going on."

"There's not much to tell." Emily was the picture of innocence. "We went to see Zach. He and Beth are old friends."

Eve's expression turned sour. "Why, may I ask?"

"I thought he might be able to help," Emily replied. "Y'know, remind Beth of how things used to be."

I had to hand it to her—she was good at thinking on her feet. Eve looked slightly appeased. I knew deep down she couldn't wait for me to "recover" so I would be off her hands. And my crazy act wasn't making her look good in the eyes of her superiors.

"Well, that was very considerate," she said briskly. "But you should have checked with me first."

"I'm sorry." Emily hung her head, looking like a lost puppy. "I didn't realize."

"It doesn't matter," Eve said in a softer tone. "Just see that it doesn't happen again."

She turned her attention to me, her black currant eyes alight with interest. "So . . . how did it go?"

I saw Emily frown at me from behind Eve's back, a signal for me to swallow my pride and play along.

"It was good to see Zach again," I said grudgingly. "I think it helped. He made me remember how rewarding being a mentor can be."

"Good!" Eve exclaimed.

"Would it be okay if we visited him from time to time?" Emily asked, folding her hands and widening her eyes so it was almost impossible to say no.

"Well . . ." Eve began. "It's rather unorthodox, but I suppose it can't do any harm."

"Thank you, ma'am." Emily gave her a grateful smile, but Eve wasn't quite finished yet.

"So, Bethany . . . you say you can picture yourself back at work?"

"I think so," I replied through gritted teeth. I seriously disliked Eve, she was such a big, bustling busybody and I'd never met anybody more fake. She only wanted me to get better for the sake of her own reputation. But I was playing my own game here and I knew it would only work if I pretended to warm to her. "That's the goal," I continued, trying to mirror Emily's politeness. "I want to get well and I miss my old life."

It was a huge lie, but Eve didn't pick up on it. "And that so-called husband of yours?" she went on. "The one you think you can't live without?"

I felt myself literally bristle with anger. How dare she bring up Xavier? She had no right to talk about him. Besides, I could lie about most things but lying about him? It didn't feel right. But I reminded myself I was doing this *for* him. If I needed to lie, cheat, and steal my way back to earth, I would.

I couldn't quite look Eve in the eye so I stared at the ground as I spoke. "He's just a human."

"Oh, really?" Eve raised an eyebrow.

Had I gone too far? I decided to backtrack. "Well, I'll always love him," I said uncomfortably. "But I see now it was wrong for us to be together. I need to leave him alone to get on with his life and I need to get on with mine."

There was silence while Eve scrutinized my face. Then a scornful laugh rang out. At first I looked around to see who else had joined us. Eve's lip curled revealing her pearl white teeth as she began a slow measured clap.

"You two must think I was born yesterday."

"Excuse me?"

"Nice try, but the game's up." She pointed a finger at Emily and threw her an appraising glance. "This one's quite the little actress. I don't know what kind of scheme you're cooking up, but it ends now. You won't get away with it."

"We're not cooking up anything," I replied angrily. "You're imagining things."

Eve laughed. "All right, Bethany, whatever you say," she hissed. "But from now on, you'll be under round-the-clock supervision. I'm locking you up—nobody comes in and nobody gets out, do you understand?" Her professional demeanor was gone. There was a hard edge to her face now that reflected her true character. "I've tried," she went on. "God knows I've tried. But there are better things I could be doing than monitoring a juvenile angel in rehab. Quite frankly, I couldn't care less. You want to stew in your own misery? Go right ahead. I'll check in on you in a few years to see if you've changed your mind."

"What?" I cried. "You can't lock me up indefinitely!"

"Who says I can't?" Eve spat. "You know what happens to stubborn little angels who fail to kick their earth addiction?" Her eyes were wide with excitement, which made her look even scarier than usual. "They end up on the celestial scrap heap. We lock them up until they fade into nothing but cosmic dust and no one can even remember their names. But don't worry, you have a few centuries before that happens to you."

"Why are you telling me this now?" I shouted.

"I was saving the best for last," Eve smiled. "When I leave here, I'll be filing my report recommending isolation due to mental instability."

"That's a lie!" Panic started shooting through me like lightning bolts. Was it possible that after everything, my plan was about to crumble in a heap?

Eve fumbled for a device in her pocket. I knew what that meant. She was going to call for reinforcements. Once her guards arrived, it would all be over. I would never get away from them and I'd be beyond Joseph's help. I took a few steps forward, determined to change her mind although I didn't know how. But before I could figure it out, Emily sprang from behind me, tackling Eve to the ground. Eve screamed and tried to wrestle her off. I jumped back, taken completely off guard. Eve was heavy and solid but she was no fighter, especially pitted against a nimble and skilled sixteen-year-old. In no time, Emily had her pinned facedown, her knees pressed into Eve's back.

"How did a skinny sewer rat like you even make it up here?" Eve panted.

"That's not your call," Emily replied tartly. Eve grimaced, rage contorting her usual placid features. With one shoe kicked off and her hair sticking up at odd angles she looked more pathetic than dangerous. But her voice when she spoke through clenched teeth had lost none of its iciness. "I don't think you realize the trouble you've just walked into. Let me go now and I won't have you thrown into the pit."

Emily ignored her. "Get out of here, Beth!" she cried. "What are you waiting for?"

"But . . ." I hesitated. "Will you be okay?"

"Don't worry—I can take care of myself."

"You insolent, worthless child!" Eve screeched. "You're going to regret this. Once I'm done with you . . ." She eventually decided to stop talking and start channeling her angelic power. Already parts of her body were glowing like a lamp. She might have been caught by surprise by the attack but the power balance was about to tip in her favor. I had only a tiny window of opportunity before everything changed. I didn't wait to see more.

"Thank you, Emily," I mouthed.

"You can call me Em," she replied, out of breath. "All my friends do."

I opened my wings and let myself shoot upward into the wide expanse of Heaven. My wings purred with energy, like a car engine roaring to life. All the muscles in my body stretched and flexed, but I couldn't enjoy the sensation. I was painfully aware this might be the last time I would be airborne. Flying in Heaven was very different from flying on earth. There was no atmosphere to combat, so it was more buoyant, effortless, like I was a balloon rising higher and higher with no destination in mind. I only hoped someone would alert Joseph to what had happened. It was us against them now.

A thick swirling fog now enveloped me. I couldn't see more than a few inches ahead but I flew on blindly. Suddenly I became aware of two angels flying beside me, and I was relieved to see they were the two angels who'd accompanied Joseph. They each took one of my hands and guided me in the right direction.

We flew for what seemed like hours. No one spoke or showed any sign of slowing down. Just when I thought I was too exhausted to go any farther, the fog cleared enough for me to see a stairway appear before us. The steps were transparent, as if light had become solid just to help us out. There was no railing and each step we climbed dissolved behind us. I held on fast to the hands of the angels beside me.

When we reached the top, I saw we were standing in the middle of a glass amphitheater that was suspended in the void of space. I could no longer see the winding white paths of Heaven below me. The structure emanated a strange energy that seemed to leech the fear out of me. It had an air of beauty and grandeur and I couldn't help wondering what it's purpose was. Did the other angels know about this place? It felt clandestine, as if it was a hidden treasure that only a select few could find.

I felt a rush of wind and turned to see a figure galloping silently toward us. The horse was black with a braided mane and his bridle and saddle both shimmered like silver. His hooves made no sound as they hit the floor. The rider slid off and strode purposefully to where we stood. Joseph was dressed differently from when I'd first met him. Now he had a somewhat regal air about him with his flowing cloak and sandaled feet. The bejeweled hilt of a sword was visible tucked in his belt. It made his presence even more imposing.

"Kneel down where you are," Joseph instructed. "We don't have much time."

I complied without a second thought. I knelt and covered my face with both hands. The scent of falling rain and droplets of dew on the grass wafted by. It was the smell of my wings. I said good-bye to them in my heart and spoke aloud the thought that was uppermost in my mind.

"Father, forgive me."

I needed to make my peace with Him. I loved Him so much and yet I was giving up an eternal life in His Kingdom. I had been disobedient and I had failed in the task He had set for me. Or had I? One thing I knew for certain was that my Father knew each one of us deeply and personally, like He knew each man and woman on earth. He knew our fates before He created us, so perhaps the hard road I had struggled along, and all the obstacles and trials . . . Perhaps they had been meant to lead me here. I trusted Him infinitely and deep in my heart I knew He wouldn't hurt me. In that moment, instead of God's wrath, like I had been expecting, I felt nothing but mercy and love surround me. It was a moment of pure clarity. I would not be rejected for what I was about to do. My Father would not disown me. Despite all my obstinacy, I had not turned my back on Him. I still loved Him with all my heart and wanted to serve Him. How could I have even made it this far if it wasn't His will?

Suddenly I no longer felt like Heaven's misfit but one of God's children, just like everybody else.

"It helps if you keep your eyes closed." I heard the angel's rich voice behind me. "Do not expect to feel pain. There's no pain in Heaven. That will come later."

I let out an audible sigh of relief. At least Xavier would be there to help me through it just as he always was. I had to believe I would make it back to him. I just prayed I wouldn't be a burden, changed beyond recognition.

I shivered when Joseph tenderly lifted and repositioned my long hair so it fell over one shoulder, leaving my wings exposed and pulsating softly after the long flight. He placed his hand on top of my head reverently and bowed his own. At his touch a vision lit by moonlight appeared in the midst of the empty tiered seats. In it I saw Xavier. He was wearing a flannel shirt I recognized as well as scuffed boots with mud on the soles. His face looked different but I couldn't work out why. He seemed older, his chin shadowed by stubble and an absent look in his turquoise eyes. His vitality had been erased by grief. He just looked tired and completely defeated. His face was still full of beauty, but it was a weathered beauty instead of the boyish charm I remembered. His face reflected the man he was destined to become . . . the man he already was. How much time had passed? A year, maybe more. In Heaven, time did not exist as it did on earth. I had no way of telling. He was still wearing his wedding ring.

A storm was raging and Xavier was standing rain-soaked in the middle of it. He was looking down on the churning ocean from a great height. I squinted at his surroundings and recognized the familiar landmark of the Crags. He stood on the very spot where I'd stood to when I revealed myself to him. The waves bashed relentlessly against the rocky boulders below and heaved the little boats moored at the dock like marshmallows. Xavier seemed mesmerized by the steep drop. The expression on his face told me he no longer cared what happened to him. He was leaning forward, the rain lashing at him like tiny arrows.

He reached into the inside pocket of his shirt and withdrew a clenched fist. Somehow I knew what was inside before he opened his hand. A perfect white feather, tipped with pink sat in his palm. It was the feather I'd left behind in his car after our first date, the one he had kept as a prized possession all this time. I willed him to return it to the safety of his pocket. It was all he had left of me. Instead he stretched out his hand and offered it to the elements. Within seconds the rain destroyed its shape and harsh winds snatched it away. I saw it spiral downward. Xavier followed it with his eyes, tilting further forward.

My breath caught in my throat when Xavier turned into a blurry outline. Then I realized it was only because a mass of clouds had scudded past and blocked out the moon. When it reappeared, I saw he had shifted position. He was now standing right on the very edge of the cliff. His boots dislodged loose stones and sent them hurtling into the void below.

My chest clenched in panic. Surely, he wouldn't jump! The storm raged around him, the wind pummeling his chest. The slightest movement in the wrong direction could be fatal.

"Don't," I whispered. "Wait for me." Then I looked imploringly at Joseph. "Do it, *now*."

"There's one last thing before you go." He spoke quickly, sensing the urgency. "You must swear a solemn oath while you are still in your celestial form. In the event that you survive and wake up human, will you do everything in your power to contribute to the betterment of humankind and the glory of God?"

"Of course," I cried. "I swear!" I didn't even need to think about it. "I swear on Xavier's life. Now do it!"

AT first there was nothing but a mild, prickling heat, as if my wings had gotten sunburned. Then the whole amphitheater flooded with blinding light. It blasted out of the shiny glass surface and the beams streamed around us in a mad dance.

Joseph was right. I felt no pain, only oneness with the light. It consumed me. I felt it penetrate every cell and flush it with new life. My mind struggled to comprehend what was happening to me. There was a sudden creaking sound that sounded so sickening it made me want to change my mind. It was a deep shuddering groan like a cavernous cry of a whale. I opened my eyes for a second and caught sight of Joseph wielding a red-hot blade. There was time to give voice only to one last thought before my entire being as I knew it shattered. I summoned the strength to scream it aloud, hoping it would resound through time and space.

"Xavier . . . I'm coming!"

33

Metamorphosis

TIME froze seconds before Joseph's blade struck. The amphitheater filled with children. I could hear them whispering even though their faces remained frozen. I knew instantly who they were; the souls of every child I'd helped transition into Heaven during my time as a guardian. They had come to say good-bye. They were murmuring words of encouragement. *Be strong. Do not be afraid. Follow your heart and you cannot fail.* They had faith in me.

I wanted to thank them, but there wasn't time—everything happened so quickly. I felt a blistering heat on my back and then I was looking at the amphitheater from the outside. I watched my body slump forward, motionless. Joseph and the children blurred like an old photograph. The glass pillars shattered around me. I wasn't a solid entity anymore but instead a million tiny fragments spiraling through space. I tried holding my breath to steel myself but there wasn't any breath to hold. There was no pain either, just as Joseph had promised.

On the journey, I caught flashes of Heaven's ineffable beauty. I passed a waterfall cascading like liquid crystal.

I passed a still blue pool with lilies floating on its surface in an explosion of colors I couldn't name. I passed an ancient tree garlanded with flowers and rooms filled with thrones so resplendent it made me wonder why I ever wanted to leave.

But they all melted like frosting in the sun when Xavier's face drifted into view. I remembered everything we'd shared up until now and how we'd fought tooth and nail for the right to be together. I needed to return in time to stop him from making the biggest mistake of his life. I vowed a lifetime of service to God if He would only keep Xavier safe until I got there. Even if I hadn't been the most exemplary of angels, I knew my Father would provide. He would not turn His back on us. But even in my disembodied state, I felt a bolt of panic rush through me. What if I was already too late? What if I came back to find Xavier was already gone, lost in a desperate bid to join me? All our efforts would have been in vain. I would be trapped on earth without him, doomed to a life of loneliness and solitude. Eventually, Xavier would end up in Heaven, but I would never find him. There were millions of realms and he would be hidden from me forever.

But I couldn't focus on that now. I had to keep it together. Getting back in one piece was my first objective. What happened once I got back was out of my control. But Xavier and I would work it out together, like we always did. My thoughts turned to Gabriel and Ivy. What would they think of me now? Would they even still consider me their sister?

When Joseph had agreed to help me, I'd imagined myself being zapped back to earth at the speed of light. I never expected the journey would take so long. Just when I thought it would never end, shapes began to appear in the void of space. I could make out vast expanses of green and jagged mountain ranges—it was like looking at a topographical map from above. The speed at which I was hurtling through space began to slow and I too took shape. The scattered particles of my old self reconfigured. I noticed my limbs begin to reappear as shimmering outlines. Surely the wait was almost over. I was about to be reunited with Xavier.

I landed on my knees in soft grass on the outskirts of a lush garden.

A flaming sword guarded its entrance, rotating to cover all four of the earth's directions. I knew instinctively where I was because it was the picture of perfection. Vivid skies stretched above me, blooms drenched the air in perfume, and ripe fruit weighed down the branches of trees. In the garden's center stood the most magnificent of all the trees, its knotted boughs stretching toward me like a hundred arms, its fruit twinkling like rosy globes. Why was I being shown this now? Just as the question formed in my mind, the answer came without any effort on my part. This place marked a crossroad in my journey. I could still change my mind. Behind me lay the eternal peace of Heaven if I wanted it. The column of light that had carried me still hovered, awaiting my decision. If I turned away from it, my old life would be gone forever and nothing would ever be simple or straightforward again. A mortal life with all its trials lay ahead: a hard and stony road but not without rewards. I took a last look at the light receding into the milky atmosphere, then stood shakily and took my first tentative steps toward the garden. Then everything went dark.

I woke in blinding pain. I knew I was on the beach because I could hear the swell of the ocean and taste salt on my cracked lips. My hair fanned around me like tangled seaweed. My angelic clothing was gone. I was wearing a flimsy white dress, ragged and dirty from the journey. I felt something strange obstructing my vision and realized my face and arms were covered in a filmy mesh like a cocoon. I could feel it already dissolving in the salty water. I wanted to tear the rest away with my nails but even the slightest movement caused such stabbing pain that I was forced to lie completely still. This was no superficial pain . . . it was bone deep, like all my muscles and bones were trying to knit together after extensive surgery. I felt like clay waiting to be fired, my muscles still fluid and my blood not yet warm. I felt at any moment I could dissolve into the wet sand. The only thing I knew for sure was that everything about me had changed.

I struggled to open my eyes. When I did, I saw something shimmering on the water like gold paint. It was angel blood . . . my blood. How much had I lost? Was I going to have the strength to walk? Was this the paralytic state Joseph had warned me about? I didn't know what came next. Suddenly I realized how my urgency had left me unprepared. I'd been in such a hurry to leave Heaven that I hadn't even asked Joseph what I should do if I made it back. I hadn't anticipated a welcome party but I wasn't expecting to face this alone. And now the beach was deserted. The night was too cold for anyone to be out. How long would I have to wait before someone found me? I felt my chest begin to heave involuntarily as broken sobs ripped through me. But every intake of air felt like I was inhaling fire.

After a while I calmed down enough to think about my options. As far as I could tell, there were only two. Wait for someone to find me, or try to summon the strength to make my way to a place where I was sure to draw attention. Neither appealed. I tried moving my fingers but they felt as stiff as the driftwood I saw lying around me. I tried summoning my angelic powers and then realized how foolish I was. I had snipped the wires, cut myself off at the source. I couldn't help myself now—I was completely human.

And then a thought occurred to me. Did this mean I had made it? I had done the unthinkable and survived the metamorphosis? I didn't know whether to laugh or cry.

Above me rose the majestic Crags, the moonlight shrouding them in a silver mantle. I craned my head as far as I could before crying out in pain. I scoured the pinnacles, outlined against the backdrop of sky like jagged towers. Relief washed over me. There was no one standing up there. It could only mean Xavier had come to his senses and gone home. I had to believe he was safe. Surely I'd sense if his body was lying broken on the rocks below. I could hear his heart beating in my head. I could almost smell the crisp pine scent of his cologne. Xavier was alive and he wasn't far away.

I heard laughter and froze. Out of nowhere a group of teenagers appeared on the beach. I felt suddenly self-conscious.

How would I explain my current state? Some of the voices sounded familiar even though they were slurred by alcohol. From where I lay they were still only dark smudges but I could see their coat collars were turned up against the wind. Some still carried bottles in their hands. As they drew closer the night air carried their voices so I could hear their conversation clearly.

"That party sucked. Remind me never to go to a Beta event again," said a girl I didn't recognize.

"Hey, I was having fun."

I knew the boy who answered. It was Wesley, one of Xavier's closest friends before we'd been forced to flee Venus Cove. What was he doing back home? I vaguely remembered hearing that he went to Stanford to study engineering. His presence here must mean college was out on semester break. How much time had passed? How much had I missed?

"Fun playing beer pong?" the girl snorted. "That game is disgusting."

"You're just pissed because Colt spent the night making out with someone else."

"As if! I couldn't give a crap about Colt. He obviously has no class if he likes someone as cheap as Anna-Louise."

"Whose idea was this anyway? It's cold as hell out here."

"Hey, where'd Molly go? Wasn't she right behind us?" My ears pricked up at the mention of her name. Molly was here?

"Maybe she changed her mind," the girl replied, sounding like she couldn't care less.

"I better head back to check on her," said Wesley.

"Man, are you still stuck on her?" slurred his friend. "You gotta know that girl's outta your league."

"Shut up, Cooper. I'm not *stuck* on anyone. Just trying to be a good friend."

Someone diplomatically changed the subject. "I thought Xavier was coming tonight."

"Yeah, right. He never hangs out with us anymore," said the boy named Cooper.

"Give him a break; he's got a lot going on right now," said Wes.

"A lot going on?" echoed his friend. "That kid's got more problems than a math book."

"That's an understatement," said the unknown girl. "It's his own fault. You make your bed, you gotta lie in it, that's what my granddaddy always said. That's what you get for falling for an outsider."

"You're an idiot, Leah," Molly's voice rang out like a bell. "What would you know about Xavier and what he's been through? Do you even know him?" Leah jumped as if she'd been caught. Molly's authority on the subject made her uncomfortable.

"Not personally, but I've heard stuff."

"Yeah, gossip isn't such a reliable source of information." I felt proud of Molly for defending Xavier. I would have hugged her if I could.

"Relax, I'm not hating on him. I just think he needs to get back out there."

"He will when he's ready," Molly said sharply.

"I'm going back to the party," Wesley announced suddenly,

cutting short the conversation about Xavier. I couldn't help feeling the topic was still raw for him. "Y'all do what you want."

Grumblings of displeasure followed but they all turned back and their voices began to wane. With a sudden urgency, I lifted my head and called out Molly's name. It came out as a cracked whisper; there was no chance she could hear me. Having her so close and yet out of reach was the last straw. I lost all motivation. The will to survive deserted me and I felt like the butt of Heaven's cruel joke. There was no point fighting for something the universe didn't want to happen. Xavier and I had been doomed from the beginning. They had let me come this far, teased me with the dream of a fresh start, and then snatched it away. I guess this was how my story was meant to end. I was too tired to be angry. Instead I was thankful that I'd made it back at all. If my life was going to end, at least it was in a place I loved. With acceptance came a numb peace. Even the pain started to subside. All I wanted now was the oblivion of sleep.

MY eyes fluttered open and I saw a woman wearing an old-fashioned nightdress looking down on me. For a moment I thought I was back in Heaven but then I realized nothing else about my surroundings had changed. The woman smiled. She wore a fringed shawl and her silver hair streamed over her shoulders. I knew she wasn't real because I could see right through her. She looked vaguely familiar. Memories of her flashed through my brain: a woman on a bench saying good-bye to her beloved dog, the metal beds and disinfected air of a retirement home, a ghostly figure at my bedroom window.

"Alice?" I croaked. "What are you doing here?"

"I've come to help you, dear." She sounded like something out of a fairy tale. "You've come this far. You can't give up now. I won't let you."

"Why didn't I ever see you in Heaven?" I asked.

"You weren't exactly allowed to have visitors," she replied.

"Eve . . ." I recalled my lockdown in the white room. My voice was full of bitterness when I said her name.

"It doesn't matter now," Alice said gently. "You've come back. I knew you would."

"Hasn't done me much good. I think I'm dying, Alice."

"Don't talk nonsense. You have to get up now."

"I can't. It hurts too much. I just want to sleep."

"You can sleep as long as you like once you're home. Now, come along. I'll help you through this."

"I *can't*."

"Xavier is waiting for you."

The sound of his name spoken aloud stirred something inside me.

"He is?"

"Of course, dear. He's been waiting awhile. But you're going to have to pull yourself together if you want to see him. I know he very much wants to see you."

And that was all the incentive I needed. Alice knew exactly which buttons to press. I concentrated hard and hauled myself onto my knees. I managed it better than I expected, but it still took a colossal effort before I made it to my feet.

"Slowly," cautioned Alice. "One step at a time." I heeded her advice and waited a moment before taking a step forward. I was like a child taking my first tentative steps. I turned to Alice, looking for approval, but there was no one there. She was gone. The rest would be up to me. Inch by inch, I made my way along the beach, spurred on only by the thought of Xavier waiting for me.

At the pier, I found a trucker sitting outside Greasy Joe's—Venus Cove's only all-night diner. He seemed startled to see me even though he was the one with sleeves of tattoos.

"Hey there, darlin'," he said uncertainly. "You need some help?"

"I'm trying to get home."

"Rough night?" I could tell he'd concluded that illegal substances must be responsible for my state. I nodded. It was easier to let him think that than try to explain any other way.

"How about we stop by the hospital first—get you checked out?"

"Please, I just need to get home and sleep it off. My brother will take care of me. He lives just near here."

The mention of a brother had the desired effect. His face relaxed a little—now that he was relieved of responsibility.

"Alright, lead the way," he said, tossing the remnants of his burger into the trash. He took my elbow and helped me climb into the passenger seat of his truck. Empty soda cans and wrappers littered the floor. There was the lingering smell of fries coupled with cracked leather and tobacco. It didn't help how I was feeling. Now I could add sickening waves of nausea to my list of symptoms. I wound down the window and let the crisp night air in. It helped fight back the urge to retch even though I knew there was nothing in my stomach.

"What's you're name, sweetheart?"

"Beth."

"That's pretty. I'm Lewis."

He saw my face and offered me the unopened bottle of water in the holder.

"Here, you're probably dehydrated. Hittin' the bar too hard can do that to a person."

"Thanks." I accepted the water and gulped it down gratefully. It washed the grit from my throat and cleared my head.

"What kinda friends you got? Leavin' you all alone like that?"

"I was out alone."

"Boy trouble?"

"You could say that."

"Take it from an old timer like me, missy. I don't care if this boy's the king of England, he ain't worth it."

Luckily, Lewis knew his way around town. Finally, we pulled into Byron Street. It was deserted except for the winter moths dancing under the streetlights. Lewis slowed down, waiting for a sign from me to stop. We passed the stately homes with their manicured gardens and gravel paths. I sat up straighter, my eyes peeled for the familiar rise in the road.

I almost forgot to tell Lewis to stop I was so transfixed when it came into view, right where the street peaked. The house with its wide porch and ivy-covered elm in the front yard beckoned me like an old friend. Ivy's pruned rose bushes stood in a row just inside the wrought-iron fence. The curtains in the front sitting room hadn't been drawn. In the soft glow of lamplight I could see towering bookshelves, a worn antique rug, and an old grand piano. The remnants of a fire still burned in the grate.

My heart stopped at the sight of a restored 1956 sky blue Chevy parked outside. I felt that same rush of excitement I'd experienced the first time I'd seen the boy with the turquoise eyes fishing off the edge of the pier. It seemed so long ago. But I knew one thing: Whatever happened now didn't matter.

I had come home.

34

Daybreak

IT was strange to stand at the gates of Byron once again. It felt like no time at all had passed. All the hardships seemed to melt away and I felt like this night marked the start of a new life. I breathed in the clean night air to steady my racing heart. I wanted to remember this moment—it was going to be the beginning of everything.

Now that I was only a few feet away from Xavier, I felt suddenly self-conscious and aware of my bedraggled state. I combed my hair with my fingers and brushed the sand off my bare toes. Then, I stepped through the wrought-iron gates and onto the path I had walked so many times in my angelic form. Now I was walking it as a real human being in my own right. The stone was cold beneath my feet and I could smell spring hanging in the air. It was strange how everything could be unchanged and yet vastly different at the same time. I stepped onto the porch and heard the third step creak as it always did. From somewhere inside, Phantom began to bark. A few moments later I heard his paws scratch at the door.

"Hi, boy," I whispered, and Phantom began to whine.

I heard footsteps in the hall.

"Phantom, come back. What's got into you?" My breath caught in my throat. I knew that voice, low and soft, with a gentle drawl from a childhood in Georgia.

I waited, paralyzed with anticipation, unable to speak or move. For an awful moment irrational fears filled my head. What if I was changed beyond recognition? What if Xavier had already moved on? Did I even have any right to show up now, to expect him to be waiting? In my head, our reunion had been filled with passion, not fear. Why was I losing my nerve now?

"C'mon boy, there's no one out there." There was weariness in Xavier's voice I'd never heard before. "Don't believe me? Okay, I'll show you."

The door opened and Xavier and I finally stood face-to-face.

He was barefoot, dressed in sweatpants and a loose-fitting white T-shirt. His hair, the color of honey, fell softly in front of his eyes, which were still the most dazzling shade of turquoise, like the ocean and the sky coming together.

His reaction was not what I expected. His mouth dropped open and he reeled backward as if I were a ghost.

"You're not real." The way he shook his head in disbelief told me his imagination must have been playing tricks on him for a while. I realized how far from human I must look. The porch light wasn't on and I was standing in shadow.

"Xavier, it's me," I said in a small faltering voice. "I've come back."

He stood in stunned silence; the hand still holding the door was trembling.

"I don't believe you."

"I'm human," I told him. "I became human . . . for you."

"I'm dreaming," he murmured, almost to himself. "Not again."

"Look!" I reached forward and grabbed his hand, digging my nails into his palm. "If I weren't real, would you be able to feel this?"

Xavier gazed at me with a heartbreaking expression of confusion mingled with hesitant hope.

"How can this be?" he said. "It's impossible!"

"You once told me a man in love can do extraordinary things," I said. "Well . . . so can a woman. I'm here, I'm real, and I love you more than ever."

Xavier's expression changed as he reached out to grasp my shoulders, feeling firm flesh beneath his hand. His grasp tightened and he pulled me into him in a desperate embrace. We crushed against each other with so much intensity I thought we might liquefy and form a whole new entity. Xavier held my face in his hands, and together we rocked silently back and forth. When he finally released me, the whole world spun and I remembered the pain that was wracking my body.

I swayed dangerously and felt my vision begin to blur.

"Hey, hey." Xavier caught me. "What's wrong? Are you okay?"

"I'm fine." I couldn't help smiling. "I'm with you."

"Come on, let's get you inside."

I took a few unsteady steps behind him before Xavier swept me into his arms and kicked the front door shut with his boot. "You're okay now," he murmured into my hair. "I'm going to take care of you."

He laid me on the couch in the living room.

"I never thought I'd see you again," Xavier said. "I thought the only way was to . . ." His voice cracked and he broke off.

"Hush," I replied, stroking his hair and noticing it was longer and the color of dark amber. "I know what you were thinking."

"I wasn't sure it would work." His voice became hard as he relived the challenge of the last months. "Living meant nothing once you were gone. Gabriel and Ivy helped; I don't think I would have pulled through without them."

"Where are they?" I looked past him into the empty house, a little less pristine than my sister usually kept it. There was a mug on the floor and a letterman jacket hanging from the banisters.

"They went on a mission . . . to Romania," he said. "Gabriel tried for months to get you back."

"He did?"

"Of course. He called on the Arch, he tried bargaining with them, pleading with them, nothing worked. I think it was killing them both. So they left. But they should be back any day now."

I felt tears spring to my eyes, overwhelmed by the prospect of seeing my siblings again.

"But, Beth . . ." Xavier sounded suddenly cautious. "You have to tell me something. . . . How did you get back here? Did you run away?" His whole body tensed up. "Are they going to come after you again? I need to warn Ivy and Gabriel. . . ."

I closed my hand gently over his as he fumbled for his cell. "No one's coming after me. Not this time. I'm back for good."

I watched his face as he took me in for the first time, noticing my wild, disheveled state. The doubt in his eyes evaporated, replaced by concern. "What happened to you? You look like you've been at war."

I felt the weariness inside me flare up and I leaned heavily in his arms, feeling useless as a rag doll. I wished he'd been able to see me radiant and healthy instead of some invalid he needed to nurse back to health. "This will pass. I just need time for the transition to be complete."

"We can talk about it later." He slipped a hand under my legs and one around my waist, lifting me easily. "Come on, let's get you cleaned up and into bed."

Xavier carried me up the staircase and into my old room, where he now slept. His gym bag was behind the door and a pile of his books sat on the white desk under a lamp. Besides the new additions, my room looked just as I'd left it. The familiarity of the whitewashed furniture and iron bed was comforting. Phantom followed us, deciding to resume his old position curled up on the rug. He didn't close his eyes, though. He kept up a vigilant watch as if he too feared I might disappear again.

"You slept in my room?" I asked happily.

"It was the only way I could feel close to you," he said. "I hope you don't mind."

I shook my head. I loved that he'd been in my room the

whole time I was away. Xavier placed me on the edge of the bed. "I'll be right back."

I could hear him moving around in the bathroom and the sound of running water. He came back a moment later with a pile of clean towels.

"Xavier, I need to ask you something. How long have I been away?"

"Awhile . . . but let's talk about that later, okay?"

"I need to know. It's freaking me out." He knelt down beside me and helped me out of the sleeves of my filthy dress.

"You've been gone two years to the day," he said softly.

"*Two years!* That can't be right."

"Beth, it doesn't matter now. . . ."

"No. No, it's not possible."

"I'm sorry," he said. "I'm nearly twenty-two, I graduate college next year."

"But . . . I've missed so much." I felt completely cheated. Missing an hour out of Xavier's life would have been too much. Two years felt like a lifetime. "You have to tell me everything."

"There's not much to tell. I got into grad school," he said casually. "My sister had a baby. I'm an uncle now."

"Oh, Xavier, I'm so happy for you. This is what you always wanted."

"Beth, you don't get it," he said. "I was just going through the motions. Inside, I didn't feel anything, even though I knew I should."

"But I'm home now," I said.

"Yes," he said, smiling. "You were the missing piece. Everything is complete now. You know we never got to have our honeymoon. I think we should go to Paris."

"Okay," I said dreamily.

Xavier laughed. "Maybe after you take a bath."

I sat on a stool in the bathroom watching the mirrors steam up as Xavier filled the tub. He picked the remnants of seaweed out of my hair.

"Rough flight?" he said.

My whole body was rubbed raw and my every muscle screamed with pain when I moved. But I tried not to let Xavier see how much it hurt.

"You're in pain, aren't you?" he asked.

"Pain is temporary," I replied. "Nothing hurt worse than losing you."

"What did they do to you?"

"Nothing I didn't ask for."

Xavier regarded me suspiciously. "Turn around," he said eventually. "Let me see your back."

"Why?"

"You know why."

I bent over at the waist. Xavier slowly lifted the tattered fabric and groaned. I felt his fingers trace the thin white scars behind my shoulder blades. When he spoke, it was hard to miss the escalating anger in his voice.

"What is this? Who scarred you like this?"

"No one. It was my decision."

"Where are your wings?"

"Gone."

"What do you mean *gone?*" His face paled. "They took your wings?"

"They didn't take them; I gave them up."

"You did *what?*"

"I had to."

"How could you do that?"

"It was the easiest decision I've ever had to make."

"How did that even happen—"

"It doesn't matter," I cut him off. "All that matters is I'm here."

Xavier stared at me for a long moment. "Are you saying you're . . ."

"As human as you are."

"I don't believe it."

"Neither did I at first. I wasn't sure I'd make it back in one piece. All the odds were stacked against me, but somehow it worked. Someone must have been watching over us."

A wave of guilt fell like a curtain over Xavier's eyes.

"It kills me," he said, "thinking about what you had to give up."

"No," I replied. "Even though now I'll eventually die, at least I'll have lived. In Heaven, I might have had eternal life, but I was dead inside. You've brought me to life. It's a gift."

Xavier bent down to kiss my forehead. Then he helped me out of my wet things and lowered me into the tub. The hot water burned at first, bringing tears to my eyes, but a few moments later the warmth seeped into me, helping to ease the aching deep in my bones. I was still a little self-conscious about being such a wreck, but Xavier hardly seemed to notice, he was so intent on taking care of me. The warm, scented water relaxed me. He got a ceramic blue jug from my dresser and used it to rinse the salt water out of my hair. He washed me gently, from head to foot, until I was completely clean. Afterward, I sat on the bed wrapped in a bathrobe as Xavier found one of his oversize T-shirts and a soft pair of sweatpants to wear. When I lifted my arms to help him dress me, he stopped for a moment, looking down at my torso.

"Well, that's new," he said.

"What is it?" I asked in alarm. Had I developed some horrible disfigurement on my journey?

"You seem to have grown a belly button . . . just like the rest of us."

"Wow." I looked down at my belly and he was right. Where there had only been smooth skin before there was now a small dent. Xavier used the pad of his finger to circle it. Even in my debilitated state his touch had the power to send shivers through me.

I climbed into my old bed, letting my head sink into the downy pillow. My body relaxed instantly as the fluffy blankets enveloped me. Although I ached with exhaustion, I couldn't bring myself to close my eyes.

"Are you hungry?" he asked. I thought about it and realized I was. "You stay here," Xavier said. "I'll go fix you something."

I must have dozed off while he was downstairs but I woke to the smell of brewed coffee and bacon. I sat up and looked at the loaded tray he placed carefully on my lap.

"The famous Woods fry-up?" I said.

"Of course. It cures everything. And please note, scrambled eggs this time, just the way you like them." I took a tentative mouthful of the fluffy eggs. The taste exploded in my mouth and I felt it revive me.

"It's really good," I said. "Are you just going to sit there and watch me eat?"

"I'm never letting you out of my sight again," he said. "You'd better get used to it."

As I ate, Xavier studied my face.

"There's something else that's different about you. I can't put my finger on it."

"There are a lot of things that have changed now."

"No, it's your skin," he said. "It doesn't glow like it used to."

"Good," I replied. "Normal people aren't supposed to glow."

"You really are human," he breathed.

Through the French doors I could see the sky already changing. There was only a sliver of moon and the midnight blue was diluting, broken by streaks of carnation and gold.

"Can you open the doors please?" I asked.

"Are you sure? You'll get sick."

"I want to hear the ocean."

I remembered how often the sound of the waves had lulled me to sleep in the past.

Xavier got up and did as I asked. The breeze fluttered the pages of the books on the desk and set the curtains billowing. Xavier sat on the edge of the bed, lost in thought.

"Are you angry with me?" I asked.

"Of course not. I'm in awe of you."

"Really?"

"Yes. You said you'd find a way and you did. You saved my life by coming back."

"That's what we do," I told him. "We look after each other."

"Do you think it's really over?" he asked. "I'm almost afraid to believe that's true."

"It's finished," I replied. "I can feel it."

I honestly believed nothing could come between us again. For the first time in my life I felt incredibly blessed. Even though I had challenged the will of Heaven I had been shown mercy. I had not been abandoned. Instead my Father had delivered me safely home.

Xavier lay down beside me and his warmth seeped into my skin like sunshine. Together we waited for daybreak.

When I looked at him, I forgot about my weariness. I didn't worry about how long my recovery might take. All I felt was a pure and childlike happiness. But Xavier was frowning. A look of concern flitted over his perfect features and dulled the sparkle in his eyes.

"What's wrong?" I asked.

He let out a sigh. "Are you sure you know what you've given up?"

"I do."

"And you don't regret it at all?"

"Not for a second."

"You don't wish you could have both—me and immortality."

"I'd choose you a thousand times over."

Xavier took my hand and I felt the smooth surface of his wedding ring against my palm. "I don't think you understand," he whispered, his turquoise eyes full of light. "From now on you're going to feel pain, grow old, and eventually die like the rest of us."

Despite the look of concern on his face, I couldn't stop myself from smiling ear to ear.

"I know," I said. "It sounds like heaven."

Acknowledgments

Thank you, Mom, for being my best friend—love you always.

Thank you, Mississippi, for being my home and my favorite place in the world.

Thank you, Katie Anderson, for being a great friend and looking out for me.

Thank you, Clay McLeod. I won't forget our crazy adventures in Memphis where we both inspired each other. Don't lose your rainbow.

Thank you, Mary Katherine Breland and Jordan Lee Phillips, for being like family. Roll tide!

Thanks to Jill Grinberg and the team at Feiwel and Friends, for embarking on this three-year journey with me.

Thank you, God, for inspiring this series and constantly inspiring me.